THE HARDY BOYS

Jonathan

11 BROTHER AGAINST BROTHER
12 PERFECT GETAWAY
13 THE BORGIA DAGGER
14 TOO MANY TRAITORS
15 BLOOD RELATIONS
16 LINE OF FIRE
17 THE NUMBER FILE
18 A KILLING IN THE MARKET
19 NIGHTMARE IN ANGEL CITY
20 WITNESS TO MURDER
21 STREET SPIES
22 DOUBLE EXPOSURE
23 DISASTER FOR HIRE
24 SCENE OF THE CRIME
25 THE BORDERLINE CASE
26 TROUBLE IN THE PIPELINE
27 NOWHERE TO RUN
28 COUNTDOWN TO TERROR
29 THICK AS THIEVES
30 THE DEADLIEST DARE
31 WITHOUT A TRACE
32 BLOOD MONEY
33 COLLISION COURSE
34 FINAL CUT
35 THE DEAD SEASON
36 RUNNING ON EMPTY
37 DANGER ZONE
38 DIPLOMATIC DECEIT
39 FLESH AND BLOOD
40 FRIGHT WAVE

41 HIGHWAY ROBBERY
42 THE LAST LAUGH
43 STRATEGIC MOVES
44 CASTLE FEAR
45 IN SELF DEFENSE
46 FOUL PLAY
47 FLIGHT INTO DANGER
48 ROCK 'N' REVENGE
49 DIRTY DEEDS
50 POWER PLAY
51 CHOKE HOLD
52 UNCIVIL WAR
53 WEB OF HORROR
54 DEEP TROUBLE
55 BEYOND THE LAW
56 HEIGHT OF DANGER
57 TERROR ON TRACK
58 SPIKED!
59 OPEN SEASONS
60 DEADFALL
61 GRAVE DANGER
62 FINAL GAMBIT
63 COLD SWEAT
64 ENDANGERED SPECIES
65 NO MERCY
66 THE PHOENIX EQUATION
67 LETHAL CARGO
68 ROUGH RIDING
69 MAYHEM IN MOTION
70 RIGGED FOR REVENGE

FRANKLYN W DIXON

THE HARDY BOYS
CASEFILES(TM)
3 STORIES IN 1

TROUBLE IN THE PIPELINE
NOWHERE TO RUN
COUNTDOWN TO TERROR

AN ARCHWAY PAPERBACK
Published by SIMON & SCHUSTER
New York London Toronto Sydney Tokyo Singapore

TROUBLE IN THE PIPELINE, NOWHERE TO RUN and COUNTDOWN TO
TERROR first published in Great Britain by Simon & Schuster, 1992
First published together in this combined edition in 1997 by Simon & Schuster Ltd
A Viacom Company

Simon & Schuster Ltd
West Garden Place
Kendal Street
London
W2 2AQ

THE HARDY BOYS CASEFILES is a trademark of Simon & Schuster Inc.

Simon & Schuster of Australia Pty Ltd
Sydney

A CIP catalogue record for this book is available from the British Library.

ISBN 0-671 00484 0

Printed and bound in Great Britain by Caledonian International Book Manufacturing,
Glasgow

TROUBLE IN THE PIPELINE

Chapter

1

"WILL YOU STEP on it, Frank? We're late." Joe
Hardy strained forward against his seat belt and
twisted the dial on the radio in their van. His
blond hair was still wet and was combed straight
back. In clean chinos and a Hawaiian shirt, he
was dressed for a party. He found a station he
liked and sat back, arms folded, to glare impatiently at his older brother.

"Calm down," Frank said, turning into a narrow road in a quiet section of Bayport. "Don't
you know it's fashionable to be late?"

"Being late is one thing—missing half the party
is another," Joe grumbled.

Frank chuckled. Put girls and food in front of
Joe Hardy, and watch out! Keeping his dark eyes
on the road, Frank said, "It'll be good to see

1

Doug. It's been almost three years, between his army stint and then that job in Alaska."

Joe stirred restlessly, staring out the side window. "We'll be lucky if there's any food left. I know Lisa invited a lot of people."

"The party is for Doug Hopkins, Joe—not your stomach," said Frank. "I hope we'll be able to get to talk to the guest of honor in the mob scene."

"We'll find out in a minute." Frank was driving at an easy pace. The road was narrow and curvy as it led through a large suburban development— small houses, each with a "Children at Play" warning on the lawn. The late-summer evening was breezeless and cool. Frank didn't feel like hurrying. His girl, Callie Shaw, couldn't make the party, and he wasn't eager to go without her.

A car was coming from the opposite direction, and Frank snugged up next to the curb under a streetlight to let it pass. Instead, the green two-door slammed to a stop beside him, and the driver leaned out his window. He wore a gray work shirt and a heavy growth of stubble on his face.

"Hey, kid," the man asked. "Where's Christensen Drive?"

"You just passed it," Frank answered. "Three blocks back, make a right, then look for a dead end. We're heading there our—"

Before he could finish, the guy slammed the car into first. Tires screeching, the car whipped through a tight U-turn, then barreled past the

Hardys' van. Frank stared as the car swerved, narrowly missing a little kid's bike that had been left against the curb. The green car roared up onto somebody's lawn, cutting a set of dirt tire tracks through the grass, and disappeared.

"Those morons!" Joe pounded the dashboard as he watched the taillights flash up the block, then make a shrieking right turn.

"Did you get their license plate?" Frank asked, his arms crossed on the steering wheel.

"License plate? I barely saw them!" Joe said.

Starting the van's engine, Frank said, "Lisa lives on Christensen Drive. We may bump into those guys again."

"If I catch those bozos, I'll burn rubber, too—right on their heads." He glanced over at Frank. "Well? Aren't we going?"

"That depends," his older brother replied. "Are we heading for the party, or are you out looking for trouble?"

"Will you knock it off and get us to Lisa's? We were supposed to be there an hour ago."

They had to park the van half a block from Lisa Shannon's house because a dozen cars already lined both curbs. They could hear the beat of music pounding down the street as they strolled under the dark canopy of trees. No one noticed them walk in. People were dancing or standing around in groups, talking and laughing. Joe headed straight for the dining room table. Frank watched as his brother slapped together a huge

3

salami and cheese sandwich, and he shook his head.

With Joe distracted, Frank decided he'd better represent the Hardy family and say hello. He went to look for Lisa or Doug.

Lisa had gone all out; her house was jammed. People were there to celebrate Doug's homecoming *and* the end of summer. Finally, out on the patio, Frank found Doug sitting quietly in the dark on a wicker couch.

"So, here's the man of the hour!" Frank said, grinning as he sat down next to him.

Doug looked up and smiled sheepishly, shaking back his light brown hair. He was sitting on the edge of the seat, leaning forward with his elbows on his knees. Always a good athlete in high school, Doug looked even more fit and sturdy than Frank remembered him.

"How does it feel to be back in civilization?" Frank asked.

"Okay." Doug shrugged.

"Well, we're glad to have you back. I guess the size of this bash shows how happy Lisa is."

"Yeah, it's great." Doug sat back and rubbed his hands together.

Frank stared. Was Doug trying to brush him off? Or were the one-word answers a sign of something going on between Doug and Lisa?

"Everything's okay between you guys?"

"Sure," said Doug, not changing his expression.

4

"Lisa was so proud of you. She talked about your job in Alaska all summer. I guess it's a good way to build up a nest egg."

If Frank thought he had found an opening, he was in for disappointment. Doug didn't respond.

"So, how was it?" Frank found himself getting a little embarrassed. "You must be tired of answering that question."

"It was okay," Doug said flatly.

"What'd you do?"

"I worked for a company that maintains the Alaska oil pipeline. I cleared land, cut brush—that kind of thing." Doug turned away, reaching for a soda on the end table.

"What's the summer like up there?"

"Pretty warm during the day, but at night it got cold. We were in Prudhoe, you know, up on the north coast—right on the Arctic Ocean. It stayed light all night long. You could read outdoors at any time just by the light from the sun."

Frank laughed. "That must be weird. I'd have trouble sleeping, I think."

Doug nodded. "Yeah, at first you do. But you get used to it."

"Didn't you go up there with one of your army buddies?" Frank asked.

If Doug had been warming up, that question cooled him down. His face became a mask; only his eyes moved, darting back and forth.

"I went with my pal Scott. We worked together," he finally answered in a measured beat.

5

Lisa Shannon came out onto the patio just then. She was a tall, dark-haired girl with a round face and a brilliant, warm smile. But Frank noticed that she seemed almost timid as she approached Doug. "Want to dance?" she asked after smiling at Frank.

Doug barely looked up. "No, thanks," he grunted. Lisa raised an eyebrow, smiled slightly, and backed away.

"Okay. If you change your mind, I'll be in the kitchen, making some dip."

Frank waited until Lisa had gone. "Come on, Doug, something's bothering you. You're acting as if this were your funeral, not a homecoming."

Doug shot him a look of pure terror, then he quickly recovered. "Just tired, I guess." He managed a nervous little laugh, but he wasn't acting like the Doug that Frank knew.

Doug was older than Frank and Joe, but he'd always been very friendly and outgoing. And even though he'd been a few years ahead of them in school, he'd spent a lot of time hanging out at their house and talking to their father. Fenton Hardy had a reputation as one of the best detectives in the country, and Doug was very interested in police work.

After high school Doug had enlisted in the army, and when his tour of duty was over, he had gone up to Alaska to have one last adventure before settling down. The adventure seemed to have turned Doug into a nervous wreck.

Frank wasn't about to try interrogating a friend. He stood up and stretched once. "I think I'll try some of that dip. Catch you later." He turned and followed the thumping of the music back into the living room. Joe had finished eating and was now starting to occupy himself with girls. He was dancing with a redheaded one in a white dress. Frank smiled at the girl and tapped Joe on the shoulder.

"Can I talk to you?"

"Not *now*." Joe made it very clear that he wanted to be left alone.

Frank raised his shoulders in a shrug and stepped off, thinking that maybe that business with the maniac driver had put Joe on edge.

Frank headed for the dining room and loaded a paper plate with chips and dip. Then he stepped back out to the patio. Doug was gone, his glass of soda half-empty on the table beside the wicker couch. Frank left his plate and walked around the side of the house to look for Doug.

The green car that had stopped them for directions was parked on the street, blocking the driveway. The driver and passenger were out of the car, standing on either side of Doug. Both were big, brawny types and loomed over him.

Whatever Doug said must have annoyed them. The driver suddenly grabbed Doug's arms, pinning them back. The other guy sank his fist into Doug's gut in a vicious body punch.

Chapter
2

FRANK WAS SMART. He stepped back into the dancing crowd, grabbed Joe, and hauled him outside.

"What are you—" Joe began. Then, by the porch lights, he saw the two guys working Doug over. Joe and Frank raced up to them. The driver with the heavy stubble was still holding Doug. Joe grabbed the guy's shoulder and whirled him around. With the goon's grip broken, Doug sagged to the ground, barely conscious. Frank knelt to make sure he was all right as the second guy began to retreat.

"Hey, Whiskers, what's going on here?" Joe demanded of the guy with the stubble.

"None of your business," Whiskers snarled, backing up.

"I think it is," Joe shot back. "You drive like

a maniac, now you beat up on a friend of ours. I think the cops—"

The two strong-armed men began retreating faster. Joe dashed after them, only to be stopped by the driver's heavy boot applied none too gently to his midsection. Frank leapt to his feet and was knocked down instantly by a chop to his throat that left him gasping for air.

The thugs, at their car by now, jumped in, gunned the engine, and tore off, leaving a strip of rubber on the street.

"You okay?" Joe asked, helping Frank up.

"Yeah," Frank rasped. "Another inch and he'd have crushed my throat. How's Doug?"

Doug struggled to his feet, moving like a broken old man. His lower lip was split. Frank pulled the van down to the driveway, and Joe helped Doug onto the passenger seat. They didn't want any of the partygoers seeing him like that.

"Who were those guys?" Joe asked.

Doug shook his head. "Don' wanna tawk," he managed, dribbling blood.

"Come on, Doug. You've got to tell us. We can help you if you're in trouble." Frank handed Doug a handkerchief. "What did they want?"

Dabbing at his lip and chin, Doug gave them a you-won't-believe-this look. "They warned me to forget about what happened in Alaska."

Frank and Joe exchanged glances. What could be so important that two thugs would come all the way to Bayport from Alaska? "Okay. What happened?" Frank asked.

"Scott and I found out that some managers in the company we were working for were taking bribes. And like stupid idiots, we told a higher-up, thinking he'd want to know. We thought we'd get promotions."

Joe raised his eyebrows. "Didn't turn out that way?"

"The guy said he'd investigate—next thing we know, a bunch of thugs grabbed us." Doug looked up at the Hardys, exhausted and terrified. "They threw me on a plane and said if I talked to anyone, anyone at all, they'd kill me." He hung his head. "I don't even know what happened to Scott."

"You mean he didn't go home?"

"I called his folks, pretending to be another army buddy. They told me he was still in Alaska. I had overheard some of the guys who grabbed us talking. They were interested in Scott because he knew a lot about explosives. He was a demolitions expert in the army."

"What's the name of this company you worked for?"

"Trans-Yukon Mining. But they also do construction and maintenance work on the pipeline. Everyone up there does some."

"Did those two come from Alaska?"

"No. They said mutual friends in Alaska sent

them to check up on me. When I told them to leave me alone, they—"

Frank interrupted. "What about those bribes? Who was spreading the money around? And *what* were they bribing people to do?"

Doug shook his head. "I don't know. We just happened to overhear these managers talking about their new-found wealth, and they mentioned it was bribe money. They found out we had overheard, decided we knew more than we did, and that was it."

He looked up at them, miserable. "I thought I wanted to be a cop, but I don't think I could handle it. I can't handle this. Could you—can you go up to Alaska and find Scott—at least find out what happened to him?" he added in a mere whisper. "I'm really scared. You saw. These guys mean business."

"We'll go," Frank said. "We'll find Scott and get to the bottom of this bribery thing, too. Now, let's get you to a hospital. Then you'd better stay at our house, where you'll be safe until we get back."

They took Doug to the emergency room and back to their house. Early the next morning the boys were in the air, heading for Alaska.

"Scott could be anywhere," Frank was saying as the plane droned its way toward Seattle, Washington. "He could be a prisoner, or in hiding. He might even be working for those guys up there by now."

"He could be dead." Joe cracked his knuckles and looked out at the peaceful blue and white of the cloud-lined sky.

They changed planes in Seattle, and in Fairbanks, Alaska, changed again. When they finally reached Prudhoe, they'd been in the air for almost twelve hours. They found the nearest motel and crashed. Although it was light outside, the town was in bed. And there was nothing they could do but sleep until morning.

The next morning they visited Trans-Yukon Mining. The company's offices were in a drab cinder-block building not far from Prudhoe's busy harbor on the Arctic Ocean. After getting past the receptionist, they found themselves in the outer office of the president of the company.

"We'd like to see Mr. Hammond." Joe leaned across the secretary's desk, turning on the charm. Frank never ceased to be amazed. Put a pretty girl in front of the guy and he became a different person. Joe's eyes sparkled with warmth and curiosity as he spoke. "My name is Joe Hardy. What's yours?"

"Cindy," the girl stammered. "Cindy Velikov." Drawn out of herself by the sheer force of Joe's smile, she shook hands. Joe held it for longer than necessary.

"Pleased to meet you, Cindy." He smiled cheerfully. "Think my brother and I could have a word with your boss?"

A blush spread across Cindy's pretty face to

the roots of her blond hair. "He—he doesn't like being disturbed. Do you have an appointment?"

"No. But we came all the way from New York to speak to him. We just want a few minutes of his time."

Cindy's ears perked up. "New York? I've never— Is it really like the pictures?"

"Oh, bigger!" Joe's hands made sweeping gestures. "Better!"

Cindy's blue eyes sparkled. "My dream is to live in New York, in one of those tall buildings with a doorman."

She hit some buttons on the intercom in front of her. "I'll check if Mr. Hammond can see you. Have a seat."

While they were waiting, Frank leaned over to Joe and whispered in his ear, "Let me handle this, okay? He may be clean, so I'm not going to hit him with everything we know."

Joe nodded.

Moments later they found themselves in Mr. Hammond's office. Dark wood paneling that matched the massive desk hid the cinder block here. A man rose, gesturing toward a pair of chairs. "I'm Spike Hammond," he said. "Sit down."

Hammond had the body of a man who'd done hard physical work all his life. In fact, he looked out of place in this office, as if he'd been stuffed into a suit and lowered in by a crane. His square jaw was balanced by an abundance of tousled red hair that fell low on his sunburned forehead. A scattering of freckles marched across the bridge of his nose.

"What brings you to Prudhoe?" Hammond asked.

Frank spoke up. "We're looking for a friend, Scott Sanders. He's supposed to be working for Trans-Yukon."

Hammond cocked his head to one side, then shook it as he leaned against his desk. "No. I don't recall that he does," he said.

"Here's a picture." Frank pulled out a snapshot of Scott in his army uniform.

Hammond took the photo between his thumb and forefinger. "Don't recognize the face; don't remember the name." He handed the picture back.

"Would you object if we had a look at your records?" Joe sat quietly with his hands folded in his lap. But Frank could hear the determination in his voice.

"That would be a bit unusual," Hammond said. "We don't normally allow anyone access to that information."

Frank jumped in. "We understand. But I don't see how you can rely on your memory to recall every name and face that passes through here."

Hammond chuckled, moving around to the other side of the desk. "I'm not one to forget a face."

"But we'd like to be sure," Joe interjected.

"We believe that Scott Sanders did work here and that he's now in some kind of trouble. I hope you'll help us out."

"I'd like to help." Hammond's forehead wrinkled in sympathy. "But it's company policy. I can't go around opening personnel records."

Frank took a deep breath. "Mr. Hammond, I'll be honest with you. We got some postcards from Scott, telling us that he was working here, and that he knew some of your managers were taking kickbacks. That's all we know. After a while the postcards stopped, and he didn't come home when he was supposed to. His folks are beginning to get nervous."

Hammond sat down. "You say this guy thought my managers were taking kickbacks? From whom?"

"He didn't say," Frank answered truthfully. "I doubt if he knew."

"Well, that's news to me." Hammond bit off his words. Frank couldn't decide if it was from anger, surprise, or the tension of a guilty conscience. "Thanks for the tip," Hammond said. "I'll look into it immediately." He got up and started to show them out. As they were passing Cindy Velikov she looked up and smiled.

"Sir, I overheard you say that Scott Sanders never worked here. But I remembered him, and I took the liberty of looking him up." She pointed to her computer screen. Joe moved quickly, not waiting for Hammond's reaction.

"He's on record," Joe said firmly. "Scott Sanders started work in June and 'quit' in mid-August." He quickly scanned the rest of Scott's personnel information, but there were no clues.

For a second the Hardys thought Hammond was going to explode with anger at Cindy. But he controlled himself and said simply, "I still don't think I ever heard that name—sorry."

Frank nodded, and Joe winked at Cindy. They left the office knowing only that Doug had told the truth. They weren't any closer to Scott.

There wasn't much to do in the Caribou Motel, where Frank and Joe were staying. They were lying on top of their beds fully clothed, including down parkas. Someone had forgotten to turn on the heat.

"Do we go to the police?" Joe asked, staring at a map of the area.

"I don't think so," Frank said. "That might scare whoever's involved—Scott may get hurt if he's still alive. Let's check around town for any kind of a clue to his whereabouts."

A faint knock on the door brought the Hardys sitting bolt upright. Frank ducked behind the door while Joe called out, "Who is it?"

"It's Cindy—Mr. Hammond's secretary," came a small voice from outside.

Joe opened the door to reveal a frightened Cindy. He made sure she was alone. "Are you all right?" he asked, staring at her.

16

"I have to tell you," she said. "Mr. Hammond was furious with me when I let you see my computer screen. Then I heard him on the phone. I don't know what's going on, but I think you'd better leave."

Frank came out from behind the door. "Why? What did he say?"

She was startled by Frank's sudden appearance. "I didn't hear everything, but he said something about 'getting rid' of you." Cindy stepped back, ready to bolt. "I can't stay—just be careful." She glanced around, terrified. "And don't tell anyone I talked to you. I just barely have my job still."

Joe sighed as he closed the door. "Do you think she'll be all right?"

"I'd worry more about us," Frank said. "Come on." In a few minutes they had piled up most of the furniture in front of the flimsy door.

They took turns standing guard, but the trip and jet lag caught up with Joe on his turn. He had just dozed off when he heard a crash. Four men smashed through the thin plasterboard of the room's back wall to fling both Hardys to the floor.

Joe was grabbed and shoved into a huge canvas bag—a mail sack, he guessed as he fought to get free. He might as well have been paralyzed. There was no way out of the heavy canvas.

Then came a blow to the back of his head—and the darkness in the bag gave way to deeper blackness.

Chapter

3

JOE CAME TO FIRST.

He was folded in half, lying on his side, and only when he tried to straighten up did he remember where he was—inside a bag. It might as well have been his coffin. Then he felt the pain, the throbbing at the back of his head that was making his skull ring. He couldn't even reach up to feel the spot—the bag was too tight. He lay still then and tried to gather his thoughts in spite of the hammering in his brain.

"Find Frank," he told himself. "That's the first thing." He listened for any signs of life around him. Then he whispered into the smothering dark, "Frank, are you there?"

He strained his ears—and heard the distant hum of an engine. A plane! He was on a plane! Then, nearer, he heard a rustling and scraping, which he assumed was Frank moving inside *his* bag.

"Frank, is that you?"

"Yeah." His brother's voice was laced with pain and confusion. "Where are you?"

"Inside a bag," Joe whispered. "And I think we're aboard a plane."

"Great," Frank responded sarcastically. "They airmailed us somewhere. Any ideas on how to get out of these things?"

Joe could hear struggling. "Keep it down," he warned. "We may have company."

Both of them listened, but all they caught was the deep *thrum* of propellers. Propellers! It must be a small plane. "If you can move at all, you should be able to get out of yours," Joe whispered. "You're more flexible than I am. I do have a knife, but I can't get to it."

Frank's head was at the bottom of the bag, and the drawstring was down near his feet. He pulled himself into a tuck and held the bag tight against the floor so it couldn't turn with him.

Moving a few inches with each turn, he was finally able to grope the top of the bag. Frank tried to force his fingers through the tiny hole to reach the knotted rope.

But he couldn't squeeze them through. He dug into his pocket and found a key, which he brought up, and began the slow process of loosening the knot.

"How's it going?" Joe asked after listening to Frank's deliberate breathing for a few minutes.

"I'll be done in a minute," Frank whispered. His fingers ached, but he'd managed to pry open the knot. Then he pushed open the mouth of the bag and peeked out.

They were in the cargo section of a small plane. Leading into the cockpit was an open door that let in the dull glare of an overcast day. Wisps of cloud whipped by the front window. Bundles, packages, and crates had been dumped everywhere, and they bounced and shifted as the plane cut through the cloud cover.

After crawling out of the sack, Frank untied the knot on Joe's. Silently, they moved on all fours toward the cockpit door, pausing to take cover behind crates. A large bearded man was asleep just outside the door, a parachute strapped to his back, a revolver in his lap.

Hunkering behind an open shipping case, Joe asked, "What do you think?"

"Give me a minute," Frank said, rubbing his sore head.

"I see only one chance," Joe said. "We grab the gun and hijack the plane."

Frank nodded and tried to ignore his pounding head. He straightened to take another look at their sleeping guard and glanced down into the crate in front of him. Inside was a kind of giant sea buoy with a beacon and what looked like radio equipment attached to it. Strange, he thought to himself. I've never seen anything like that.

But he didn't have time to think more about it. The man with the gun began to stir. As he moved Frank saw that he was sitting on a pile of packed parachutes.

The bearded guard startled himself awake with a snuffling snort and rubbed a hamlike fist across his eyes. His head snapped up, and he focused immediately on the empty mail sacks. Jumping up with more speed and grace than most men fifty pounds lighter, he scurried nervously around the cargo bay, searching for his escaped prisoners. He got to Frank's hiding place first.

In two moves Frank shot up and kicked out with both feet to try to knock the revolver from the goon's hand.

But his kick was off the mark, and Frank fell, landing violently on his side. The bull of a man was on him in a flash. Frank watched as the butt end of the revolver came crashing toward him. The blow only glanced off his head, but Frank still saw red and orange circles swim across his eyes as he lay stunned for a moment.

Joe gave a war whoop and swooped down on the man from his perch on a crate. But the hulk's reflexes were quick. He reached out and grabbed Joe's wrist, flipping him over on his back. Joe's head caught the full impact, and he was knocked unconscious.

Dropping the gun, the guard reached out for

both of Joe's wrists and dragged him over to the hatch. Boosting Joe up onto his hip, he held him tight against his body with one arm and released the lever on the hatch with the other.

Frank watched and, in a sudden burst of understanding, knew that the goon was planning to drop Joe from the plane as soon as the hatch was fully open.

Frank focused all his concentration, shook his head to clear it, and dove for the parachutes.

Supporting Joe against his hip, the guard continued to struggle with the door against the wind and pressure. He had it slid halfway open. Joe would be tossed out in another few seconds.

Frank slipped on the chute, snapped it closed, and pocketed the gun he had retrieved from the floor.

The goon, in one final shove, had the door open.

Frank dove for Joe just as the hulk released him into the whistling air. He caught Joe by the belt. The blast of cold had an almost instant reviving effect on Joe, and he woke up as soon as Frank snatched him. He wrenched his body around and clung to Frank's shoulders. The boys were sinking through the white puffs of cloud vapor, too insubstantial to support even a feather.

As soon as they were free of the plane Frank yanked the rip cord on his chute and tightened his grip on Joe. The air caught the silk, and the boys felt the welcome tug that broke their free fall. They drifted slowly down to a moonlike landscape.

Rocky hills covered with green lichen and moss stretched as far as the eye could see. Fifteen feet before touching down Joe hopped off, bent his knees, and landed in a tuck two feet from Frank. They were on a fairly gentle slope a few hundred yards from a narrow but swift little river. They had to be miles inland, from the wide expanse of water they had seen from the air.

After gathering up his chute, Frank tucked it under a stone. Both boys scouted around for any shelter in the barren tundra. The only sounds were the constant hiss of the wind and the water as it tumbled over the rocks in the riverbed.

Frank found a smooth, flat place at the foot of a huge rock. It was out of the wind and close to the river, so they'd have plenty to drink. Joe ran back for the parachute and, using his pocket-knife, cut it in half to make a tent. The remaining material would serve as bedding—on a mattress of moss, parachute wouldn't be a bad blanket.

"What's for breakfast?" Joe asked once their shelter was set up. He looked at his watch. It was three o'clock in the morning, and the sky was still filled with light.

"Well, you can have moss with water, or lichen with a few roots shredded on top," Frank joked. They stood for a moment, looking for a place to search out something to eat.

"Look over there," Joe said, pointing upstream. "See that bunch of bushes? We've got firewood, at least."

Frank turned to see a cluster of dead alders by the river's edge. "Great," he said. "Now all we need is something to cook."

"How about fish?" Joe smiled.

"But how are you—?"

"Wait. A little trust, please. Genius at work."

Joe whipped his belt off, cut the buckle away, then pried its pin free. He began to rub the small piece of metal back and forth until he'd sharpened it into a point. With another rock he gently hammered the pin into a hook shape.

"There you go—one grade-B, size-ten fishhook," he declared, proudly holding it up for Frank to see.

"All *riiight*," Frank said. "Now let's tie some string to it and—uh-oh, no string."

Joe held up a finger. "It's a good thing I'm here." He yanked up some clumps of sparse grass and began braiding it into a few feet of line.

While Joe was busy, Frank hunted for bait. Among the alders he found grubs.

Joe dropped the baited hook into the stream and it quickly disappeared under the swift water.

The line twitched almost instantly. Then, in a flash, there was a fierce tug, and the line was pulled tight.

"I've got a bite," Joe yelled excitedly.

"Get him in fast," Frank called. "Don't give him time to bite the line or rub it on a rock!"

Joe walked straight back from the edge of the river, holding his hands high above his head. The fish followed and flopped onto the rocky bank—a huge, fat northern pike.

Frank scooped up the fish in his bare hands. Removing the hook, he held it up.

"Must be at least four pounds," Joe gloated, coming over for a closer look. While Frank built a fire, Joe cleaned the catch, casually tossing the guts toward the stream.

After building a little grill out of wet alder sticks, they roasted the fish quickly. The meat was moist and flavorful and hot enough to burn their fingers as they picked it apart.

Just as they were finishing, the quiet of the sunlit night was interrupted by the sound of someone splashing along the river's edge. A large brown bear.

"Got the revolver?" Joe whispered.

"In the tent," Frank said, not taking his eyes from the lumbering beast. "I'll get it." He moved quickly and silently and returned holding the gun down by his thigh. "I don't know if it'll do much damage in this case."

"You may be right." Joe kept his eyes on the bear, who continued waddling downstream toward them. "It'd probably do just enough to make him mad. Is it a grizzly?"

"Looks like it," Frank answered. "It's got that kind of silver fur around its throat." He glanced

25

at the fire. "It probably smelled the fish. Where'd you put the guts?"

"I threw them in the—" Joe stopped suddenly, staring. The fish guts had landed on a nearby rock. "Uh-oh."

"Nice going," Frank said. "Let's sneak into the tent. Maybe he'll eat the guts and go away."

They inched backward toward the tent. The bear came right up to the fish guts. In one gulp, he licked them up. Then, twitching his nose, he headed for what was left of the fish beside the fire.

"He's coming nearer," Joe whispered, eyes wide.

The bear had obviously caught Joe's and Frank's scents. Abruptly it rose up on its hind legs, throwing a shadow thirty feet long that fell like night over the boys. No one breathed. Time was frozen for a second.

Then Frank raised the gun. The movement attracted the beast, and the unnatural silence was shattered with one giant roar as the grizzly began its charge!

Chapter

4

FRANK STOOD HIS ground and, arms extended, took careful aim before squeezing off a single shot. Nothing! Only a click—the gun was jammed. The bear kept coming.

Then a second later a gunshot blast cut through the air. Frank and Joe didn't stop to think where it had come from because their eyes were still on the bear. It quit its attack, stood on its hind legs, and rolled its massive head to find the distraction. Coming up the riverbank were a man and a dog. The man had a rifle in his hands, pointed straight up. Another gunshot, and the bear whoofed once and fled.

The man waved, and the Hardys managed a quick nod of their heads. Holding his rifle casually at waist level, the man trotted toward them with the dog at his side.

"Hello!" the man greeted the boys. "You had a little scare there, eh?"

As he got closer Frank and Joe could see that he was a native Alaskan. His face was a perfect circle of copper-colored leather that had to have taken many years outdoors to acquire. Squinting in the sunlight, his shiny black-pebble eyes were surrounded by deep lines.

"I thought we were dead. Thanks," Frank said simply, and extended his hand in greeting. "Boy, were we glad to see *you*."

The man laughed and then shook his head. "Not much you can do when a bear's hungry."

"I guess not," Joe said, glancing upstream to make sure the bear had really gone. He saw only the river and the endless barren hills.

"Are you hunting?" the man asked, looking them over skeptically.

"Uh, not exactly," Frank said.

"I hope not. Not in those clothes," the stranger remarked, pointing to their sneakers. "Need some help?"

They nodded eagerly. "Guess you could say that. We don't even know where we are. We had an emergency and had to jump from our plane."

The man scanned the area without speaking. He thought he might see the wreckage of a crash. "Too bad. You both okay?" was all he said. He obviously didn't want to pry.

"Yeah, we're okay. Just a little tired. We'd like

to get to Prudhoe," Joe said. "Do you know the way?"

"No problem. I'm a hunting and fishing guide. My name's Virgil Asuluk."

Frank and Joe breathed a sigh of relief. "I'm Joe Hardy, and this is my brother, Frank."

"Pleased to meet you. This is Tanook. He's a lead dog. Very good animal." Tanook was a large, silvery husky, with the big chest and broad head characteristic of his breed. When Virgil began to walk off, Tanook sprang to his side.

They picked up their parachute and followed Virgil along the river. He explained that one of his fishing camps was at the mouth of the river. "My helicopter is there. I'll fly you back to Prudhoe."

"Helicopter?" Joe asked.

"Times have changed. We have planes and snowmobiles. But we also keep our good friends, like Tanook."

The dog barked once at his name, and a helicopter circled them lazily.

The Hardys explained why they were in Alaska as they trudged along.

"Those companies are not good," Virgil said, shaking his head when he'd heard their story. "Often they won't hire the Aleut or the Athapaskan, and we make complaints." He explained to the Hardys about the different tribes of Indian and Eskimo peoples in the north. "Sometimes you have to pay to get a job." His eyes were open wide to emphasize the shock.

"That's what our friends found out. And one got chased home, and the other one has disappeared. Now we've been kidnapped and almost killed. It looks as if it might be more serious than just kickbacks for jobs." Frank was grim as he marched along, matching his pace to Virgil's.

"Not good, not good." Virgil shook his head and paused. "You must find your friend."

An hour later they came to a small flat plain at the mouth of the river. Across the open space a dozen tethered dogs barked happily to greet their master. Strips of raw fish were hung out on large wooden racks to dry in the sun. A fishing boat lay on its side in the grass, and a red and white helicopter stood off by itself like a giant, futuristic insect.

Virgil led the Hardys to the chopper. He climbed up on the strut and put his rifle inside. Then he turned the ignition key to activate the battery. Rock music boomed out of the open door. Virgil grinned. "New speakers—put them in myself."

"Great." Joe's eyes shone. The thought of whipping through the sky on the wings of full-blast rock 'n' roll was kind of exciting.

"I have lots of tapes. You can pick what you like for the trip later." Virgil shut down the system. "But right now let's get you something warm to drink."

He led the way toward a small sod hut that had grass sprouting on its roof. Some rough wooden beams framed the door and the small windows on each side of the structure. A chimney seemed to grow out of the roof.

"Come in, come in," Virgil said, ducking through the door and gesturing for them to follow. Inside it was dark but warm and comfortable. The floor was hard-packed dirt. Hunting and trapping equipment hung on the dried mud walls, along with beautifully carved fishing spears. Six cots were stacked neatly on top of one another in one corner. Virgil went to the cast-iron stove and opened it up.

"I'll get this going a little better. Tea okay?" They both nodded.

"I bring folks here for the fishing," Virgil explained as he busied himself with the tea. "Every month in the summer I have a new group."

He chatted about his copter and the fish and game as the Hardys quietly sipped the hot, sweet tea.

Abruptly in the middle of a good fishing story Virgil stopped, his head bent toward a window and his eyes unfocused. He was listening. "Someone is coming." Frank and Joe heard nothing, but they followed Virgil outside. The dogs were all standing up and looking in the same direction. Virgil stared off into the sky.

"What are we supposed to be hearing?" Frank asked.

"A chopper—maybe more than one," Virgil said. "Maybe someone looking for you?" He looked at them intently.

Frank shrugged. "Could be," he said. He and Joe exchanged nervous glances.

"I hear it now," Frank said. They watched as Virgil lifted his arm to the sky.

"There they are, three of them!"

The dogs began to whimper with excitement, but Virgil didn't seem to notice. He kept his eyes on the choppers.

"Are they coming here?" Joe asked.

"Don't know," Virgil said, shading his eyes. "Looks like they're flying a search pattern. They're moving slow and low to the ground."

The distinctive shuddering *whirr* of helicopter rotors grew louder and louder. The choppers were zigzagging back and forth, but Frank realized they were probably following the path of the river.

"Hmm," Virgil said, slightly surprised. "I think I recognize them." He squinted into the sun. "Yes—North Slope Supply. I thought they went out of business."

"What are they?" Joe asked.

"A small company," Virgil replied, still keeping his head raised to the approaching craft. "Small construction projects—they work for larger companies as subcontractors."

Frank and Joe nodded. The choppers must have noticed the camp, since they were coming toward them. The hovering machines couldn't have been more than a hundred feet above the ground.

Frank and Joe could see the North Slope Supply logo emblazoned across the sides of all three copters. The noise became almost unbearable as the choppers came closer. The wind from the whirling blades felt hard and unpleasant against their faces.

When the copters were about forty feet above the ground, the side door on one of them slid open abruptly. A man stood framed against the interior darkness. In his hands was a submachine gun with a string of shiny brass cartridge cases flying from the chamber.

Flaming death was spitting from the gun's muzzle, and it was aimed at the boys and Virgil.

Chapter
5

FRANK AND JOE lunged directly under the hovering chopper to get out of the line of fire. Virgil sprinted for the sod house, zigzagging across the open space. Unable to take aim at the Hardys, the man in the chopper followed Virgil with his heavy weapon.

His bullets stitched the earth, but because of the position of the chopper and Virgil's quick and erratic movements a hit was impossible. The Hardys could hear the gunner yelling at the pilot to spin the copter around.

As the bird began its turn Joe pointed to the fishing boat lying on its side. They dashed from under the shadow of the chopper, ducking and weaving as Virgil had. Halfway to the boat they were hit with clods of earth as bullets ripped up the ground behind them. The chopper was zeroing in—and fast. The sound of the copter got louder, and they could feel the shadow on their backs.

"Hit the dirt," Joe yelled. They dove apart, belly-flopping on the ground and rolling away as a burst of fire marched between them. The chopper overshot, and they sprang the last few yards to the cover of the fishing boat.

Catching their breath, they peered around the craft to see what was happening. The choppers must have been talking to one another by radio. The machine gun was silent as the chopper hovered nearby; the other two were hovering out of firing range.

Suddenly the copter on the attack flashed toward the sod hut. Frank and Joe saw Virgil running around to the back of the house with a fishing spear in his hand. The attack chopper was stalking him.

Keeping the house between himself and the enemy above, Virgil was playing a cat-and-mouse game with the machine gunner. He ran, luring the chopper this way and that. Then he'd duck inside or leap through a window just as the gunner must have thought he had a clear shot. Once Virgil disappeared, the pilot had to guess where he'd jump out next and maneuver the helicopter into position.

Virgil burst through a window and rolled across the ground with a spear.

The chopper was caught out of position, and

Virgil jumped up and ran to its blind side. In a split second he snapped the spear forward. The razor-sharp projectile left his hand with the force of a missile and pierced the fiberglass housing on the chopper's engine, burying itself in the gearbox.

At first it seemed as if the blow had had no effect on the hovering craft. The gunner continued blasting the sides and roof of the hut as Virgil dived around it for cover. Then the chopper began spinning in an erratic bobbing and weaving pattern. It limped off a safe distance and landed.

But as soon as it moved off another copter started toward them. "Let's run for the hut," Joe suggested.

"Too chancy," Frank replied. "They know we aren't armed, so they won't be cautious."

Suddenly Virgil burst out of his house, zigzagging toward his dogs. He ran by each one and unhooked it from its tether. The new chopper didn't pay much attention. It hovered in front of the fishing boat as Virgil sprinted back to the house.

"We've got to think of something," Joe said. "They'll pick us off like fish in a barrel." He ducked back behind the boat, knocking his head on a large wooden box mounted in the bow of the boat. The lid fell open, and a jumble of marine equipment burst out—lines, nets, a can of engine oil, and a flare gun with flares.

"Is this what I think it is?" Joe asked, showing it to Frank.

"Uh-huh. Does it work?"

"We'll soon find out."

Joe peered over the edge of the boat. The chopper's pilot and passenger were on the ground now, moving toward the sod hut. Only the passenger had a gun, and he was obviously more concerned with Virgil and his possible stash of weapons than with the boys.

Taking aim, Joe launched a flare into the open door of the sitting chopper. It exploded inside the enclosed space like a bomb. Blinding light and thick smoke came belching out. The two men whirled around at the sneak attack and began to back away, pointing their weapons first at the house, then at the boat.

The last chopper played it safe. Since it was the only bird able to fly, its pilot put down at a safe distance. The one crew member jumped out and went running to help his friends. As he was crossing the open space Virgil shouted something from the door of the hut.

His sled dogs suddenly sprang to life, charging the crewmen.

And at the same time a huge explosion erupted from the helicopter with the flare burning in it. Flames had reached the fuel tank, and the whole chopper was being blown to pieces.

"Let's go!" Joe shouted. He and Frank leapt out from behind the boat. Virgil had the same idea. With the enemy momentarily startled and pinned down by the dogs, they made a run for Virgil's chopper, Tanook leading the way.

Gunshots cracked as they dodged across the clearing, but there was so much smoke in the air there was little danger of being hit. They clambered into the helicopter and took off, rising above the dark, billowing clouds. Tanook was whimpering in the back as they rose from the ground.

"Will the dogs be all right?" Frank asked.

"No one in Alaska will shoot a dog," Virgil said. He glanced down at the clearing to make sure what he said was true. Frank and Joe looked down, too. They could see the enemy running for the one good chopper. The dogs pursued them, barking and growling, but they stopped short of attacking.

Virgil headed for Prudhoe. Even at some distance, they could still see the plume of smoke rising from the burning chopper.

"We'll go in over the mountains," Virgil was saying. "Who knows how fast their copter is."

They looked back. The last North Slope helicopter was in the air and coming after them. It was bigger than Virgil's, and probably faster.

"What'll we do if they catch up with us?" Frank asked.

Virgil shrugged. "First try to lose them. If we can't do that, then we'll worry about being

38

caught." He turned the copter abruptly and began to drop closer to the ground.

"I know these valleys," he said. "If we can get behind a mountain, we can hide from them, put down, and disguise the chopper. They may be faster, but we're quicker. There's a difference."

Virgil looked grim, but he couldn't resist turning on the stereo. A heavy rock beat came thudding dramatically from the speakers, drowning out the sound from the engines and rotor. Joe turned to Frank, grinning. "Music to escape by," he mouthed. It was like a movie soundtrack. There they were, swooping across the Brooks Range, pursued by a helicopter while listening to the same music they'd heard at Lisa Shannon's party.

"This is something else," Joe cried, taking in the scenery and keeping an eye on the approaching chopper. "Virgil, they're gaining on us."

"Not much I can do," Virgil responded. He craned his neck around to see the enemy. When he realized how close they were, he hung a hard right and dropped into a narrow valley.

"Better try it now," he said. But the North Slope chopper was right behind them and seemed to have no trouble keeping up.

Suddenly Virgil leaned forward and began to fiddle with the throttle controls. He tapped the gauges, muttering to himself.

"What's wrong?" Frank asked.

"Doesn't feel good," he said, adjusting two

more knobs. "It's like we're running out of fuel, but that's not possible. I filled it up this morning."

Frank and Joe felt helpless.

"No," Virgil said grimly. "Something's definitely wrong. We're losing altitude, and the fuel is way down." The engine skipped and sputtered. Joe leaned back in his seat and tried to see the enemy. Little drops of moisture appeared on the window next to him.

"Hey, it's raining," he said, tapping on the glass. But it didn't make any sense. The sun was out. There wasn't any moisture on any of the other windows.

The engine began to cough more and more. Joe looked up to see what was happening. Not a cloud in the sky. What he did see was a stream of fuel pouring out of a bullet hole in their gas tank.

"We've got a leak," he said over the sound of the music, which must have masked the gunshots. "It's coming down my side."

As Virgil glanced over to see the growing stream roll down the window, the engine stopped for a good five seconds. The music shut down, and the chopper began to fall like a stone.

Chapter
6

THE SUDDEN SILENCE was eerie. No music, no rotor. Just the click of the engine ticking down as it cooled. The plunge to the earth felt the same as if they'd been on a good roller coaster—but a lot less fun.

"Hold on," Virgil said calmly. He flipped a switch and began to pull on a knob on the control panel. "Let's hope this works." Virgil's face was tense as he turned the ignition off and then back on again.

"What are you doing?" Joe asked, his voice tight.

"Got a reserve tank," Virgil explained. "Never use it. Don't know if it's full or how the line is."

The starter cranked over and over, but the engine only coughed and died. The ground came

41

closer and closer. They were over a forest in the middle of a deep valley. Joe was already picking out their crash site as Virgil cranked the starter once again.

"Do you have any chutes?" Frank asked.

"Nope." Virgil had already considered the alternative of jumping and dismissed it.

Then, with faint rumblings and stirrings, the engine suddenly began to turn over. "She's catching." Virgil smiled. "Feel her? There she goes!"

Frank and Joe felt the sudden surge of power as the blades bit into the air and lifted the chopper out of her death plunge. They were down low enough to watch treetop branches wave in the sudden blast of air.

"We'll have to put down real soon. There's not much in this little tank, and once it goes, that's it." Virgil scanned the area for a place to land in the dense forest below.

Frank's mind was churning. How would they get out of this and get back to Prudhoe? They had to find Scott, bring him home if they could. Instead, they were in the middle of nowhere, on the run in a damaged helicopter, pursued by unknown thugs dead set on killing them. It was starting to make him mad.

He looked up. "I've got an idea. Virgil—do you have any rope? Any tools aboard?"

Virgil nodded. "In the back. There's a big coil of rope and a complete tool chest. Why?"

"Find a clearing, a small clearing."

Virgil and Joe looked over at him.

"What are you talking about?" Joe burst out. "That's what we're doing!"

"I mean a *really* small clearing, just big enough for two choppers—and one trap."

"You'd better talk fast," Joe said.

Quickly Frank described what he had in mind. Virgil and Joe listened intently. Then Virgil began to grin.

"Sounds like it's worth a try. Let's go." He swung the chopper around and headed for what Joe pointed out as the only good place to land. The North Slope chopper was still following, but at a safe distance. Maybe its occupants feared some kind of trick.

Virgil put the bird down as close to the trees as he could, the rotor blades whirling only inches from branches. To the left, only a slightly larger space remained. There was no place else for the other chopper to land.

"Let's go," Frank called. "We don't have much time. Don't let them see what we're up to."

He grabbed the tool chest, throwing his parka over it to conceal it from their enemies. Joe had the coil of rope under his jacket.

"Come on, into the woods," Frank urged them. Virgil and Joe ducked into the cover of the trees.

"What's first?" Virgil asked, peering up at the North Shore copter through the branches.

43

"Pick a tree on the other side of the clearing and get a rope around the top of it. Then we make a cut in the trunk with the saw."

"Right!" Joe burst out into the clearing.

"Get back!" Frank yelled.

Joe plunged back under the canopy of leaves. "What's the matter?"

"Don't let them see you," Frank said as he started pushing his way around the perimeter of the clearing. "We want them to think we've made a run for it."

"This looks like a good one," Virgil said, tapping a tall tree on the opposite side of the tiny meadow.

"Too tall," Frank responded, staring up at the top. "It would land on our chopper, too."

"How about this one?" Joe called out, standing next to a slender, dark-barked tree a few yards in from the edge of the clearing.

"That's better," Frank said. "Looks just the right height. And the fact that it's in from the edge is good. Not so obvious. Can you climb it, Joe?"

With the rope wrapped diagonally around his torso, he began to shinny up the tree trunk.

"How high do you think we should put it?" he called down.

"That's about right—right now," Frank yelled up.

Joe slipped the rope off and tied it snugly around the trunk. He dropped the end of the rope to the ground and came down as easily as he'd gone up.

"Okay. Now let's cut a *V* on the side opposite the direction of the fall," Frank said. Grabbing one end of the saw, he and Virgil removed a wedge from the back of the tree. The upper half of the tree was now standing on a quarter of its trunk.

They could hear the enemy chopper circling down closer. Virgil looked up. "They've been trying to figure out what we're up to," Virgil said. "I guess they've decided we ran. Now they have to come down to find out which way."

"Let's get this thing finished," Frank said.

Taking the end of the rope, he trailed it along behind him as he headed back to the other side of the clearing. It wasn't easy keeping the rope clean and yet remaining hidden in the trees. Joe and Virgil followed.

"Okay, Joe. Loop it through a branch on this side, and then let it go slack. The rope has to lie flat. We don't want them to see it." Joe went up with the rope and was back in a flash.

"Okay, all set!" he said.

They positioned themselves at the end of the rope. The North Slope chopper hovered just forty feet over the clearing. They were within easy firing range. The Hardys and Virgil could see the machine gunner and two friends with revolvers peering around the edge of the open door.

"This is it," Joe said.

As the chopper lowered itself into the final fifteen feet of descent, Frank gave the signal. They pulled the rope tight, lashing it firmly around the trunk of the tree. The enemy pilot never saw it. But the chopper certainly felt it.

The rope snapped up from the ground, right under the helicopter's belly. It caught one of the wheel struts, making the copter tilt. That put more weight on the rope, and the cut tree toppled, knocking the helicopter out of the air. The chopper smashed to the ground, one of its rotor blades flying off with a metallic *twang*.

Frank and Joe ran up to the open door of the helicopter. Five men lay piled in a heap. All were alive but unconscious. Joe gathered up the guns and threw them into Virgil's chopper. Frank checked the copter's pilot, who was out cold but breathing. His last act had been to cut off the engine before crashing.

"Okay," Frank said, jumping down. "Let's patch our fuel tank and siphon their gas off. These guys'll be all right."

Virgil was already at work on the fuel tank. Once he gave the okay, Joe used a length of rubber hose to suck the fuel out of the North Slope chopper and direct it into Virgil's.

"Let's hope the patch holds," Virgil said over the noise of the engine as it lifted them up over the mountains. They didn't have to worry—the tank held all the way to Prudhoe.

Virgil dropped them on the outskirts of town before he flew off to check on his dogs.

"Don't worry," he yelled out as the chopper lifted off. "I'm with you—and I've got friends." As he waved Tanook barked a goodbye from the seat next to him.

Frank and Joe changed motels after picking up their things. The walls in the old room had been repaired, covering up any sign of a forced entry. It was obvious the motel management had been paid off.

"So, what do you think?" Frank asked. "Do we march into North Slope Supply and ask why they tried to kill us?"

"No," Joe answered, checking out the walls in the new motel. "But we do have to go there and snoop around. They must have a very good reason for trying to get rid of us."

"Let me try something," said Frank, picking up the phone. "Could I have a number for Scott Sanders, please?"

"No such listing in Prudhoe," he mouthed to Joe. "Then could I have the number for North Slope Supply?" He dialed the number and got through to North Slope.

When he asked for Scott Sanders, the company said they had no record of an employee with that name.

"There has to be a connection," Joe said. "We go to Trans-Yukon, Hammond gets upset. Cindy

47

warns us, but we still get kidnapped and almost killed. Then, when we escape, North Slope comes after us with half an army. They've got to be in on it.''

"In on what?" Frank asked, throwing up his hands.

"I don't know. But I'm beginning to suspect Scott might be able to tell us.''

The boys stood outside the gate of North Slope Supply as the employees trooped out at closing time. They were showing their photograph of Scott and asking if anyone knew him. Some said he looked familiar, but not one person could identify him.

When the men had all driven away, the gate guards beckoned the Hardys over.

"Can we help you boys?" a guard with a beefy, friendly face asked. His big belly strained over his gunbelt.

"Maybe," Frank said. "We're looking for a friend of ours. We thought he worked here, but we haven't been able to find him." He held up the picture for the guard to see.

"No, don't think so," the fat guard said. "How about you, Smitty? Recognize this face?"

He handed the picture to the other guard, who shook his head, but Frank noticed that his eyes continued to glare at the picture.

"Tell you what," said the first guard. "Come

on into the guard house and we'll look up his name on the computer.''

"Great! Thanks a lot,'' Joe said. They stepped into the small booth. Two chairs and a built-in table, with a computer and phone, filled most of one wall. Joe was surprised to see submachine guns hanging on the wall.

"What was that name?''

"Scott Sanders,'' Joe said.

The heavy guard punched a few buttons on the computer, and Frank knew immediately that he was bluffing. Before he could say anything, Smitty moved up behind them to block the door, his hand on the butt of his revolver.

"Okay, boys. How about telling us what you're really here for?''

Chapter
7

THE FAT GUARD whirled around and slapped a hamlike fist into his open palm. "Answer the man!" he snarled.

"We told you the truth," Joe said, trapped between the two guards. "We're looking for our friend Scott Sanders."

"Yeah? What else?" It seemed Fatso was taking over the interrogation.

"Nothing else. We just want to make sure he's all right."

"You expect us to believe that? Two kids come all the way to Alaska—"

"How do you know about us?" Frank asked.

"Never mind. We know. What are your names?"

"I'm Frank Hardy, this is my brother Joe, and

we're friends of Scott Sanders. Does he work here? That's all we want to know."

Fatso laughed. "A lot of people work here, kid. And it's none of your business what their names are. Especially when you're trespassing."

"How can we be trespassing when you invited us in?" Joe asked as innocently as possible.

The guard's face tightened and became masklike. "It's time," he said, nodding to Smitty.

Joe was ready and ducked when Smitty swung. While the guard was off balance, he landed a solid blow to Smitty's solar plexus. The shocked guard doubled over with a gasp. But when Joe moved in to follow it up, Smitty rapped a nightstick across Joe's knee.

The sudden pain made Joe totter, and Smitty threw the stick around Joe's throat. Joe swung his elbows wide and rammed them into Smitty's stomach. *Whoosh!* The air rushed out of him. Joe whirled around and landed one punch that reduced Smitty to an unconscious heap on the floor.

While Smitty was trying to dispose of Joe, Fatso had gone for his gun.

Frank snapped off a karate kick to jar the gun out of the guard's hand just as it cleared the holster. The kick landed perfectly, ramming the revolver into Fatso's hip. But then the guard raised the gun to aim it point-blank at Frank.

Frank couldn't believe the man was still holding the gun after the kick he'd delivered.

But before Fatso could pull the trigger, Joe was

51

flying across the room and landing spread-eagle on top of the man. His gun jerked up and discharged into the ceiling. The thunder continued to bounce off the walls for several seconds. Joe grabbed the downed man's wrist and pried the gun out of his hands. A quick chop to his fleshy jaw and Fatso was out cold.

"I thought I was a goner," Frank said. "Thanks."

"It all evens out," Joe said with a quick grin. "Let's tie these bozos up. I want to get inside and see what's going on."

They handcuffed the guards, then cut the phone wires. After borrowing their guns, the boys walked through the main gate to North Slope Supply and closed it after them.

"Think anybody's here?" Joe asked.

"Doesn't look like it," Frank whispered, looking around the empty yard.

North Slope Supply consisted of a collection of small buildings surrounded by a chain-link fence. Two Quonset huts stood side by side along the western edge of the compound. A concrete bunker and a cluster of old sheds were scattered on the eastern side. In the middle of the lot stood a modern, one-story office building, its shiny white walls in direct contrast to the tired buildings around it. Long rectangular windows of tinted glass started at ground level and ran up to the roof. The entire place was deserted.

"It *is* after hours," Frank muttered, trying to convince himself that everything was normal.

"Let's check out one of these huts," Joe said.

They headed across the hard-packed dirt and ducked into the unlocked door of the first hut. It was hot inside. The air smelled of mildew, as though wet cardboard had been decaying there for years.

"Nothing here," Frank said. "This is weird. The company is called North Slope *Supply*, but there aren't any supplies."

"It is spooky," Joe agreed. "This is a company that can afford three helicopters, and their plant looks like it could barely buy three wheelbarrows."

"Come on. Let's check out the rest." They walked through the Quonset hut and out the other end. Continuing through the second hut, which was also empty, they came to the concrete bunker. This door was bolted shut.

Joe found a rusty iron bar and pried the bolt off the door. Frank hesitated at the entrance, looking behind him. "I have the feeling we're being watched," he said.

Joe shrugged. "From where? I haven't even seen a squirrel." He stepped into the bunker, and into pitch-dark. But as his eyes adjusted, he could make out a dim shape. "There's something over there," he said.

"What is it?" Frank had his back to the room, still scanning the quiet yard.

"I can't really tell—it looks like some kind of buoy."

Frank wrinkled his brow. A buoy? Where had he seen a buoy recently?

Joe came out. "Nothing else." He closed the door, leaving the bolt hanging.

Frank continued to mull over the strange emptiness of the place. "I can't believe there's nothing here. No equipment, no office supplies, no uniforms, no files—no nothing!"

"I don't see why it's so strange. Look, the office building is new. Maybe when it was built they moved everything in there."

"I can't see them storing backhoes, bulldozers, and graders in there." Frank shook his head. "It looks like this is a dummy company. But whose dummy?"

"Maybe it's Hammond's," Joe suggested. "Cindy heard him talking about getting rid of us, so I think we can assume that he sent the guys to mail us into the wilderness, right?"

"I'm with you."

"But when we escaped, who came looking for us?"

Frank nodded. "North Slope! So Trans-Yukon and North Slope might be connected somehow." He frowned. "But remember in the hut how Virgil was surprised North Slope was still around? Maybe they went bankrupt and sold off their equipment—choppers and all. That would explain all this empty storage space."

"But it wouldn't explain how the guys at the gate knew us." Joe headed for the office building. "What I want to know is, where does Scott fit in?"

"Think," said Frank. "The only thing we've said to these people is that we want to find Scott. And they keep trying to kill us. Somehow we represent a big threat to them—or Scott does."

They reached the side of the building. Standing between two long windows, Joe leaned over and tried to peer inside.

"Can't see a thing. The glass is tinted," he said.

Frank joined him, cupping his hands around his eyes as he pressed his face against the glass.

"You can see a little if you block out the light. I think . . . yeah, I do see someone in there."

"Does he look like that picture of Scott?" Joe asked.

Frank looked again. The figure was seated at a desk in profile. He seemed to be assembling some kind of electronic device. "Kind of. It could be him."

He grabbed Joe's arm before he could bang on the window. "Scott doesn't know who we are. And we don't know if he's alone."

"There's only one way to find out," Joe suggested. "Let's go in."

"Are you nuts?" Frank whispered. "These guys have tried to kill us at least three times, and you want to walk right into their nest?"

"How else are we going to talk to Scott? If that's him, it's worth a try."

Against his better judgment, Frank agreed. Stealing around the corner, they approached the thick glass door. Joe tested it, and it opened easily. He motioned for Frank to follow him in. Holding a gun ready, they walked cautiously into a brightly lit corridor.

"I don't see any security cameras, do you?" Joe asked.

"No, but they could be hidden. I don't like this, Joe. It's too easy."

"Well, I'm sorry I couldn't make it any harder," Joe said. "Come on. He's in there." He pointed to a door at the end of the hall.

About ten feet from the door they heard a strange hissing sound. They stopped. Nothing. "Heating system, I guess," Joe whispered.

A few more steps and they tasted something in their mouths—a strange tang. "Gas!" Frank yelled.

They tried to run back down the hall to get outside, but their legs became leaden. They staggered, and then their legs turned to rubber.

Frank watched the floor swim up to meet his eyes. Then there was nothing but darkness.

Chapter
8

JOE HARDY STRUGGLED to consciousness and out of his drugged sleep. The muscles he needed to open his eyes weren't able to do their job. Even when he did force his eyes open, he felt as if he were looking at the world from somewhere in the back of his head.

He reached up to rub his eyes, but his hands wouldn't move. At first he thought that, like his eyes, they were just heavy and taking their time to wake up. Then the awful realization dawned that he was strapped down—his wrists, chest, and ankles all immobilized.

With horror he decided he was strapped to an electric chair. There were wires attached to his arms, and other wires emerged from under his shirt.

Straining against the leather straps, he only

exhausted himself pulling against them. It was hopeless. Whoever had tied him up had done a professional job. He couldn't even remember what had happened to him; his mind couldn't focus on a single event.

"Mr. Hardy. I see you're with us again. How was your little nap?"

Joe tried to focus and eventually saw a short, blond man framed in a doorway. He was wearing a business suit and carrying a sheaf of papers under his arm.

"Where am I?" Joe asked. He didn't recognize the man or the room he was in. Maybe he was dreaming, he decided. None of this made sense.

"You are on the property of North Slope Supply," the man said gently. "How are you feeling?"

"Not good," Joe responded. "What happened?"

"Perhaps I should ask you the same question."

What *had* happened? Then slowly it dawned on him. They'd been stealing down the hallway on their way to see Scott, when—

"I can't really remember," he lied, playing for time.

The blond man laughed. "Let *me* refresh your memory. You were sneaking along one of our hallways last night, and you triggered one of our security mechanisms. Do you remember now?"

Joe pretended to try to remember. "Oh, yes,"

he said, as if it were a great relief to know what had happened to him. "Who are you?"

"My name is Sandy White. I'm president of North Slope Supply. I'm sorry I can't shake your hand." Joe glanced at the man's face to see if he was toying with him. But White merely smiled, and Joe couldn't read the cryptic smile.

"Why do you have me tied up like this?" Joe demanded, staring the man right in the eye.

"Why were you trespassing on the grounds of my company?"

"We—I was looking for a friend of mine." Joe changed the *we* quickly. In case Frank had gotten away, he didn't want to incriminate him.

"Who might that be?"

Joe had to think fast. By now, the guards must have come to and told their boss whom he and his brother were looking for.

"I don't think I have to tell you that," Joe told the man.

"You're right," Sandy White said, standing in front of Joe's chair and staring down at him. "You were looking for someone named Scott, weren't you?"

Joe glared at him. "Then why did you ask? What are all these wires for?"

Sandy White dropped his papers on a table and slipped his hands into his pockets, leaning back against the table. "Why don't you tell me what you know about North Slope," he coaxed, examining the shine on his shoes.

"I don't know anything," Joe said. "All I know is that Scott worked for Trans-Yukon. They say he doesn't work there now. Maybe he went to work for North Slope. All I'm doing is trying to find him."

"Are you aware that North Slope does top-secret work for the government?"

Joe rested his head against the chair back. "Really? Does that give you license to kidnap people and try to kill them?"

White chuckled. "The powers of government can run pretty far. And I have big plans."

"So what are you saying? That Scott's working for the government?" Joe kept staring at the older man, trying to get any clue from his reactions.

"I didn't say that. As a matter of fact, I don't think I've ever heard of this Scott person."

This guy was giving absolutely nothing away. Joe wished that Frank was around. He squirmed against his straps.

"So you don't know anything about North Slope?" White continued.

"Nothing, but I'm learning."

"So you are," White said mildly. "You may learn a few more things shortly."

"I think I know more than I want to already," Joe told him.

"I wouldn't say that, if I were you," White said. "You asked what the wires were for."

Joe looked down again. He saw now that the wires ran across the floor and into a hole in the wall. A tinted glass panel was framed into the wall at window height just above the hole.

"I'm curious why you've been so persistent," White remarked. "You've had to overcome pretty tough obstacles so far."

"I have to keep trying," Joe said flatly.

"You don't represent any larger organization?"

"Me? No. I told you—I'm only looking for my friend."

"I see." White paused. "I'll tell you what I'm going to do. You know what a polygraph is, don't you?"

Joe nodded. "Of course. It's a lie detector."

"That's correct. The wires attached to you right now are hooked up to a polygraph machine in the next room. I'm going to turn it on, and then I'm going to ask you a few questions. Is that all right with you?"

"I don't think I'm in a position to refuse," Joe said, but his words were aimed at Sandy White's back. The man hadn't even waited for an answer.

White paused just inside the doorway and rotated his body to face Joe again. "Be back in a moment." He gave Joe another enigmatic smile. Joe wondered what kind of guy would stick someone in a torture chamber and then tell him to have a nice day.

Joe's mind was racing. What was he going to do? He really didn't know anything. Maybe that makes it better. I'll just tell the truth, he decided.

Who knows? Maybe I can even pick up some info from the questions they ask. I just wish Frank were around.

The door opened, and White returned with the polygraph machine on a little cart.

"Sorry to keep you waiting," he apologized. But his next words turned that politeness on its head. "Here are the ground rules. I ask the questions, you answer them. If you don't answer them, or if the machine shows you're not being truthful, I'll kill you. Is that clear?"

Joe took a deep breath and nodded. White's true colors were finally revealed.

"Fine. Shall we begin?"

"My time is yours."

"What's your name?"

"Joe Hardy."

White watched the machine as a mechanical arm swung a pen point over a rolling sheet of paper.

"You didn't think I'd lie about my own name, did you?"

White stared. "How old are you?"

"Seventeen."

"Where are you from?"

"Bayport. It's a town—"

"Do you have any brothers or sisters?" White cut in.

"Yes. One brother."

"What's his name?"

"Frank Hardy."

"What does your father do?"

Joe stopped. He'd been spitting back the answers as quickly as he was questioned, but this one caught him off guard. He tried to mask his hesitation with a cough.

"Sorry, I got a tickle in my throat."

"Don't bother." White pointed to a big loop on the paper where the needle and pen had swung wildly. "You know this machine doesn't say whether you're telling the truth. It measures stress—heartbeat, breathing rate, muscle tension—even how much you sweat. I can see you had a big reaction to that question. Let me ask it again. What does your father do?"

"He's retired."

"I see. Retired from what?"

"Retired from public service. He worked for the City of New York."

White leaned forward and stared at the needle of the polygraph. He let out a stream of air as if he were disappointed.

"Mr. Hardy," he began. "Your life is hanging by the proverbial thread. It is obvious to the machine and myself that you're trying to hide something. If you won't tell me, I'll have to up the ante. You see, it's *very* important to me to find out what you know."

He got up and went outside. Almost instantly the door reopened, and White reentered, wheeling a gurney, and on the gurney was Frank. His mouth was taped shut, and wires from some kind of machine were attached to his stomach.

White took those wires and attached them to the polygraph. Then he turned to Joe.

"I have just added a small electrode to this machine. Your brother has a substantial amount of plastic explosive attached to his stomach. If the polygraph needle jumps to the electrode, it will detonate the plastique.

"Of course, the explosion will kill him." White turned the corners of his mouth up in a thin-lipped grimace. "Shall we begin again?"

Chapter

9

"WAIT A MINUTE!" Joe yelled.

"I would suggest that you remain as calm as possible, Mr. Hardy. I see by the needle you are getting upset."

"Upset? Of course I'm upset. You've got my brother wired up like—like a human bomb!"

"But *you're* the detonator. Just answer the questions honestly, Mr. Hardy, and no harm will come to your brother."

Joe could see the wide sweeps the polygraph needle was making. He tried to calm down, but he couldn't stop his heart from pounding. Forcing his eyes away from the machine, he looked over at Frank. Frank's eyes were calm.

"That's better," White said soothingly. "The more you surrender, the easier this will be."

Joe exhaled in a long hiss. If he could just stay

calm and answer the questions, maybe he could figure a way out of this situation.

He remembered some of Frank's karate exercises—those to make his mind a blank. He concentrated on deep, regular breathing.

"I'll begin again," White said, drawing up a chair and placing it near the machine. "What brings you to Alaska?"

Joe stared straight ahead and spoke in a quiet voice. "We're here to find Scott and bring him home if he's in trouble."

"What makes you think this is a job for you?"

"My brother and I have done this kind of thing before." Joe felt angry that he had to spill his guts, but he forced the anger down.

"What kind of thing?" White asked, obviously pleased that he was getting somewhere.

"We've done some rescue missions and undercover work," he said.

White seemed to be amused. "For whom?"

Easy breathing—keep your mind blank, Joe told himself. He did *not* want to answer this question. "To help friends—"

"And?" White said, watching as the needle headed for the contact point.

"And for a government agency." Joe's words came out in a rush.

"Which agency?" White was pretending to have all the patience in the world.

"The Network. We've only worked indirectly—they'd never admit they knew us," Joe said.

"Don't worry, Mr. Hardy. I won't ask them for references."

Joe glanced over at Frank, who nodded his head slightly. His eyes seemed to say that Joe was doing the right thing.

"Tell me what you know about Trans-Yukon Mining," White continued.

"Only what our friend Doug told us."

"What did Doug tell you?"

"That they had a contract to work on the pipeline and some of the managers were taking bribes."

"Did he tell you what the bribes were for?"

"He didn't know, but maybe they were buying people jobs."

"Who was buying jobs?" White asked quickly.

"Doug didn't know," Joe responded.

"Do *you* know?"

"No, I don't," Joe said emphatically.

White paused. "Well . . . the polygraph says you're not lying. But I'm not so sure."

The sound of human voices drifted into the room. White glanced up and moved quickly to the door, opening it a crack. Men were shouting outside. White slipped out without saying a word.

"Frank, are you okay?" Joe was trying to keep his breathing steady and his mind empty.

Frank nodded.

"Is that a real bomb?" Joe couldn't force himself to look at the lump on Frank's stomach.

Frank nodded again. Joe closed his eyes and tried to smother the panic that had risen, sour-tasting, to his mouth. How much longer could this go on? What would happen when they were done? Would White dare to let them go?

Dimly Joe and Frank heard a now-familiar sound—the *whirr* of a helicopter. What was going on?

After a loud crash the door flew open. The needle swerved so wildly Joe didn't dare look. But when Frank began mumbling through his gag, his eyes wide with relief, Joe turned to see Virgil and Tanook in the doorway.

"I thought I'd find you in here," Virgil said. "Are you all right?"

Frank nodded his head, which was all he could do. Joe spoke as if he were in a trance.

"We're fine, Virgil, but there's a guy who'll be back any second. Please hurry." Joe was barely whispering.

Virgil looked hard at Joe. "What's wrong with your voice? Have they given you medicine?"

Joe breathed out very loudly. "I'm wired to this machine—"

Virgil nodded. "They were asking you questions to see if you tell the truth—"

"But it's also wired to a bomb on Frank's stomach. If the needle jumps too high, the bomb will explode." Joe's voice was hardly louder than a sigh.

Virgil could barely understand what Joe was saying. "What? Frank is taking the test, too? With a bomb on his stomach?"

Joe closed his eyes. He couldn't afford to get frustrated. "It's no test. If I get upset or excited, the machine will set off his bomb. Do you understand?"

Virgil looked from the bomb to the polygraph. "That bomb—Frank—you *had* to tell the truth!"

Joe nodded. "Right. Now please cut these wires and get us out of here."

Virgil went to the polygraph and tore out the wires. He unstrapped Joe, who ripped the wires off his own body while Virgil removed the bomb from Frank. They both helped get the tape off Frank's face.

"I'd have been here sooner," Virgil said as he went to work on the tape, "but I had to take care of the dogs, and then round up my friends. I thought there would be more trouble—and I guessed you'd head here and straight into it."

Frank was finally free from all the tape. "Let's get out of here before that creep comes back," he exclaimed, rubbing his face with both hands.

"First we've got to look for Scott," Joe said.

"No," said Virgil. "There's no one else here. I checked. Follow me!" Virgil ran to the door and peered out. "No one."

They tore down a long corridor to the front of

the building, where they heard Virgil's friends shouting at the front gate about North Slope being unfair to workers. "That drew all the guards," Virgil said. "One of my friends will bring the chopper in. Stay low."

They crouched at the side of the building, out of sight of the guards and White. Virgil pulled a small walkie-talkie from his jacket and called in the chopper. In less than two minutes it dropped in, low and fast.

When the chopper was ten feet off the ground, they sprang up and sprinted in a zigzag pattern for its open door.

The noise of the blades whipping overhead was deafening, but even it wasn't loud enough to drown out the sound of gunfire. They dove through the door headfirst.

Frank was the last one in, and as he landed the helicopter lurched. His kneecap felt shattered. The pain sent him rolling across the floor as the chopper tilted up into the dust-filled sky.

Virgil and Joe examined the damage to Frank's knee. His jeans were torn, and a mean-looking gash cut a line down his entire kneecap.

"It's not a bullet wound," Joe said. "You must have smacked your knee on the edge of the chopper as you dove in."

Frank held his leg. "This definitely has not been one of my better days."

"Take it easy," Joe said. "We'll have you fixed up in no time."

Virgil dressed the wound as the pilot headed for a hunting camp in the mountains. "You'll have to keep the leg straight for a couple of days, but it'll be all right," he said.

That night, after dropping off Virgil's friend, they sat around the fire after dinner to talk. Even though the night sky was light, the air was considerably cooler than in the day. The warmth of the flames soothed them.

"I think we've got to jump on this right now," Joe insisted. "Sandy White may think we represent the Network, and he may try to speed up his plans now."

"Well, I'm not going to be much help," Frank said, looking at his outstretched leg. "And you may think I'm crazy, but I don't think the North Slope compound is where the action is."

"What do you mean?" Joe asked.

"Well, for one thing, there were so few men there. My hunch is, White's got another base of operations, and I think it's north of here."

"North? There's only ocean north of here!" Joe exclaimed.

"Well, maybe his troops are on the ocean."

"But why north?"

"It's a matter of buoys," was all Frank offered. Frank shifted, trying to make his leg more comfortable. "It also seems evident to me that he's involved with Hammond at Trans-Yukon. Did you notice how he knew who Doug was?"

"Right," Joe said, remembering. "He didn't ask who Doug was when I mentioned him."

"Well, that's one thing that needs checking out at Prudhoe. I think I'll stay up here. I've got this crazy hunch about a boat or something."

"I was planning to go fishing soon," Virgil said. "Might as well go tomorrow. We can check out the immediate area, and that way Frank can stay off his leg."

"Great!" Frank said. "That's perfect."

"It's perfect, if you'll take me back to Prudhoe," Joe cut in. "There are a lot of ends to tie up there. There's the Hammond-White connection. And was that really Scott we saw? I mean, what would he be doing there? In some lab, after hours?"

"I'll take you," Virgil said. "Better go now. This way I can come back and then get a good start in the morning."

"Fine with me," Joe responded, getting up from the ground.

"Just don't get into trouble," Frank said. "We won't be around to help you out."

"What? Me? Get into trouble?" Joe smiled. "You've got to be kidding. I'm just going to do a little creative snooping, that's all."

"Right." Frank laughed. "Just don't get caught."

"You can always contact the weather pilot at the airport if you want to get in touch with us,"

Virgil volunteered. "He's a friend of mine, and he flies out over the ocean just about every day."

Joe nodded. "Fine. He's one of the first people I'll check in with."

"Who else do you know in Prudhoe?" Frank asked as Joe hurried to leave. "Wait a minute. Are you going to talk with Cindy?"

"That's for me to know, and you to find out." Joe grinned. "Catch you later."

He climbed into the helicopter. In a matter of minutes the chopper was a speck in the huge northern sky, and Frank was alone by the fire.

He stared into the flames, thinking. An image of buoys in some part of his mind kept insisting that this whole thing had something to do with the ocean.

Frank closed his eyes, trying to concentrate. But the fire and his rough day drugged him. Soon he was dozing. The flicker of the firelight played against his eyelids like a blinking light, like the safety buoys floating back home in Barmet Bay . . . .

Frank's eyes snapped open as he realized what was nagging him. He'd seen them *twice*. They'd found one on the plane, before they'd had to jump. Then there was the other one in the bunker at North Slope Supply.

He tried to call up an image of what they'd looked like. The one on the plane had a radio transponder. Well, that cinched it. That definitely explained *why* he kept thinking of the ocean. But why would anyone want or need a floating radio set?

Frank's head jerked back as he pulled himself totally awake. A floating radio could pinpoint the high-seas rendezvous for an airplane—or a submarine.

Chapter
10

VIRGIL HAD HARDLY landed the chopper before Frank ran limping up to talk about his idea.

"You could be right," Virgil said. "Some of my friends think there's submarine activity up there."

"How would they know?" Frank asked.

"When things come out of a sub, they head up to the surface—oil, that kind of stuff," Virgil answered. "We'll see tomorrow."

They slept soundly and at midmorning set off in the helicopter for Virgil's fishing camp. The dogs were still there. Apparently someone came in to feed them every day while Virgil wasn't there. The boat was still sound and seaworthy, and soon they were chugging through the white-caps of the Arctic Ocean.

Virgil laughed as Tanook jumped aboard. "This dog loves fishing," he said.

The boat was sturdy, built more for endurance than speed. The engine was mounted on the back, and Virgil stored extra fuel and supplies under the seats. It was a craft made for the icy waters of the northern seas.

Frank sat in the center, Virgil at the stern, one hand on the tiller. Tanook took his station up front. He enjoyed the wind in his face, even though he did bark when hit by spray.

As they headed north Virgil tended to business, throwing out lines and catching fish. He threw them, alive, into the large wooden box in the middle of the boat. Some he would use for bait— others for food. One he threw to Tanook, who quickly gobbled it down.

"When autumn comes, all this will be dotted with pack ice," Virgil told Frank with a grin. "All the native people know. The best time to travel is in the wintertime."

Frank looked out over the black water. It was hard to imagine what it would look like a couple of months from then—white and frozen in the darkness of the Arctic winter.

After an hour of fishing Virgil pointed to a shiny spot on the water where the reflections from the sun were tinted with blue and red. "See that?" he called. "Oil. Not good for fish or seals!"

Frank had seen pictures of oil slicks in news

magazines, but this wasn't the same. "It doesn't look very big," he said.

"Big enough," Virgil muttered bitterly. "This had to come from a big ship—a freighter or a submarine."

They continued north, past the slick, then past still another one. Virgil scanned the horizon silently. Frank, too, fell into silence, prickling with the feeling that they were not alone. Something was out there with them. But all he heard was the droning of their engine as they plowed north.

Virgil turned off the engine without warning. The complete silence was a shock to Frank. He looked at Virgil to see if everything was all right. Virgil just held up a finger to his lips to silence him. His ear was cocked into the wind and he was gazing at nothing.

"I think I hear something," he said after a moment. "Listen."

Frank caught only the sounds of waves slapping against the side of the boat and of the wind.

"What do you think it is?" Frank whispered.

"A boat, or maybe a plane," Virgil said. He remained perfectly still. "I think it's coming up from the south."

Frank was amazed at Virgil's hearing. At the fishing camp, he'd heard the approaching choppers minutes before anyone else. Now he'd picked out the sound of a distant engine over all the wind and water.

But Frank was the first to catch the glint of sunlight on the plane's wings. "There it is!"

It showed only as a tiny speck against the white of the overcast clouds. But it became clearer as it drew nearer. "It's a seaplane," Frank said, "with pontoons."

"Not many planes come out here prepared to land on the water." Virgil cranked up the engine again, pointing the boat due north and opening the throttle. The bow rose out of the water as the propellers bit into the sea.

"How can we race a plane?" Frank asked.

"We're ahead of it already, and we can keep an eye on it for quite a while," Virgil said. "If we line up with its course, sooner or later we're bound to come across it when it lands."

They continued on in silence. Virgil no longer fished—he wrapped up all his lines and stowed them.

A thought occurred to Frank. "Do we have enough fuel?"

Virgil glanced down at the tanks. "Depends on how long we have to go. We can keep on for a couple more hours."

Frank sat back to enjoy the ride. What more could he want? His leg was feeling better; he had the smell of salt water and the wind—and maybe answers for a lot of questions.

The plane was long out of sight, but after two hours of following its course they caught up with it. There it was, bobbing on the water in the middle of nowhere.

Frank tapped Virgil's arm. "Better turn off the engine. We don't want them to think we're spying on them."

"What if we're fishing?" Virgil said with a grin. "That shouldn't be suspicious."

Throwing out some fishing lines, Virgil handed Frank a parka. "Pull the hood up," he suggested. "They may have binoculars."

Looking innocent and busy, Virgil started the engine, and they trolled slowly, moving constantly toward the seaplane. There was no sign of life either in or around it. Where was the pilot?

As they got closer Frank's eyes narrowed. "Hey, Virgil, that plane isn't moving around. I think it's anchored."

Virgil steered around it in a wide circle. After several minutes they were able to see the other side of the plane and they got a glimpse into the cockpit. Two men *were* inside, deep in conversation. They obviously hadn't seen the little fishing boat.

Bobbing up and down in the water, next to the plane, was a sea buoy with a radio transponder on it.

Frank grinned in triumph. "That could be the buoy they had on the plane we fell from, or one exactly like it. We may have tied these guys into the attempt to kidnap us. Now all we have to do is see what they're waiting for."

Virgil cut the engine and drifted. Because they were so low in the water, they were hidden by waves most of the time. They sat still with poles in their hands, but with both eyes on the plane.

Their work was soon rewarded, for the sea suddenly erupted yards from the plane. And a black hulking form lifted out of the waves like some sea behemoth. Frank and Virgil watched in stunned silence.

Shedding tons of seawater, the metal sea monster revealed itself to be the superstructure of a submarine. A hatch opened, and a man clambered along the sub's deck, holding a chain.

One of the men on the plane tossed a line to him, and he towed the plane up next to the sub.

A second man emerged from the hatch. Frank could see right away who it was. The sun picked out his blond hair, marking him as Sandy White.

"That's the guy who wired us to the polygraph," Frank whispered. "He's the president of North Slope Supply."

"Are you sure?" Virgil asked.

"Positive," Frank said. White was giving orders to the man who'd fastened the ropes. Then he stopped, his eyes scanning the horizon. Frank had the uncomfortable feeling that White had spotted them.

White moved to the plane and reached out. The pilot tossed him something. For a second White held his hands up to his eyes. Then he turned to the sailor, who quickly turned and disappeared down the hatch.

White's hands went back to his eyes. This time, sunlight reflected off the polished lenses. "Binoculars!" Frank said. "He has spotted us!"

A crew of four came tumbling out of the hatch, dragging something. Frank recognized it as an inflatable boat and an outboard motor.

"We'd better get out of here," he said. "If they catch us, White will recognize me."

"Okay, here we go," Virgil said.

He gunned the motor, turning the boat south as they heard another engine ripping into life behind them. "That sucker inflates fast," Virgil said.

Frank looked around, his mouth set in a straight line. "It moves fast, too."

The inflatable craft was tiny but high-powered. And it was gaining on them with every second.

Chapter

11

WHEN JOE ARRIVED in Prudhoe, the first thing he did was change hotels once again and get some sleep. Then later that day he set himself up on a stakeout.

When quitting time came for Trans-Yukon, Joe was reading a newspaper, sitting on a low wall across the street from their offices. He kept his face covered while keeping an eye on the workers. Finally Cindy Velikov opened the heavy glass door and stepped out into the late-afternoon sunshine. She buttoned her coat as she strolled across town on foot.

Joe followed her, but it wasn't easy to keep his distance. Her steps were small compared to Joe's normal impatient stride. He had to force himself to maintain a leisurely gait and stop frequently, as though he were basking in the warm weather.

She went into a grocery store, but Joe didn't dare to go inside. When Cindy came out she had a small brown bag of groceries in her arms. She continued to walk, now into a residential area.

After a few more turns she walked up to the back door of a small red ranch house. Joe walked past. He went to the end of the block, checking to make sure he wasn't being tailed. Then he walked around to the back door and knocked.

She stood behind the screen, staring out at him. For a minute she didn't know Joe. Then, after she recognized him, she smiled broadly and opened the door.

"Joe Hardy!" She grinned.

Joe smiled back. "That's me," he said. "I hope you don't mind. I followed you home because I want to talk to you."

"No, I don't mind," she said. "Come in."

Cindy opened the door, and Joe stepped into the kitchen. The floor was terra-cotta tiles, and the appliances were all new. White café curtains covered half the window above the sink.

Cindy laughed. "What are you staring at?"

"Sorry," Joe said. "I guess I was a little surprised—your kitchen looks so modern."

"I guess you were expecting a log cabin with a water pump in the kitchen and an outhouse." Her eyes twinkled as she spoke. "We are part of the United States, you know—just bigger and better." She made a sweeping gesture with her hands, reminding Joe of what he'd said about New York City. They laughed.

"So, what would you like to talk to me about?" she asked.

Joe came straight out with it. "I want to find out about what's going on with your company."

Cindy nodded. "Okay," she said. "But I think we'd better take a walk. My father will be home soon, and I don't want him to hear this."

She picked up her coat, and they left through the kitchen door.

"Oops," Cindy said, turning around. "I'd better leave my dad a note, so he doesn't worry." She ducked into the kitchen again and was back a moment later.

They headed out to the street, both with their hands in their pockets. Joe spoke first.

"I never thanked you for warning us that night," he said. "Did you hear anything from your side about what happened to us?"

Cindy shrugged. "No. I thought you'd left the state."

"We almost did—the hard way. A bunch of guys jumped us and threw us on a plane. We barely escaped."

"You should have left when I warned you." Cindy turned to Joe. "My boss isn't a very nice man."

"So why do you work for him?"

"Jobs aren't so easy to get up here. I've had this one for a few years, and I'm saving money to go to college." She shrugged. "And Mr. Hammond wasn't always this way."

"What way? He seems friendly."

"Sure, he's friendly. But I think he's involved in something crooked. He's been hiring weird people we don't need, and firing men who've worked for him for years. The place has really changed over the last six months."

"How do you know all this?" Joe asked.

"I update the personnel records, so I see everything that's going on. Mr. Hammond thinks I don't pay any attention, but I do. We were letting people go because of money problems, then all this weird hiring began.

"But I can't prove that anything wrong is going on," Cindy continued. "And also, no one who's suspicious wants to be labeled as a trouble maker. This is a small town," she said, glancing around at the little houses that lined the streets. "And we have just a few big companies. Mr. Hammond is a powerful person here. He knows all the other bosses. If the men who got fired grumble too loudly, they won't get any work."

Joe saw what he was up against. "You said it wasn't always like this—so who changed things? Who's spreading the bribes around?"

"I have no idea." Cindy shook her head. "At first I thought it was just a trickle of guys from the lower forty-eight states, up here looking for work. In hard times, they'll pay for their first job."

"Does that make sense?" Joe asked, trying to imagine how anyone could afford to do such a thing.

"For some of them, it does. When jobs are scarce up here, people are willing to do just about anything. See, the pay is very high. If you're willing to live cheaply here, you can save quite a bit."

"You mean a guy could come up here, bribe someone to get a job, make a living, and still save money?"

"Exactly. They do it all the time. It's not a comfortable life, but they can make a bundle, even with the bribes they have to pay."

"You said 'at first.' Do you think it's just a guy here and there paying Hammond for jobs?"

Cindy shook her head, her blond hair brushing her shoulders. "It's been happening too regularly. And the people all wind up getting the same job."

"What job?" Joe asked.

"I don't know exactly what they call it. Trans-Yukon has a contract to maintain parts of the pipeline. They cut brush, scrape ice off—even clean the inside of the pipes. It seems like that's the job that the bribes were about—the inside job."

"You mean people actually go into the pipe to clean it?"

Cindy nodded. "It'a a really dirty job, but it's

got to be done—to make sure everything's okay."

Pieces began coming together for Joe. "Millions of dollars of oil flow through the pipeline. Suppose somebody could go up in the mountains where no one is around and sabotage the whole operation?"

"There's a security system," Cindy said. "The pipe has to be guarded."

"Well, if I was going to pay Hammond for a job, I'd want to be a guard on the outside, rather than do the dirty work inside."

"There's one other thing. I heard about some kind of a deal between Hammond and White going down on Sawtooth Mountain tomorrow morning."

"Guess who'll be there to greet them," Joe said, curious.

They'd arrived in the business district of Prudhoe, just a few blocks from the waterfront.

"Would you like to walk over to the water?" Cindy asked.

"Fine," Joe said. He was still trying to figure how North Slope and Scott Sanders fit into the story.

The docks weren't pretty. They were a jumble of serious industrial equipment spread along a cold, flat, unfriendly coastline. Still, there was something exciting about walking past the huge tankers, pipes, and pumps. It gave the feeling of important business being conducted, even at the edge of the world.

Joe and Cindy stopped on the street that looked out over the busy port. The sound of engines and the heavy clang of hammers beat through the air. It was just past seven o'clock in the evening, but the sun was high and the light was reddish gold.

"I've lived here all my life," Cindy said. "My father is a descendant of the original Russian settlers. My mother was the daughter of an air force captain stationed here. She died a couple of years ago."

"I'm sorry to hear that," Joe said.

"This is all I know. I'd really like to get out of here. You know, see the world. I feel as if I know next to nothing."

"Well, there's plenty to see," Joe said. "It seems to me you know a lot about things around here."

"Maybe too much," a rasping voice hissed from behind them. When they pivoted around, they were smack up against a huge, towering guy.

"Maybe Mr. Hammond should hear just how much you know about things around here." The man had a thick wool cap pulled down over a square, fleshy face. When he took his hands out of his pockets, Joe stared. These were the biggest hands Joe had ever seen, thick and broad, with bulging knuckles and callused skin. If this guy made a fist, it would nearly be the size of Joe's head.

"Come on, you two," the man growled. "We've got a date with Mr. Hammond."

One huge paw shoved at Joe's shoulder, forcing him to walk in front.

Joe's fists clenched. How could he not have known they were being tailed? He was furious.

"Don't try anything, pal," the thug warned. "I'm holding on to the girl's arm right now. But I could just as easily grab her neck." He laughed. "You wouldn't want that, would you?"

Chapter

12

"PLEASE, JOE, DO what he says." Cindy sounded terrified. When Joe glanced back, he saw the tears that lined her eyes.

"Keep walking," growled the man. "Never mind what's going on back here." Joe forced himself to step out. He could hear Hammond's goon wheezing as he lumbered along behind.

Joe's mind flicked frantically from one plan to another. He had to nail this guy. But how? He was stuck out front, and the guy had Cindy for a hostage. Anything Joe might do to let Cindy get away would get him creamed. But he couldn't just run for it and leave Cindy. Nor would he be delivered to Spike Hammond, all wrapped up like a Christmas present.

Somehow, he had to get the edge on this guy. He'd have to watch and hope for an opportunity.

The streets they were on now, down by the docks, were narrow and gray. Low buildings, mostly warehouses, squatted under the arctic sky. Many of the roads were dirt—grass, moss, and lichen grew wherever cars and feet hadn't trampled them.

"Turn here," Hammond's goon commanded.

Joe followed his directions. They were walking away from the waterfront and toward the center of town. It was quiet and deserted, but not too far off they could hear the sound of music and men's laughter. Maybe there was a chance after all.

To set things up, Joe decided on a little distraction. "So tell me," he said over his shoulder as he continued to walk, "does Hammond give you a piece of his action?"

"None of your business."

"Hammond's raking it in with his bribe scam," Joe went on. "I hope you're getting some."

"I do all right. I'm on retainer," the goon said in a proud voice.

"Like a lawyer," Joe said. "But I bet he doesn't pay your medical expenses."

"Why should he?"

"Because someday someone will knock your stupid head off, and the doctors are going to have to sew it back on."

Joe had timed the zinger perfectly. They'd just reached an area with fast-food joints, stores, video-game parlors, and a movie theater. Man-mountain couldn't do anything to him here.

He could hear the thug's teeth grinding together. "Just keep your mouth shut, punk. I'll take care of you later."

They were passing a video-game parlor as a crowd of men came spilling out onto the sidewalk. They were laughing and cheering as two of them broke into a sparring match. The fighters held their fists high and danced in circles around each other, ducking and weaving, flicking hard knuckles toward grinning faces. It was all in fun—none of the jabs were connecting. But the crowd made a big thing out of each near-miss.

One of the fighters lost his balance and bumped into Joe. A chance! Joe spun the off-balance boxer back into Cindy and the goon. The guy found himself with his arms around Cindy, and before he could get loose, Joe jumped in.

"Keep your hands off my friend's girl," he yelled, taking a huge wind-up with his right hand. The punch was more like a slap. Everyone in the street heard the *crack* of Joe's hand on the boxer's cheek.

The crowd became quiet—too quiet. They were mad. It was one thing to have a friendly sparring match with a buddy. It was another to see some stranger haul off and slug that buddy in the face.

"Get him!" somebody yelled, heading toward Joe. "Fix that punk's face for him!"

Joe stood his ground in front of Cindy as the

crowd surged forward. He took some punches but also threw a few good ones, to keep these guys good and angry. Retreating a bit, he risked a look back toward Cindy. Hammond's goon still held her arm in a tight grip.

Jumping behind the confused thug, Joe yelled, "Come on, pal, I'm not fighting them all for you. She's your girl, after all."

Figuring the goon was with Joe, the crowd began to jostle him. Man-mountain shoved them away, but they shoved back and then began throwing punches. It was perfect. He lost his temper, dropped Cindy's arm, and waded into the crowd, slugging at everybody.

While the thug was busy getting mobbed, Joe grabbed Cindy by the wrist and pulled her down the street. "Come on! Now's our chance!"

As they ran the yelling and groaning faded behind them. Joe glanced back as they rounded a corner and saw that the goon had belatedly realized what was going on. He was pulling out of the fight.

Joe and Cindy ducked around another corner and found themselves in a narrow back street, barely wide enough for a single car. Joe led the way, running as fast as he could while towing Cindy. He tried the first door they came to, hoping to duck before Hammond's thug could see where they'd gone. The door was open, so they stepped inside, yanking it shut behind them.

Their hiding place was dark, with flickering

light glistening in the air behind them. Joe stared around in confusion until it hit him. They were standing behind a movie screen. The flickering light came from the film being projected onto the thin silvery sheet in front of them. They were standing in the back of the movie theater, looking at the reverse images of the film.

"We'd better get away from the door," Joe whispered. "Follow me."

They tiptoed along the back wall to a dark corner on the far side of the stage. As soon as they reached it the outside door banged open, and the thug peered in.

Joe looked around for an escape route. An iron ladder, mounted on the cinder-block wall, was just to his left. He silently motioned for Cindy to climb up. As soon as she reached the catwalk at the top, Joe followed.

Once they were on the dark catwalk, he whispered in her ear, "We had to make our move before his eyes adjusted to the dark."

They both stared down as their pursuer searched the backstage area. The images from the film swam across his clothes. Music blared loudly from speakers placed directly behind the screen. The thug reached the dark corner where they'd stood a minute before. And Cindy gasped out loud. Too loud. The guy glanced up.

Joe climbed over the railing and dropped on top of the man standing below. He made a perfect landing, knocking the guy flat to the floor. Immediately they began to grapple. But thanks to his huge bulk the thug quickly got the upper hand, pinning Joe to the floor.

With a quick jerk Joe managed to get his hands free, and he clapped them together hard over the thug's ears. The pain threw the guy off balance, and Joe took advantage of that to shove him back onto the floor again.

Leaping to his feet, Joe jumped on him. But the thug was a born street fighter. He rolled aside and lunged toward the wall, where a large flashlight hung from a hook. Grabbing it, he swung it viciously at Joe's head, catching him on the ear.

Joe staggered, his ear ringing, his vision going red. He was two seconds from being out cold— but he was also madder than he'd felt in a long time. Ignoring the pain, he waited for the guy to swing again, and when it happened, he ducked. The flashlight passed over his head, leaving the goon wide open.

Putting all his weight behind a solid uppercut, Joe caught the guy right on the chin. He toppled slowly to his knees, the fight knocked out of him.

Joe yanked the flashlight from the man's hand, pushed him to the floor, and sat on his chest. "Now talk," he whispered angrily. "What's Hammond up to?"

"I don't know," he groaned.

"You'd better stop stalling," Joe warned, his voice covered by the soundtrack from the film.

"Unless you want to be swept up by the ushers after the midnight show."

"All right. We're getting a big payment up on Sawtooth Mountain in the morning. That's all I know. The boss wants everything to go smoothly," the goon mumbled.

"Who's giving you the money?"

"I swear I don't know. Different people every time."

"You'd better be telling the truth," Joe growled. "Now get over there by the ladder."

The man crawled across the floor and leaned against the wall. Joe motioned for Cindy to come down. They undid the goon's belt to use to tie him to the iron bars of the ladder and shoved a handkerchief into his mouth.

Turning on the flashlight, Joe escorted Cindy around the edge of the screen, down the steps, and up the main aisle of the theater.

"We look official, don't we?" he joked. "Just like an usher and a customer."

There was no one in the lobby out front. They left the light on the ledge outside the box office and stepped out into the bright night.

"I've got to get in touch with Frank. Do you know anyone with a ham radio?" he asked.

"Yes—my father," Cindy said excitedly. "He keeps it in the basement."

He grinned. "Great. Let's go!" Once again they were running through the streets.

Cindy's father wasn't home, but Joe was able

to get the set going. He put out a call every five minutes for over two hours, but there was no response.

"This isn't good. I know Virgil keeps his radio on." He tried a few more times, but he was getting anxious. "We've got to get ahold of them."

Cindy left him twiddling dials on the radio set. "I'll make some supper." But she'd hardly reached the kitchen when Joe came bounding up the stairs.

"We've got to go to the airport. I just talked to the guy who flies the weather plane. He's a friend of Virgil's, and he'll take us out over the ocean to find them."

Cindy turned off the stove and got the keys to her dad's car. She drove like a pro to the airport, where they found the pilot sipping coffee in front of the hanger.

In less than ten minutes they were in the air, scouting the gray waters of the Arctic Ocean. Joe's eyes were getting tired when he saw something floating in the water.

"What's that?" he asked, pointing.

The pilot glanced over. "First iceberg of the season." He dipped the plane for a closer look.

But floating behind the ice was a boat. Joe trained his binoculars on it. Yes, he recognized that boat—it was Virgil's.

And it was empty, drifting aimlessly on the cold vastness of the silent sea.

Chapter

13

SEVERAL HOURS EARLIER Frank and Virgil had been speeding through the rough waters, trying to outrun the inflatable speedboat.

"There's no way we're going to outrun these guys," Virgil shouted over the noise of the churning engine. Ice-cold water sprayed up from the bow of Virgil's little fishing craft as it bounced over the waves. Tanook, who'd been lying peacefully on the floor of the boat, was up now, his nose pointing anxiously into the wind, his ears flattened against his head.

Frank looked back. Their pursuers seemed to be flying over the water.

"That must be some kind of a high-tech machine," Frank shouted. "If we can't outrun it, what do we do?"

"We need to find some pack ice," Virgil yelled.

"It might give us an advantage." He scanned the horizon for icebergs.

They plowed through the choppy seas. Frank clung to his seat, not only to keep his balance but also to keep his leg as straight as possible. He didn't want to tear open his wound by falling when the boat hit the trough of a wave. Virgil, meanwhile, had stood up in the stern, one hand on the tiller. His dark eyes squinted into the gray distance.

He sat abruptly, steering the boat on a new course. "Ice," he said briefly. They quickly reached a cluster of icebergs, and he nosed the boat in, looking for a crack between the huge chunks. Finding one, he drove the boat into the narrow passage. The sides of the boat scraped along the ice, but by keeping the engine going, Virgil was able to nudge some of the smaller ice fragments away.

"We might be able to hide in here," he said, running the engine slower. "They'll be afraid to come in."

The pack ice glistened around them, white and blue. Some pieces were tall, towering over the boat, giving them protection not only from the wind but from their pursuers. Other pieces were flat, riding in the water like traveling islands. Virgil drove the boat skillfully through the little channels between the chunks.

Once they reached the shelter of several big bergs, Virgil cut the engine altogether, and they drifted. They could hear the engine of the other boat bearing down on them.

"I think we'd better give them one more look at us," Virgil said.

"What for?" Frank asked. "Aren't we safer in here?"

"Uh-uh," Virgil said. "They've got to think we're dead. So we'll pretend to capsize."

"How're you going to . . .?"

Virgil gunned the boat back out into the open water. The attackers were within firing range, bouncing along on a high crest. Two shots rang out, then Virgil banked into a steep turn and circled the first part of the ice pack. Suddenly they were on the other side of a tall berg.

"The last thing they saw was our turn," Virgil said. "That's very dangerous in this water. Now—we have to move fast." He cut off the engine. "Unravel that fishing line. We've got to set up a trick."

They drifted up against the edge of the ice. Virgil leapt out and drove a metal spike deep into the granular snow that covered the surface of the berg. Then, taking the transparent fishing line, he tied one end to the stake and the other to a hook protruding from his boat at the water line. He made sure the stake was set securely, then covered it with snow. Then he took a weight and tied it to the line.

"Good. That'll make it sink," he said. "Okay, everybody out." Frank and Tanook jumped onto the iceberg. Frank was hobbling. Tanook was wagging his tail and looking from Virgil to Frank.

"I hope this works," Virgil said. "I'm going to make it look like we tipped over." With an empty plastic container, he shoveled water into the boat. When a substantial puddle had collected on the bottom, he shoved the boat away and toward the open passage to the sea. The wind and the waves pushed it the rest of the way into open water. The fishing line was completely invisible.

"Okay, let's hide," he said. "This way." They hurried across the relatively flat surface of the iceberg, their feet crunching the snow.

"Tanook first," Virgil said. He picked out a place where Tanook could hide. After making the dog lie down, he began covering him with snow. In a few minutes, Tanook had completely disappeared.

"Stay!" Virgil commanded. Tanook did not move. "Good boy!"

Virgil walked away, feeling for the depth of the snow with his feet. When he found a place that he liked, he motioned for Frank to lie down.

"You hide here. The snow will protect you."

Frank lay down, warm in the heavy parka Virgil had given him. With large chunks, then handfuls of finer powder, Virgil proceeded to bury Frank, leaving him airholes.

"Okay?" Virgil called.

"Fine!" Frank replied, making sure his leg was in a comfortable position.

"Just in time. Here they come."

Frank heard Virgil burrowing into the snow next to him. Then the *brrr* of the pursuit boat's engine reached his ears. It sounded as if they were circling Virgil's abandoned boat. Frank hoped they wouldn't find the transparent lifeline, or worse, run afoul of it. If their propeller cut it, Virgil's boat would be adrift for real.

The engine drone moved back and forth in front of the ice pack. They must be looking for our bodies, Frank thought. Then he heard nothing. The engine had been cut off—it hadn't died away. Moments later the sound of human voices broke the silence.

Then came the crunch of footsteps on the snow. What if they see our footprints? Frank suddenly thought.

Judging from the direction of the voices, the men from the sub had landed quite a distance from where Frank and his friends were hidden.

"We check it out," one voice said in a thick accent. "Is better to be sure."

Frank heard rattles and scrapes—someone was climbing the little hill in the center of the ice island. A new voice asked something in a foreign language.

"Remember orders—we talk English," the first voice growled. "I see nothing here. We go back to sub—get ready for the drop at Sawtooth."

Next came a skidding sound, then the crunching and squeaking of feet on snow.

"Probably drowned, those kids," the second voice said.

So, White recognized me, and figures Virgil must be Joe, Frank thought. Good. We have another surprise to hit them with. He lay as still as possible as the voices drew nearer.

Suddenly they were very close.

"Footprints?" one man said.

They stopped to examine the tracks. "Could be seals—or polar bears."

"Seals, I think. No polar bears here. Or kids, either, I think—not unless they throw their boat away."

The searchers laughed. "We go back, tell about drowned boys."

Frank heard them walk away with relief. But wait a second—they were heading toward Tanook.

How could a dog—even as intelligent a dog as Tanook—remain under the snow? Frank was thinking to himself. "Please, Tanook, be good," Frank muttered under his breath. "Please!"

From the sound of things, Tanook did remain still—right until one of the searchers stepped on him. Frank heard a yelp and a growl, a wild yell from one of the men, and then a gunshot.

Frank pushed his way up to peek from his hiding place. Tanook must have gone for one searcher's wrist—since he could see a revolver on the snow. The man was howling, nearly drowning out Tanook's growls.

The other crewman kept circling the struggling pair, trying to get a good shot at Tanook. The dog was twisting and jumping so much that it was hard to take aim. Frank saw the man raise his gun, then lower it, afraid of shooting his comrade.

Then Tanook switched his grip and lunged for the man's throat. The man reeled back, throwing his hands up to protect himself. Tanook smashed into his chest. The other man took steady aim at the dog, and then Frank leapt up from his snow grave with a shout.

The man with the gun whirled toward Frank and snapped off a wild shot. At the same time his buddy pushed Tanook away—and tottered off the iceberg.

He hit the freezing black water and had time for one desperate cry before he went into shock. Perhaps it was merciful. The man's white face was stiffening even as he sank below the surface.

Everything had halted for that horrible moment. Even Tanook stood still, staring at the water as if he couldn't believe what had happened.

The remaining seaman looked shocked, but he was well trained, and he knew his business. His gun hand was rock steady, the revolver aimed dead on target—right at Frank's heart.

Chapter
14

VIRGIL SPRANG FROM his hiding place like a missile launched from an underground silo. Now the gunman had to turn and face yet another enemy. He didn't know which way to point his gun.

Tanook crouched and growled, his teeth bared. Frank turned sideways so he'd be a smaller target. Virgil began to speak to Tanook in his native language.

The man with the gun spoke. "You come with me," he said nervously, pointing the gun first at Frank, then at Virgil, all the while keeping an eye on Tanook, who was creeping closer.

"Come and get us," Frank said boldly.

The man glared, then fired at Frank—and missed. His revolver was a snub-nose, and Frank was a good thirty yards away. Virgil hit the ground at the sound of the gun. That was wise, since the gunman whirled, squeezing off a shot in his direction. The bullet whizzed inches above Virgil's prone body. The gunman turned on Tanook. Too late.

Tanook was leaping as the gunman snapped off another shot. Tanook twisted in midair and came in at waist level, his teeth sinking into the wrist of the guy's gun hand.

With Tanook holding the gun down, Frank had a chance. He bent his good knee and hurled himself across the snow to join in the struggle. The man was still clutching his pistol, fighting to grab the gun with his free hand. That's when Frank landed, flattening the guy.

"Nice work, Tanook," Frank said, patting the dog. The man's body was limp, and Tanook let go of the wrist. Frank took the gun.

"Only one bullet left," he said, glancing in the chamber. Then he looked down at the man who lay unconscious in the snow. "Sorry to gang up on you, pal, but we had no choice."

"Who is he?" Virgil asked, staring at the man's pale face.

"He works for Sandy White, that's all I know. When he was talking with his buddy, they mentioned something about Sawtooth. Does that mean anything to you?" Frank asked as he knelt down to check the man's vital signs.

"Yes. There's a mountain called Sawtooth."

"I think that'll be our next stop," Frank said. "We've got to figure out, once and for all, what

White and Hammond are up to. Let's get your boat and head out of here."

Virgil shook his head. "We'd waste time— better take their boat." He looked around worriedly. "Maybe the ice walls kept in the sounds of the gunshots. If not—well, sound travels pretty far over open water. I'd like to be out of here. We can leave my boat for Sleeping Beauty here."

After checking the amount of fuel left in the inflatable speed boat, they started the engine and headed for Virgil's fishing camp. It was a fast but uncomfortable trip.

Joe's face was grim as he sat deep in thought aboard the weather plane. What had happened to Frank and Virgil? The abandoned boat, floating in the middle of the ocean, was a haunting sight. He hardly dared think about it.

"You've got to take us to Sawtooth Mountain. Can you do that?" he asked the pilot.

"Sure can. But there's no way I can land. You'll have to jump. I've got some chutes in the back."

"I don't think Cindy should jump," Joe said, looking at the girl beside him. "Maybe you should go back to Prudhoe."

"No way!" Cindy shouted. "I'm not going there. They know where I live, and chances are that fat guy got away and told Hammond I was with you."

"But you could hang out at a friend's house until this thing gets settled," Joe suggested.

Cindy fixed her eyes on Joe. "Read my lips," she said. "The answer is *N-O*. I'm going with you!"

"Okay, if that's what you want," Joe said, throwing up his hands. "It's not going to be much fun. Your boss likes to play hardball."

"Ex-boss," Cindy told him.

They climbed into the back of the plane and strapped on parachutes. Joe had to show Cindy how to do it and teach her how to pull her cord.

"I'll be right with you," he said. "It's easy. Don't be afraid. And when you land, keep your knees slightly bent."

Cindy nodded and bit her lip. It was clear she was scared but determined to go through with the jump anyway.

"We'll be there in a few minutes," the pilot said.

"What time is it?" Joe asked.

"About two in the morning. You'll have to wait for a while once you get there."

"That's okay. We'll find a hiding place where we can keep an eye on things. If you don't hear from us in a day or two, would you come looking? And tell Virgil, if you see him."

"Will do," the pilot said. "We're coming up on Sawtooth now. Get ready to jump."

Joe slid the side door of the plane open, and a

fierce rush of cold air hit him like a wall. Taking Cindy's hand, he walked her to the edge of the door. He gave her a reassuring smile, then held her hand as they dived out of the plane.

They fell through the pale sky for only a few seconds before pulling their rip cords. Joe had no idea where they'd land, but he figured it would look like much of the Brooks Range—rocky, treeless tundra covered with arctic moss and wild blueberries. The only danger could be the occasional stand of white spruce, which could reach a height of twenty feet. But the trees usually only grew in sheltered valleys, and they were supposed to land near the summit of Sawtooth Mountain.

Joe could see the ground coming up fast now. It was hard to tell what it looked like. With only half light, the terrain looked flat. But Joe knew that was an illusion. As he got closer he saw they'd be landing right on the side of the mountain.

He hit first, drifting up into the slope of the hill. He kept his balance and landed perfectly.

Instantly he looked up for Cindy. There she was, drifting out of the sky under the webbing of her chute. She looked a little like a fly struggling in a spider's web. She moved her legs in anticipation of the landing and held on to the lines for dear life.

When she hit the slope of the mountain, Cindy hit hard. But Joe had disengaged himself from his own chute and was running to help her. She would be bruised, but basically unhurt.

"Gather up your chute and follow me," he said. "We're going to climb."

They collected the billowing folds of their parachutes like huge armfuls of laundry. Then, tucking them under their arms, they clambered up the steep, rocky slope of Sawtooth Mountain.

At the peak they found a safe hiding place—a rocky ledge, out of the wind and, even more important, hard to see from the air. They would be mostly covered by a huge boulder that perched on the side of the slope.

"This is perfect," Joe said. "We can get some sleep here, and we won't have to worry about being seen." He began to spread out his parachute.

"You mean you're going to try to sleep here?" Cindy asked in disbelief. "It's so rocky!"

"It's perfect. Protected, cozy—we've even got blankets."

Joe lay down on his parachute and then rolled himself up in it. Cindy reluctantly did the same. They were so tired that despite the rocks and the roar of the wind they were both sound asleep in a few minutes.

They were awakened in the morning by the *whirr* of an approaching helicopter. Crouching close to their rock, Joe and Cindy watched as the chopper landed on the desolate mountaintop a few yards away from them. Four men got out, including Spike Hammond. They stood around their silent copter, staring off into the sky.

A few minutes passed. Another chopper came rattling in from the north and landed even closer to Joe. He crept around the boulder to get a look inside the pilot's bubble. The pilot was alone—but Joe did see a MAC-10 submachine gun leaning up against the copilot's seat.

As Joe watched, the pilot grabbed a large leather bag off the floor and hopped out, leaving the engine on and the door open. Joe didn't recognize him. He walked over to Spike Hammond and shook hands. Joe tried to hear what they were saying, but the roar of the engine and the thrumming blades made it impossible.

Hammond and the pilot talked for a minute or so, then the pilot handed Hammond the bag. Apparently Hammond wanted to check it out. He set the bag down, undoing a buckle that held it closed. Joe took a chance. Leaning farther around the boulder, he tried to get a look inside the bag. When Hammond tipped it over, Joe got a glimpse. It was filled with money.

He decided to act.

"Stay down. If anything happens, hide out until the weather pilot sends someone to look for us," he whispered to Cindy.

"What are you going to do?" she asked, staring at him, eyes like saucers.

"I've got to stop them. I can't hear what

111

they're planning, but it can't be anything good. I've got to do something."

Cindy grabbed his arm. "But, Joe, there's no one to help you!"

"I can't wait." Joe's face was grim as he pulled away.

Carrying his parachute slung over his shoulder, he ducked around the rock and sprinted for the nearest chopper. As he neared it he threw the chute up into the slowly rotating blades. The nylon caught in the rotors, fouling the engine. It sputtered to a halt, and Joe grabbed the MAC-10 inside. Then, coming around the fuselage of the chopper, he took command of the startled group.

"On the ground, all of you!" Joe shouted, pointing the submachine gun at them. The five conspirators froze in shock.

"Now!" Joe squeezed the trigger, sending a hail of bullets into the air just above their heads. They dove for the ground like soldiers in a drill.

Cautiously, Joe stepped out from behind the helicopter. He kept the gun level as he moved to recover the bag. Just as he was reaching for it he caught a flicker of movement from the corner of his eye.

Great, Joe thought. He could see a figure at the far end of the summit—a human silhouette moving against the gray of the sky.

Joe kept moving as if he hadn't noticed a thing,

his eyes flashing from his prisoners to the bag to the oncoming figure.

His hand tightened on the grip of the MAC-10. He calculated he had about two seconds to whirl, nail the ambushers, then return to cover the men on the ground.

Chapter

15

"Don't shoot!" A familiar voice cried out as Joe whipped around. But Joe was already triggering the submachine gun.

At the last moment he jerked up the short barrel, and the figure flattened itself against the ground. The deadly spray of bullets flew into the blank silver sky.

"Hold your fire, Joe! It's me, Frank!" Joe would have a hard time identifying his brother. Frank lay flat with his cheek against the moss. But his voice was unmistakable.

"Frank, you maniac. I could've killed you!" Joe said, half-scolding, half-delighted. But this wasn't the time for a chat. As soon as his attention had been distracted from the prisoners they had started for their revolvers.

"Hold it right there!" Joe ripped off another

round of automatic fire, tearing up some of the tufts of moss between the prone figures.

"Don't anyone move a muscle," he ordered.

Frank stood up and approached Joe with the revolver he'd taken from the man on the iceberg. Virgil came over the lip of the mountain with Tanook at his side. When he saw the number of men on the ground, he looked amazed.

"How'd you get here?" Frank asked.

"It's a long story. Hammond had a tail on Cindy. Some thug of his tried to bring us in—I got him to talk. What happened to you? I saw your boat bobbing out on the ocean."

"That's the least of it," Frank said. "We saw lots of interesting stuff, including Sandy White on a submarine. I think you might call North Slope an offshore company."

"I guess so, if the head office is in a submarine," Joe joked. "But it begins to explain why he was so interested when we mentioned the Network. That might make a foreign agent nervous."

Frank nodded. "Especially if the foreign agent was spreading bribe money around and kidnapping people. But we still don't know what he's up to or how Scott fits in. Maybe we can find out from the guy who brought the payoffs."

Joe pointed to the skinny, dark pilot with the stubbly beard who'd stepped out of the chopper. "He's the one. I fouled his rotor with my parachute and, uh, borrowed this gun from his copter. That bag over there is full of money."

"Keep me covered," Frank said. "I'm going to ask a few questions." He took a step, limping slightly, but suddenly spun around. Something had moved behind a boulder on the edge of the summit. He dropped into a crouch, aiming his revolver.

"Don't, Frank. It's Cindy. I forgot to tell you she was with me."

Cindy came out from behind the boulder, looking nervously at Frank.

"Joe, you should have told me. I almost shot her! Sorry, Cindy," he said, apologizing. She smiled weakly. "Maybe you can help us fill in some details."

"I'll do my best," Cindy said, looking at Spike Hammond, whose face had gone beet red.

But Frank ignored the construction boss, concentrating on the man who'd brought the money. Leaning over the guy, he asked, "Are you ready to talk?"

The man continued to lie facedown on the ground. "I have nothing to say."

"We'll see about that," Frank said. "What are you doing here?"

"What does it look like? I'm giving this man some money."

"What for?" Frank asked.

"It's my job," the man snarled into the dirt. "I fly a chopper and make deliveries."

"Where's Scott Sanders?"

"Who's that?"

"We saw him in the office building at North Slope headquarters."

"If you saw him, why ask me where he is?"

Frank was getting nowhere. This guy wouldn't give away anything. In fact, he didn't even look at Frank. He kept his gaze flat on the ground.

Time to change tactics, Frank decided. "What about you, Mr. Hammond?" he asked, turning to the large, redheaded man. "Guess you can't keep pretending you don't know what's going on, can you?"

"I'd like to know what *you* think you're doing," Hammond blustered, "bursting in on an innocent business meeting, hijacking—"

"Innocent?" Frank cut in. "Do you usually hold meetings on mountaintops—with people delivering bags of money?" He looked around the bare slope. "Or maybe this is the Bank of Sawtooth, and this fellow is the head teller."

Hammond said nothing. He was obviously feeling very uncomfortable.

"Do you know who this guy is?" Frank prodded Hammond, pointing at the skinny bag man.

"No, I don't," Hammond snapped back.

"If you want to keep lying on this cold ground, that's fine with me," Frank said. "But you might try being a little more helpful. So you don't know this guy personally. How about the people he's working for? I'd guess you'd check out an organization before doing business with it—even if it's dirty business. Who are they, and what are they up to?"

Hammond shifted his gaze warily. "I—uh, we tried, and got no—" Then his face hardened. "I don't see why I should tell you anything, just because you come along with a cock-and-bull story about a submarine."

"A submarine that I saw Sandy White, the president of North Slope Supply, climb out of. He saw us, too, and sent a couple of thugs after me and my friend here," Frank said.

"Well, that doesn't mean anything!" Hammond's voice was loud, but his tone was worried.

"Come on, Hammond. White isn't using that sub to set up underwater oil wells. He's using it as a base. And if he can afford a submarine, it means there's a pretty big organization behind him—like a government. How many unfriendly governments are close to Alaska?"

The big businessman's face went pale as this sank in.

"So, we've got a foreign agent handing around lots of money. What does he get in return?"

"North Slope asked if we could put some of their guys on our payroll, that's all. We were hurting, and they gave us a cheap loan—in several installments. What's the harm in that?"

"No harm, except to the guys you had to fire—

and to the morale of the rest of your workers, who hoped for promotions," Frank said.

"It happens all the time," Hammond said. "You have a friend whose nephew needs a job, so you help out—knowing he'll help you out on a deal down the line. That's the way it works."

"I guess White must have quite a few nephews," Frank shot back. "You're accepting money for these guys, and you don't even know who they are!"

"I don't need to know," Hammond replied. "They aren't hurting anybody."

"Oh, no? They attacked and threatened a friend of ours, kidnapped another, and tried to kill us. Remember how you called White to tell him about us?"

Hammond glared at Cindy when he heard this.

Frank stepped in front of him. "Your pals from North Slope grabbed us and stowed us aboard a plane heading into the Arctic Ocean. It was going to drop the signal buoy for the sub's rendezvous." He stared hard at Hammond. "And you know what? They were going to drop us right along with it."

"I—I didn't know," Hammond said, still more shaken.

"He can't prove a thing," the bag denly spoke up. "Who would listen t story about submarines and spies?"

"How about you, Hammond?"

119

"Are you beginning to have your doubts about your friends? What jobs are you selling to them?"

"Little stuff," Hammond finally answered, his face torn with doubt. "Cleaning, inspection, pipeline security—stuff like that."

"These all sound like pretty menial jobs," Frank said. "Do you really believe a company would want to stick their people in them?"

Hammond's face showed he didn't think so—now. "I didn't want to look a gift horse in the mouth," he admitted. "And we needed the money."

Now it was the bagman's turn to glare. "If you had kept your mouth shut—"

"No, I just kept my nose shut," Hammond said. "This whole deal stank, but my managers and I went along with it. Well, now I've got an idea where you come from—so what are you guys up to?"

"Your guesses are still far off," the man said, his sneer taking in both Hammond and Frank. "It doesn't matter. Your greed and foolishness have allowed us to get in place for our task."

"You dirty little—" Hammond lunged for the bagman, but Frank stopped him.

"Okay, that's enough. Everybody up. We'll get the whole story soon enough, after we get to the authorities and—" He stopped in midsentence. The bagman was writhing in convulsions on the ground.

"You'll never stop us!" he hissed. "And your authorities will never question me!"

Frank dropped to his good knee. But the bagman had already stopped moving—he lay rigid. Frank pried open the man's mouth, recoiling from a sharp stink. What looked like a dental filling fell out, a big piece—the whole crown of a tooth.

"Look at this!" Frank picked up the filling and held it up. Joe came forward cautiously, his weapon still trained on Hammond and his men.

His eyes opened wide in disbelief. "A hollow tooth!" he whispered.

"Obviously, it was holding a suicide pill," Frank said, his face grim.

"More spy stuff," Joe said, shaking his head.

But Frank Hardy's face grew grimmer. "Think for a second, Joe. What group has standing orders for its people to die rather than be captured?"

Joe looked even more unbelieving. "You're not thinking—the Assassins?"

They'd run into the Assassins before. In fact, this group of terrorists-for-hire had sent the Hardys on the most painful case of their career. An Assassin bomb had wiped out Iola Morton, Joe's girlfriend, in a ball of flame.

"Assassins—in Alaska?" Joe muttered. "Hard to take. But if you're right, we've got big trouble."

"Not just us," Frank said. "The whole country could be in for a bad time."

"What do you mean?"

A shiver ran down Frank's back. "Think about it. We all depend on the oil from the pipeline. And right now the whole maintenance staff—security and all—has been infiltrated by terrorists."

Chapter

16

SPIKE HAMMOND ROSE up on his knees, staring at the dead bagman. The businessman was obviously upset—he was terribly pale.

"Terrorists?" he mumbled. "Attacking the pipeline?"

Hammond looked as if someone had kicked the world out from under him. "You know, I always prided myself on being a working man, successful in business, going for the American dream. I started out as a roughneck in an oilfield, then worked my way up in the construction business. I thought I'd made it. . . ."

His voice tightened. "Then things went bad. The company lost money, we needed cash. And this deal came along." Hammond looked down again at the lifeless terrorist and then buried his face in his hands. The rest of his men looked on in stunned silence.

"I can't believe this," Hammond muttered through his hands. "I never thought . . ."

"That's just it," Joe said. "You never thought! *Now* what do you think? Do you realize the size of your mistake?"

Hammond pushed himself up to standing. His head was still bowed and he was unable to speak.

"And what about Scott Sanders? Where's he?" Joe asked. "We came up here to find him, and you lied to us."

"I didn't lie—I honestly don't know what happened to him." Hammond looked over at his managers. "Carter here told me that we had a problem with some of the workers."

One of the men in the group nodded cautiously.

"I was told that some guys knew about the money and were beginning to make trouble. We got on the horn to North Slope, and they said they'd take care of it. That's all I knew."

"So you don't have any idea where Scott is?" Frank asked.

Hammond shook his head. "Maybe he's with them—probably at their main office. They used to have a big equipment depot outside of town, but they had an explosion out there, right before all this started."

Frank leaned in when he heard the word *explosion*, his face grim. "I'm beginning to see why they kept Scott and let Doug go," he said. "Scott was a demolitions expert in the army."

"I don't understand," Hammond said.

"They got their hands on Scott right after an explosion wrecked their depot outside of town. I bet they lost more than equipment out there; I bet they lost their bomb expert in that explosion, too."

"Bomb expert?" Then the pieces clicked together for Joe. "They're going to blow up the pipeline!"

Frank was now face-to-face with Hammond. "How many people did you give jobs to? Where are they working?"

"It's hard to say," Hammond responded. "We had a lot of requests. . . . And I don't know exactly where they all work."

"So they could be anywhere along the line? Anywhere?" Joe asked, as if it were impossible to imagine such a thing.

"I'm afraid so," Hammond admitted.

"So, as far as you know, your entire company is infiltrated by terrorists! Do you know what that means? It means that the Assassins can disrupt the entire world oil supply!" Joe said.

"At the very least, they can upset the supply for our country," Frank said, frowning. "How much of our oil comes from the Prudhoe Bay oil fields?"

"About fifteen percent," Hammond mumbled.

"That's enough to cause chaos if it suddenly got cut off," Joe said.

"And they're using Scott to help build their bombs." Frank shook his head.

"You know what you've done, Mr. Hammond?" Cindy said. "You've sold your country down the river." She came closer to the group and stood near the men she'd worked with at Trans-Yukon.

Hammond crossed to a large rock and sat down, burying his face in his hands again.

"What can we do? Go to the authorities?" he asked.

Another of his managers spoke up. "Spike, if you do that, it'll be over for all of us."

Joe looked at the guy as if he'd just crawled out from under a rock. "It will be over, but for a different reason."

"Joe's right," Frank said. "Once the Assassins realize this guy isn't coming back, they'll probably push their schedule up. I've never known them to call off an operation."

"So what should we do?" Hammond asked again.

Frank looked at him. "We'll have to think fast, and we'll need all the help you can give us. If you and your men come through, I'm sure the authorities will be easy on you, if and when we save the pipeline."

"You've got our help. Count on that. Right, men?" Hammond turned to his three managers, who were standing together, some distance from him. They stared at him blankly.

"Right, men?" he asked again.

The three looked at one another, then one of them stepped forward. He was called Carter, and he looked as if he had been elected to act as spokesman.

But as he passed Cindy, he dodged behind her. One of his arms whipped around her neck. A gun appeared in his other hand, and he pressed it to Cindy's head.

"Sorry, Hammond. No deal!" Carter said, holding Cindy in front of him like a shield. "Just give us the money and we'll get out of here."

Hammond stared at Carter. "Are you out of your mind?" he shouted. "Where are you going to go? You can't walk away from this!"

"Watch us," Carter said. "Right, guys?"

The other two managers grouped behind Cindy and Carter as Joe raised his gun.

"Don't try it, kid!" Carter shouted. "Just give us the money and no one will get hurt!"

Hammond looked at Frank and Joe.

"We've got no choice. Give them the bag," Frank said.

Hammond stepped forward, picked up the bag, and set it down in front of his managers. One of them reached out and picked it up.

"Don't do this!" Hammond begged. "We've got another chance. We can make up for our mistakes."

"Hammond, you kidded yourself about how to save the company—now you're kidding yourself about this." The sneer in Carter's voice was almost like a slap in the face. "You'll rot in prison no matter what you try to do now. And we don't want to rot with you."

"That's not true," Frank said. "They'll—"

"Save it," Carter snarled. "Back off."

He motioned with his head, and the group began to back up toward the one remaining chopper. Tanook, sensing something was wrong, began to whimper. Carter glared at the dog.

"You'd better keep that mutt away from us, or we'll kill him," he warned.

Virgil put a hand on Tanook's head, and the dog fell silent.

"You can't do this!" Hammond screamed. "Wake up and smell the coffee! If you guys split now, you'll go down in history as traitors. The whole world will know about this. The feds will be after you for the rest of your lives."

"What are you, running for office?" another one of the managers said. "There's enough here for us all to get away—if we don't have to waste it on saving your crock of a company."

The three managers continued to back up toward the chopper. Once they reached it, two scrambled to the doors. Carter remained in front, continuing to hold Cindy.

"Throw your guns over here," he said, digging

the barrel of his revolver harder into Cindy's temple.

Joe and Frank put the safety switches on and tossed their weapons forward. The side door of the chopper slid open, and Carter stepped up, still dragging Cindy along.

"You're not taking her!" Joe yelled. "There's no point!"

"I'll toss her out when I'm ready," Carter yelled back. "Just keep your distance and everything will be all right!"

Joe and Frank watched as the engine of the chopper coughed to life. The blades began to rotate. They could still see Cindy, standing by the side door of the helicopter, Carter holding a gun to her head.

At the last minute, as the chopper began to lift from the ground, Carter gave Cindy a shove. She landed on her feet and then fell onto her hands. She half ran, half crawled to avoid the overhead blades.

The copter lifted rapidly, rising to a height of thirty feet. Carter was still standing in the open hatchway, laughing down at the Hardys, Hammond, and Virgil.

And just at that instant a huge noise erupted within the chopper's belly. The helicopter exploded. Its thin walls blew out, and the rotary blades wobbled wildly into space. The sky filled with glass and chunks of metal. Huge pieces of fiberglass spun through the air like misshapen Frisbees.

Where there had been a helicopter full of men, there was now a boiling fireball. Smoke roiled around the flames.

On the ground Joe yelled, "Down! Quick!"

Pieces of wreckage started to rain down from the sky to pierce their bodies like shrapnel.

Chapter

17

JOE AND CINDY were protected under a dead bush as the sky gradually emptied itself of debris. Frank, Virgil, and Tanook had found shelter of a sort behind the boulder. Only Hammond remained standing, looking on in stunned silence. Perhaps he thought he was atoning for what he had done.

"I don't believe it," he said over and over, shaking his head. "What happened?"

"The money bag must have been booby-trapped," said Joe. "As soon as they reached a certain height, a detonator set off the bomb. It was meant for you, too," he said to Hammond.

The big redheaded construction boss swallowed hard. "You mean they were going to get rid of us?"

"That's right," Frank said. "You'd served

your purpose. They didn't want you around to talk and foul things up. Human life means nothing to them. Not even their own!"

"The scary thing is, Scott probably made that bomb," Joe remarked.

"But we still haven't found him—*and* we've got to stop the people who have him now," Frank announced. "Any ideas where we should start?"

Cindy spoke up. "I'm pretty certain most of the North Slope people were hired as hatch men. They open the hatches on the pipe and make sure everything is going smoothly."

Joe looked at her. "You didn't say that before."

"I just remembered that that was what I usually typed on their personnel records."

"Then that's it!" Frank said. "They've put bombs in the hatches. Anything else you remember?"

Cindy frowned, trying to force anything else out of her memory. "Most of them started working down south, near Valdez. Lately, they've been working in the north, toward Prudhoe."

Frank nodded. "They probably worked their way right up the pipeline. And now, if they've got to get out of here quickly, they're in range of that submarine up north."

He stood up. "We've got to get to the pipeline and take a look. Virgil, can you fix that chopper?" He pointed to the Assassin's helicopter, with the parachute snagged in its rotors.

132

"Right away," Virgil said. He leapt up on the top of the enemy bird and began to unravel and cut away the mess. "We could hike down the mountain and use mine," he called out as he worked. "But I think it'd take too much time."

"You're right," Frank said. "We've got to act fast."

Frank, Cindy, and Hammond gathered rocks to pile over the dead Assassin's body. When the temporary grave was completed, Cindy took a moment to mutter a few words in prayer.

Suddenly the chopper engine roared to life. Virgil waved from the pilot's seat. They ran over and climbed aboard, grateful for Virgil's expertise. They rose straight up from the mountaintop, then swooped to the south.

They gained speed and rose up again to get over the Brooks Range. In the early-morning light, the desolate area below seemed totally untouched by humans. But after a brief flight, they were flying over what seemed to be a miles-long brown snake, coiling over the rolling terrain.

It was a service road cut into the virgin landscape. And next to it was the gleaming pipe, stretching as far as the eye could see.

Hammond pointed out the first inspection hatch.

Virgil put the chopper down on the service road. Dust billowed around them as they jumped from the chopper and approached the pipe. Hammond reached out and touched the hatch.

"You need a special tool to unlock these babies," he said. "I didn't think about that."

"Wait a minute," Joe said. "I saw something in the back of the copter." He trotted over and reached behind the passenger seat of the Assassin's copter. Standing up, he held up an unusual-looking wrench.

"Is this what you're talking about?"

"Bingo," Hammond cried, and he began to unlock the hatch. After several minutes, he unscrewed the final bolt. But the hatch didn't budge. "Stuck," Hammond growled.

He attacked it again and, with a huge burst of strength, threw the hatch open. Then he stuck his head inside the hole.

"Don't see a thing," he said, his voice echoing inside the pipe. "Looks fine to me."

"Let me see," Frank said. He joined Hammond at the edge of the opening. Peering into the darkness, Frank could see nothing. The fierce smell of oil made his head swim, and all he heard was the velvety gurgle of the dark stream rushing inside the pipe.

Suddenly a loud click sounded in the dark. It seemed to come from the inner wall. Frank glanced to his right and saw something large and heavy splash into the river of oil. He grabbed for it, but he couldn't reach it.

"Something just fell off the wall of the pipe," he yelled, bringing his head out of the hatch. "It clicked and fell into the oil."

"Grab it," Joe said.

Frank held up a filthy hand. "I tried, but it's gone."

"There shouldn't be anything hanging inside the pipe," Hammond said. "And there's nothing to hang it on."

"A magnet would hold on to the pipe," Joe said.

Frank nodded. "Probably an electromagnet that could be turned off by a radio transmitter. I'll bet they still use them in the military."

His face darkened. "Scott again! They've probably got one of those mines at every hatch."

"And they've just set them all free now," Joe said. "They're floating in the oil. When they get to the right spots, they'll probably go off."

"When they get to the pumping stations!" Hammond said. "We're not just talking about some holes and huge oil spills. They want to rip the guts out of the whole system!"

"Where must we go to stop this?" Virgil asked.

"I'll bet they've set themselves up inside a pumping station," Frank said. "That way they can monitor the flow of oil to make sure the mines have reached the most vulnerable locations."

Hammond spoke up. "I hate to say it. I sold them the construction plans to the main pumping station up in Prudhoe. One of their guys is the plant supervisor." He hung his head.

"That's it!" Frank said. "Let's go!"

The copter thundered through the air toward

the pumping station. Hammond was determined to do his part to make up for his mistake.

"I know the place inside and out," he said. "I worked on the crew that built it." He turned to Virgil. "Land on the roof. We can go down the climate-control vents."

Virgil nodded. He brought the chopper over the station and settled it down on the flat asphalt roof. Joe jumped out, and Frank cautiously followed. Hammond started to go, too.

"We'll take care of this," Joe said. "Stay with Virgil and Cindy. We need you on lookout."

"What about Frank's leg?" Virgil yelled down.

"It's about ninety percent, Virgil," Frank yelled back.

Hammond reluctantly agreed to let the boys go alone. "Okay. Just rip off those screens," he said, pointing to the large, chimneylike outlets on the roof. "You can slide down the ducts. The different rooms are labeled on the inside. You'll probably want the control room." He gave quick directions.

"Thanks," Frank called. "Now get out of here, fast!" Hammond jumped back in the copter, and Virgil took off.

The Hardys wasted no time. Joe ripped the screen off one duct and climbed in, followed by Frank, who could only crawl on one knee. The other leg he dragged behind him. It was dark inside, but when they came to a vent, light shone in from the space below. They could hear the constant drone of the pumping machinery deep inside the building.

Sometimes, as they crawled along, muffled voices drifted up from the various rooms they passed. Frank and Joe were careful to make no noise as they crept through the darkness.

Following Hammond's directions, they dropped down several levels and crawled over the center of the building. Finally they reached a vent marked "Cntrl. Rm."

The floor was a long way down when they peered through the vent. They were in a high-ceilinged room containing a control booth filled with computer equipment. Two men stood in front of a large panel of controls.

Joe tapped Frank on the shoulder, then pointed. There was another vent in the room, directly over the booth. They crawled until they could lean over the small grid that covered the opening.

They listened to the voices below.

"So, my friend, it's just a matter of minutes before the project is completed." It was the voice of Sandy White. Frank pressed his face against the grid, trying to see who the other person was.

"It's Scott," he whispered to Joe. "It's Scott and Sandy White!"

They listened again.

"Once I push this button, we'll be on our way to the sub. The crew here is on coffee break, so they'll never know what happened. By the time the whole thing blows, we'll be over the Arctic Ocean.'' White glanced at his watch.

Frank and Joe gave each other the high sign. This was it. They had to make their move.

Joe went first. Quietly, he lifted the grid off the vent and placed it to the side. It seemed to take him forever, but he was able to do it without making any noise. Then, drawing himself up in the cramped space of the duct, he leapt headfirst through the hole.

He flew into White, knocking him back from the control panel. Both of them went sprawling across the floor. As they fell Joe yelled out, ''Scott, we're friends of Doug!'' But that's all he had time to say.

White was immediately up on his knees, jamming an elbow into Joe's solar plexus. Joe groaned and doubled over, trying to catch his breath. But every time he inhaled, his lungs refused to expand. Scott had ducked into the corner, unable to decide what to do.

Frank came down, feet first, like a cannonball, but White was ready, lashing out with a kick as Frank landed. But Frank threw his arm out and knocked the foot off course. Then, lunging, he grabbed it, twisting the leg and trying to throw White to the ground.

White twisted his body in midair, bracing himself with the foot Frank held captive and kicking Frank in the face with the other.

Frank's head snapped back, and he fell, losing his hold.

White fell to the floor but sprang up immediately and ran for the control panel—or rather, for the little radio transmitter with the big red button that lay there. Joe tackled him and brought him down. But he couldn't pin the man. White wriggled out of Joe's grip, leapt to his feet, and raised his foot to stomp Joe on the neck.

Joe rolled out of the line of fire, and White's foot only scraped the side of his head. His ear felt as if it had been ripped off. White again went for the detonator, but this time Scott stepped in. He snatched it away from White and threw the transistor pack to Frank.

White went after Frank but then stopped.

"Okay, enough," he said, taking a similar pack out of his pocket. "Your friend here is wired with enough plastic explosive to wreck this room. He's a human bomb! And this is the detonator!" He held the small transistor box in his right hand. "Now give me the switch to the mines, or I'll kill all of us right now."

Frank looked at Scott. He could see the unmistakable lump taped to his stomach.

"That's right," White said. "Just like the persuader I used on you. Now give me the switch before I use this one!"

Frank stared into the madness behind White's eyes.

"Give it to me!" White screamed. The veins in his neck bulged. His face was red with rage.

Frank had to gamble. He knew the Assassins were capable of suicide, but he doubted whether a big cheese like White would be expected to make that sacrifice.

"If you flip that switch, you'll just die, and the pipeline will be back in operation in a month." Frank popped open the little electronic box in his hand and ripped out the wires. "It's over, White. Give up!"

When White saw the control box destroyed, he looked like a robot who'd been short-circuited. But his moves were still fast. He grabbed Scott and backed out the door of the control booth, holding up the detonator.

"Stay where you are," he spat. "I can still take your friend with me—and maybe do a little more damage."

Chapter

18

JOE LUNGED FOR the door, but his brother grabbed him.

"Let them go," Frank whispered roughly.

"Are you out of your mind?" Joe yelled. "He's about to escape. He may even kill Scott just for kicks."

Frank continued to hold his brother back. "He's less likely to do that if he thinks he's won. Let's give him a chance to escape."

They ran to the door and watched as White dragged Scott across the floor of the station.

"See?" Frank told Joe. "We've left his plan in ruins. The mines are useless now, without this." He held up the detonator, its wires and microchips hanging out like an electrician's nightmare.

"And we know another thing. White isn't about

to risk his own life. He proved that in here just now." Frank stared out as the terrorist dragged his captive into the maze of pumping machinery.

"Yeah, but we're going to lose sight of him, Frank! If he can stash Scott somewhere and get out of the building, he could still trigger the bomb, kill Scott, and do some serious damage." Joe pounded the wall in frustration. Then he stopped. A blueprint of the entire station was thumbtacked right where his fist had landed.

"Check this out!" Joe said.

"Quick," Frank said, when he saw what it was. "Where are the exits?"

"Looks like there're only three, aside from the main one," Joe stated.

"Remember where they are. Now let's go. We've given him enough time."

They broke through the door and practically fell down the flight of stairs that led from the control booth to the floor of the pumping station.

"He went this way!" Joe called as he sprinted across the cement floor toward a jungle of pipes and machinery.

Frank followed behind as fast as he could, casting a worried look at the incredibly complicated mass of hardware, with its hundreds of hiding places.

"Maybe I took a chance letting him go. But I

didn't want to push him too far,'' Frank said as they pushed into the steel jungle.

Joe was in the lead, but he skidded to a stop when the floor ended. Looking over the edge, they could see two or three stories down. The entire space was filled with pipes, painted green, red, and orange.

Frank stared down in shock. "That's a bit more hiding space than I counted on.''

The network of pipes filling the vast, dark space looked like the inside of a giant mechanical stomach. Miles and miles of bent, wandering tubes were all humming and gurgling with life.

But Joe wasn't interested in the looks of the place. His eyes were straining for any sign of motion. "There they are!'' His arm stabbed down into the dimness.

"I see them.'' Following Joe's arm, Frank instantly caught sight of White and Scott. They looked like miniature figures climbing through a maze of giant tree trunks.

Joe leapt out onto the first pipe and began to swing to the next one like a monkey. Frank followed, using his arms the whole way.

"He's taking him down to one of the big compressors,'' Joe said, leaping from one pipe to the next.

Frank glanced down and saw them struggling through the endless labyrinth of twisting metal. Scott seemed to have a rope connecting him to White.

Joe sprang recklessly from pipe to pipe, landing on the narrow surface of one, then crouching down and lowering himself to the one below. It's a lucky thing we have sneakers, he thought.

When he landed on a pipe without a handhold available he had to keep his balance and not think about what a fall would mean. The image of being knocked from pipe to pipe until he reached the distant floor wouldn't help keep him steady.

Frank followed more slowly, going hand over hand, keeping his cool in a deadly situation.

"Do you see them?" he asked.

Dropping onto a pipe, Joe peered down. "He's reached the compressor, and he's tying Scott to a pipe." He glanced up at Frank. "I'm going after White. You go for Scott—get the bomb off him."

Joe took chances, dropping farther, straining to catch pipes. Once he bounced off a tube he'd aimed for and nearly went tumbling down through the maze. But he managed to grab on to another pipe and hang there for a moment, catching his breath. Looking down, he realized he'd nearly reached the compressor.

Below him, White was scrambling around on a large pipe, lashing Scott down. Scott fought against the ropes, but he was obviously scared about setting off the bomb on his stomach.

White tied the final knot around Scott's neck and looked up. Seeing Joe coming fast, he leapt off the big pipe like a spider monkey. Catching a thin pipe several yards away, he swung himself down into the darkness like Tarzan and silently disappeared.

Joe covered the last of the distance to Scott's pipe with a series of hair-raising jumps. He landed on all fours about a yard away from where Scott was tied.

"Scott, my brother's coming to help you out. I'm going after that maniac," he yelled. "Frank's coming."

Scott nodded, but Joe could see the panic in his eyes. The poor guy must be half out of his mind by now, Joe thought. He's been a captive for almost a month, building bombs for terrorists—and now he's a human bomb.

Joe continued his wild descent. Sandy White was still ahead of him, dashing through the tangle of pipes at the bottom of the station. He'd reached the floor but still had to climb over some broad feeder pipes as he headed for a side door.

Joe realized that White had made a mistake by going straight down. He still had to struggle across the floor. And that gave Joe a chance to catch up. He began angling his way down through the overgrown monkey bars, cutting a course to just above the doorway.

He glanced back. Frank had reached Scott and was struggling to untie him, balancing on the pipe and tugging at the knots at the same time.

Now it was up to Joe to win the race to the

door. Joe remembered from the blueprint how this door led to a flight of stairs up to ground level and an exit to the pumping station. The area outside the station was open space.

Joe figured White would want to run a good way before finally detonating the bomb. He wouldn't know how far the exploding compressor would throw debris and would want to be a good distance from the building. Joe bore down, leaping and swinging through the pipes, almost in a trance now, knowing that his brother and Scott were depending on him.

White reached the door just seconds before Joe was in position to drop on him. The terrorist rammed into the exit with his shoulder, setting off an alarm.

Neither of them paid any attention to the shrill, bone-jarring siren. Joe swung down by the doorway and pushed through. He knew White was probably running up the stairs to the exit.

Clawing his way up the steps, Joe could feel his lungs burning with desperate fatigue. Now there was another door ahead of him. He rammed through to find a wide, empty space outside the building.

There was White, sprinting toward a helicopter with the North Slope logo. His escape vehicle had parked far out from the building. Its engine was already running, and a side door was open. White glanced over his shoulder, saw Joe, and forced his pace a bit faster. Joe didn't know if he could catch him. He only knew he had to.

From above came the clattering sound of another chopper. Joe looked up. It was Virgil. Spike Hammond stood in the open bay with the MAC-10 in his hands.

The North Slope pilot saw them, too. He turned up the throttle and lifted a few inches off the ground. Obviously he expected Sandy White to dive into the chopper headfirst, and then he'd take off.

Joe heard a shot. The engine of the North Slope chopper screamed to a halt. The blades whirred around helplessly, and the nose of the copter smashed into the ground. Hammond had hit a bull's-eye.

White stumbled to a halt. Joe could see his chest heaving as he tried to catch his breath. The men in the damaged chopper bailed out of the open door and made a run for it. White watched his comrades scatter. He looked up to see Virgil's copter hovering. He faced Joe, who was sprinting toward him.

A thought flicked across Joe's mind as he sprinted toward White: This is where an Assassin is the most dangerous, when he's got nothing to lose and nowhere to go.

For a second Joe couldn't figure out why White was just standing there. Then he watched as the terrorist's hand flashed into his pocket. It came out with the detonator.

Joe put his head down and charged like a bull. But he knew he was too far away to stop him. White pressed the switch. Joe expected to hear a terrifying, expanding boom, the blast that would take out the compressor, Scott—and Frank Hardy.

Instead—there was nothing.

White stared, pushing the switch again and again. Still nothing.

A surge of joy erupted through Joe. He bore down on White like a freight train. Frank had done his job; now it was Joe's turn. He was going to take this Assassin alive!

White threw the detonator switch away and bit down on something in his mouth—hard.

He's got a hollow tooth—and a suicide pill! thought Joe as he forced a little more speed out of his aching legs.

But White didn't go into convulsions in front of Joe. Apparently he was having trouble with the cap on his tooth. He was yanking on it with his fingers as he backed away from Joe.

Joe barreled up, realizing he'd have just one shot at stopping this guy. Still running full tilt, he reared back, then unleashed his right fist in a wild haymaker with all his weight behind it.

He caught White in the side of the jaw, snapping his head to the side. One punch was all he needed. White was out. And the poison pill was on the ground. Joe's punch had jarred the hollow tooth loose. When the Assassin was flung back, the tooth cap—and its deadly little filling—flew out of White's mouth.

Frank and Joe sat on either side of Scott as they waited for their plane at the airport. Cindy was with them, too. "I can't believe what you guys have done," she said. "It was nice of you to let Mr. Hammond turn Sandy White in."

Frank shrugged. "Yeah, well—he was pretty upset once he realized how he had been used. And he was in pretty deep trouble. This might help him. He'll probably still go to jail, but he won't have such a guilty conscience."

Joe grinned. "By the way, who's in charge of Trans-Yukon?"

"All the men who were fired came back and elected someone to run the company. They offered Scott a big job," Cindy said, smiling.

Scott Sanders shook his head till his long dark hair tumbled into his brown eyes. He looked like a young, handsome kid—until you saw the dark bags and fatigue under his eyes.

"No way!" he said. "All I want to do is go home and see my folks. Give me some time. Maybe I'll come back in a couple of months."

"Did they really give you a hard time?" Cindy asked sympathetically.

"Well, they lost all their explosives experts when they had an accident, so they kept me working pretty hard. I was tired, which is not the way to be when you're fooling around with bombs. And they never left me alone. That was hard, too.''

"Man!" Joe exclaimed. "I don't know how you stood up to all that.''

Scott looked at Joe with deep feeling in his eyes. "Well, then, Joe, we're even. I don't know how I can thank you and Frank for what you did. I owe you everything.''

Joe patted him on the back. "We're just glad it worked out, and that we were able to stop those crazies. The authorities are collecting all the mines. And it turns out White is a big cheese in the Assassins. Once they've gotten all the info out of him, they hope to put a big dent in our friendly neighborhood terrorists.''

Their plane was announced, and they began to gather their belongings.

Joe took Cindy by the hand. "If you'd like to come to Bayport sometime, let me know." He grinned. "We're not all that far from New York.''

Cindy smiled. "Well, I was thinking about going to college in the East—who knows?" She shrugged. "It sounds good, but awfully far away.''

"Far away from Alaska, maybe," Joe said. "But you'd be a lot closer to the rest of the world." Everyone laughed.

"Where's Virgil?" Frank asked, looking around. "He said he'd be here. We didn't have a chance to say goodbye.''

"I don't know," Cindy said. "But you'd better go. Please write!"

Frank and Joe and Scott trudged across the tarmac to their plane. At the foot of the stairs, the attendant took their bags and stowed them in the baggage compartment. They climbed aboard and took their seats.

As the plane began to taxi toward the runway Scott and the Hardys looked out the windows and saw Cindy waving from the observation deck.

Then the plane took off, and they were on the way home.

Frank leaned back in his seat, finally able to relax—until he glanced out the window. "What's that?" he asked, pointing to a speck in the sky.

"Looks like a helicopter." Joe's voice was casual, but he sat up straight. The chopper came closer and closer to the plane. Could it be a revenge attack from the Assassins?

It was close enough now to see inside the pilot's bubble.

"Holy smokes!" Joe laughed. "It's Virgil!"

The native Alaskan was grinning broadly as he waved goodbye to his friends.

"Look, there's Tanook," Frank said. "He's in the passenger seat!"

Tanook sat tall and proud next to his master. His pink tongue was hanging out of his mouth, and his fierce blue eyes stared quizzically at the passing plane. Frank and Joe laughed. Tanook's head cocked to the side, and then he seemed to bark.

"So long, Tanook!" Frank said.

"So long, Virgil," Joe said quietly, almost to himself.

The chopper pulled away. In a matter of seconds it was lost in a bank of clouds.

NOWHERE TO RUN

Chapter
1

"SURE YOU CAN have this back—if you're man enough to take it from me." Swinging from the saddle of his 1000 cc Harley-Davidson motorcycle, the stranger held out the bright green Frisbee to Joe Hardy. The biker was dressed in black from helmet to boots, his face masked by a black reflective visor.

"What's your problem? Did the Darth Vader School for Rejects let out early today?" Joe Hardy's blue eyes hardened as he walked over to face off against the black-clad stranger.

An eerie laugh echoed from beneath the Darth Vader helmet and visor, as the biker teased Joe. He tossed the Frisbee into the air and caught it several times.

1

"Little Joe Hardy thinks he's all grown up now," the guy scoffed.

Joe's face turned an angry red. Six feet tall and well muscled, Joe Hardy was anything but little.

"Just toss him the Frisbee and move on," Frank Hardy spoke up, standing beside his brother. He was an inch taller but leaner than Joe.

"You think the two of you can take this from me?" The stranger swung his leg over the Harley, pushed down the kickstand, and stepped away from the bike to confront Frank and Joe.

The guy stood as tall as Joe and appeared every bit as strong. Something about his swagger seemed familiar to Joe, who took a careful look at the cycle. The biker took advantage of Joe's shift of attention to fire the Frisbee at him.

Joe batted the plastic disk aside and started to jump for the stranger. He was stunned when Frank stiff-armed him to a halt.

"Let's make this a little more even," Frank suggested. "Take off your helmet."

The stranger laughed again and unsnapped his chin strap. Slowly he lifted the helmet from his head. . . .

Minutes earlier, Frank, Joe, and Frank's girl-friend, Callie Shaw, had been enjoying a lazy afternoon at Bayport Park, tossing the Frisbee around. It was the first real rest for Frank and Joe since getting back from Alaska after their last case, *Trouble in the Pipeline*. They'd gone up looking for a missing person and found themselves tangling with terrorists. Now they were home, and things were getting back to normal.

"I hope Mom and Aunt Gertrude get home from vacation soon," Joe had said as he tossed the Frisbee to Frank. "I'm getting a little tired of Dad's frozen fish sticks every night."

"Dad" was the famous private detective Fenton Hardy. Although his sons admired him as a top investigator, they were not impressed with his talent as a cook.

"I know what you mean." Frank jumped to catch Joe's toss. "I looked in the mirror this morning and thought I saw gills." He whipped the Frisbee around his back and fired it at Callie.

"Don't worry." Callie grinned as she caught Frank's pass with the tip of her finger and let it spin for a few seconds. "*I'll* fix you dinner tonight. How does Caesar salad and lasagna sound?"

"Oh, Callie," Joe teased. "I knew you were good for something."

That got him a dirty look from Callie—as well as a rocketing Frisbee aimed straight at his throat.

"Hey!" Joe backpedaled and cushioned the blow of the Frisbee against his chest. He leapt into the air, whirled around, and tossed the Frisbee between his legs. It sailed wildly over Callie's head and landed on the park's motorcycle trail.

"Nice throw, Joe," Callie said, fuming.

Joe brushed back his blond hair. "Sorry, Callie." He didn't sound too sorry, though.

Callie jogged over to pick up the Frisbee, but she never reached it. The black-clad biker had screamed to a stop and snatched up the plastic disk. He refused to give it to Callie. Sensing trouble, Frank and Joe had run to Callie's aid.

Now Joe stood poised, ready to jump this hood the moment he made his move. The stranger pulled the helmet from his head.

Frank gasped.

But Joe yelled in joyful surprise. "Biker, you maniac!" He did jump on the guy now, but only to slap him on the back. "What are you doing back in Bayport?"

"*Biker?*" asked a confused Callie.

"Bob Conway, senorita bonita," the cyclist said. " 'Biker' to my friends." He gave her a disarming smile. Callie looked confused.

"Biker's an old friend of Joe's," Frank said. "He graduated from Bayport High three years ago."

"This guy was my hero when I was a kid," Joe explained. "He's the one who taught me about hot-rodding engines and racing motorcycles." His grin stretched from ear to ear. "Biker was a champion motocross racer on the junior circuit when I was a freshman.''

"It was the only way I could get you out of my hair.'' Biker laughed and said to Callie, "He'd hang around the garage where I worked and bug me until I showed him a few tricks. He was a good student.''

"My dad said Joe got his temper from you, too,'' Frank added with a laugh.

"Yeah, well, you've got a great dad, but I'll never understand why he was always angry at me,'' Biker said.

"Probably because of stunts like this,'' Callie said as she picked up the Frisbee.

"Oh, that,'' Biker said. He looked a little embarrassed. "I couldn't help myself. Besides, I know the Hardys are always up for a little adventure. And you have to admit, Joe looked pretty silly standing there ready to fight over a Frisbee.''

Callie stared at him, squinting as she tried to dredge something out of her memory. "Wait a second,'' she said. "Didn't you go to jail or something?''

"He was innocent.'' Joe's voice rose. "And we helped prove it.''

"Be cool, Joe,'' Biker said.

"It was something about stealing motorcycle parts,'' Callie went on.

Joe's face reddened with anger. "I told you—''

"Hey, wait a minute—you're Callie Shaw.''

5

Biker smiled, his soft brown eyes staring into Callie's. "I used to tell Joe that you were the cutest freshman at Bayport High."

Callie blushed.

"Three years ago, right before graduating, I was arrested for buying stolen cycle parts," Biker explained. "The dirt-cheap prices should have warned me, but I was a little thickheaded back then. About a week before I went on trial, Frank and Joe caught the real thieves and cleared me. I graduated from BHS and went off to make my fortune."

"You're going to stick around for a few days, aren't you?" Joe asked.

"Time is about all I have left," Biker replied with a slight smile.

Frank sensed Biker was holding something back.

"You can stay with us," Joe added. He knew Biker's folks had moved out of Bayport.

Biker glanced around. "You're sure you want an escaped convict sleeping in your house?"

"*What?*" Joe stared—so did Frank and Callie.

"Is this another dumb prank?" Callie demanded.

" 'Fraid not." Biker threw a leg back over his bike and sank down on the saddle.

"If you're telling the truth," Frank said, "we shouldn't even be talking with you."

6

"What are you saying?" Joe turned on his brother.

Biker nodded. "He's saying that aiding an escaped felon could get you into trouble—serious trouble."

"Never mind that." Joe brushed the idea aside. "How can we help?"

Frank looked unhappily at his brother, not liking Joe's eagerness. "First tell us what happened," he said.

"After I left Bayport," Biker began, "I cycled up and down the East Coast. Finally I settled in New York City. I got a job as a mechanic at a small watch company out in Queens called Dal-Time. One day a sales representative got sick and I took his place."

He shrugged. "The next thing I knew, I was selling designer watches. Last year DalTime's Watch Ya Wearing? was the top sports watch in the country—and I was the top salesperson."

"Sounds as if you made your fortune," Frank said.

"Yeah, but the fame that came with it wasn't exactly what I had in mind." Biker sighed. "Three months ago I returned from a cross-country bike trip, right into the arms of a welcoming committee. Two of New York's finest." Callie didn't understand and looked confused. "Two cops," Biker explained. "I was arrested, tried, and convicted of hijacking a shipment of DalTime watches valued at half a million bucks.''

Joe whistled.

''Based on what evidence?'' Frank asked.

''Oh, little things.'' Biker was trying hard to look calm, but there was fire in his eyes. ''They found a sudden increase of twenty-five thousand dollars in my bank account and several boxes of Watch Ya Wearing? watches in my garage. The serial numbers just happened to match the ones on the invoice for the stolen watches.''

''That's all?'' Frank asked.

''Yes, if you don't count the eyewitness.''

''Eyewitness?'' Callie couldn't believe what she was hearing.

''Yeah. The truck driver managed to convince everybody that I was the hijacker.'' Biker paused. ''Even though the hijacker was wearing a mask.''

''This begins to sound like a frame to me,'' Joe said.

''How did you escape?'' Frank asked.

''I was on the way to the state prison at Attica, and—remember that little lock-picking trick you taught me, Frank?''

Joe grinned, remembering how Frank had challenged Biker to get out of a pair of handcuffs.

''The cops' cuffs were actually easier to pick than the ones you had me practice on.'' Biker broke up at the expression on Frank's face.

"So now you're here." Callie obviously didn't like the idea.

"I sneaked back into the company and got a charge card to buy a bike and riding gear. I also got some cash. I plan to pay them back. At first I thought of heading to Canada; then I thought of Frank and Joe."

"What can they do for you?" Callie demanded.

"Look, I'm innocent—and I need help to prove it."

"Count on us," Joe said, ignoring the troubled look on Frank's face. "The first thing we have to do is crack the driver's story."

Frank glanced from Joe to Biker. "I don't know," he said.

Joe turned to Frank. "You believe him, don't you?

"That's not what's bothering me." Frank looked Biker in the eye. "If we take you in, we're harboring an escaped felon."

Biker shrugged again and got back on his Harley. "Gotcha. I owe you guys too much to get you into trouble with the law." He kicked his hog to life.

"Wait a minute!" Joe yelled. "We can talk this over."

"We could use Dad's advice on this," Frank said and paused. "Well, we could talk, I guess—on one condition."

"Name it," Biker said.

"Tell our dad your story, then turn yourself in. You're not doing yourself any good by running." Frank braced himself for a fight—not with Biker but with Joe. Once Joe got an idea in his head, he could be deadly stubborn.

"Wait a minute—" Joe began.

Biker cut in, "Your father's fair. If he'll listen to me, I can't go wrong—not with three Hardys helping me."

After dropping Callie off at her house, Frank and Joe drove home in their van, followed by Biker on his Harley.

"What's that old wreck doing across the street?" Frank asked as he pulled into the Hardy driveway.

"Huh?" Joe had been deep in thought.

"I've never seen that beat-up old Chevy around here before," Frank said.

"I'm more interested in what we're going to tell Dad," Joe said. "He never really liked Biker."

Biker pulled up beside the van and slipped off his cycle.

They were almost to the front door when it burst open and a short, plump man stepped out on the porch. Frank and Joe had never seen him before.

"Freeze, turkeys," the man snarled, his voice like gravel on concrete.

Frank nearly broke up. The guy sounded like a bad imitation of a TV detective.

One thing was for real, though—the hair-trigger 9 mm automatic pistol the man had aimed right at Biker's head.

Chapter

2

"No!" BIKER YELLED, shoving Frank and Joe aside and dashing back to his bike.

The short, heavy man shouldered past the Hardys. Joe watched in horror as the man braced himself in a firing position, taking aim as Biker swung onto the Harley.

Hurling himself at the stranger, Joe tackled him just as the gun went off. The shot buried itself in the lawn. Biker's cycle screamed with power, and he tore off down the street.

Joe jumped to his feet only to find himself looking down the barrel of the pistol.

"All right, punk," the short man wheezed. "You want it the hard way?"

"Hey!" Frank shouted.

12

The man looked like a joke, but he moved like a pro. He pivoted, covering both Frank and Joe. "Down on the ground," he ordered. "Facedown. *Move!*"

"Sims! Put that gun down!" shouted Fenton Hardy, running through the doorway. "These are my sons."

"Your sons?" Sims asked in confusion, still flicking his gun between Frank and Joe.

"Yes, and getting shot might be bad for their health."

Sims lowered his gun, sliding the deadly automatic into its shoulder holster.

"Your sons walked up with Biker Conway. They helped him escape," Sims said. "You didn't tell me they were so buddy-buddy with crooks."

Joe went for Sims, but Frank grabbed his arm and pulled him back. "Who is this guy?" he asked.

"First let's get inside," Fenton said.

Once in the living room, the elder Hardy began the introductions and explanations. "This is Mort Sims. Sims, these are my sons, Frank and Joe."

Neither the Hardys nor Sims offered to shake hands. The tension in the air was thick.

"Sims is a private investigator from New York City," Fenton went on. "He's looking for Bob Conway."

13

"I *had* him until Joe jumped me. I would have stopped him, too."

"Stopped him?" Joe shot back. "You were going to blow him away!"

"Listen, sonny, I've been hired to nail him. Nobody cares *how* I bring him in."

Frank saw a muscle just above Joe's jaw flex and took a step to place himself between Sims and his younger brother. He didn't like Sims's attitude, but he wanted more information from the private detective.

"Who hired you?" Frank asked with a quick glance at Joe. Joe recognized his brother's silent signal to cool it and relaxed.

"Scott Dalton, founder and president of Dal-Time, the watch company Conway stole from."

"Why? Biker's innocent." Joe couldn't keep the words in.

"Yeah? Who made you judge and jury? Mr. Dalton had complete faith in Conway, even put up three hundred grand in bail money so Conway could be free during his trial. The old man was willing to help with Conway's appeal, too, until Conway escaped. Now the bail money's been forfeited, *and* Conway's charged on the company card. Mr. Dalton wants either Conway or his money back."

Joe stared at Sims as if he were some kind of very ugly bug. "You're nothing but a bounty hunter," he said.

14

Sims clamped his jaw. Joe had hit a nerve.

"What are you doing here?" Frank asked, trying to catch Sims off balance.

Sims laughed. "It's no secret that Conway's from Bayport. I figured I'd check the place out—and ask an old friend from the New York force to help look for this escaped con." Sims glanced at Fenton Hardy.

"Wh-what?" Joe stared at his father.

"Sims doesn't know Bayport," Fenton explained. "I'm a consultant on this case."

"But you can't—" Joe began.

"Can't what? Can't uphold the law?" Sims threw himself into a chair, the springs groaning under his bulk. "Can't be a bounty hunter?"

Frank saw that Joe was ready to jump on Sims again, and gave his brother a jab in the ribs. Joe glared back.

"What were you two doing with Conway?" Fenton asked.

Frank looked at Joe, then answered for both of them.

"We met him in the park about an hour ago," Frank said. "He explained about the robbery and wanted us to clear him. We were bringing him here, hoping you could help."

"He was thinking of turning himself in before Wyatt Earp here began waving his gun around," Joe added. His cold blue eyes bored into Sims.

"You were doing the right thing," Fenton said.

"But if you see Biker again, restrain him and call me. This is Sims's case, and he's within the law. In spite of your feelings, Joe, Biker is a convicted felon."

"Yeah. Let older, wiser heads handle this job," Sims added with a sarcastic smile.

Joe turned to Fenton. "You never did like Biker."

"What I didn't like," Fenton replied, an edge in his voice, "was his hot temper—and the way his wildness rubbed off on you."

"You won't even think about his side of this," Joe said, frustrated. "Look at the case against him. The watches were planted in Biker's garage, and anybody can deposit money into a bank account. It's obvious that the eyewitness was lying."

Sims jumped up to stand toe-to-toe with Joe.

"Just like that!" he shouted with a snap of his fingers. "You solved the case. You've decided that a judge and jury didn't do their jobs right—no, you know better." Sims stabbed a plump finger at Joe's chest. "Every punk in Queens knows you don't run out on the law. If you do, you answer to Mort Sims. My job is to bring Conway back—dead or alive!"

Joe exploded. He pushed Sims backward. Caught off guard, Sims fell over the chair. But on the way down he lashed out with a karate kick, knocking Joe's legs out from under him.

16

Frank and Fenton stepped between the two. "Break it up," Fenton snapped. Frank pushed Joe out the front door.

Before following Joe, Frank faced his father. "He'll cool down in a little while. In the meantime we'll be at Mr. Pizza."

"You understand what I said about dealing with Conway," Fenton said.

Frank paused in the doorway. "We understand," he said. "But we don't have to like it."

The boys drove in absolute silence. Both brothers were thinking. Joe didn't like the idea of his father working with a bounty hunter to trap one of his best friends. He knew he *had* to prove Biker's innocence before trigger-happy Sims got him in his sights again.

Frank's eyes flicked between the road ahead and Joe. His brother often blew up, and he usually could shrug it off quickly. But that wasn't happening. Now Joe seemed filled with cold fury.

A chilling thought flashed through Frank's mind. If it came down to a choice, would Joe stand by his friend and idol, Biker Conway, or his father, who had teamed up with a bounty hunter? Frank became determined that such a decision shouldn't have to be made.

"The pits!" Joe suddenly slammed his hand on the dashboard.

"I know," Frank replied. "But we'll solve this one—"

"No," Joe interrupted. "Remember the pits? Where Biker used to practice?"

"You mean the old quarry outside of town?"

"Yeah. He could be camping there."

Frank shook his head. "Too obvious."

"Only if you know that Biker used to practice there, and Sims doesn't know Bayport, remember?" Joe looked at his brother. "It's worth a try."

"Okay, we'll check it out." Frank turned the van toward the pits.

Joe smiled. Just as he'd done three years earlier, he intended to clear Biker of a crime. He would put Sims in his place and prove to his father that Biker wasn't a thief.

The pits consisted of five square miles of large and small holes left after a mining company had dug out all the profitable sandstone. The area of dirt and stones looked more like a moonscape or an air force bombing range than a part of Bayport. But it made a great motocross practice course.

Frank and Joe parked the van, then split up and began to search from opposite ends of the quarry.

Joe's high hopes of finding Biker at the pits soon vanished. He didn't see even a trace of evidence that Conway had been there. Frustrated, Joe kicked up a cloud of dust.

"Hey!" Frank yelled as he jogged toward Joe. "I saw your smoke signals."

"Find anything?" Joe asked, an expectant look on his face.

"Nothing. You?"

Joe shook his head.

"It's getting dark," Frank said with a glance at the sky. "I called Callie on the mobile phone, and she's going to meet us at Mr. Pizza in half an hour. Let's eat something and brainstorm."

"Yeah," Joe grunted and headed for the van.

Frank shook his head. After girl-collecting, eating good food was Joe's favorite pastime. When even an invitation to a hot pizza supreme couldn't cheer Joe up, he was in a bad way.

The sudden roar of an engine cut the air. Frank saw a big black cycle swerve out from behind a gravel mound and drive toward Joe. Lost in thought, Joe didn't notice the cycle or its black-clad rider.

The cyclist had noticed Joe, though. He was aiming straight for him, hefting something in his hand.

Frank stared for one quick second, wondering what was behind that reflective helmet. Then there was no time for thinking—only for acting. He leapt for Joe.

Joe felt someone shove him from behind, so hard that he was lifted into the air before he fell—hard—to the ground. He jumped to his feet as a motorcycle roared past him and out of the quarry.

"That guy nearly ran us down," he said angrily. "You get his license number, Frank?"

When he got no answer, Joe spun around.

Frank lay facedown in the dirt, motionless, a thin line of blood trickling down the side of his head.

Chapter

3

JOE'S EYES WIDENED. "Frank!" he yelled, dropping to one knee.

He gingerly brushed away the dust from his brother's head. The bleeding had almost stopped, but the area around the gash was starting to swell. What could have caused this? Joe wondered.

Then he saw a small crowbar lying on the ground. "Another inch and it would have been over," he muttered.

He pressed a handkerchief against Frank's temple.

"Ouch!" Frank's eyes fluttered open.

"You'll have a good lump there." Joe gave his brother a quick smile.

But Frank didn't smile back. "Did you see who was driving that bike?"

"Couldn't tell. First I wasn't paying any attention. Then the only thing I saw was dust." Joe picked up the crowbar and examined it. "This is a standard motorcycle tool."

"Think it might have been Biker?" Frank forced the question out.

Joe's eyes flashed. "No way. Why would he do that?"

"I saw our attacker—he had the same type of motorcycle, same clothes. Who else do we know who dresses like that?"

Joe frowned. "I didn't see anything. But I did hear the engine. It sounded terrible."

"I was too busy saving you to listen. What does the sound of the engine mean?"

Joe walked over to the tire tracks and followed them around the gravel mound. "Over here!" he yelled at Frank.

Joe squatted down beside a black stain that stood out in the dead gray dirt of the quarry. He pinched some of the black stuff and rubbed it between his fingers.

"Oil," he announced. "And it's hot, as if it had just leaked out of a running engine." He glanced around, then smiled. "Notice anything about the tire tracks?"

"The tires are worn down, as if they'd been on a long trip." Frank was growing impatient.

"Worn down?" Joe said. "They're bald. And the footprints next to them prove that the driver was wearing regular street shoes."

"What's the point?"

"You know Biker. He wouldn't ride his cycle with an oil leak like this, or let his tires wear down. And he wouldn't wear street shoes even for casual riding. He may not be serious about a lot of things, but cycling is his religion."

"That was three years ago." Frank folded his arms across his chest.

"Don't give me that big-brother routine," Joe spat out angrily. "You did that the last time I wanted to help Biker, and you looked pretty foolish then, too.

Frank looked at the oil spot and the tire tracks and footprints. Then he looked at his brother.

"Okay," he said with a sigh. "I'll go along with you for now. I just want to be sure that we aren't on the wrong side of the law this time. But if it wasn't Biker, who was it?"

"Maybe the same person who framed Biker. Someone who wants to stop us from proving he's innocent."

"Or someone who wants to nail Biker before we can help him," Frank countered.

"What?"

"No one knew we were coming out here. We came looking for Biker. I'd guess whoever attacked us must have been waiting for Biker, too.

"We've got to find Biker and warn him." Joe raced for the van.

"First, let's get Callie at Mr. Pizza," Frank said as he hopped in the passenger door.

"She'll just get in the way," Joe protested.

"We can find Biker faster with three of us looking," Frank replied sternly. Even after all Callie had done to help the Hardys, Joe was still reluctant to involve her. Maybe it was because she was Frank's girlfriend. Or maybe it was simply because she was a girl.

The cool air of the Bayport Mall was a welcome relief to Frank's throbbing head. He didn't like Joe's automatic defense of Biker. If he began to get desperate, Joe might just do something stupid. Best to find Biker, get him to a safe place, and then concentrate on finding their attacker.

They walked into Mr. Pizza, the aroma of spices, cheese, and pepperoni reminding them that they hadn't eaten. Callie was waiting at their favorite booth, impatiently tapping her straw on an empty soda glass.

"It's about time you two—" Callie began. Then she noticed the lump on Frank's temple. "What happened?" she gasped.

Frank quickly explained about meeting Mort Sims and their encounter in the pits with the mysterious rider.

"I think your father's right," Callie said. "It

looks as if Biker causes trouble wherever he goes."

"His main trouble is getting blamed for stuff by people who don't know him," Joe shot back.

"Settle down, Joe," Frank said with a frown. "No need to start jumping down our throats."

"Everyone's treating Biker like a hardened criminal," Joe said. "How can he expect us to help him if Callie and Dad are trying to put him back in jail?"

"I didn't say I wanted him back in jail," Callie said. "I only—"

"Excuse me," interrupted a tall, dark-haired young man wearing a leather cycle jacket. "The manager said you two are Frank and Joe Hardy."

The guy's jacket didn't really go with his pretty-boy good looks. He actually had a dimple in his chin, and his hair was carefully styled.

Joe was ready to tell the guy to beat it when he noticed a pretty auburn-haired girl standing next to him. Her blue jumpsuit showed off a great figure, and her green eyes were fixed on Joe—a nice feeling, since she had to be twenty-one or twenty-two.

"Can we help you?" Frank asked cordially, relieved that the verbal battle between Joe and Callie had reached a temporary cease-fire.

"My name is Brandon Dalton. This is Sue Murphy," he said with a nod toward the auburn-haired girl.

"Hi." Sue gave them a shy smile.

"Dalton," said Frank thoughtfully. "Any relation to Scott Dalton?"

"My father," Brandon replied. "You must be Frank." He stuck his hand out toward the older Hardy. "And you must be Joe. I'm told you're just about the best detectives around."

Brandon's pale blue eyes rested on Callie. "And who's your friend?" he asked with a big smile.

"This is Callie Shaw," Frank said, aware of Brandon's admiring stare at Callie.

"Who told you we were detectives?" Joe asked as Brandon and Sue squeezed into the booth.

"A close friend of both of ours," Brandon said. "Biker Conway. He means a lot to us at the watch company, and we want to find him before Sims does."

"Yeah. I'm—we're afraid that if Sims finds Biker first—well . . ." Sue's voice broke off.

"Sims has a rotten reputation," Brandon said flatly. "We want to make sure Biker doesn't get hurt."

"How did you know we were here?" Frank asked.

"We stopped off at your house and spoke with your father," Brandon replied. "Sims told my dad yesterday that he suspected Biker might hide out in Bayport. We—that is, Sue and I—decided to follow him and make sure Sims brings Biker back in one piece." Brandon leaned back, unzipping his riding jacket. "You see, I'm his best friend, and Sue is his fiancée."

Joe felt a pang of disappointment. Then he silently congratulated Biker on having great taste in women.

"I'm the vice-president in charge of sales," Brandon said, folding his arms over his chest. "Sue works in the records and accounts section. I persuaded my dad to put up the bail money. No one really believed that Biker stole that shipment of watches, but when he escaped and used the company's charge account for running money, my dad blew his top. He hired this Sims character to track Biker down."

Brandon shook his head. "In Queens, they call Sims 'Old Dead-or-Alive.' He's a real hard-nosed character."

"We want to try to find Biker, talk him into coming back to appeal his case," Sue added softly, leaning forward.

"That's what we had in mind," Joe said. He liked the smile Sue gave him. "I don't think Frank and I will have too much trouble discrediting the evidence."

"We're not sure what we're going to do yet," Frank said, more to Joe than to anyone else.

"I don't know—the evidence seemed pretty conclusive," Brandon said. "The defense attorney did say that the money in the bank account

27

and the watches in Biker's garage could have been planted. But after Nick Frost testified, everyone seemed convinced that Biker was guilty."

"Nick Frost?" Frank murmured to himself as if he had heard the name before somewhere.

"He was the driver of the truck that was hijacked—the eyewitness," Brandon said.

"He lied," Joe growled.

"To prove that, we'll have to find Frost," Sue said.

"He's missing?" Callie asked.

"About the same time that Biker escaped, Frost disappeared also," Brandon said. He suddenly rose. "If you'll excuse me, I have to call the company and check in with my dad."

"There's a pay phone by the counter," Callie told him.

"Thanks, babe." Brandon winked, and Callie blushed a deep red.

"Have you known Biker long?" Joe asked Sue.

"Almost three years." Sue stared at the table, twisting a paper napkin in her hands. "Practically from the day he began working at DalTime. At first I thought he was just a macho jerk."

"What made you change your mind?" Callie asked. Joe glared at her, but she just wrinkled her nose at him.

"Underneath all that leather and motorcycle oil is a gentle, caring man."

"When do you plan on being married?" Callie went on.

"Callie . . ." Joe said sternly.

Sue fought back a sob. "Last week." She wiped her eyes with the napkin and turned to Joe, a fragile smile on her face. "Biker told me a lot about you."

"Really?"

"Yes. When he was teaching me about bike riding, he'd tell stories about this gawky kid who used to bug him about engines."

Joe felt his face turn hot from embarrassment.

"I think he made most of it up," Sue said.

"Was there any evidence that Biker was innocent?" Frank wanted to get back on track.

"I was called as a defense witness." Sue turned to Frank, her voice low. "Biker had been—" Sue finished her sentence in a scream.

Frank, Joe, and Callie turned to look where Sue was staring.

Biker Conway had Brandon Dalton pinned to the floor, his fist drawn back to let loose with a crushing blow.

Chapter
4

TONY PRITO, the manager of Mr. Pizza, was the first to reach Biker and Brandon. He grabbed for Biker first, but Biker shrugged him off, thrusting Tony against the counter.

"Tony—" Frank began as he came up.

Tony was a friend of the Hardys, but right then his temper was up. "You know this clown? Well, tell him I'm calling security." Tony jumped over the counter and picked up his phone.

"Biker, stop!" Joe yelled.

"Back off, Joe," Biker growled. "This is between me and Dalton."

Joe was stunned by the fury in Biker's voice.

Dalton's handsome face was white with fear.

He looked at Frank with pleading eyes. "Get this maniac off me!"

"This isn't doing you any good," Frank said. The growing crowd of gawkers worried him.

"I'm tired of everyone telling me what's good for me." Biker's fist was still cocked, but he hadn't punched yet.

"The security guards are on their way, pal," Tony shouted from behind the counter.

"Let's get out of here, Biker," Joe said quickly. Biker wouldn't budge.

"Biker, please." Sue's voice was the only calm element in the rising storm.

Biker looked up, embarrassed. He lowered his fist and stood. Frank pulled Brandon up.

"Here come the guards," someone yelled.

Joe grabbed Biker's jacket sleeve and jerked him out the back exit of Mr. Pizza.

"Joe!" Frank shouted. He let go of Brandon and bolted after his brother. Joe's impulsiveness would lead him straight to jail.

Frank plunged down a dark flight of stairs to the loading dock. Voices led him toward the indoor parking garage of the mall. As he sprinted past a support pillar, an arm reached out and grabbed him around the throat.

"Joe! Hold it! It's Frank," yelled Biker.

Joe let go of his brother. "Sorry. I thought you were one of the security men."

"And what if I was?" Frank shouted. "Would you have punched me out?"

"I might have," Joe shouted back.

"What's wrong with you?"

"I'm trying to help Biker."

"How? By helping him escape? Remember what Dad said. We're to hold on to him and call Sims."

"You think turning Biker over to that bounty hunter is a good idea?" Joe's face turned a blazing red. "You heard what Dalton said about that guy."

"That's not our decision."

"Biker was framed!"

"I agree with you, Joe. But we've got to do this the right way or we could all end up in jail. In the eyes of the law, Biker's still an escaped felon. You're helping him escape."

"And you're turning your back on a friend, handing him over to a bloodthirsty bounty hunter."

Frank shoved Joe back against a Dumpster. Brother or not, Joe wasn't going to accuse him of being a coward or betraying a friend. Joe charged Frank.

Biker stepped in, holding the brothers away from each other. "Knock it off, you two. I don't need this kind of help."

Frank and Joe stared at each other until they heard running footsteps.

Callie came dashing up. Breathless, she gasped, "The security guys just entered Mr. Pizza. They'll be heading down here in a second."

Without hesitation, Joe and Biker raced for the van in the parking lot.

"You stay with Sue and Brandon," Frank said to Callie. "See if you can find out more about them and Biker." He backed toward the van. "I'll call you as soon as I can straighten out this crazy mess."

By the time Frank reached the van, Joe had slipped on Biker's jacket and gloves, and had the key's to Biker's cycle clutched in his hand.

"What do you think you're doing?" Frank asked.

"No time," Joe said, slipping on the black helmet and visor.

Two security men were coming down the stairs. One pointed at the group, and both men ran for them.

"You take Biker for a ride," Joe ordered, his voice reverberating in the echo chamber of the helmet. "I'll call you on the mobile phone once I get rid of the guards." He dashed to Biker's Harley before Frank could protest.

Frank made a move toward Joe, but decided against it as the guards drew closer. He hopped into the van and fired it up. He put the van in drive but kept his foot on the brake.

"What are we waiting for?" Biker asked.

"We're not going to leave Joe here if he can't get away," Frank replied.

Joe jumped on the Harley and jammed the key into the ignition. He punched the start button and the engine rumbled to life. The guards changed direction, turning from the van to the bike. Joe kicked up the stand. The guards were only twenty yards away. He squeezed in the hand clutch, pushed the foot lever to first, and twisted the throttle full open. The engine roared with power. When Joe popped the clutch, the Harley burned rubber and shot off through the underground garage.

Glancing in the rearview mirror, Joe watched the guards recede and finally disappear. He crossed the parking lot, then raced up a ramp to the street. Joe planned to ride in circles and then head for the outskirts of town to call Frank.

Frank. Joe was shocked at how he had accused his brother of being less than loyal. But how could Frank cautiously step back when a friend needed help?

The glaring headlights of a beat-up old Chevy flashed in Joe's rearview mirror. Joe made a right turn—the car followed. He sped up—so did the Chevy. Joe could see the shadowy forms of two men in the car's front seat.

"Enough of this playing around," he decided out loud, opening the throttle all the way and shifting into fourth. The bike whined and shot forward.

Joe was shocked to see the Chevy lurch forward and keep pace. Underneath that rusty, dented old body, he realized, was a fireball engine that exploded with power and speed.

Joe tapped the foot shifter into fifth, and the bike bolted forward. The car pounded along after the Harley. Joe crouched down to cut wind resistance. Even so, the Chevy caught up, bumping the bike's rear wheel. The cycle swerved, but Joe was able to maintain control.

How was he going to shake this tail? Joe realized he was near the railroad tracks. If he could keep the Chevy at bay for a few more minutes, he could zip down the embankment, hop onto the tracks, and follow them out of town. The car wouldn't be able to follow.

Joe heard a whine from the Chevy's engine. He turned to see the car leap forward and then felt it slam into the back of his cycle again. The bike pitched forward violently. Joe held on to the handlebars and kept himself from flipping off.

Now the cycle was weaving wildly down the street. Joe rode it out, steering into the erratic moves, going at high speed. He had almost regained control when the front tire struck a curb.

Moving at eighty miles an hour, the bike bucked like a wild bronco, unseating Joe and hurling him straight for a brick wall!

Chapter

5

FRANK DECIDED TO HEAD in the opposite direction from Joe. With luck, the security men would be too busy chasing Joe to get a good look at the van and its license number.

A hollow feeling settled in Frank's stomach—and it wasn't from hunger. It wasn't enough that the police were after Biker. Now they were probably after Frank and Joe as well. Then there was the way he and Joe had deliberately disobeyed their father. The law was one thing to have to answer to—Fenton Hardy was quite another.

"Joe once told me that whenever anybody needed help, Frank Hardy would be there." Biker's words cut through Frank's uneasy thoughts.

Frank glared at Biker in silence.

"He also said that when the odds were all against him, he wouldn't want anyone but you in his corner."

"Fine," Frank mumbled. "But he didn't have to be so eager to test it out."

"I *am* innocent, Frank."

"I know, but your attack on Brandon back there doesn't do much for your case."

"Oh, that." Biker laughed.

"Just like Joe," Frank said, "always too cool under pressure."

"I was trying to scare Brandon, not kill him," Biker went on. "He's a nice enough guy, but he has this habit of moving in on other people's girlfriends. Maybe things come too easy for him, since he's rich and handsome. If he doesn't watch himself, he can become the biggest jerk in the world.

"If his daddy didn't own the company, he would've been fired a long time ago, and I'd be vice-president in charge of sales."

"Why? He seems competent enough to me."

Biker laughed. "He tries too hard to be the boss. Once he came up with the brilliant idea of having all the field representatives call in at nine A.M., to make sure they were 'on the job.' Of course, as an executive, he wouldn't come in until ten, so his secretary handled the mess. Every morning at nine o'clock sharp, the company switchboard lit up like the Fourth of July—

then at one second past, the board would blow a fuse.''

"Why didn't Mr. Dalton stop it?"

"I tried to warn him, but he couldn't believe that anybody would have given such a stupid order. Then one day Mr. Dalton tried to call out at one second past nine and *zzzaaappp!*'' He laughed. "That day, Mr. Dalton was the one who blew a fuse."

"What happened?" Frank asked as they turned down another street.

"Mr. Dalton got furious at Brandon. After that, Brandon made it tougher for me to route my shipments. I could handle that. But then he started getting personal by hitting on Sue. Just now, when I saw his cycle next to hers in the mall parking lot, I lost it."

"Your temper just digs your hole deeper," Frank said.

"I've calmed down a lot since I met Sue."

Frank frowned at Biker. He hadn't noticed any sign of a change.

"I can't believe you were convicted on such slim evidence," Frank said, his brow furrowed. "What could that truck driver have said to convince a jury?"

"If I get my hands on that liar, I'll choke the truth out of him!" Biker slammed his fist against the dash. He looked out the window into the dark night. "Nick Frost testified that the hijacker was wearing black leather riding clothes exactly like mine, down to the emblems and logos I had sewn on from my junior motocross days. The only thing he couldn't see was my face—because of the racing mask.''

"Racing mask?'' Frank asked.

"Yeah. It looks like a ski mask, but it has one large oval for the eyes instead of two small holes.''

"It still sounds like circumstantial evidence,'' Frank said.

"Frost claimed that he recognized the hijacker's voice as mine. I suppose he ought to know—I've chewed him out plenty of times for messing up my orders.''

"Did you know Frost is missing now?''

"No.''

Frank slowed the van to a halt.

"What's wrong, Frank?'' Biker asked. He looked around, afraid that they had been stopped by the police.

"Nick Frost . . .'' Frank said thoughtfully.

"What about him?''

"Each time I hear that name, a little bell rings.'' Frank hopped in the back of the van and unlocked the panel that held his laptop computer.

"Wow, High-tech Hardy,'' Biker said. "What are you trying to find in that little magic box?''

"A rat,'' Frank replied. A red light blinked on the computer and the screen jumped with amber letters. Moments later, Frank smiled for the first time in an hour. "And here he is, right in my dad's files. It seems Mr. Frost was once a petty crook here in Bayport, but hasn't been around for some time. How did you meet him?"

"Nick started working for DalTime about six months after I did. We drove together until I got promoted. He never said anything about being from Bayport."

"You wouldn't either if you had his record," Frank replied with a nod at the screen.

The data continued to scroll upward, listing Frost's past crimes. Biker whistled.

"Did he have anything against you?" Frank sat behind the steering wheel and started the van.

"The only time— Nah, that's silly."

"What?"

"About a year ago I got this great idea for promoting the watches and getting paid to ride cycles. Mr. Dalton let me form a company cycle club called Riding on Time. All of us—me, Sue, Brandon, Frost—would visit shopping centers and malls to put on safety and riding demonstrations. We had matching jumpsuits and—"

"What about Frost?" Frank said, interrupting the reminiscences.

"Brandon may be a jerk sometimes, but Frost makes stupidity an art form. The guy was careless, wouldn't follow instructions or stick to the routine. He nearly ran over some kids at one mall. Worse than that, he treated his bike like garbage. I finally told him to take a hike.''

Frank's eyes narrowed as he thought. "So, Frost rides a bike?''

"Yeah, why?''

Frank described the attack at the pits. "Joe said the guy's bike was a wreck.''

"Sounds like Frost. We used to joke that he never had to change his oil because it always leaked out first. He made a big fuss about being kicked out of our club but quieted down when Fat Harold's men started looking for him.''

"Fat Harold?''

"A loan shark with very long and very sharp teeth. From what I understand, Frost was deep in debt to Fat Harold and sinking fast.'' The van lurched from side to side as it hit several potholes. "Hey, where are we going?''

"The computer gave Frost's last address. It's a garage owned by the Sinbads. If he's in town, he may be there.''

"The Sinbads?''

"They're a local cycle club known more for their fighting than their riding. I guess they were formed after you left Bayport.'' Frank turned down a dark street. "Why would Frost be after you?''

"What do you mean?''

"Sue said that Frost disappeared shortly after you escaped. Did you threaten him at the trial?''

"I just looked at him," Biker said. "But you know what they say—if looks could kill . . ."

"Did you ever tell Frost about the pits?"

"I might have. Drivers talk about a million things on long hauls." Biker sat up. "Come to think of it, I did most of the talking."

Frank wasn't surprised.

He turned into a dark driveway. The van's headlights lit up the stained walls of a cinderblock garage. Rusted engine parts and skeletons of cycle frames cluttered the area. A large, poorly drawn picture of a skull with a blood-drenched knife between its teeth warned unwelcome visitors to stay away.

"Friendly folks, aren't they?" Biker mused.

Frank stopped the van several yards from the large wooden door of the seedy garage.

"Let me do the talking," Frank cautioned Biker, his hand on the door handle. "The last thing I need is for you to start a riot."

"Yes, sir," Biker said with a laugh and a salute.

Frank began to push open the door when it was suddenly jerked away from him. A large, hairy hand grabbed his shirt collar and yanked him out of the van. Then he was blinking in the glare of the headlights as a massive brass-knuckled fist flew toward his face. He had just enough time to move his head slightly. The brass knuckles only scraped along his jaw, but the force of the blow sent him stumbling backward.

A bearlike shadow was silhouetted against the headlights. The man swung his arm out and twisted his wrist. Frank heard the distinctive *snick* of a switchblade. A six-inch, razor-sharp blade glittered in the lights.

"My friends call me Switch." The huge man chuckled. "I usually keep this around in case of trouble. But when I heard you guys might be coming—I knew *I'd* be giving *you* trouble."

Chapter

6

JOE FLEW OFF the cycle, his fall cushioned by a pile of garbage. He rolled to one side as the bike slammed into the wall—hard. It fell to the ground, a hunk of twisted, screaming metal. The engine whined, then coughed, then died.

Joe lay quiet, the breath knocked out of him. He stayed still and took in small gulps of air. Revived, he tried to push himself up, but a burning line of pain shot down his left arm. Broken, he figured.

The Chevy screeched to a stop less than a yard from Joe, the headlight beams blinding him. He stood on wobbly legs. Although injured and dazed, Joe was ready to confront the two men getting out of the car. He wiped the grit and crud of the garbage from his visor and looked around, trying to find anything to use as a weapon.

The two men were still a blur. The driver leaned across the hood of the Chevy, pointing something at Joe. Joe instantly recognized the glint of steel from a large pistol.

"Okay, Conway," came a gravelly voice. "Back up to the wall." Joe had no choice as he heard the hammer lock into firing position. He backed up.

"Take the helmet off," the man ordered.

Joe tugged on the chin strap with his right hand. He loosened it and slowly pulled the helmet off his head.

"*Joe!*" Fenton Hardy yelled from the passenger side of the car.

Joe was momentarily confused. "Dad?" He caught himself as he began to fall forward.

Fenton ran to the front of the car and helped his son out of the garbage.

"What's going on here?" asked a puzzled Mort Sims. He still held his 9 mm on Joe, unsure what to do next.

"You've got the wrong guy, Sims," Joe said with a weak smile.

Sims lowered the hammer and replaced his gun in its holster.

"You've done it now, Fenton." He glared at Joe's father. "You told me that your sons were levelheaded, that they'd cooperate with the law.

I ought to arrest Joe here and now for aiding an escaped felon.''

"What you'll do," Fenton replied harshly, eyes narrowed, "is drive Joe to the hospital."

Sims hesitated, then threw his hands up in the air and climbed into the driver's seat of the Chevy.

Joe cradled his left arm as Fenton helped him into the backseat.

"I think it's broken," he groaned.

"You're lucky you didn't break your neck," Sims retorted.

"Just drive, Sims," Fenton ordered as he hopped into the front passenger seat.

Reluctantly, Sims shifted the car and gunned the accelerator.

"What were you trying to prove by luring us away from Conway?" Fenton turned and asked after he gave Sims directions to the hospital.

"I wasn't luring you away from him." Joe tried to avoid his father's steel blue stare. "We didn't even know you were there. Biker got into some trouble at the mall, and I wanted to shake the security guards."

"Conway's a loser," Sims said matter-of-factly.

"Get off his back," Joe shot back.

"What kind of trouble?" Fenton Hardy wanted to know.

"Did you tell Brandon Dalton that Frank and I

were at the mall?'' Joe inquired instead of answering his father's question.

"He called the house about an hour after you left," Fenton answered. "He wanted to talk Biker into turning himself in."

"How'd he know to call our house?"

"I told him yesterday I was going to ask your father to help me," Sims replied. "Now, why don't you answer your father's questions?" Sims shot Joe a suspicious look.

"After we met Brandon and we talked a bit, he went to make a phone call. Next thing I knew, Biker was there and ready to punch him out."

"Was Murphy with Dalton?" asked Sims.

Joe hesitated. "Yes."

"So, Conway thought he'd do a little tap dancing on the guy who stole his girl." Sims laughed and turned to Fenton. "Word is that she dumped Conway for the rich kid after the trial."

"That's a lie," Joe said bluntly.

"Why didn't you call in, tell us where Conway was?" Fenton asked.

"Biker had just shown up when he got into the fight with Brandon."

"Where is he now?"

"With Frank."

"Where's Frank?" Sims asked impatiently.

"Driving around until Biker cools off."

"You were told to restrain him," Fenton said coldly.

"We had to get him away from the security guards," Joe replied. He knew what was coming the moment he said that.

"Why?" Fenton's voice was steady, like a flow of angry lava. "They would only have held him until the police arrived, and then Conway would have been put in jail—*where he belongs.*"

"He's innocent," Joe protested. "If you'd really look at the evidence—"

"Judge Joe Hardy," Sims scoffed. "When's your appointment to the Supreme Court, Judge Joe?" Sims turned the car toward the hospital's emergency entrance. "You've got no reason to believe that Conway's innocent."

"My reason is based on something you wouldn't know much about," Joe said calmly.

"Yeah? What's that?"

"Friendship."

Joe watched in the rearview mirror as Sims's eyes narrowed into angry slits.

"You're lucky you *didn't* break that arm," the emergency room doctor said as he studied the X rays of Joe's left arm. "It's only a torn ligament— and a world-class bruise." He shut off the X-ray lamp and began writing on a chart. To a nurse he said, "Wrap it and put it in a sling." He turned to Joe. "You'll have to wear the sling for a few

48

weeks. No baseball or tennis or anything that might agitate that arm.''

"Like helping escaped convicts," Sims added with a wry smile.

The doctor raised his eyebrows at Sims. "Just take it easy," he said, leaving the curtained room.

"I've known you for a long time, Fenton," Sims began as the nurse was adjusting the Velcro straps on Joe's sling. "You're one of the best investigators around. I never thought I'd be telling you this." Sims took a deep breath. "But if your boys get in my way again, I'll be forced to bring the law down on them. Hard.''

Fenton's eyes bored into Sims. "My sons may have their faults. But breaking the law intentionally isn't one of them." Fenton approached the examining table where Joe was sitting. Joe was chilled by his father's icy stare. "Tell Sims everything you remember about Biker's old hangouts," Fenton ordered when the nurse left the cubicle.

Joe felt a great weight pull down on his shoulders. Fenton rarely used that tone of voice with either of his sons. Joe slid down from the table.

"You heard him," Sims said triumphantly. "Everything. I want that convict by morning."

Joe's mind was clear and calm. "No."

"I can't help you, Joe, if you insist on hampering Sims's investigation." Fenton Hardy's voice was no longer angry—just resigned to the fact that his son was sticking to his convictions.

"I won't betray an innocent friend to a trigger-happy bounty hunter like Sims." Joe paused. He felt the weight press down even more heavily. "Or to a bounty hunter like you."

Chapter

7

FRANK HARDY HEARD the sounds of a struggle from the other side of the van. But Biker would have to take care of himself—Frank had time only for the switchblade slicing toward him. He caught his attacker's arm as it swung down with the knife. Then Frank rolled, and Switch stumbled off balance. Whipping around, Frank snapped a kick behind the guy's left knee.

Switch grunted and fell to the ground.

Frank was on his feet in a flash. Switch rose slowly, the switchblade missing from his hand. Frank took a defensive karate stance. His teacher had taught him to let the bigger, more powerful guy make the first move, the first mistake.

A head taller and a foot thicker than Frank, the

51

bearlike man was slow. He swung a beefy fist at Frank. Frank slapped it away and moved back. Anger flashed in the man's eyes. He tried faking with his right and then jabbed with his left. Frank blocked the left jab and punched Switch in the nose. The man staggered back, shock and pain registering on his face. He snorted like a bull and charged Frank, his arms swinging in wide, wild arcs. Frank ducked and swiftly jammed his knee into the man's stomach. Switch doubled over but did not fall.

Frank decided to finish off the big man and help Biker. He moved toward the man for the knock-out punch. But Switch darted forward, catching Frank off guard. Two pile-driver gut punches had Frank wobbling on his feet. Then Switch threw a roundhouse right that connected right where the crowbar had hit Frank before.

Frank must have blacked out for a moment, because the next thing he knew, Switch had him in a bear hug. The man squeezed Frank just below the ribs and lifted him off the ground. Frank felt the air being forced from his lungs as Switch slowly tightened his grip. The big man knew the fight was already over. He was just ending it, the most painful way he knew.

Frank's lower ribs ached and his lungs screamed for air. He was too weak to kick, and his arms were pinned. Little pinpoints of light swirled behind his eyes—he was going to black out again. His head fell forward.

Switch chuckled a throaty, evil, triumphant laugh and shifted his grip.

When the arms around him loosened for a second, Frank snapped his head back, smashing it into the man's nose. Switch screamed and let Frank go, both hands going to his nose. The instant Frank's feet hit the ground, he spun and delivered a crunching kick to the man's jaw. Switch folded to the ground.

Frank stood over the thug, ready to deliver another blow if the man moved. His lungs felt as though a fire were raging inside as he took in short, choppy breaths. A dull ache rippled along his sore ribs. Switch remained still.

A steady rhythm of punches echoed from the other side of the van. Frank darted around the van, expecting to help Biker. Instead, he found Biker holding his assailant up, delivering quick jabs to the guy's face.

"Where is he?" Biker growled.

"D-d-d-don't . . . know," stammered the man.

Biker was set to deliver another set of blows when Frank shoved him back. Without Biker's support, the man crumpled to the ground.

"What are you doing, Frank? He would have told me where Frost is." Biker's eyes glowed with rage.

"If you didn't kill him first!"

Biker glared down at the man.

The roar of a motorcycle echoed in the air.

"The garage!" Biker shouted as he and Frank ran toward the cinder-block building.

The engine screamed high RPMs, and the cycle exploded out of the garage, shattering the old wooden door. A wood panel hit Biker and knocked him to the ground.

Frank found himself face-to-face with the cyclist—a tall, gaunt-faced guy with an old scar across his right cheek. The rider swerved his bike, kicking out and catching Frank on the hip. Frank tumbled backward.

"Frost!" Biker yelled, running into the garage.

Frank jumped to his feet.

A second cycle fired to life inside the cinder-block walls. The darkness of the night and the dust thrown up by Frost's escape hid what was happening. But Frank could figure it out.

"I'm going after Frost," Biker yelled as he downshifted. The cycle spat fire, and Biker shot off into the night in hot pursuit of Frost.

Frank rushed to the van and hopped in. He had to stop Biker before the wild man got hold of Frost. Frank knew that, given Biker's present state of mind, Frost's life was in danger.

Thanks to Joe's wizardry, the Hardys' black van was one of the hottest vehicles in Bayport. But Frank couldn't keep up with the two cycles. He slammed his fist against the dashboard as the red taillight of Biker's cycle disappeared into the dark. He jumped as the mobile phone chirped.

"What?" he bellowed into the phone.

"Hey, take it easy," said Joe.

"I've lost Biker."

"How?"

"We found Frost and got into a fight with a couple of those Sinbad creeps."

"What are you doing messing with the Sinbads?"

"I'll explain later. Where are you?"

"Home."

Frank sighed. "I'll be there in about ten minutes."

Frank found Joe in the kitchen where the younger Hardy was trying to manage an over-stuffed sandwich with his one good hand.

"What happened to your arm?" Frank asked as he poured himself a glass of milk.

"Sims tried to run me down."

"What?"

"Dad was with him." Joe quickly explained about totaling Biker's cycle and refusing to give Sims any information. "I don't think I'll be asking Dad for any favors soon."

"I warned you about this," Frank said. He sat across from his brother.

"Don't give me that Frank Hardy I-told-you-so look." Joe raised the sandwich to his lips, only to have half the ham and pickles fall out the back. He put it down with a sigh.

"You really called Dad a bounty hunter?" Frank asked.

"Yeah."

"Where is he now?"

"Asleep. To calm Sims down, Dad had the police put out an all-points bulletin saying that Biker was dangerous and perhaps armed. Then he persuaded Sims to go back to his hotel and wait."

"You shouldn't have called Dad a bounty hunter."

Joe looked down at his mangled sandwich. "I know. I lost my temper. You'd think he would trust us. We would never do anything to hurt Dad."

"He knows that, but he's got Sims to deal with. I don't think it's a good idea to go sneaking behind Dad's back."

"We're not sneaking! We're helping a friend."

"Look, I believe Biker's innocent, too." Frank's voice rose. "I just don't want you putting your friend before the rest of the family." The shout strained Frank's bruised ribs. He winced, putting a hand to his side.

Joe sat back in his chair and stared at Frank. "What's wrong with your ribs?"

"A grizzly tried to squeeze me to death." Frank filled Joe in about the conversation in the van and the discovery that Frost was from Bayport. "I just hope Biker doesn't find Frost."

"Why?"

"I'm not sure if Biker's determined to prove himself innocent or if he just wants revenge. What if he knew Frost was from Bayport and came here looking for him? We could have been an afterthought." Frank glanced at the kitchen clock. "It's almost midnight. I ought to call Callie."

"Don't bother," Joe said as he pushed his sandwich away. "Brandon and Sue went back to their motel rooms, and Callie's at home." He paused. "Did Biker say anything about him and Sue and Brandon?"

"Just that Brandon had tried to move in on Sue."

"Sims claims that Sue's a gold digger, after Brandon for his money." Joe's lips twisted. "That guy's got some really wonderful ideas about people."

"He's just trying to rile you, Joe."

"Maybe it's working." Joe looked up at Frank. "Let's get some rest and start over in the morning."

Neither Frank nor Joe slept well. For both, the night passed slowly.

Frank's alarm awoke him from a restless sleep six hours later. He found Joe already up and in the living room waiting.

"Didn't you sleep?" Frank asked.

"Yeah. A little. You ready?" Joe asked as he zipped up a light fall jacket.

"Let me get some juice first," Frank protested.

Just then a loud thump echoed at the front door. Joe jumped.

"It's just the newspaper," Frank said. "Why don't you check out the headlines?"

Joe opened the door. Frank gasped.

Brandon Dalton swayed in the doorway, his boyish features swollen, bruised, and bloody. He stumbled, then caught himself. His eyes were wide with terror.

"*Biker!*" he whispered in a hoarse voice. "Biker."

He took a faltering step, trying to grab Frank. Then he fell to the floor in a heap.

Chapter

8

JOE GRIMACED AS he watched the nurse gently rub gooey salve on a cut over Brandon's right eye. Once Brandon was cleaned up, his face didn't look so bad. He would have a swollen lip and a black eye, but there were no serious injuries.

Not wanting to wait for an ambulance, Frank and Joe had rushed Brandon to Bayport Hospital after he collapsed. Awakened by the disturbance, Fenton had called Sims, and both men followed the boys to the hospital.

"Well, it doesn't look as if anything's broken." The emergency room doctor yawned as he walked into Brandon's room. "However, I'd like you to stay here for a couple of hours, just for observation.''

Brandon nodded weakly.

''Mind telling me what happened?'' Sims asked from a corner of the hospital room.

''All I wanted to do was talk Biker into turning himself in,'' Brandon said.

''Where did you find him?'' Frank asked.

''I didn't—he called me. Wanted me to meet him at the pits.''

''How do you know about the pits?'' Joe asked.

''Biker always talked about growing up in Bayport, being a junior motocross rider and all that drivel. He gave me directions to the quarry, and I met him there about four this morning. All he would say was that he had unfinished business from Mr. Pizza.''

''Mr. Pizza?'' Sims perked up.

''Biker and Brandon had a run-in there,'' Frank said quickly, ''but Biker was just trying to keep Brandon away from Sue.''

''I'd say he really finished the job.'' Sims tugged on his ear and nodded toward Brandon.

''We haven't heard Biker's side of the story and you've already got him convicted,'' Joe said hotly.

''His guilt should be obvious even to a junior detective,'' Sims sneered. ''First he breaks out of jail—that's real innocent. Then he tries twice to beat up on a friend who's trying to help him, just because he's jealous. The question is, why did he return to Bayport in the first place?"

"He wanted help," Joe replied.

"Yeah, right," Sims snorted. "Maybe he wanted to get rid of the only witness who put him behind bars."

"That's crazy," Joe said with a glance at Frank.

His brother was silent, astonished that the bounty hunter was saying the same things he'd thought last night.

Sims puffed himself up and announced, "I'm bringing him in. I've never lost a bail jumper yet."

"Just make sure Biker doesn't have any accidents before you get him back to New York," Joe warned.

"That depends on your friend." Sims smiled. "He can go back the easy way or the hard way. I don't judge people, you know. I just bring back fugitives. The courts decide whether they're guilty or innocent." His face hardened. "But nothing, especially two junior detectives, will stop me."

Joe stepped forward, his fists clenched. He was ready to punch Sims when Fenton walked into the room. Joe froze, but Fenton stepped right past him. "Biker's been spotted," he announced.

"Where?" asked Frank.

"Just outside of town, near that old quarry."

Frank gave Joe a sidelong glance.

Sims was out the door before Joe could stop him.

Noticing the concerned look on Joe's face, Fenton said, "I'll stick with him. If we catch Conway, he goes back to Queens with Sims."

Joe nodded silently.

"What are you two going to do?" Brandon asked from his hospital bed.

"We're going to try to find Biker before Sims does," Joe replied.

"I suggest we stay out of his way for the time being," Frank cautioned. "And I don't mean Sims's."

"Then what do we do? Sit around and twiddle our thumbs?" Joe was red with anger.

"I want to take another look at the Sinbads' garage," Frank said, ignoring Joe's outburst.

"That's a good idea," Brandon said. "I'll come with you." Brandon started to get up from his bed, but only fell back.

"You'd better stay here," Joe said. "The doctor said you could leave in a couple of hours."

"Yeah. You're right," said Brandon. "Call me if you find anything."

"Sure," Frank said. He nodded toward the door, and he and Joe left.

"Do you believe Biker beat up Brandon?" Joe asked as they neared the garage.

"I believe Biker is capable of doing just about anything if he gets angry enough."

Joe stared straight ahead. Biker *was* capable of losing his temper. Especially when he cared a lot about something—or some*one*, like a girlfriend.

Joe had seen Biker lose it completely three years earlier at a motocross event. Another cyclist had tried several times to kick Biker's cycle. Biker detested cheaters. After the race, Biker punched out the other rider and then took a hammer to the guy's motorcycle. When he was done, the cycle was totaled.

"Looks deserted," Frank said as he pulled the van to a stop and looked around.

Joe was too intent on looking at the run-down garage to hear Frank. He hopped from the van and scouted the area.

"It's clear," he said.

Frank shook his head. He'd have to keep an eye on Joe.

The door of the garage still lay in splinters where Frost had burst through. Frank and Joe entered the bay area and looked around. Frank tried a door leading to an office while Joe rummaged through some junk in the back.

The office wall was covered with motorcycle pictures and graffiti of skulls, cycle logos, and blood-drenched daggers. Frank cupped his hand over his nose—the office stank of decayed food. Something moved by the door—a large black rat. It squealed and scurried for the dark safety of a corner.

"You okay?" Joe yelled from the garage.

"Yeah," Frank replied. "Just introducing myself to one of the houseguests."

Joe was growing impatient. He kicked at the rubbish and boxes that lay about the bay area. He still didn't believe that Biker had deliberately lured Brandon out to the pits just to beat him up.

"Ow!" he yelled as his foot struck a wooden box hidden under a pile of dirty blankets. He looked closer, then threw the blankets aside. Stenciled on the side of the box was DalTime and a Queens address. Joe dug around in the blankets and discovered two more boxes. "Frank!"

"What's wrong?" Frank asked as he ran into the bay area.

"Got the time?" Joe smirked as he held up a handful of designer sports watches.

"Does anybody really know what time it is?" Frank replied, a wide grin on his face. For the first time in two days, he really began to believe that Joe had been right about Biker all along.

"This proves that Frost was in on the hijacking," Joe said.

"If the serial numbers match the invoice for the stolen watches," Frank replied.

"Why don't you just throw a wet blanket on the party?" Joe said sarcastically. Frank was being too cautious again.

"Look, Frost could have swiped these from any of the shipments he delivered."

Joe hated to admit it, but Frank was right.

"Let's take these three cases to Brandon. Maybe he can identify them," Frank said as he picked up one of the boxes.

Joe stacked the remaining box on the one he'd kicked and followed Frank out of the garage.

"Going somewhere?" a gruff voice asked.

Joe lowered his boxes. In front of Frank was a bearlike man, four other Sinbads at his side.

"Uh, how's business, Switch?" Frank tried to sound calm.

"Breaking and entering's a serious crime," Switch said with a chuckle. The big, burly biker seemed in a dangerously cheerful mood for a man whose nose was wrapped in bandages.

"Come on, Switch, let's quit fooling around. We've got to meet Frost at Daryl's," said a short, balding guy with an eye patch.

"Do what you want with old One-Arm here," Switch said, pointing at Joe's sling. He twisted his wrist and like magic his six-inch blade appeared.

"I've got some unfinished carving business with the other one."

Chapter
9

BRACING THEMSELVES BACK to back, Frank and Joe prepared for a hopeless fight. Frank knew that with his karate skills he could handle one of these guys, maybe two, but strength and numbers were on the Sinbads' side. And that didn't take into account the chains and clubs each Sinbad was holding.

Switch laughed and lunged carelessly at Frank. Frank moved to one side and delivered a smashing chop to Switch's wrist. The snap of bone and the cry of pain told Frank that Switch's knife hand was now useless.

Joe quickly decided that the best defense was a good offense. He yelled at two Sinbads as they approached. Surprised, the Sinbads hesitated.

Unable to use one arm, Joe charged, knocking both guys to the ground. But a third guy slugged Joe in the jaw, stunning the younger Hardy.

Frank saw Joe hit the ground. The Sinbad who had slugged Joe was raising a baseball bat over his head. With a spinning heel kick to the head, Frank sent that Sinbad to dreamland.

"Thanks," Joe said as he jumped to his feet.

"Any time," Frank replied.

"Kill 'em!" yelled Switch as he held his broken wrist, his face twisted in anger and pain.

The remaining Sinbads backed Frank and Joe against the garage wall. Clubs were raised and chains spun in the air. The two Hardys were in a fight for their lives.

A roar split the air. Behind the Sinbads, Frank and Joe could see a black-clad cyclist bearing down on the group.

"Biker!" Joe shouted.

The cyclist turned and braked the bike, ramming the three Sinbads. The bikers yelled as they flew into the air. The cyclist twisted the throttle handle and darted away.

Taking advantage of the confusion, Frank and Joe knocked the three guys out.

The cyclist rode up to Frank and Joe.

"Nice going, Biker," Joe said as the cyclist shut off the engine. Then the cyclist unstrapped the helmet and pulled it off. Joe was stunned. "What?"

Long auburn hair fell from beneath the helmet.

"Sue!" exclaimed Frank with a laugh.

"Glad I could help," Sue replied as she stepped from the Harley.

Callie pulled up in her car behind Sue and jumped out. "Surprise!"

"How did you know to find us here?" Frank asked as he put an arm around Callie.

"I called your house and found out about Brandon. Then I called the hospital to check on him," Sue replied. "He suggested that while you two were checking this place out, I should go back to Queens and look at Frost's apartment. I called Callie and asked if she wanted to come with me."

"And I suggested we meet here and tell you two," Callie added.

"I'm glad you did," Frank said with a smile.

"Where did you get that other cut?" Callie asked when she noticed the scrapes left by Switch's brass knuckles.

"From him," Frank said, pointing to the unconscious Switch. "We met here last night, too. This morning was round two."

"We found some evidence that will clear Biker," Joe said as he picked up one of the watch boxes.

"Great," Sue replied.

"It doesn't clear Biker yet," Frank said. "First we've got to prove that these are the watches that were stolen, and then that Frost actually hijacked the shipment.''

"You think Frost hijacked his own shipment and then framed Biker?" Callie asked.

"Stranger things have happened," Frank replied.

"Frost hated Biker after he kicked him out of the company cycle club," Sue said thoughtfully.

"We'll explain later," Frank said in response to Callie's puzzled expression. "Let's tie up these clowns and try to find Dad."

Callie called the police while Frank and Joe tied up Switch and his pals.

"Why did Brandon want you to check out Frost's apartment?" Frank asked Sue.

"He's never believed that Biker stole those watches, and he thinks that maybe Frost had something to do with the hijacking."

For the second time that day, Frank felt as though his mind were an open book.

"But why would Brandon send *you* to Queens? Why not Sims?" Joe asked.

"I don't know," Sue replied with a shrug. "Brandon just said he was going back to the motel room to rest."

"He's out of the hospital?" Frank asked.

"Checked himself out," Sue responded. "He claimed the hospital was too noisy and he couldn't get any rest."

69

"Did you hear him leave this morning when he went to meet Biker?"

"I heard a phone ring in the next room early this morning," Sue said. "It woke me up, but I was too sleepy to notice anything else."

"You didn't hear a cycle pull away?" Joe asked.

"I guess I went back to sleep," Sue said apologetically.

"She's not a sleuth like us," Callie said as she rejoined the group. "She doesn't distrust people the way we do."

Joe looked at Callie skeptically.

"Let's leave Callie's car and Sue's bike at the house," Frank suggested. "If we can't find Dad and Sims, we'll all go to Queens and search Frost's apartment."

While Callie looked for lunch stuff in the Hardys' kitchen, Frank tried to locate his dad and Sims. "No luck," he said to Joe.

"Don't you guys have anything besides fish sticks?" Callie yelled from the kitchen.

"No!" Frank shouted back. "Joe ate all the cold cuts last night."

"Brandon isn't answering his phone," Sue said as she returned from the den. She had tried to call Brandon on Fenton's private phone.

"He's gone?" asked Frank suspiciously.

"I doubt it," Sue replied. "He said the hospital

gave him a pretty strong sleeping pill and he was going to take a taxi back. He's probably out like a light."

"You thinking that Brandon is involved in this somehow?" Joe knew his brother well enough to read his thoughts.

"Why not?"

Sue laughed. "Brandon Dalton doesn't have the guts to say boo to his own shadow. He's all good looks and air."

"Guess what?" Callie said as she emerged from the kitchen. "You guys will have to buy us lunch along the way—unless you want fish-stick sandwiches."

"We've got to get gas," Frank announced as they headed for the highway.

"Hey, remember what one of those Sinbads said to Switch?" Joe suddenly asked with a start.

"What?"

"They were supposed to meet Frost at Daryl's. That's the gas station on Tenth."

"That was a while ago," Callie pointed out.

"It's worth a try," Frank said as he turned the van down Tenth. "Maybe someone can tell us which way Frost went."

Daryl's was one of the last full-service stations left in Bayport.

"Why are you stopping here?" Callie asked as

Frank pulled the van into a vacant lot across the street from Daryl's.

"Look." Frank pointed to a Harley parked by the gas pumps.

"Let's check it out." Joe hopped from the van before Frank could say anything.

"Wait here," Frank said to Callie and Sue. "That might not be Frost's bike."

Joe was kneeling beside the bike when Frank approached.

"Ever seen an oil leak like that?" Joe asked. Directly beneath the engine was a dirty black patch of oil.

"Must have been here awhile," Frank noted, "to leak that much oil."

"Not so long," Joe said. "The tank isn't filled yet." The nozzle was in the bike's gas tank, and the pump was still working.

"Can I help you guys?"

Frank and Joe spun round. The station attendant leaned against the doorway leading into the office, wiping his greasy hands on an even greasier T-shirt. Joe recognized him from school.

"Hey, Randy," he said with a friendly wave. "Know whose bike this is?"

"No." Randy walked over to Frank and Joe.

"Know where the guy is?" Frank asked.

"Why?"

"I've been looking for a bike like that." Joe forced a smile.

"That piece of junk! I thought you knew some-thing about bikes," Randy scoffed.

Joe sighed. "Just tell us where he is."

Randy shrugged. "Guy said he was going to the bathroom." He turned and wandered back inside the office.

"I'll check around the side," Joe said. "Try to phone Dad. Maybe he's—"

Joe's last words were cut short by the blast of a gun. The bullet smashed glass on the pump next to Joe. Frank and Joe jumped behind the pumps.

"Where'd that come from?" Frank yelled.

"Over there!"

Frank followed Joe's pointing finger. A small-barrel .38 was sticking out around the edge of the building, held by someone wearing a black cycle helmet.

"What's going on out—" Randy began as he stepped outside the station office.

"Get back!" Joe shouted and jumped up, wav-ing the attendant back.

Frank yanked Joe back down as the gunman fired again.

Two more shots quickly followed. The last bul-let struck the gas hose leading to Frost's Harley. The rubber hose split in two and fell to the ground. Gas spread around the cycle and the island.

"The gas pump!" Frank yelled.

Joe reached over to shut off the pump, but

before he could, a fourth shot rang out. The bullet hit the concrete, sending sparks in all directions and hitting the rapidly spreading pool of gas. The gas exploded.

In a fraction of a second, the entire island of pumps was enshrouded in bright blue flames—with Frank and Joe caught in the middle!

Chapter

10

"WE'RE SURROUNDED!" Joe yelled as he held up his arms to protect his face from the flames.

A thick black plume of smoke rose into the air like a dark mushroom.

Frank spun around. Joe was right. Flames encircled them. Worse yet, the flames were getting thicker as more gas ran out. Running through the flames would mean getting seriously burned. But staying there would ensure a horrible death.

"The pump's going to explode!" Joe stared in horror as the fire ran up the split hose and engulfed the pump.

Frank spotted their one chance to escape.

"Over here, Joe!" he yelled above the crackle of the fire. He grabbed the faucet of the island's water hose and twisted it open. There was no way water could put out a gasoline fire, but . . . he held the hose over his head until he was completely soaked; then he turned it on Joe. "Ready?"

"Yeah," Joe replied.

"One, two, *three*."

The Hardys threw themselves into the flames and emerged singed but safe seconds later. Simultaneously, they rolled on the ground to smother any flames. Callie and Sue covered them with their jackets.

"You okay?" Joe asked as he brushed himself off.

Frank nodded.

Screams sounded from inside the station's office.

"Randy!" Joe yelled. "He'll be trapped inside."

Frank turned—to find Callie dashing into the small building. She grabbed the terrified attendant by the arm and tried to pull him toward the door. But Randy was crazy with fear. As Frank burst through the door, Randy's terrified thrashing had sent Callie spinning into a candy machine. She hit hard, gasped, and slid to the floor. Frank helped her up, grabbed the attendant, and began pulling him toward the door.

A sudden rush of air and heat hit Frank. He jumped back, watching helplessly as a wall of gas-fed flames rose up to block their only exit.

"We're gonna die!" the attendant screamed as he pulled away from Frank and ran to a corner of the office.

Frank grabbed a chair and threw it into the picture window on the side of the building. He dragged the attendant from the corner and hurled him out, sending him staggering to safety. Callie wobbled to her feet. Frank put his arm around her and both scrambled through the broken window.

Joe rushed forward to grab the dazed attendant. All four sprinted away from the building.

A loud crack shattered the air as the pumps exploded. The concussion and blast slammed them all to the ground. Thick black smoke rolled over them and began to choke them. Frank and Callie crawled away from the smoke as Joe and Sue dragged Randy away from danger.

Seconds later the gas station was surrounded by fire engines, police cars, and ambulances. Half an hour later the fire was extinguished, leaving the station a charred skeleton.

"Are you boys okay?" asked Officer Con Riley with concern. He had arrived with the fire engines and had waited till the paramedics had checked Frank, Joe, and Callie over.

"Yes," Frank replied. "But I don't think I'll want to roast hot dogs anytime soon."

"Mind telling me what happened here?" Officer Riley asked.

Frank hesitated, then explained that he, Joe, Callie, and Sue had been looking for Frost when they spotted his cycle at the gas station. "Next thing we knew, someone was shooting at us," Frank finished his story.

"And you think it was Frost firing at you?" Con asked.

"Yes," Joe said without hesitation. "We had a run-in with some members of his gang earlier. He knew we were on his tail."

"Hey, Con, come over here and look at this!" a fire fighter yelled as he pointed into a ditch next to the station.

"You four stick around. I'm not through getting your statements," Con Riley said as he walked toward the fire fighter.

"Shouldn't we tell him about the watches you and Frank found at the Sinbads' garage?" Sue asked Joe.

"Not yet," Joe replied. "The watches by themselves don't prove Frost was in on the hijacking. We need to check out Frost's apartment first."

"Frank, Joe, come over here," Officer Riley shouted.

Frank and Joe walked over to the ditch.

"Know who he was?" Officer Riley asked, pointing into the ditch.

They saw the body of a dead man with a switchblade in his back. On his left forearm was a tattoo of a snowflake with a blood-drenched knife sticking through it. But Frank stared at the gaunt, scarred face.

"It's Nick Frost, isn't it?" Frank asked.

"Right you are," Con replied. "Know how he got here?"

"No," Joe said quickly.

"I guess someone else must have been shooting at you two," said Con Riley. He walked down into the ditch and knelt beside the body. "What's this?" he asked, pulling a wallet from beneath the body. He opened it, took out a driver's license, and then stood. "You two know somebody named Robert Conway?"

Frank and Joe looked at each other with stunned expressions.

"He's a friend of ours," Frank finally said.

Officer Riley signaled for Randy to join them, then gestured at Frost's body. "Is this the man who came in to get gas?" he asked the attendant.

"Y-yes," Randy answered. His face went pale when he looked at the dead man.

"See anybody else?"

"Another guy on a bike pulled up after he did," the attendant replied.

"What did he look like?" Joe asked. He glanced at Con Riley, who didn't appreciate Joe's butting in.

"I couldn't tell. He had on a black helmet and a black leather motorcycle jacket and pants."

The attendant looked at Con Riley. "Can I go now? I think I'm going to be sick."

Officer Riley nodded, and the attendant hurried away.

"Conway," Con Riley said thoughtfully. "I arrested him about three years ago for buying stolen motorcycle parts. He's an escaped con, isn't he?"

"He's as innocent now as he was three years ago," Joe rapped out.

Officer Riley, tapping the license against his hand, looked skeptically at Joe. "The description we have at the station says he rides a new Harley."

"His bike was destroyed when it smashed into a brick wall," Joe said.

"How would you know that?" Riley asked, his eyes full of suspicion.

Joe raised his injured arm in its sling. "I was on it at the time."

"What about the bike he took from the Sinbads?" Callie asked.

"Callie!" Joe shouted. He couldn't believe that Frank's girlfriend would betray Biker.

Frank quickly explained to Con Riley about the first run-in with the Sinbads the night before. "But Biker wasn't wearing his helmet or his jacket," he concluded.

"That's right," Joe added. "*I* have them. They're still in the van." Joe rushed over to the van, pulled out Biker's helmet and jacket, and handed them to Con.

"There's no proof that these are Conway's," Riley said.

"You have my word they are," Joe told him.

Con Riley looked at the jacket and helmet and then at Joe. "This may cost me my badge, but I believe you. It still doesn't clear Conway, though."

"Look at this," Frank said from the ditch.

Joe and Officer Riley joined Frank, who was holding up one of Frost's hands.

"Frost's knuckles are scraped and bruised, as if he'd been in a fight," Frank said.

"You're right," Riley replied. "But I don't see why that's important."

"*Look* at him," Frank said.

Joe and Con Riley looked at Frost's unbruised face.

"If he'd been in a fight, he should be all marked up, shouldn't be? There's not a cut on him."

Con Riley tilted back his hat and scratched his head.

Just then, Sims's beat-up old Chevy pulled up next to the police cars. Sims and Fenton Hardy got out and walked over to the ditch.

"Nick Frost," Frank explained when his father stood beside him.

"Any suspects?" Fenton asked Con Riley.

"The attendant said that another cyclist pulled

up shortly after Frost. That was the last he saw of Frost or the other guy.''

''Whoever killed Frost tried to kill us, too,'' Frank added.

''Conway,'' Sims growled.

''What?'' Joe demanded angrily.

''With Frost gone, Conway has a better chance of having his conviction overturned,'' Sims replied.

''He wouldn't shoot at us,'' Joe said through clenched teeth.

''Your friend's a convicted thief. I've dealt with scum like him before. You can't trust him.''

''We've got proof that Biker didn't steal those watches!'' Joe blurted out.

His words were drowned out as a police radio blared a report. ''Suspect apprehended at edge of town.''

A triumphant grin spread across Sims's face as he grabbed Biker's license from Con Riley.

''It doesn't matter whether he stole the watches or not. He's a murderer—and now he's locked up.''

Chapter
11

"I WANT TO SEE Biker and hear his side of the story," Joe demanded.

"Forget it, kid," Sims replied.

"It's best that you stay away from Conway," Fenton agreed.

"Your father's right," Sims went on. "You shouldn't be hanging around a killer."

"He's not a murderer!" Joe shouted. He lunged at Sims, grabbing the older man by the lapels of his jacket. Frank pulled his brother away.

"Settle down," Frank said. "You're not doing Biker any good by losing your temper."

Frank had to drag Joe over to the van, out of Sims's hearing.

"Look, Biker's safe in jail," Frank whispered harshly. "Whoever killed Frost and shot at us will probably try to get Biker, too. Anybody desperate enough to kill once won't hesitate to do it again."

Frank was relieved to see a glint of understanding come into Joe's eyes. "Now, let's go to Queens and search Frost's apartment before Sims gets the idea to do the same thing."

Joe nodded and climbed into the passenger side of the van.

"You still want to come along?" Frank asked Sue.

"Staying here won't help Biker," she replied. "Besides, you'll be able to find Frost's apartment more quickly with me to guide you."

With that, Frank, Callie, and Sue got into the van.

"Where are you going?" Joe asked as Frank pulled away from the burnt gas station. "The highway to New York is in the other direction."

"I know," Frank replied. "I don't want Sims to see us leaving town. So I'll head downtown for a couple of blocks and then take another route to the highway." Frank checked his rearview mirror several times to make sure Sims wasn't following.

"This is it," Sue said a couple of hours later.

Frank stopped the van in front of a dingy five-story apartment building.

"Frost's place is on the third floor," she added, "apartment three-F."

"You two keep watch outside," Joe said as he hopped into the back of the van and opened a box containing various disguises. "Frank and I will handle this."

Callie was ready to protest when Frank raised his hand.

"We'll need some warning if Sims or the cops show up," he explained, then winked at Callie.

Callie smiled as she and Sue got out of the van.

"Acme Speedy Delivery," Joe said as he threw one of two blue jumpsuits at Frank.

They quickly pulled on their disguises. Joe grabbed a clipboard and handed a wrapped, empty box to Frank.

"That ought to do it," he said.

The inside of the apartment building was as dingy as the outside. Frank and Joe had to use the stairs because the elevator had broken down.

"Here it is," Joe said as they walked down a darkened hallway.

Frank put the box on the floor and pulled out a case full of lock picks. He crouched down, inserted a pick in the lock, and in seconds had opened the door.

They entered the apartment and Frank locked the door from the inside.

"This place could stand a tidal wave of disinfectant," Frank said, wrinkling his nose at the smell of dirty laundry and unwashed dishes.

Joe was too busy going through Frost's dresser drawers to notice the smell.

Frank walked over to a window and opened it to air out the room. He looked around. The place was a mess. Food wrappers, dirty TV-dinner trays, old clothes, cycle magazines, and record albums littered the floor. Frank kicked some of the stuff out of his way and decided to check under the bed.

Joe took everything out of the drawers but found no clues. He pulled the drawers out to check the bottoms and back. Still nothing. He moved the dresser away from the wall. When he found nothing again, he pushed the dresser over in frustration. It hit the floor with a crash and Frank jumped up.

Then came a pounding on the wall.

"Hey, knock it off in there. I'm trying to sleep," yelled a rough voice.

"Take it easy, Joe," Frank said. "If there's something here, we'll find it."

Joe headed for the closet. He kicked a stack of magazines out of his way. The magazines scattered, several landing next to Frank. He shook his head and looked down. Sticking out of one was an envelope. He pulled it out of the magazine and smiled. Printed on the front of the envelope was the DalTime company logo. Beneath it was Frost's name.

Frank was about to call out to Joe when he heard the distinctive metal click of a gun's hammer. He turned. A large, burly man was climbing through the open apartment window from the fire escape, a steel blue .45 automatic in his hand.

"We've got company, Joe," Frank said quietly.

Joe spun around. Two more men came in the window; the second looked just as big and mean as the first and held a twin to the first man's .45. The third man was small, thin, and pale. His pig-eyes were deep-set and small.

"Gentlemen," the thin man said in a tinny, high-pitched voice, with all the charm of a cobra, "making a special delivery?"

"We were just leaving," Frank said quickly. He turned to leave, hoping none of the men saw him tuck the envelope into his jumpsuit.

The first man moved to the door and leveled his .45 at Frank's chest. Frank noted the gunman's casual, businesslike expression.

"It's rude, just running off and leaving your guests," the small man said. His thin-lipped smile stretched from cheek to cheek.

"Hey, man," Joe said, "we got about ten more deliveries before we can knock off work. I don't want to miss the big game on the tube tonight."

The thin man's expression hardened. He nodded, and the second thug moved to the other side of Joe, his .45 aimed at Joe's stomach. The two thugs now flanked the Hardys.

"Gentlemen, I'd like you to meet Mr. Rock," the thin man said with a nod to the thug next to Frank. "And this is Mr. Hard Place," he added with a nod to the thug next to Joe. "You two must be Mr. Stuck and Mr. Between."

The thin man laughed, his high-pitched giggles echoing in the room. "Get it? Stuck between a rock and a hard place?"

"Real funny," Frank shot back. "My partner wasn't kidding. We could get fired if we don't—"

"*Shut up,*" the thin man growled. He walked over to Frank. "You look very familiar to me," he said. "Have we met before?"

"No," Frank replied coolly.

"Let me introduce myself. I'm Fat Harold." The thin man was visibly disappointed that neither Frank nor Joe seemed to recognize his name.

"*Fat* Harold?" Joe said in disbelief. "A weed like you couldn't get wet running around in the shower."

Fat Harold laughed. Frank grimaced at the grating giggle.

"*This* is why they call me Fat Harold." The man reached into his pocket and pulled out a two-inch-thick wad of folded bills. He began flipping the bills as though he were counting them.

Frank's and Joe's eyes widened—all the bills were hundreds.

"You're a bookie," Frank stated.

"Very good, kid," Fat Harold said with a smile as he put the money back into his pocket. "And you're no delivery men."

"Should I kill them now, Mr. Harold?" Rock asked.

Although the question startled Frank, it was the thug's calm tone that disturbed him most. Rock sounded as if he had asked about ordering a pizza.

"No, I don't think that will be necessary," Fat Harold replied. "It's obvious that these two are looking for the same person we are. You see, boys, my *pocket change* is actually a little short this week, thanks to a thief named Biker Bob Conway."

Frank and Joe glanced at each other.

"Ah, so you know the little welsher. Good. What's he into you for?"

Joe stared at him, confused.

"About ten grand," Frank answered quickly, realizing that Fat Harold was assuming he and Joe were bookies also.

"Petty cash." Fat Harold was unimpressed. "Conway owed me nearly a quarter of a million in bad debts."

"Owed?" Frank asked.

"He missed his last payment deadline when they caught him with the watches."

"Watches?"

"Yeah. Some harebrained scheme of his to pay me two hundred and fifty grand by stealing some watches from the company he worked for," Fat Harold explained. "I didn't get my money or my watches."

"Why did you think he'd be here?" Frank asked.

"I got a call from a little birdie about an hour ago saying Conway would be here," Fat Harold replied. He stared suspiciously at Frank. "What brings you two to these lovely surroundings?"

"Uh, we knew Frost and Conway were friends and thought we'd find one of them here, get our dough," Frank said quickly.

"What happens now?" Joe asked.

"Now I'll take Conway in nice little pieces," Fat Harold said slowly. "It'll be worth a ten percent finder's fee for you two boys if you find him and give me a call."

"Sounds great," Frank said.

"Here's my card."

Frank looked at the business card Fat Harold handed him. No address or name—just a distinctive number: 555-BETS.

"Cool," Frank said. He stuck the card in his back pocket.

Fat Harold stared at Frank's face again. "Are you sure we haven't met before?"

"Positive," Frank answered.

"I don't know," Fat Harold said thoughtfully. "Something about you . . . Rock, check his ID."

Frank stepped back to confront Rock, but froze when the big man stuck the .45 against his chest. Rock pulled Frank's wallet from his back pocket and flipped it open.

"His name is Frank Hardy," Rock said, handing the wallet back to Frank.

"Frank Hardy," Fat Harold said slowly. He walked across the room to the window, rubbing his chin in thought. He snapped his fingers. *"Hardy!* That's who you look like."

Fat Harold stared at Frank's face. "When I first started out in this business, an NYPD detective named Fenton Hardy made my life miserable. He was the only cop who ever put me in jail." Fat Harold walked around Frank. "Yeah, you look like a younger Fenton Hardy." Fat Harold's voice began to sound amused. "Maybe like his son!"

"Hey, man," Joe said. He stepped toward Fat Harold, only to be shoved back by the barrel of Hard Place's .45.

Fat Harold held out his hand, and his thug handed over Joe's wallet. "Another Hardy, huh?" Fat Harold's nasal laugh echoed in the room. "The sons of Fenton Hardy. You almost had me believing you were bookies."

His expression became cold, hard, deadly. "Kill them." The bookie's voice sounded almost bored as he turned and headed for the window.

"Yes, sir, Mr. Harold," Rock replied.

After he had exited through the window, Fat Harold leaned back in from the fire escape and said, "Rock, make sure you get my business card back. Nothing personal in this, boys. We're just settling an old debt. I spent two years in prison because of Fenton Hardy. Two years for two sons. Sounds fair."

His laugh bounced off the walls in the alley as he climbed down the fire escape.

"Let's have the card," Rock ordered. Frank took it from his pocket and flipped it at Rock.

"Stand over there," Rock ordered with a wave of his gun. "Lace your fingers behind your heads."

Frank and Joe moved toward the center of the room, hands behind their heads. Both were looking for an opportunity to escape, but Rock stood behind them and Hard Place in front.

"Like Mr. Harold said," Rock began as he walked around in front of Frank and Joe, "nothing personal. We're just doing our jobs. Kneel down."

Just a job, Frank thought. If not for the guns,

Rock and Hard Place would look as if they were taking orders behind the counter at Mr. Pizza.

The two thugs slipped six-inch silencers from their pockets and screwed them onto their pistols. They checked their safeties and locked the hammers into firing position.

Frank and Joe glanced at each other. They'd always expected to go out with a bang.

Instead, they'd go out with a whisper—shot in a gangland-style execution by the silenced guns of two bored killers.

Chapter

12

ROCK'S HEAD JERKED up as someone began banging loudly on the door.

"Hey! Open up! We know you two deadbeats are in there!" An angry voice shrilled from the other side of the door. It was Callie, yelling as loud as she could.

"Yeah. You're not getting away this time," Sue shouted through the door. "We want those paychecks before you gamble them all away!"

"Who's that?" Rock asked Frank.

"How should I know?" Frank replied sharply.

The pounding on the door grew louder.

"Knock off that noise!" someone yelled from another apartment.

"You tell those good-for-nothing husbands of ours to come out now!" Callie yelled.

"Yeah," Sue added. "They're not wasting their paychecks on card games this time!"

"Go away," Rock yelled back. "You got the wrong place."

The pounding continued. Somewhere down the hall a baby screamed itself awake and began crying loudly.

"Let's do it and get out of here," Hard Place said, nervousness showing in his voice.

Joe knew it was the right moment to make his move. Hard Place glanced over at Rock for a split second, and that was enough time for Joe to slam a steel fist into the thug's gut. Hard Place gagged and doubled over.

Frank grabbed one of the drawers Joe had taken out of the dresser and threw it at Rock. The drawer cracked against Rock's skull and shattered into tiny pieces.

Like twin bolts of lightning, Frank and Joe dashed for the open window. They scrambled down the metal steps and then jumped from the fire escape ladder and hit the asphalt pavement of the alley in a dead run toward the street.

A second later they heard the *phfft, phfft, phfft* of .45 slugs slamming into the ground behind them.

The Hardys' black van screeched to a halt at the end of the alley.

"Hurry!" Callie yelled from the front seat.

The side door of the van slid open. Sue waved frantically for Frank and Joe to run faster.

"Step on it!" Frank yelled as he and Joe leapt into the van.

Callie mashed the accelerator to the floor, sending Frank, Joe, and Sue tumbling around the back of the van. She turned the first corner and gunned the engine again.

"Slow down!" Joe shouted after several more two-wheel turns.

Callie stomped on the brake and Joe lurched toward the front of the van and fell forward against the dash. His injured arm smacked into the mobile phone, breaking it.

Joe let out a yell of anguish, cradling his arm. "I felt safer back there with those two thugs than I do with you."

"Oh, yeah?" Callie fumed. "Maybe you'd like me to take you back there."

"Crazy girl driver," Joe shouted back.

"Knock it off, you two!" Frank was in no mood for one of Joe and Callie's famous fights. "Let's get out of here before they catch up with us."

Joe jumped into the passenger seat and buckled his seat belt.

"Ready," he said.

Callie huffed in exasperation, put the van into drive, and started forward at a normal pace.

"The least you could do is say thanks," Sue said from the back of the van. "Something terrible could have happened to you two if we hadn't thought so quickly."

Joe remained silent.

"How did you know we were in trouble?" Frank asked.

"Callie asked me to check out the alley. I spotted Fat Harold and his two bodyguards climbing up the fire escape. I called Callie over, and when she saw Fat Harold leave without his goons, she knew you two needed help and came up with the idea of pretending to be your wives. She's a real hero."

"How do you know Fat Harold?" Frank asked.

"He came around the company a few times, looking for Nick Frost. Mr. Dalton, Brandon's father, had to call security to run him off. Fat Harold's a real pain in the neck."

"Does he know Biker?" Joe asked.

"Only Biker's shoes." Sue laughed. "Biker almost took his head off one day at work," she explained. "We were walking out to the car, and Fat Harold was hanging around waiting for Frost. He whistled and made a rude remark to me. Biker took out Fat Harold's two bodyguards first and then started for Fat Harold. That guy is so thin that when he saw Biker heading for him, he crawled under his limousine and refused to come out till Biker left."

"Did Biker owe Fat Harold any money?" Joe wanted to know.

"No."

"According to Fat Harold, Biker owes him two hundred fifty thousand dollars in gambling debts."

"That's impossible," Sue protested. "Frost was the only one at the company who placed bets with Fat Harold."

"Then why did Fat Harold say he was looking for Biker?" Joe said more to himself than to the others. "I wish we'd found something to help us make some sense of all this."

"Maybe we have." Frank pulled the DalTime envelope from his pocket.

"What's that?" Joe said, excitement in his voice.

"Let's find out." Frank ripped open the envelope, pulled out several sheets of paper, and scanned them.

"Well?" Joe was impatient.

"What do you make of these?" Frank handed the papers to Sue.

She took the papers and glanced through them.

"What are they?" Joe asked, unbuckling his seat belt and joining Sue and Frank in the back of the van.

"We have something here." Sue held up the first sheet. "This is a shipping invoice and schedule for three hundred cases of Watch Ya Wearing?

watches to a large retail store chain in Kansas City. And"—she held up the second sheet—"this is a schedule of employee vacations with Biker's name underlined in red."

"And this," Frank said, holding up a third sheet, "is a road map with a major highway leading out of Queens and New York City outlined in red."

"So what does all this prove?" Callie asked.

Joe's attention was on Sue. "Did Frost have access to shipping invoices?"

"Only for the deliveries he made." Then she added, "But he had no business with the vacation schedules. Those are supposed to be confidential."

Joe noticed a look of disappointment come over Frank's face. "What's wrong?"

"The marks on this map end somewhere in northern New Jersey—on a highway in the middle of nowhere. There's March thirtieth and an *X* marked, and above that is 'B—seven-thirty.' " He looked grim. *"B* for Biker."

"March thirtieth at seven-thirty! That's when the hijacking took place, according to Frost's testimony," Sue said.

"Where was Biker on that date?" Joe asked Sue.

"He'd just returned from his cross-country vacation. He got to my place at about eight, and we went out for dinner at eight-thirty."

"The spot where the truck was hijacked is a good thirty miles away," Frank said. "Biker couldn't have hijacked the truck, hidden it, and then gotten to your house by eight. Didn't his lawyer point that out to the jury?"

"Yes, but the prosecutor said that as an expert driver and a former motocross champion, Biker had the skill to just make it to my house from the highway."

"That stinks," Joe objected. "For all we know, that *B* could stand for 'Plan B' or Boise, Idaho. Frost hijacked his own truck. Let's just go back to Bayport and prove it."

"We can't do that just yet," Frank said.

"Why not?"

Frank ignored Joe's angry question and turned to Sue. "Could Frost access the vacation schedule from any of the company's computers?"

Sue shook her head. "Frost was a little slow. On his good days, he could barely remember his own address, much less try to figure out how to use a computer."

"Then somebody must have given him the information—somebody who knows the company's computer access codes and who needed half a million bucks' worth of designer watches." Frank stared at Sue.

She looked at him. "The only one who was in any sort of trouble was Frost."

"And his troubles are over now," Callie reminded them from the front seat.

"What are these numbers up here?" Frank asked as he pointed to the top of the shipping invoice.

"Sales rep's code number and shipping date," Sue replied.

Frank looked at the invoice sheet and then at the vacation schedule. A wide grin came across his face.

"What is it?" Joe asked.

"I'm not sure," Frank replied. He faced Sue. "I'll need to get into your company's computers and check something out first. Can we get in there without too many people finding out?"

Sue looked at her watch. "By the time we get to the offices, almost everybody should be gone for the day. But the security guards won't stop me from showing my cousins around," she added with a smile. "Problem is, we'll have to double back the way we came. Suppose Fat Harold is there and recognizes the van?"

"No problem," Frank said, heading for the van's storage space. "We've got a bag full of tricks back here."

Callie pulled the van into a vacant parking lot. Fifteen minutes later, plastic signs on both sides of the van advertised the Bug-B-Gone exterminating company. Atop the van was a four-foot-long black-and-orange inflatable bug, held securely to the van's roof by magnetic feet.

"That thing sure is ugly," Callie said as she looked at the bug through the van's sun roof.

"Yeah, but those two thugs are looking for an Acme Speedy Delivery van," Frank said.

"Don't you think the bug makes us a little too obvious?" Sue asked.

Frank smiled. "Sometimes the best place to hide is in plain sight. Okay, Sue. Which way?"

The watch company was near the Queens-Brooklyn line in an old factory building that was being renovated. Frank was glad to see that the employee parking lot was nearly empty.

"Don't turn the light on," Frank said as they entered Sue's second-floor office. "I don't want to attract any attention."

Sue sat at her desk and booted up her computer. She typed in several security access codes. "It's all yours, Frank."

Frank took Sue's place at the terminal. He typed in the sales rep's code and Biker's Social Security number.

"Where's that door lead?" Joe asked, pointing to a large wooden door opposite Sue's desk.

"That's Mr. Dalton's office," Sue replied.

"What are you looking for?" Callie asked Frank impatiently.

"I'll let you know when I find it," Frank replied absently. He was looking for a microneedle in a computer haystack, and he didn't need any distractions.

Joe paced the small office. Biker was sitting in jail facing an assault charge for beating up Brandon and a murder charge for the death of Frost, and two hoodlums working for a small-time bookie were gunning for Biker, Frank, and Joe. The last two days hadn't been shining ones for the Hardys.

"Yeah!" Frank announced triumphantly.

"What is it?" Joe rushed around the desk and stared at the display terminal. The letters and numbers on the screen meant nothing to him. "Would you mind explaining this to me?"

Before Frank could answer, the door across from Sue's desk creaked open.

Joe turned—just in time to stare into the black eyes of a Doberman springing over the desk toward him, its sharp teeth aiming right for Joe's throat.

Chapter

13

"JOE!" FRANK YELLED as he tossed a ruler to his younger brother.

Joe caught the ruler and smacked the Doberman on the nose. The dog fell to one side, sneezed, shook its head, and crouched to spring again.

"Sit, Trooper!" yelled Sue.

The black Doberman sat down and growled at Joe, exposing large yellow teeth.

"This is *your* dog?" Joe asked Sue, keeping his eyes on the Doberman and the ruler ready to smack the dog again.

"He's the company's dog," answered a silver-haired man from the open doorway.

"Mr. Dalton," Sue gasped.

"Sue," Mr. Dalton answered in a surprised yet relieved voice. "What are you doing here? Who are these people?"

"Frank, Joe, Callie," Sue said, "this is Scott Dalton, founder and president of DalTime, Inc."

"Brandon's father?" Callie asked.

"Looks that way," Joe muttered.

"Why are you here? I thought you were looking for Biker," Mr. Dalton said.

"Frank and Joe are detectives from Bayport," Sue explained. "Biker asked them to help him. We came here looking for evidence that might prove Biker's innocence."

Joe moved toward Mr. Dalton and was about to explain why they had sneaked into the offices when Trooper stood up and growled.

"Out, Trooper," Mr. Dalton ordered, a deep scowl on his face. The black Doberman gave a small whine and meekly left the room. "Sorry about the dog, Joe," Mr. Dalton said. "I got him shortly after the trial, when the phone calls started."

"What phone calls?" Joe asked.

"Someone began threatening to hurt me. Although the voice was disguised, I thought it was Biker." Mr. Dalton sat in a chair opposite Sue's desk. Frank could read the weariness and worry on the older man's face. "I used to treat him like a second son."

"Did you really think it was Biker?" Frank asked.

"I know Biker's a pretty wild young man, and the evidence at the trial was damaging. I almost believed he was guilty myself."

"What made you change your mind?" Joe asked.

"The calls kept coming even after Biker's escape. Knowing Biker, I expected him to head for Canada or Mexico. He wouldn't waste time calling up to threaten me."

"What exactly did the caller say?" Frank said.

Mr. Dalton rubbed his forehead as if trying to forget a bad dream. "The caller said he would return the watches for two hundred fifty thousand dollars, about half their value. If I didn't go through with the deal, he would kill Brandon and then me. I'm no coward, but this guy really scared me."

"Mr. Dalton hates guns. That's why he takes Trooper with him wherever he goes now," Sue added.

"When I heard voices, *male* voices, coming from Sue's office, I naturally thought the caller was about to make good on his threats," Mr. Dalton said. "I'm really sorry if Trooper frightened you, Joe."

"Forget it. No harm, no foul," Joe said lightly.

"Is Brandon okay?" Mr. Dalton asked Sue.

"He was before we left Bayport," Sue replied. "Why do you ask?"

"I can't get ahold of him. The hospital said he checked himself out, and there's no answer at the motel."

"Maybe he's at the police station giving a statement about Biker beating him up," Callie suggested.

"I can't believe that Biker attacked Brandon," Mr. Dalton said. "He knew Brandon wouldn't have a chance against him. This is very puzzling."

"Maybe what I've found could clear up some of the mystery," Frank said.

"I've always liked Biker," Mr. Dalton said. "I wish my own son had half his common sense. What have you found?"

"This should reopen the case and reverse Biker's conviction," Frank said. "Look here."

Joe, Callie, Sue, and Mr. Dalton gathered around Frank and the computer terminal.

"Here's Biker's original invoice sheet for the shipment of watches to Boston," Frank said. "Notice the date—March third, the day Biker left on his cross-country trip."

He handed the paper to Mr. Dalton, who looked the sheet over and nodded his head. Frank turned to his computer.

"But look at this." Frank played the computer

keys like a classical pianist. Seconds later a similar invoice sheet appeared on the screen.

Frank pointed to the screen. "Notice that the sales rep's code and invoice number are exactly the same as the numbers on Biker's invoice. But look here." Frank ran his finger straight across the screen to the date column.

"March thirtieth," Joe said.

"Right. Biker's original order wasn't shipped on March third—it went out the thirtieth."

"That's the day Biker returned from his trip," Joe said excitedly.

"And the day of the hijacking," Frank added.

"This date could be a typing error," Callie said.

"Maybe," Frank agreed, "except for *this*." He hit the keyboard again. Another form appeared on the screen.

"Biker's original invoice form!" Joe exclaimed.

"Right again. It was canceled on March fourth, the day *after* Biker left for his vacation." Frank punched the keys, and the two forms appeared side by side.

"Except for the date, they look exactly alike," Sue said.

"*Too* much alike," Frank said, "as if someone was trying to hide something." He turned to Mr. Dalton. "Do you often reroute shipments?"

"No. That's not the way I run my company,"

Scott Dalton said. "We process orders as they come in—unless I personally say otherwise. I don't like sales representatives stealing shipments from one another and routing them to special customers. It causes too much friction."

"Well, it looks as if that's what happened here. Biker's original shipment was headed to Boston," Joe said, pointing to the screen. "Then that same order got bumped back and routed to Kansas City!"

"Along the route of the hijacking!" Frank tapped on the desk.

"Then Biker is innocent," Joe said.

"How does this prove Biker's innocent?" Callie asked.

"Somebody changed Biker's order—setting it to go out on the thirtieth instead of the third," Frank explained. "That same person rerouted the shipment west instead of north. And all that time, *Biker was out of state*. He couldn't have known when the shipment left the plant or where it was going."

"Only two people could have known," Joe added. "The sales rep who rerouted the shipment and the driver of the truck, Nick Frost."

"I'd guess Frost set up the phony hijacking with the help of his Sinbad buddies," Frank concluded.

"Why?" asked Mr. Dalton.

"Frost was a heavy gambler and lost often,"

Joe explained. "Maybe he used up all his credit with Fat Harold and then started a new account, using Biker's name. When it came time to pay up, Frost dreamed up this hijacking scheme."

"But it didn't work out as planned," Frank added. "Somebody killed Frost."

"What?" Mr. Dalton said, shock in his voice.

"Before leaving Bayport, we were shot at and almost killed in a gas station fire," Joe said. "The police found Frost's body in a ditch nearby. They're holding Biker for the murder."

"I don't believe this," Mr. Dalton said as he sat down.

"Your theory sounds good," Callie said, "except for two things."

"What?" Joe asked, rounding on her.

"Who killed Frost, and who told Fat Harold we'd be at Frost's apartment?"

"According to Fat Harold," Frank said, "a little birdie told him. Maybe that same little birdie killed Frost."

"Isn't it funny how Sims always manages to be around whenever there's trouble?" Joe said thoughtfully.

Then his eyes widened. "Frank, we've got to get back to Bayport. If Sims is involved in any of this, Biker is in real trouble."

"Let me run a hard copy of these invoices to show to the police," Frank said as he began typing in commands on the computer.

Mr. Dalton stood, strength seeming to enter him. "I'll try to call Brandon and tell him to fire Sims, that you two have proof that Biker is innocent. Sims won't like it, though."

"He's got a real mean streak in him," Callie said.

"Mean?" Mr. Dalton said with a bitter laugh. "Sims's dead-or-alive reputation is no joke. Brandon told me that thirty percent of his fugitives are brought back in boxes. I'm sorry I was ever talked into hiring such a man."

"Callie, you'd better stay with Sue," Frank said as he pulled the black van into the motel parking lot. "If Sims is in on this, he might go after her, too."

"Sure," Callie replied. She and Sue hopped out of the van and headed for Sue's room.

Frank put the van in drive and started out of the parking lot.

"Hey, guys!" Brandon shouted as he pulled his cycle up next to the van. The swelling had gone down, but the bruises on his face were dark blue.

"Did your father get ahold of you?" Frank asked.

"Yeah. Sims is off the case. You guys did a great job."

"Where is Sims now?" Joe asked.

111

"He said something about leaving Bayport," Brandon replied.

"Keep an eye open for him," Frank warned. "We think he might be mixed up in all of this."

"Sure thing," Brandon said. "Say, where's this evidence you say you found?"

"Right here," Frank said, patting his shirt pocket.

"Great." Brandon gave him a smile.

"Tell Callie we're going home first, then to the police station," Frank said.

"You got it," Brandon said with a wave.

Frank pulled the van out of the parking lot and headed for home.

"If you hadn't broken the mobile phone, we could have warned Dad by now," Frank said with a smile.

"If you'll remember, it was your *girlfriend* who knocked me against that thing," Joe replied without humor.

Minutes later Frank and Joe were walking into their living room. Scuffling sounds came from the cellar.

"Dad's office!" Frank whispered.

They bolted down the stairs to Fenton Hardy's basement office. Biker, one handcuff around his wrist, was struggling with Sims for the bounty hunter's pistol.

"Sims!" Frank shouted.

Joe leapt at Biker.

The office echoed with the roar of the 9 mm automatic.

Sims jerked backward and crashed to the floor—lifeless.

Chapter

14

JOE WAS MOMENTARILY deafened by the blast of the gun. He watched Sims hit the floor, then lowered his shoulder and smashed into Biker, ignoring the pain from his hurt arm. With lightning speed he grabbed the gun and twisted it from Biker's hand.

Something whipped past Joe and slammed into Biker's chest. Biker doubled over and crumpled to the floor.

Joe spun around. The "dead" Sims stood in a karate stance.

"You're alive," Joe gasped.

"It looks that way," Sims replied. "Not that your friend didn't try his best."

"You *looked* dead," Frank said.

"That was the idea." Sims nodded at Joe. "Thanks for your help," he said with a smirk. The bounty hunter knelt next to Biker and holstered his gun. He grabbed Biker's arms and cuffed his hands. Biker groaned in pain as the cuffs clicked tighter and tighter.

"Hey! Those are too tight." Joe was furious.

"You don't think I'm going to give him a second chance, do you?" Sims asked. He lifted the groggy Biker and sat him in Fenton's chair. Frank was amazed at how the short, overweight Sims could move with such strength.

"What's Biker doing out of jail?" Joe asked, suddenly startled.

"Question your friend," Sims huffed.

"What happened, buddy?" Joe asked gently.

"I guess I got kind of stupid—I broke out," Biker answered, his speech thick.

"Why?" Frank was shocked. "Here we are trying to clear you and you make a break for it." He turned away and slapped his fist into the palm of his other hand.

"What can I say? I'm a dumb biker." Biker's head fell over on his chest again. He was out of it.

"Well, buddy, sorry, but as soon as you're better, we're going to have to return you to Con and the boys at the station."

"Over my dead body," Sims said.

"What do you mean? He has to go back," Frank stated simply.

"Look, kid, I found him after he escaped, and I'm taking him back to New York to collect my reward." An evil, triumphant smile cut into Sims's round, wrinkled face.

"You can't do that. He's being held on a murder charge here."

"What was that? I seem to have gone temporarily deaf. I couldn't hear a single word you said," Sims said, cupping a hand to his ear.

"I suppose you didn't get a phone call from Brandon, either?" Joe said.

"What call?" Sims asked.

"The one telling you to back off," Joe replied. "Why not check in with your boss?"

"Don't tell me what to do," Sims growled.

"Frank has found evidence that proves Biker didn't hijack that shipment of watches."

"Really?" Sims said with a mocking look.

Frank took the two invoices from his pocket and handed them to Sims. He quickly explained Biker's vacation schedule and the rerouting of the watches.

"It was impossible for Biker to know where and when those watches would go out," Joe concluded.

Sims looked at both invoices. He rubbed the back of his neck and then asked, "Get these from a computer, Frank?"

"From Sue's computer at the watch company," Frank replied.

"You're pretty good with a computer, aren't you, Frank? I bet you'd do just about anything for a friend, wouldn't you?" Sims's steel gray eyes bored into Frank.

Joe glanced at Frank, then at Sims. He knew what Sims was implying.

"Frank didn't tamper with those invoices," Joe said, controlling his slowly rising anger.

Sims threw up his hands in mock protest and handed the invoices back to Frank. "What can I say?"

"There's something else you should know," Frank said. "Biker didn't beat up Brandon."

"Just how do you know that?" Sims asked, curious in spite of himself.

Frank walked over to Biker, who was still unconscious. He gently lifted Biker's hands and turned them over.

"See here?" he said. "No bruises."

"Huh?" Sims looked confused.

"You saw Brandon at the hospital," Frank said. "Whoever gave him that beating would have some badly bruised knuckles."

"Unless the attacker was wearing motorcycle gloves," Sims countered.

"I've seen the difference between someone beaten with gloves and someone beaten with bare knuckles," Frank said confidently. "Brandon was beaten with bare fists, and he was beaten by Frost.''

''Impossible!'' Sims shook his head in disbelief.

''Remember how badly scraped Frost's knuckles were?'' Frank asked.

''That's right!'' Joe said.

''What would Brandon have to do with Frost?'' Sims asked.

''I don't know, but I want to ask Brandon about Frost, and I want to find out why he lied to us about calling you,'' Frank replied.

''You two will have to follow that up by yourselves,'' Sims said. ''As soon as Conway revives, I'm taking him back to Queens.''

''What kind of detective are you?'' Joe was incredulous.

''I'm the best detective there is, sonny boy.'' Sims's eyes flashed with anger and his cheeks turned a dark red. ''I do my job. I was hired to bring Conway in. And I don't know anything about a murder charge here. Got that?'' Sims grabbed his rumpled hat. ''I just stopped in to say goodbye to Fenton and pay him for his services.''

''Where *is* Dad?'' Frank asked, hoping to slow Sims down.

''Don't know. 'Bye.'' Sims grabbed Biker's arm and tried to pull him from the chair. Biker groaned. Joe pushed Sims aside. Both squared off.

"Move off, buddy boy," Sims growled at Joe.

Frank was about to help Joe when the phone rang. He grabbed the receiver, keeping an eye on the other two.

"Hello," he said.

"Frank!" It was Callie, her voice high and shaky.

Frank was about to ask Callie what was wrong when he heard scuffling noises in the background—and then the unmistakable voice of Fat Harold.

"Is this Frank Hardy of Acme Speedy Delivery?" Fat Harold wheezed into the phone.

"What do you want?"

From the dark scowl on Frank's face, Joe knew something was wrong. He forgot about Sims and stood next to his older brother. Frank punched the speaker phone so Joe could hear.

"I've got two special delivery packages for you. They're extremely fragile. One is Callie Shaw, the other is Sue Murphy."

"Let them go," Frank ordered.

"Oh, I'll let them go," Fat Harold replied. "But *how* I let them go depends on you."

"What do you mean by that?" Frank asked.

"We're at a junkyard just outside of Bayport. And Rock—you remember Rock, don't you, Frank?—he's always wanted to play with one of those car crushers. Right now he's got Miss Shaw and Miss Murphy in the front seat of a rusty old

Ford. He's just dying to push the button that will turn the car into one cubic foot of metal.''

"No!" Frank yelled.

"I knew you'd want these special packages." Fat Harold paused and breathed in deeply. "I want one of three things—the two hundred and fifty grand that Biker Conway owes me, the watches he stole, or Conway himself."

"Where? When?"

"Bruce's Paradise Salvage. Know where it is?"

"Yes."

"Thirty minutes, or Rock pushes the button. It's a fair trade, Frank. You get two, while I only get one."

"We can't get any of those things together that fast," Frank protested.

"Twenty-nine minutes and forty-three seconds," Fat Harold said. "Or your girlfriend becomes just another small part of American culture."

Fat Harold's screeching laugh tore at Frank's ears until he slammed down the receiver.

Frank dashed from the room, but reentered instantly. "Sims, you wait here with Biker, or you're dead. You got that—dead!"

120

Chapter
15

BRUCE'S PARADISE SALVAGE looked like anything but a paradise. A crazy maze of rust-eaten cars, engine parts, and transmissions littered the potholed dirt road. The dead smell of wet and rotting upholstery filled the air.

"One minute," Frank said.

Joe nodded.

They jogged toward the rear of the salvage yard. Joe carried a largish black briefcase under his right arm, and he tried not to let his injured left arm swing out too much.

Darkness had set in, and the salvage yard's single streetlight cast deep shadows. Frank and Joe kept their eyes on the shadows, wary that Fat Harold could have set a trap for them.

They turned a corner of stacked cars to find Callie and Sue flanked by Rock and Hard Place, who held two ugly automatics leveled at the girls.

"Freeze," ordered Rock. He shoved his gun into Callie's side.

Callie grimaced.

"Be careful with that thing." Frank's voice was tight. "We brought what you wanted." He looked around. "Where's your boss?"

"I'm here, remembering the good old days," Fat Harold called to Frank and Joe. He stepped out from behind a faded yellow school bus.

"I didn't think they had buses in reform school," Joe said.

Fat Harold laughed. He nodded to his two thugs. Rock and Hard Place locked and loaded their automatics. They pointed the deadly pieces at the heads of Callie and Sue.

"Wait!" Frank yelled.

Fat Harold walked till he stood about ten yards from Frank. He looked at his watch.

"Right on time. Excellent." He glanced at the briefcase under Joe's arm. "I assume you have either the money, the watches, or Conway in that little case." His nasal laugh bounced off the rusted cars.

"Money," Joe replied without a smile. "Two hundred and fifty thousand."

"Very good," Fat Harold wheezed.

"Biker has confessed to stealing the watches,

then fencing them and hiding the money until he could get out of the country. It's all here.'' Joe tossed the case at Fat Harold's feet.

Fat Harold jumped back.

''There's no booby trap,'' Frank assured the bookie.

''How did you know where to find Callie and Sue?'' Joe asked at almost the same time.

''I've got friends I never knew I had,'' Fat Harold began as he kicked at the briefcase. ''The same little birdie that warned me to go to Frost's apartment told me Conway's girlfriend was staying at the Bayport Motel.'' He nodded back to Callie. ''And she's the insurance I needed to make sure you two wouldn't try anything funny.''

Fat Harold knelt down. He lifted the briefcase and smiled as he pushed down on the snaps. His face reddened.

''It's locked,'' he growled.

''Oh, sorry,'' Frank replied. ''I've got the key.'' He put his hand into his jeans pocket. Rock turned his automatic on Frank, who quickly raised both hands to show he had no weapon.

''Slowly,'' Fat Harold said.

Frank pulled a small silver key from his pocket and held it up.

''Throw me the key or say goodbye to one of the girls.'' Fat Harold's face tightened with rage.

''One girl, one key,'' Frank said calmly, gambling that Fat Harold wouldn't order his two thugs to shoot Callie and Sue.

Fat Harold's face untwisted into a thin smile.

"Fair enough," the bookie replied. He nodded to Hard Place. The thug lowered his automatic and pushed Sue toward Frank.

Fat Harold laughed. "The little birdie told me that Callie Shaw means a lot to Frank Hardy. We'll hold her until we're safely out of Bayport. Now the key, if you please."

"Don't do it, Frank," Joe said. "Make them give up Callie."

"Kid, don't make a fatal mistake," Fat Harold said. "Don't get the foolish idea you can *make* me do anything. He held out his hand. "The key—*now!*"

Frank flipped the key at Fat Harold. The bookie picked it up and put it in one of the locks. He gently turned it. Frank heard a small sigh escape from the bookie when nothing happened. Fat Harold put the key in the second lock and turned it. He smiled triumphantly and lifted the briefcase lid.

Frank shoved Sue to the ground as he and Joe covered their eyes. A blinding light burst from the briefcase. Fat Harold screamed as the scorching glare of a caseful of exploding flashbulbs tore into his eyes.

Frank and Joe charged. Frank leapt for Rock. He was relieved to see that Callie, even though blinded, had thrown herself to the ground and was scrambling away from the thug. Rock was shaking his head and swinging his arms wildly in front of him. Frank landed a solid kick to Rock's stomach. The thug sat down—hard. Even so, he raised his gun, aiming blindly in the direction of his attacker. Frank kicked the gun from Rock's hand and rammed a fist into the side of the thug's head. Rock hit the ground and didn't move.

At the same moment Joe ran for Fat Harold, who was staggering and screaming, one hand over his eyes, the other trying to pull a pistol from his pocket. Joe whipped a sawed-off baseball bat from his sling and tapped Fat Harold's wrist as he came up with the gun. The gun went flying, and Joe sent the bookie flying in the opposite direction. Then he turned to Hard Place.

The thug, tears streaming from his blinded eyes, began firing his automatic wildly in the direction of any sound. Frank and Joe hit the ground.

"Stay down!" Frank yelled to Callie and Sue.

Hard Place turned toward the sound of Frank's voice and squeezed off a shot. Frank rolled away from the slug as it sliced the ground inches away from him.

A single pistol shot pierced the air. Hard Place was knocked to the ground as a bullet slammed into his shoulder.

Sims and a handcuffed Biker ran from behind a

stack of cars. Sims's 9 mm was still smoking from the shot he'd fired at the thug.

Just then Rock staggered to his feet, a backup gun in his hand. He had apparently regained his eyesight and was aiming the pistol at Mort Sims.

"Sims!" Frank yelled. He was too far away to help the bounty hunter.

Suddenly Biker knocked a surprised Sims to one side and sprinted toward Rock. He lowered his shoulder and slammed into the thug with such force that Rock was lifted from the ground and flew several feet backward before smashing into a stack of rusted cars. The unconscious gunman slid to the ground in a lump, his pistol landing harmlessly a few feet away.

"You all right?" Biker asked as he helped Sims up.

"Yeah," Sims replied. He shoved Biker's hands away and stood on his own.

"You could say thanks," Joe said as he helped Sue to her feet.

"Conway's lucky I didn't shoot him," Sims said. "I thought he was trying to escape."

"Good job," Frank said to Callie, who had wiped her eyes and was now brushing dirt from her jeans.

Sirens cut through the air. Moments later several Bayport police cars pulled into the salvage yard. Con Riley and Fenton Hardy hopped from the lead car.

"Frank! Joe! Are you okay?" Fenton asked as he ran up to his sons.

"Sure, Dad," Frank replied. He turned to Con. "Better have your men cuff these three."

Riley nodded to the other officers.

"We've got proof that Biker didn't know about the watch shipment," Joe said as he handed the invoices to Fenton. He explained about the trip to Queens and finding the invoice with the rerouted watches.

"That adds up with what Con found," Fenton replied.

"What's that?"

"The wallet and driver's license found at the scene of Frost's murder were reported stolen several months ago by Biker," Fenton said.

"That's right," Biker added as he joined the group. "I lost my wallet during a Riding on Time tour."

"He could have pretended to lose it," Sims insisted.

"Maybe," Fenton said. "But Frost was murdered by someone riding a cycle. When Biker was arrested, he was on foot."

"He could have ditched the bike anywhere," Sims retorted. "And what about his debts?" He turned to face Joe. "You told me yourself that Fat Harold was after Conway for not paying up on his gambling debts."

"I never gamble," Biker replied. "That's a fool's game."

"Never? We'll see about that." Sims stalked over to a patrol car and pulled Fat Harold from the back. He marched the bookie toward the group and stood him in front of Biker.

Fat Harold, still dazed, looked Biker up and down.

"What am I doing? Judging a beauty contest?" the bookie sneered.

"This is the man who owes you two hundred and fifty grand," Sims insisted. "This is Biker Conway."

"No," Fat Harold replied.

"That flash-bomb must have blinded you," Sims said in disbelief.

"Excuse me," Fat Harold said indignantly. "I know the faces of everyone who owes me money, especially big money." He pointed at Biker. "And this guy is *not* the Biker Conway I know!"

Chapter

16

"I WAS WRONG," Brandon Dalton said as he stood in the Hardys' living room, trying to avoid Biker's eyes. "Frank's right. Frost did beat me up, but he said Biker had paid him to do it."

"You knew I couldn't stand Frost," Biker said.

"I wasn't thinking."

"Why did you lie to us about calling Sims off the case?" Joe asked.

"I didn't say I had gotten ahold of Sims," Brandon replied. "What I meant at the motel was that I agreed with my dad about kicking him off the case."

"None of this makes any sense," Sims said.

"Why?" Joe asked. "Because you might have the wrong man?"

129

Sims glared at Joe. Joe smiled.

"Did you disguise yourself when you placed your bets with Fat Harold?" Sims asked Biker with a cold stare.

"Get off his case," Joe hissed.

"That's all right, Joe," Biker said with a smile. He returned Sims's stare. "It doesn't matter whether you believe me or not. I'm innocent. I know it—more important, my friends know it. And tomorrow the courts will know it."

"And I'll drop my assault charges," Brandon added.

"You can take off those handcuffs," Joe said to Sims.

"You've got to be kidding," Sims chuckled. "I've got my reward money to collect."

"Biker's innocent and you know it," Joe insisted. Joe didn't get anywhere with Sims so he turned to Fenton. "I give my word. Biker won't go anywhere."

Fenton looked at his son. "Uncuff him," he said to Sims.

"Not on your life."

"For a professional, you've acted pretty foolishly," Fenton said without hesitation. "Frank and Joe have proved that Biker didn't hijack the truck, the murder charges have been dropped, and Brandon has just admitted that it was Frost who beat him up." Fenton walked up to Sims. "You're in my home, and I'm not going to let you keep cuffs on an innocent man. Tomorrow we'll go to court, and I know with a good word from us any judge will drop the charges against Biker for escaping. I think you're out of your money, anyway, Mort."

Fuming, Sims stomped over to Biker and unlocked the cuffs.

"Thanks," Biker said sincerely as he rubbed his chafed wrists.

Sims turned to Fenton. "There's still something about this case that isn't right."

"Well, it's time you used your detecting skills to help and not hinder this investigation," Fenton said.

Sims rubbed his neck. He was visibly embarrassed.

"I suggest we question Fat Harold," Fenton added.

Sims lowered his head and walked out the front door.

"You sure Callie and Sue will be okay at the motel?" Fenton asked before leaving.

"Con Riley said he'd post a patrol car outside," Frank replied.

"Besides, I'll be there," Brandon added as he put on his motorcycle helmet.

"Biker, I'm glad my sons were able to prove you innocent," Fenton said as he shook Biker's hand. "I'll call if we get anything out of Fat Harold."

"I'm lucky to have you two on my side," Biker said after Fenton and Brandon left.

"Three now," Joe said. "Didn't you hear my dad call you 'Biker'? He's never done that before."

"Yeah," Biker replied. "I could be in jail on a murder charge. Any lawyer could have convinced a jury that I knew Frost had framed me and that I killed him in a blind rage. He must have lifted my wallet months ago."

"Who could hate you enough to frame you for the hijacking and the murder?" Frank asked.

Biker shrugged his shoulders. "Beats me. What I want to know is who pretended to be me when he placed all those bets with Fat Harold."

"Does Sue have an ex-boyfriend who could be jealous?" Joe asked.

"Not that I know of," Biker replied.

"We can ask Sue about that tomorrow morning. Right now, I say we get some rest," Frank said as he headed for bed. "No telling how long my dad and Sims will be with Fat Harold."

"You can sleep in Aunt Gertrude's room," Joe said to Biker. "I hope you like perfume."

As they reached the top of the stairs, Biker turned to Joe and said, "I'll understand if you want to lock the doors and windows."

"What?" Joe asked, astonished. Then he saw the grin on Biker's face. He jabbed Biker in the shoulder. "You'd make a wisecrack to the devil."

Joe slept restlessly, disturbed by strange dreams. The worst one had him trying to prevent Biker from riding off a large cliff into a bottomless grave. The night seemed to go on forever.

He heard a noise in his bedroom and sat up. "Who's there?" he said loudly.

"It's me," Frank replied.

Joe jumped from his bed. "Did Dad call?"

"Keep your voice down. They got here about an hour ago and went to bed. Sims is staying, too."

"What time is it?"

"Almost five-thirty. Get dressed."

"Why are you whispering?" Joe asked as he pulled on his jeans.

"I think I'm onto something, and I don't want to wake Biker."

"What is it?"

"Shhh. In the basement." Frank left Joe's room.

Joe didn't like it when Frank started acting secretive. Joe preferred the straight approach. Frank liked to keep his ideas to himself until he was absolutely sure that he was right. Sometimes he waited until it was almost too late.

Frank had his computer booted up by the time Joe reached the basement office.

Like Joe, Frank had slept restlessly. But his restlessness was because of a nagging problem—Fat Harold's "little birdie." Someone had always been one step ahead of the Hardys and had nearly gotten them killed twice. Joe suspected Sims. But it would have been easier for Sims to kill Biker in the "line of duty." No, Fat Harold's "little birdie" had to be someone who was close to Biker and to Frank and Joe as well.

"What's the big mystery?" Joe asked. He sat in the chair next to Frank's and rubbed the sleep from his eyes.

"How did Fat Harold know someone would be at Frost's apartment—and where to find Callie and Sue?" Frank asked.

"Someone told him," Joe answered with a yawn.

"Right—his 'little birdie.' And how did that little birdie tell him?"

Joe sat up. "What do you mean?"

"How did the little birdie contact Fat Harold?"

"By phone!"

"Right, again. Someone's been keeping tabs on us and reporting back to Fat Harold. And now for the grand prize: What kind of phone calls did the little birdie make?"

"Long distance!"

"Give the man a stuffed bear!" Frank said. Just then the computer chirped and the screen lit up. "The little birdie made two calls to Fat Harold. If he was close enough to know our every move, then he had—"

"To make the calls from Bayport," Joe finished.

"You win the bonus prize," Frank said. He turned to his computer and began punching in the code numbers for accessing long-distance phone calls.

"Sims could have known," Joe said.

"No. Whoever made the first call tried to set us up. Sims didn't know we were going to Queens. The second phone call was to inform Fat Harold about Callie and Sue and set us up again. Fat Harold was in Bayport shortly after we arrived—and we were with Sims the whole time."

The computer beeped, and Frank punched the Enter button. "Aha?" he said triumphantly.

"What is it?" Joe moved to view the screen. A seemingly endless list of phone numbers rolled before his eyes.

Frank hit a button and the list stopped scrolling. He pointed at one line. "Here's the first phone call."

"How can you tell?"

"Remember Fat Harold's crazy number?"

"Yeah. Five-five-five-BETS," Joe replied.

"BETS translates to two-three-eight-seven—and there it is."

"Here's the second," Joe said, pointing farther down the screen.

"The time of the first call was shortly before noon, about the time we were on our way to Queens. The second call was made several hours later, just after we got back to Bayport."

"The two phone calls came from different phones," Joe said with disappointment. "Probably pay phones."

"Let's find out." Frank punched in the first and second phone numbers. A second later the screen flashed with the answers.

"One's an extension at Bayport Hospital; the other is a room at the Bayport Motel," Joe said.

Frank turned to Joe. "Are you thinking what I'm thinking?"

"If I am, then Sue and Callie are in danger," Joe replied.

"Let's be sure." Frank picked up the phone next to his computer and dialed the hospital number. The nurse on duty refused to give out any information about the extension number. Frank next dialed the Bayport Motel. The phone seemed to ring endlessly.

Finally a groggy voice answered, "Hello?"

It was Brandon Dalton.

"Sorry, wrong number," Frank said quickly and hung up the phone.

"Dalton," Joe said as fact.

"The *B* on the road map stood for Brandon, not Biker," Frank added.

"We'd better wake up Dad and Sims," Frank said.

The Hardys turned to leave, then froze. Biker stood in the doorway. Joe had never seen such rage on a human face. His friend appeared to be out of his mind with anger.

"Biker—" Joe began.

Before Joe could finish his sentence, Biker Conway slammed the door shut with such force that it cracked. Frank and Joe could hear him running up the stairs.

Joe was the first to reach the door. He pushed, but the door wouldn't budge.

"It's jammed," he yelled to Frank.

"Stand back," Frank shouted. Joe stood to one side as Frank ran and jumped at the door. His karate kick split the door in half, and he and Joe rushed up the stairs.

They were stunned to see the kitchen table and chairs scattered, as if someone had thrown them around the room. Under one upended chair lay Sims.

Frank picked up the chair. A quickly swelling bruise was taking shape below Sims's right eye.

"Biker," the bounty hunter yelled. "He's gone insane!"

A car engine roared to life outside. Joe ran to the doorway in time to see Biker peel away from the curb in Fenton's car.

"The motel," Frank shouted as he ran to the van.

Frank and Joe jumped aboard, Frank shoving the key into the ignition. But nothing happened.

"He's killed the engine," Frank yelled, slamming his fist against the dash.

Joe hopped out, ran to the front, and threw open the hood. "He ripped out some spark plug wires."

"Great," Frank said. "Are they on the ground?"

"No, he must have taken them with him." Joe slammed the hood closed. Then he yelled, "What about Sims's car?"

They dashed back to the kitchen, to find Fenton Hardy kneeling over Sims, who was still trying to pull himself together. When he heard the whole story, Fenton dug into Sims's pockets himself to find the car keys.

His face was gray as he passed the keys to his sons. "You'd better find Biker quickly," he said, pointing to the stunned bounty hunter's empty holster.

"Biker left the keys, but he took Sims's gun."

Chapter

17

THE BATTERED CHEVY screeched to a stop just outside Brandon's motel room. The door stood wide open. Fenton Hardy's car was parked in the space right in front.

The door to Sue's room flew open and Sue ran out, followed by Callie.

"Your father just phoned," Sue said, sobbing, as Frank and Joe hopped from the car.

Joe grabbed her by the shoulders. "Where's Biker?" he shouted.

"H-h-he showed up a few minutes ago. He told Brandon he wanted to show him where the pits were." Sue burst into tears.

Joe shook her. "Did you see a gun?"

Sue's eyes widened. "No."

"How did they leave?" Frank asked.

"They took Brandon's bike," Callie replied.

Joe threw his sling off. "Give me your keys," he said, flexing his arm. Sue pulled her bike keys from her pocket. Joe grabbed them and ran to Sue's cycle.

"Where do you think you're going?" Frank yelled after his brother. "Your arm—you can't drive a bike."

Joe kicked the cycle to life. "Watch me. Follow me in Sims's car. We're going to the pits." He shifted to first and zoomed out of the parking lot.

Frank, Callie, and Sue hopped in Sims's Chevy and followed. Joe quickly became a small dot to them and then disappeared altogether.

Joe was at the pits in a matter of minutes. He shot through the entrance and guided the cycle around potholes and gravel mounds. He knew that Biker's favorite practice spot was the largest hole near the rear of the quarry. It was also the most secluded. Nice place for a murder, Joe thought.

A gunshot echoed throughout the quarry. Joe gunned the throttle and jumped a ridge. Before the echo of the shot had died, he'd stopped the cycle at the edge of the large pit and shut the engine off. He gasped.

Biker was on his knees, a widening stain of red on his shirt. Brandon stood over Biker waving two weapons—Sims's 9 mm and a snubnose .38

pistol. Joe recognized the .38 as the same gun that had been fired at them at the gas station. Brandon was shouting hysterically at the slumping Biker.

"Then my old man cut my salary after you finked on me about the salesmen phoning in. He said he was going to fire me if I fouled up again. I'm the son of the company's owner. I have an image to maintain. Frost promised me some easy money—fast. And, yeah, I used your name. You're just a low-life mechanic who tried to be a big shot."

Brandon paced back and forth in front of Biker, swinging his arms wildly. Biker fell to his side. Brandon grabbed Biker's collar and pulled him up.

"It was easy to talk Frost into pulling the hijacking while you were away. But why should I pay Fat Harold? He thought Biker Conway owed him the money. By planting your wallet next to Frost's body, I made sure that you'd be blamed for the murder, too."

Brandon laughed and let Biker fall to the ground.

"I'm the only one who knows where the watches are. My dad's company will get the insurance money, but I'll be able to live up to my image after I sell the watches."

He aimed the two pistols at Biker.

"Of course, you'll have to die. I'll plead self-defense. After all, everyone from Bayport to Queens knows about your hot temper.''

Brandon locked the hammers of the guns. An evil grin crossed his face.

Joe kicked the bike to life, jerked the throttle open, and flew down the hill. Brandon turned, his face twisted in confusion and fear. He fired wildly at Joe. Joe zigzagged the bike so Brandon couldn't draw a bead on him.

Brandon seemed to realize he was wasting bullets. He threw the .38 aside, crouched in a shooting position, and carefully aimed the 9 mm at the onrushing Joe.

Joe ducked low over the cycle and let up on the throttle. He stomped on the rear brake and turned the bike to the left, skidding into Brandon. The rich kid jerked backward as the 9 mm roared. His bullet whizzed past Joe's head, knocking Joe from his bike and slamming him into the hard ground on his left arm. Pain from his earlier injury shot through his body like a thousand volts of electricity.

Brandon took the opportunity to run. As Joe lay dazed, Dalton hopped on his bike and sped away.

Joe stood and stumbled toward the bleeding Biker. Biker, his eyes glazed, pointed after Brandon.

''Get him,'' he gasped, then fainted.

Joe jerked his bike up and kicked it into a roar.

He twisted the throttle and rocketed after the fleeing Brandon. Brandon wasn't a good rider—slowly but steadily, Joe closed the gap.

Desperately, Brandon fired the gun at Joe. The recoil nearly made him lose control of his cycle. When the gun emptied, he threw it at Joe, missing widely. He jumped a small hill and almost flipped the cycle.

Joe expertly jumped the hill, moving ever closer to Brandon.

The hills in this part of the quarry were more numerous and higher. With each jump, Joe narrowed the gap. On the steepest grade, Joe was able to pull up on Brandon's right side.

Brandon kicked out. Joe swerved aside, but quickly caught up to Brandon again.

Joe pulled his cycle slightly ahead of Brandon's. He reached over, grabbed the front brake handle, and squeezed. The bike jolted to a stop and flipped Brandon forward. He screamed as he flew through the air and slammed into a mound of gravel. His cycle flipped end over end, flying dangerously close to Joe. Joe swerved his cycle to the right. Brandon's bike crashed into a boulder and died with a screaming whine.

Joe turned his cycle and headed toward Brandon, who was shaken but not seriously hurt.

"On your feet," Joe ordered.

Brandon stood slowly on wobbly legs. He shook his head and stumbled.

"Let's go," Joe growled.

Brandon staggered forward with Joe following on the cycle.

Moments later, they returned to their starting place. Joe was glad to see Frank and Callie giving first aid to Biker.

"How's he doing?" Joe asked, concern in his voice.

"He'll survive," Frank replied. "Sue's gone to call an ambulance." He looked up at Brandon. "I see you got him."

"Not without a fight," Joe said. He hopped from the cycle and knelt next to Biker.

"Hey, hotshot!" Biker tried to laugh, but ended up groaning.

"Take it easy," Joe said.

"Great." Biker grimaced.

Callie picked up the .38 by the trigger guard. "Whose is this?"

"That's Brandon's." Joe took the gun from Callie. "Recognize it, Frank?"

"Sure. Well, I should; it looks like the gun from the gas station."

Joe wrapped the gun in a handkerchief. "I also heard what Brandon said to you, Biker, and I'll repeat it at his trial."

"Good work, Joe." Frank shook his head. "But I wish you'd waited for the rest of us."

"If I'd waited for you to catch up," Joe protested, "Biker might be dead."

"He still might be!" called out a tinny voice from the top of the hill.

They turned to see Fat Harold aiming a MAC-10 submachine gun at the group.

His nasal laugh echoed through the pits as he squeezed the trigger, sending a blizzard of bullets at Frank, Joe, Callie, Sue, and Biker.

Chapter

18

"I KNEW THAT would get your attention." Fat Harold giggled as he trotted down the hill. He'd purposely aimed high over their heads. The bookie stopped just short of the group, covering them with his MAC-10. "Why the surprised look, friends? You may be on the side of law and order, but I own the keys to the courthouse. It's good business to have a few state judges on your payroll. One of them owed me, and I'm out. Although I couldn't get my friends out."

Fat Harold laughed and moved toward the frightened Brandon.

"So, I catch up with you at last, *Biker Conway*." Fat Harold leveled the gun at Brandon's heart as the kid cowered. "Or should I say *Brandon Dalton?*"

"N-n-no," Brandon whimpered.

"Sorry," Fat Harold said. "But you don't have the watches or the money. So I'll have to write off the debt—and erase you as well." He nodded to the others. "And I'm sorry that you five will have to join young Mr. Dalton in the bad debt column. I can't have any witnesses. You do understand."

Fat Harold gave them his thin-lipped smile as he worked the bolt on his gun. Brandon stepped back, his hands in front of him as though they could stop the lead slugs. His face was a portrait of terror.

"All bets are off." Fat Harold laughed. "It's time to cash in your chips." He stepped forward, his finger tightening on the trigger.

That step forward brought the bookie to the spot where Biker lay. In a desperate move, Biker lashed out in a kick. Fat Harold screamed as his knees buckled. As the bookie was thrown off balance, his MAC-10 sprayed shells wildly into the dirt. Brandon fell to the ground.

The Hardys moved quickly, Joe yanking the gun from Fat Harold's hands while Frank landed a powerful uppercut to the bookie's jaw. Fat Harold groaned and slithered to the ground, unconscious.

Callie ran to Brandon and turned him over.

"He's okay," she yelled back to Frank and Joe. "I think he just fainted."

"Good," Frank replied.

"Not so good," Joe said as he knelt beside Biker. "He's reopened his wound—and he's in danger of bleeding to death."

"And because of Joe's statement, Brandon's been booked for the murder of Frost and for hijacking the watches," Fenton Hardy said as Sue was adjusting the pillow behind Biker's head.

Biker shifted on the hospital bed. "Too bad," he said. He was startled by the stunned looks Frank and Joe gave him. "For all his faults, I kind of liked the kid. He was good for a few laughs around the office."

"How long are you going to be in here?" Mort Sims asked. He leaned against the door, crumpled hat in hand.

"Doc says about a week," Biker replied.

"Well," Mort Sims said as he put on his hat, "this is one time I'm glad I didn't bring back my man." He opened the door. "See you around, Fenton." Then he was gone.

"That guy has some nerve," Frank said.

"It's the closest you'll get to an apology," Fenton said. He faced Frank and Joe. "And you two—"

"Dad, I'm sorry if I caused you any trouble," Frank said.

"Yeah, I know I said some things that—" Joe began.

"Forget it," Fenton interrupted. "If I had to lose a case, I'm glad I lost it to my sons." He headed for the door. "I'm off to the airport to pick up your mother and Aunt Gertrude. You two be home in time for supper."

"As long as it's anything but frozen fish sticks," Joe said with a grin.

Fenton shook his head and left the room.

"You're going back to Queens after you get out?" Frank asked Biker.

"Right." Biker grinned. "The D.A. is making a motion tomorrow to drop all charges. Then I'll be returning to DalTime."

"Why?" asked Callie. "Dalton caused all your problems."

"*Brandon* Dalton caused all my problems," Biker replied. "Brandon even talked his dad into hiring Sims."

"Why?" asked Callie.

"Because Brandon figured Biker wouldn't make it back to Queens," Joe said.

"Brandon even had himself beaten up," Frank added. "And then he killed Frost to shut his mouth about the watches and the beating."

"But why are you going back to DalTime?" Callie asked.

Biker looked at Sue. "I like Mr. Dalton. He's

going to need all the support Sue and I can give him.''

"Besides," Sue added, "we need our jobs if we're going to get married. Speaking of which, we'll have to set a new date. But you guys are definitely invited to the wedding.''

"You've got it," Joe said with a grin. "Just do me a favor.''

"Name it." Biker grinned back at him.

"When we turn up for the wedding—no adventures. Okay?''

Biker nodded solemnly. "You have my word. My wedding will be as quiet as my homecoming.''

Callie, Frank, and Sue cracked up. But Joe just shook his head gloomily.

"That's what I'm afraid of," he said.

COUNTDOWN
TO TERROR

Chapter

1

"I TELL YOU, Frank, we're being suckered." Joe Hardy scowled at his older brother, slightly raising his voice over the drone of the jet engines. "I think Dad's sending us on a wild-goose chase to get us out of the way. He hasn't trusted us since his last case."

Detective cases were something both the Hardys and their father knew a lot about. Fenton Hardy was an internationally known private investigator, and his sons had often tangled with criminals. But their last case, *Nowhere to Run*, had pitted father against sons. Fenton had had the job of capturing a friend of Frank's and Joe's, while the younger Hardys had tried to clear him. It put a serious

1

strain on the family for a while—Joe was still feeling it.

Frank Hardy's dark eyes went from the news magazine he was reading to his brother's troubled face. "Chill out, Joe. Dad just asked us to do him a favor—fly up to Halifax, Nova Scotia, and pick up some depositions. I don't think he's sending us into exile."

"No, just all the way to Canada," Joe said sarcastically.

He got a shrug from Frank in reply. "Okay, this insurance scam may not be the biggest case ever to come our way. But we take what we can get." Frank tapped the magazine in his hand. "Maybe you'd rather be tackling this terrorist thing—twenty people killed in Europe and the Middle East, and no one knows who's doing it, much less why."

"Crazies don't need a reason," Joe said, his blue eyes suddenly icy. He'd lost a girlfriend, Iola Morton, in a terrorist bomb blast that had been meant for him. "Anyway, we'd be doing the world a favor if we went after scum like that. Who really cares about a bunch of penny-ante crooks fooling around with shipping cargoes to rook insurance companies?"

Frank grinned. "Well, the insurance companies do. And so does Dad, since he was hired to find these guys. And it's not so penny-ante. The accounts may be small, but these guys are operating up and down the whole Atlantic seaboard.''

The pitch of the ever-present hum of the engines changed, and the plane banked. "We must be coming in for a landing," Joe said, looking out the window at a perfect late-summer day. "Maybe a crash landing. I don't see anything out there but trees."

Frank leaned across his brother to glance out the window. Thick pine forests, broken only here and there by lakes, rushed by under them. "If you'd bothered to do a little homework instead of grousing about this trip, you'd know the airport is about six miles outside the city."

"The control tower is probably made of logs," Joe muttered, still staring out the window.

But as the plane went into its landing glide, it approached an airport as modern as most. "Looks like they use radar instead of smoke signals," Frank quipped to his brother.

The plane bounced once on the tarmac, then rolled to a stop beside the terminal. As soon as the moving walkway had been attached to the plane, the Hardys were ready to go. Both had carry-on bags—they hated waiting for luggage to be unloaded. Frank had a special padded flight bag for his lap-top computer. It hung from his shoulder as they walked off the plane.

"Let's grab a cab and get into town," Joe

said. "The sooner we finish this job, the happier I'll be."

Frank grinned at him. "You mean you don't want to hang around and enjoy all the tourist sights?"

Joe whipped around in the middle of the terminal, pulling something out of his pocket. "Well, if I'm here to play tourist, I brought the perfect prop."

With a flick, he opened a folding instant camera and hit the shutter switch. The built-in flash went off, and a moment later Joe handed Frank a picture of himself scowling against the glare of the flash.

"Perfect!" Now Joe was grinning.

Frank gave him a sour look. "I think you could use a little practice with this thing. Who are all these people behind me?"

"Local color," Joe loftily informed him.

They headed outside to the rank of taxicabs. Frank happened to glance back and saw one of the "local-color" people rushing over to a phone booth. He was a tall, dark guy with a bushy mustache and a white turban. "I hope he's not calling his lawyer about being blinded by a camera flash," he muttered. Then he slid in next to his brother in the cab.

It was an old luxury car, a "gas guzzler" with a surprisingly plush interior. Frank had noticed that the taxi sign on the roof was held on by tension cords. He suspected the car also served as the driver's personal transportation.

"The Harbour Hotel, please," Joe told the driver, and the car pulled smoothly away from the curb.

As soon as they were on the road, Joe rolled down the window, breathing deeply to take in the piney smell of the trees around them. "It's not exactly the way I expected to be introduced to a city," he said.

"Oh, Halifax is big," the driver said. "But it's green too." Passing through rolling hills heavily studded with stands of trees, the Hardys agreed that it did look pretty terrific.

"Not much traffic this afternoon," the driver continued. "You boys must have been the first off the plane."

"That's the best part of carrying your own bags," Joe said, staring out at the nearly empty road. "You mean you get traffic jams out here?"

"We get a lot of people on these roads," the driver said. "It's the worst on the bridges into town." He smiled. "Halifax has about everything you'd expect from a modern city, including traffic jams and crowds."

"And crazy drivers," Frank put in, looking out the front windshield. A red sports car had appeared at the top of the hill ahead, barreling down the gentle slope at full speed.

Joe laughed. "Maybe he's afraid he's going to miss his plane," he suggested.

The driver shook his head. "I don't think any flights are leaving right now," he said. "My bet is that he was supposed to pick someone up."

Soon after the red sports car flashed past them, they heard the shriek of its brakes. Frank looked out the rear window and saw the car go into a wild, fishtailing U-turn. Now it was moving up behind them.

Frank's eyes narrowed. There was something weird about this.

Joe's danger antennae were working just as well. "Driver, speed up a little," he said. "This guy is getting a little too close to our tail."

"You said it," the driver agreed. He hit the gas, and the big old car lengthened the distance between them.

But the red car sped up even more, as if it were trying to catch them.

"First he's in a hurry to go one way, then the other," the driver said. "I'm going to pull over and let this maniac pass."

"That's not—" Frank began.

"Don't!" Joe said.

But as they were speaking, the driver was tapping his brakes and pulling off to the side of the road.

Now the red car was slowing, too. As it came

up broadside, Frank watched as the passenger window steadily slid down. "Somehow, I don't think this guy needs directions," he said. "Let's get moving."

The driver turned back to stare at Frank blankly.

"Forget it," Joe yelled. *"Duck!"*

A hand had appeared in the sports car's window. It held a gleaming 9 mm automatic.

And it was pointed straight at them.

Chapter

2

THE HARDYS AND their driver hit the floor as the gunman cut loose with five wild shots. The windshield shattered, as well as both windows on the driver's side.

Although they couldn't see the red sports car from their positions on the floor, they heard the engine rev, the tires spin out.

"They're pulling out in front of us," Joe said. "We've got to get out of here."

He reached for the door handle, but missed as the taxi suddenly jerked forward. The engine roared as it picked up speed and passed the sports car.

Frank peered between the front seats to see the driver still on the floor, one hand holding

8

the bottom of the steering wheel, the other on the gas pedal.

"How do you expect to steer—by touch?" Frank asked.

"Son," the driver said, "in the wintertime, when white-outs hit the road, that's just how we do drive. It beats getting shot at."

He jockeyed the wheel and chanced a darting glance into the rearview mirror. As his head rose above the seat, bullets smashed what was left of the rear window.

The driver tromped on the gas pedal, and the cab shot forward.

Frank and Joe looked back through the glass shards to see the red sports car starting up.

Both cars raced along the empty road in a weird dance. The agile red sports car darted back and forth behind the huge blue cab, trying to catch up. But the Hardys' driver sent his cab weaving across the road to block the attackers.

The gunman was leaning out the window, trying for a clear shot, when the cab slowed suddenly. The red car bounced off its rear fender. The impact nearly threw the gunman out of the car.

He shouted angrily, pumping bullets into the cab's trunk.

The driving battle continued, speed versus size. But finally the little car managed to maneuver around the larger one again. It swung wide, so that the gunman was even with the rear seats of the cab.

He grinned, raising his automatic.

Joe stared across the three-foot distance and into the eyes of his would-be murderer. He ducked and looked desperately around the backseat of the car, looking for something, *anything* to use in his defense.

Frank's computer lay on the seat beside him. Joe snatched up the flight bag by the shoulder strap and swung it out the shattered window.

It caught the gunman in the arm, deflecting his aim up. Still holding on to the bag, Joe leaned out of the car and swung his shoulder. This time the computer hit the gunman with stunning force, knocking him back against the sports car's driver.

The car veered closer to the cab as Joe leaned out farther, swinging the bag over his head. Frank reached out to his brother, trying to steady him.

Then Joe released the whirling bag, sending it straight into the oncoming car's windshield. It smashed against the glass, shattering it into a spider's web of cracks.

The driver flinched, losing control of the car, which careened wildly across the road into a stand of white birches.

Frank pulled his eyes away from the scene.

10

"Nice aim. But did you have to use my computer?"

The wrecked car quickly receded behind them. Joe leaned forward to tap their driver on the shoulder. "Hey, aren't we going to stop?"

"Not as long as those guys have guns," the driver told him. "We'll call the cops at the first gas station we come to."

The Hardys shrugged. They weren't eager to face the gunman again either. "Maybe we should call Dad's contact on the Halifax force," Joe said.

Frank nodded. "It'd be easier than trying to explain this to a desk sergeant."

They were pulling up at a gas station then. "We'll call the police," Frank said.

"And you'd better call a cab," the driver said. "This one is a little too open to the wind."

Frank got the number for the Halifax police, dialed, and asked for Sergeant Gerald Dundee. The desk officer transferred his call.

"Dundee," a voice snapped on the other end of the line.

"Sergeant Dundee, this is Frank Hardy—my brother and I are supposed to meet you this afternoon. But something very strange has happened on the way in from the airport." He gave the story of the attack.

Frank ended the story, "Either they wanted

us, or they wanted the car we were in. Who knew we were coming?"

"Myself and the insurance people," Dundee replied. "It was hardly top secret. But why would a bunch of insurance cheats attack you?" Dundee had grown much less annoyed as he listened to Frank's story. "Tell the driver to stay at the gas station until I get there. You go on to your hotel—the Harbour, isn't it? I'll come and question you after I'm finished out there."

Even as Frank was hanging up, a new taxi arrived. The Hardys transferred their bags, then gave their first driver Dundee's message and paid him. They felt it was the least they could do.

The rest of the ride into the city of Halifax was quiet. They came to a wide expanse of water—Halifax Harbor—which they had to cross to enter the city. "This is the old bridge," the driver said as he started across a two-lane span. "Up north is the newer bridge."

The Hardys looked out at the bustling seaport. The cranes were moving boxcar-size crates into the holds of waiting container ships. Other ships were moored at the docks—including a navy corvette.

When they were across the bridge and driving through the city, they were impressed with the mix of state-of-the-art office towers with buildings from one or two centuries before. The driver pulled past what looked like two-hundred-year-old warehouses to stop in front of an ultramodern hotel complex. "The Harbour Hotel," he said. "Right next to the old and restored part of town."

"Very impressive," Frank said. He and Joe paid their fare, got their bags, registered, and settled into their hotel room to wait for Sergeant Dundee.

He arrived about an hour later, a big, craggy-faced man with ginger red hair turning to white. Heavy, grizzled eyebrows topped his piercing blue eyes. He was vigorous, but he was old. Frank realized Dundee must be near retirement age. That was why he'd been given the job of dealing with insurance companies and their investigators. Judging from the heavy frown lines cut into the man's face, he didn't enjoy his job.

But Dundee's eyes sparkled with life as he filled the Hardys in on the investigation into the attack. "There's little enough to be said—the car was empty when we got to it. We're checking the plates, of course. And I found some blank import forms in the glove compartment."

He smiled. "We may have some sort of smuggling operation involved here."

"Isn't that a little out of your line?" Joe

asked. "I thought you were the local insurance liaison—"

Dundee cut him off bitterly. "I've spent years on the force—most of them on the waterfront. And my contacts down there can track these guys down faster than anyone else."

Joe shrugged, aware he had touched a nerve.

"Is there anything we can do?" Frank asked.

Dundee shook his head. "I'll take care of this investigation. If you remember anything more though, contact me."

Sergeant Dundee rose from the couch in the hotel room and headed for the door. "If you show up at my office tomorrow morning, I'll have those depositions ready." He opened the door and turned back to them. "You should be able to leave town by tomorrow afternoon."

He closed the door so sharply behind him that it was almost a slam. Frank turned to his brother. "Do you get the feeling he wants us out of his way?"

"I think he's too busy trying to prove that he's still a cop to worry about us." He stretched and patted his stomach. "Right now, I'm more worried about what's for dinner."

They went exploring the city's waterfront restoration project and found intriguing small shops and lots of restaurants. Joe stopped in front of one place that had a sign with a man in uniform scoffing up a huge meal. "The Hungry Guardsman," he said, reading the sign. "Home of the three-dollar steak. Sounds good to me."

"There are lots of people inside," Frank said, looking through the window.

"And lots of cute girls," Joe added, pressing close to the window.

They went inside, and a waitress in a striped jersey showed them to a table. "Give us a couple of Cokes," Joe said, "and two of those three-dollar steaks."

"Oh," said the girl, "I'll send the food waitress right over."

"Food waitress?" Joe gave her a puzzled look.

"I only serve from the bar," the girl said.

Joe shrugged. "Well, do what you have to do. We're here to eat." He grinned. "But I don't think another waitress could be as cute as you."

He was wrong. When the other girl arrived, she put her coworker in the shade. Mischievous blue eyes twinkled above a cute snub nose with just a sprinkling of freckles. She gave them a quick grin. "Hi, I'm Shauna MacLaren. I'm your server tonight." she said. "I hear you'd like some food." She was a tall girl, just an inch or two shorter than Joe's six feet. On her model-perfect frame the restaurant's infor-

15

mal uniform of striped jersey and jeans looked like a fashion statement. Her shoulder-length hair was midnight black.

"I—wow!" Joe sat back and stared.

"What my talkative friend here wanted to say was that we'd like a couple of those three-dollar steaks," Frank told Shauna.

She brought them the steaks in moments, and the boys dug in.

"Frank"—Joe looked up, his mouth half full of steak and fries—"remember how I told you never to let me fall for a waitress again?"

The second great love of Joe's life had been a Bayport waitress, Annie Shea, who'd nearly gotten him killed in the *Witness to Murder* case.

Frank nodded. "I remember."

"Well, I want you to forget it." Joe's eyes followed Shauna as she walked among the tables.

"I should have guessed," Frank groused. "But I warn you, she's getting you into trouble already."

"What are you talking about?" Joe demanded.

"You've been so busy keeping an eye on her, you didn't notice those guys at the table behind us. They came in right after us, and they've been watching us ever since."

Joe turned, pretending to watch Shauna

while actually scanning the room. ''You think we've got a tail?''

''Well, there's one way to find out.'' Frank abruptly rose from his seat, tossing a ten on the table. Joe gave one sad glance to what was left of his steak and stood up, too. The three guys who'd been eating behind them abandoned their meals. It was the proof the Hardys needed.

''They're between us and the door,'' Joe said.

''I know—we'll take another exit.'' Frank had already noticed another door that opened onto a small sidewalk dining area. Leading Joe, he walked through the diner, over the knee-high fence that separated the tables from the traffic, and down the street.

The tails took the same route, blank faced.

''They've got to know we're on to them,'' Joe whispered. ''What will they do now?''

His answer came as four more rugged-looking types joined the three guys.

''I don't like this,'' Frank said. ''Come on!''

He darted into traffic and across the street, then turned right. They were on a very busy boulevard that led up a steep hill to an open park. The seven trackers began closing in.

Joe glanced over at his brother. ''If we're going to run, it's easier downhill,'' he said.

Frank nodded. "On the count of three, we cross back, and run down. One—two—"

He waited until a bus blocked the pursuers from crossing the road, then called, "Three!"

Frank and Joe dashed in front of the bus, then down the hill.

The tails were caught flat-footed and couldn't pursue until after Frank and Joe had a decent lead.

Joe glanced back, grinning at the guys behind them. "What do we do now?" he asked.

"We stop," Frank said.

Joe stared at his brother. "Why?"

"We just ran out of running room," Frank answered.

Their escape route dead-ended—right into Halifax Harbor.

Chapter

3

THE HARDYS HAD only two ways out of this disaster—to the right or to the left, along the water.

To the left Joe saw quays and tourist joints. Far in the distance rose the Harbour Hotel, a possible haven that might as well be on Mars.

"This way!" Frank was looking right—to a sign that read Ferry Passengers.

The ferry terminal was just beyond that, and beyond that the ferry. Late commuters were boarding, and it was obvious the ship was about to leave.

Joe didn't need to be told twice. Both Hardys darted to the right. As they entered the terminal building, they were confronted by a

19

line of turnstiles. But Joe saw a sign by the snack bar that said Tokens. Still on the run, he slapped down the necessary fares and got two tokens.

He and Frank were through the turnstiles and boarding just as the pursuing posse stormed into the terminal. The loading gates came up, and the ferry pulled away. Joe waved goodbye to the seven furious faces.

"Looks like they missed the boat," he said.

Frank nodded. "I just wonder where we're going." He dug into his jacket pocket and came out with a guidebook. Paging through, he smiled. "We're going to a town called Dartmouth, just across the harbor. And I know exactly where we're heading once we get there."

Joe stared at him. "Where?"

"To a phone—we've got to call Sergeant Dundee."

Until then, they enjoyed the view of Halifax Harbor—from the middle of the water.

When the ferry pulled into Dartmouth Terminal, Frank and Joe joined the stream of commuters onto dry land again. There was a pay phone in the terminal building, and Frank dialed Dundee's number.

On the third ring the phone was picked up. "Dundee's line," a clipped voice on the other end answered from what was obviously a squad room.

Frank identified himself and asked for Sergeant Dundee. He was told the policeman wasn't in at the moment, but that he'd return Frank's call if he'd leave a number. "If you mean right away, he can get us at 555-8912," Frank said, reading the number on the phone. "It's a pay phone."

"We'll get him," the voice promised.

The police were as good as their word. Almost as soon as Frank hung up, the phone rang. Gerry Dundee was on the other end.

"Sergeant Dundee, Frank Hardy here," Frank said. "I've got a follow-up report for you." He went on to explain how he and Joe had been followed and how they'd escaped.

"So now you're in the ferry terminal on the Dartmouth side, eh?" Dundee said. "Cross the rail line there, cross Windmill Road, then head up Portland Street. The first place on the right-hand side is a cops' hangout. Wait for me there and you shouldn't have any trouble. I'll be along in fifteen to twenty minutes."

Frank hung up the phone, turned to Joe, and said, "We get to take a little walk."

They followed Dundee's directions, found the place, and spent the next few minutes peering out the window at the street one floor below. It wasn't long before an unmarked car pulled up outside the place. Gerry Dundee stepped out.

He was in a very good mood when he met the Hardys. "So you had to cut your dinner short over there across the water," he said. "Let's make up for it over here—my treat."

Dundee ushered them over to a table, and moments later they were sitting in front of thick, steaming steaks. "Always a favorite of mine," he said, tucking in with the gusto of a man twenty years younger.

He smiled at Joe's slightly surprised look. "The smart mouths in the department wonder how I can tackle these, too," he said. "In their books, old crocks like myself don't have the teeth—or the brains—for real meat or real cases."

Spearing another hunk of medium-rare beef, he popped it into his mouth and began chewing. Then he swallowed and smiled. "They think that once you get to a certain age, you can't take it anymore."

He tapped the side of his head. "But this old brain has more experience and data locked away than all their precious computers. I've found out some stuff—"

Frank asked suddenly, not meaning to interrupt but impatient for news, "Anything said about our case?"

Dundee drew himself up, his face going stiff. "What are you talking about?"

"I mean what was the reaction from your buddies downtown. You'd think they'd show some interest when somebody involved in an attack like the one we went through gave you a call. But the guy I talked to acted as if he'd never heard of me."

Dundee didn't reply. He just stared stonily at Frank.

Frank leveled his gaze and returned the stare.

"Are you investigating this case on your own?"

Nothing. No reply.

"If I'd wanted a one-man show on this case I'd have turned to my brother Joe and let him carry the ball. But we did the right thing; we contacted the police."

Frank leaned across the table. "So, you're holding on to the report on our attack—hiding the facts in your head, with all that other great data. Well, I don't like it. I don't like being staked out like a sacrificial lamb while you try to breathe some life into your career."

"Hey, Frank," Joe began, looking from his brother to Dundee as they continued to glare at each other, "I'd like to hear what he has to say."

He turned to Dundee, but the older cop's face was still a frozen mask.

Gerald Dundee reached into his pocket, threw enough money down on the table to cover the tab, and rose abruptly from his seat. "I don't have to justify myself to anyone, especially to a kid like you," he said. "I've put in enough time on the job to know what I'm doing."

He stepped away from the table and headed for the stairs that led down to the street. "If you want a lift back to the Harbour Hotel, I'll give it to you. But we won't discuss the case."

Joe wanted to discuss it, but judging from the looks on his brother's and Dundee's faces, he knew his chance for learning anything that night was blown.

Joe looked unhappily at his half-eaten meal for the second time that night. At least the lift would get them back to their hotel quickly. Maybe the Harbour Hotel had steak on its room-service menu.

"Uh, thanks, Sergeant," Joe said. "*I'd* appreciate the lift." He glanced over at Frank, giving him a look that said, "Cool it—one of us should stay friendly with this guy."

They walked down the stairs to the restaurant exit, Joe walking with Dundee, Frank trailing behind. It felt funny for Joe to be playing the nice guy—especially when they were playing the game with a cop.

Dundee led the way to the unmarked car, opening the doors. "I'm afraid one of you will have to ride in the back."

Frank silently took the rear seat, usually reserved for suspects and prisoners. Joe took the shotgun seat, right in front of the car's police radio.

Gerry Dundee stepped around the car to get behind the steering wheel. He started the engine and pulled the car away from the sidewalk.

"Hand me that mike, Joe," he said as they drove down the street. "I should call in and let the dispatcher know I'm back in the car."

Joe handed over the microphone, and Dundee hit the button on the side. "Car ninety-seven to base—I'm heading back to town."

There was a brief burst of static, then a voice came back, "What's the matter, Gerry? The steak over there too tough for you nowadays?"

That got a flash of a grin from Dundee. Obviously he and the dispatcher were old friends. "Helen, *life* is tough—not the steaks."

While Dundee and the dispatcher bantered, Frank leaned over from the back seat, listening intently.

"What's that noise?" he asked suddenly.

Dundee glanced over his shoulder, his face hardening again. "What noise?"

25

They all could hear it now, over the open line—brief, tiny blips of interference, coming regularly.

Frank frowned as he listened, his eyes searching the interior of the car. "Those blips are some kind of FM broadcast—and since they're not getting any softer or louder, I guess whatever's causing them is in this car."

"So?" Dundee wanted to know.

"So," Frank answered, "the only thing I can think of that would make that noise is a radio-controlled bomb."

His face was grim as he turned to the others. "And I think we're riding right on top of it."

Chapter

4

GERRY DUNDEE LICKED his lips nervously.

"Son," he said, "you picked a great time to tell me that."

Frank and Joe looked up from the search they'd been making of the car to stare at what was happening around them.

Dundee had just turned onto a busy road. They were jammed in the middle of traffic now.

"We can't bail out here," Joe said. "Where does this road go?"

"Straight to the bridge," Dundee said, his voice tight. "If we blow up anywhere along here, we'll take dozens of people with us."

Frank's eyes darted right and left. "Can't

we turn off and head for someplace less congested?"

Dundee shrugged. "We can try to turn left up here—if we don't get killed by the bridge traffic."

He was going to try for the left-hand lane, but a car screeched up beside theirs just then, cutting them off. The bridge toll stations were ahead of them now. They were stuck on the bridge, like it or not.

Frank turned to the left and stared at the passenger in the car that cut them off. He looked familiar. Frank placed him almost immediately. He was the guy with the mustache and turban he'd seen hurrying for a phone in the airport. It was definitely the same guy.

Now Mr. Mustache held up a small box with a whip-aerial and a button on it. The message was clear. This was the detonator for the bomb they had on board.

"I don't think they're going to blow us up as long as we're good boys," Frank said. "That guy hasn't made a move to touch the button."

"That wouldn't be smart, with us right beside him," Joe pointed out. "I don't think it would do the bridge much good, either."

"I think they're just going to use it as a threat to get us to park someplace nice and quiet where they can question us, but about what I don't know."

Frank sounded calm, but his brain was churning furiously, trying to come up with a way out of this death trap. Right then, he reasoned, they did have one slim advantage. The enemy, whoever they were, didn't want them dead—at least not yet.

"If we let them pace us all the way, we'll never have a chance of escaping," he said. "Sergeant, can you get ahead of them?"

"On a jam-packed bridge?" Dundee asked. But he nodded his head, realizing they might be able to use the distance. "I'll do my best."

A tiny opening developed in the left-hand lane, ahead of their pursuers. Gerry Dundee shouldered his car into it. Then he darted back into another small open spot in the lane next to it, earning a blast on the horn from the driver he had cut off.

They'd gained a bare car length, but the pursuit car was having a hard time catching up. Drivers who've been cut off once aren't willing to let it happen again soon.

Dundee continued to weave through the heavy traffic. It was slow going, pulling a half a car length here, a half a car length there. But as the far end of the bridge came up, they were still within plain sight of their pursuers.

The pursuit car pulled over to the right-hand lane to be in the same one as Dundee. The older policeman grinned.

"Good. They think I'm going to make the right off the bridge and take the underpass to Barrington Street. Well, they're in for a surprise."

He accelerated past the turnoff and whipped into the left lane. Then he made a wild left turn, nearly getting clipped by a horrified van driver. "Get ready to jump, boys," Dundee said as he jockeyed the wheel. "This street dead-ends into a sort of park that should be deserted now."

Frank and Joe saw the greenery up ahead as Dundee swerved to the right side of the road. "Get while the getting's good!" he yelled, jamming on the brakes.

The Hardys jumped. Dundee brought the car around in a screeching U-turn, pretending that he'd just discovered the road didn't go through.

Then the pursuit car rolled up to block the open end of the street.

Gerry Dundee was already halfway out of the car, with one foot on the pavement.

Mr. Mustache must have hit the button, because two seconds later the unmarked car blew up.

Frank and Joe were staggered by the blast. It tore the hood off the engine and shattered the windshield. It also tossed Gerry Dundee like a rag doll in a tornado.

He flew across the street, arms flailing, and

landed hard on the grassy ground near the Hardys.

Joe stared at the man lying unmoving near his feet. Frank was looking at the guys in the pursuit car. Apparently they decided they'd called too much attention to themselves. With a screech of rubber, they peeled out and away from there.

Frank turned to his brother, who was kneeling beside Dundee. "Don't try to move him," he said, putting a hand on Joe's arm to stop him. "He may have internal injuries—and we don't want to make a bad situation worse."

Dundee had landed half on his side, half on his stomach, his arm twisted under him. His face lay in the dirt. Slowly, painfully, he turned his head around. Spotting Frank, he sucked in a shallow breath.

At first Frank thought Dundee was just wheezing. Then he realized Dundee was trying to tell him something. "Easy, easy," he said, dropping down to his knees beside the injured man. "Don't move around."

Gerry Dundee ignored him, trying to twist around, trying to talk. Half the man's face was bruised and beginning to swell. He winced as he coughed—it sounded more like a death rattle. Frank had horrible visions of broken ribs and vulnerable lungs as Dundee kept

31

mouthing words at him. He had no breath to sustain an actual sound.

To try to stop him, Frank brought his ear close to Dundee's mouth. Even then he could barely understand what the old cop was gasping out.

"Listen . . . important," Dundee said. "Found out . . . where . . . are." He glared at Frank, his eyes blazing for a moment as he tried to force the words out before his body betrayed him. "Find them . . . Fort . . ."

The effort was too much. Gerry Dundee's eyes rolled up, and the tautness went out of his muscles. He sagged down into the grass.

Frank and Joe stared at each other. He'd left them a world of trouble, a desperate need to get help—and half a clue.

Chapter
5

THE HARDYS STOOD surrounded by a sea of blue uniforms in the waiting room of the Camp Hill Hospital. They all wanted word of Gerry Dundee. Instead of a white-coated surgeon, however, a guy in a suit separated himself from the figures in police blue to talk to the boys. He didn't need to present his ID and badge. Everything about him said plainclothes cop.

"What can we do for you, Detective Otley?" Frank asked, glancing at the man's identification. He and Joe knew only too well what was coming.

"It's a shame about poor Gerry," Otley told them. "My father worked with him once. He was a legend on the waterfront—nothing went on there that he didn't know about." The police officer shook his head again. "Those days are long past now."

Otley looked at them with about four thousand questions in his eyes. "Now, about this report you gave the uniformed officers," he went on. "You said you reported being attacked on the road from the airport. I've checked, and we have no record of any such report."

Frank shrugged. "I was asking Sergeant Dundee about that when we realized there was a bomb in his car."

The detective gave them a sharp glance. "That's another part of your story I'd like to hear more about. I'm sure you know that Gerry Dundee is semiretired, working only as our insurance liaison. He wasn't even investigating any large cases. So why would anyone plant a bomb in his car?"

"Maybe he wasn't investigating anything *officially*," Joe said, "but something must have been up. "Take a look at the car—that damage didn't happen because he'd forgotten to change his oil filter."

They spent another hour talking with Otley, then the news came from surgery. "Sergeant Dundee is in very critical condition," the doctor said. "We've moved him to the intensive care unit."

"He's not conscious yet?" Otley asked.

The doctor shook his head. "At this point, it's touch and go whether he'll ever regain consciousness."

Otley and the Hardys decided there was nothing they could do and began to leave. Frank looked at the detective. "How about what Dundee said after the explosion?" he asked. "I could hardly make out the words, but it was something about finding someone at a fort."

Detective Otley bit back a laugh. "Halifax was the main British base in eastern Canada. This area is *crawling* with forts."

Frank and Joe were silent as Otley gave them a lift. They'd given him the name of a different hotel—the Cavalier—and all the way there, they looked back for tails.

After registering, Frank said, "Well, if they're not going to check out the forts, I guess we will."

The next morning found the boys buying new clothes—they had left their luggage at the first hotel. Frank spent time the night before with a map and guide to Halifax, choosing sites. "We'll work our way back," he said. "Our first stop is Fort Needham Park."

They found the park easily enough, perched on top of a high hill. But they didn't find a fort—just a brass plaque, indicating that a fort had once stood there.

Joe stared around. "Somehow, I don't think this is the fort Dundee meant. I'd have a hard time imagining the bad guys hanging out here," he said, gesturing to a playground.

Frank was looking at the strange monument that stood in the middle of the park, a thirty-foot-long cement wall with an arch and old-fashioned church bells hanging from it. He and Joe went over to check it out.

"It's a monument to the *Imo* disaster," he said, reading a plaque. "Back in World War I, a ship full of artillery shells collided with a ship, the *Imo*, in the harbor here." The park had a perfect view of the waterway out of the harbor.

"According to one of the guidebooks I read last night, a quarter of the city was destroyed. The whole area behind us was blown flat."

Joe looked back along the quiet streets lined with neat houses made of concrete block. "Yeah—those houses all look like they were built at the same time," he said. "That must have been quite a blast."

Frank nodded. "It was the biggest man-made explosion until the atomic bomb went off over Hiroshima." He shook his head. "They found pieces of wreckage twenty miles away."

"Well, that's interesting, but we are looking for a fort," Joe said. "Where do we go now?"

Frank told him and then led the way down Gottingen Street to central Halifax. It must once have been a bustling shopping area, but now many of the stores were boarded up, and others looked pretty seedy. Then they began climbing again, a different hill, steeper than the first. Joe read a sign that said The Citadel.

"This is the biggest of the old fortifications," Frank said. "I think we should check it out."

"But wouldn't he have said *citadel* instead of *fort?*" Joe asked.

The wound their way up a path that climbed the hill. Slowly the fortress came into view. The outside of the wall was a grassy hill, which protected the inside granite wall from cannon fire. Frank and Joe joined a stream of tourists entering through the only gate, a thin bridge across a ditch.

"Quite a place," Joe said, looking around the stone walls, which butted up to the hill.

"Complete with Hungry Guardsmen," Frank said, watching as a file of red-coated young soldiers in kilts came marching up. Another young soldier not in formation walked by just then and stopped beside them.

"You've been to the Hungry Guardsman?" he asked, smiling. "It's one of our favorite hangouts—out of uniform, that is." He glanced down at his finery. "When school's on we go there for lunch."

"School?" Joe asked.

"You didn't think we were full-time soldiers, did you?" the young corporal asked. "This is a summer job, to help pay for college." He grinned under his jaunty Scots highland bonnet. "We study the drillbooks from 1869 and our routines are completely authentic. Watch us put on our show." He pulled out an old-fashioned pocket watch. "And you should stay for the firing of the noon gun."

Another officer strolled over. "Corporal Bell, shouldn't you be at your post?"

Bell snapped to attention. "Yes, *sir!*" He trotted off to join the marching troops.

Lining up, the summer soldiers went through the drill of loading and firing their weapons like well-trained professionals. The crowd was firing away, too, clicking cameras like mad.

"That must take a lot of practice," Joe said, watching as the troopers reloaded and fired again. Even though they were firing blanks, the sharp crack! of the volleys was pretty deafening.

"There sure is a crowd," Frank said. "I don't think the guys we're looking for would hang around—"

He bit off his words suddenly as he recognized a face and turban at the edge of the crowd. It was the guy from the airport and the pursuit car, Mr. Mustache.

Apparently, he realized he'd been spotted. As the Hardys tried to push their way to him, he was already moving across the drill grounds, heading for the ramp up to the earthen parapets of the fort. Once on top he ducked to the left, disappearing behind the roof of the powder magazine, the room where explosives were stored.

Frank and Joe ran after him, but when they reached the top of the ramp, they didn't see the white turban.

"He can't have gone far," Joe said. "But those crowds are blocking the way around to the other walls."

Frank nodded. "Looks like the noon gun is about to be set off."

More student-soldiers had appeared, these in dark blue uniforms with pillbox caps. They were wheeling back a cannon at the far edge of the wall, preparing it to be fired.

"I don't see him in the crowd," Joe said. "So where is he?"

Frank was staring thoughtfully along the top ridge of the earthen fortification. Two holes broke the line of the wall. Apparently they were dugout rooms that burrowed down into the hillside.

Joe followed his brother's gaze. "Let's check 'em out."

The entrance to the first dugout was locked, but the door to the second one lay open. They went down a couple of steps, through a doorway, and into a cramped stone room like a cellar. There was a large sign warning troops not to smoke or carry lit matches into this ammunition room. Joe was just peering into a separate chamber beyond when the door slammed shut behind them.

Frank pounded once on the door before realizing that it opened inward. But when he pulled the latch, the door didn't open either. It had been jammed shut.

Still heaving at the door, Frank said, "Joe, look in that other room and see if there's anything we can use for a tool."

Joe was in and out of the room in a second, his face white.

"What's the matter, old gunpowder storage areas make you nervous?" Frank kidded.

But after he spoke, he realized he was seeing some sort of blinking red glow from the other room.

"The ammunition in there is not old," Joe said. "Not unless they had digital timers back in 1869."

Chapter

6

FRANK FORGOT ABOUT the door and rushed into the other chamber. It was a bare, chilly, whitewashed room, with empty old gunpowder barrels.

But sitting on one of the white-painted shelves was something a lot newer. At first, all Frank saw were the flashing red numbers on the timer, ticking down from the three-minute mark. Then he saw the wires leading into a small metal box. A little bit of grayish-yellow gunk that looked like clay oozed out one corner.

Frank knew it wasn't clay—it was plastic explosive.

He moved to the bomb. "This is my job,"

he said quickly to Joe. "You work on trying to get that door open."

Joe ran for the outer door, yelling back, "Can you disarm that thing?"

"Do my best," Frank said. "But there's not much time. Whoever set this wants us to go off with the noontime gun."

"That guy must have been hiding on the far side of this dugout, then sneaked back and pulled the door closed." Joe's voice was full of disgust as he tugged at the door. "He suckered us just fine."

Frank was busy trying to follow the wires from the timer to the plastique. Some of them didn't seem to have any purpose. He took a deep breath and wiped his sweaty palms on his pants. They had to be decoys or booby traps. Two minutes, thirty seconds left.

He quickly traced a red wire into a complicated loop, where three other wires, black, yellow, and blue, twined in. Were they spliced in or just wound around it? Frank took a deep breath. "A Fellawi loop," he muttered out loud, startling himself.

"A what?" Joe asked. He'd given up trying to pull the door open and was now on his back, attempting brute force. He was kicking at it. But the thick old panels resisted him, and the noise of preparing to fire the gun covered any other noises he made.

"Omar Fellawi is the dean of terrorist bomb makers," Frank said, gently probing at the rat's nest of wires. "If the stories about him are true, he taught himself, and doesn't follow any of the usual methods." It calmed Frank to talk—it made it seem that he had time to kill. But he only had two minutes to detonation.

"I didn't know there were rules for making bombs."

"Oh, there are, and they're very strict," Frank said. "I've seen some of the manuals, and there are rules you have to memorize. 'Blue before yellow can kill a fellow.' That's one of them. It means if you disconnect the blue wire before the yellow one, it could set the bomb off." Frank sucked air in through his teeth. A wire had come away in his hand—a blue one.

"And you're saying Fellawi doesn't care what colors he uses?" Joe had jumped to his feet again, scraping away the paint from the door hinges with his pocketknife. But it didn't seem likely that he'd loosen the hinges before time ran out.

"A lot of bomb squad people died before they figured out what he was doing," Frank said, glancing at the timer. One minute, thirty seconds. "Not only that, but he uses these big loops of wire with colors twined together. It's his signature."

"But I guess now that they know about his tricks, they know how to get around them." Joe bit back a curse as the largest blade on his pocketknife snapped when he tried to wedge it under the hinge to lift it off.

"Fellawi thought of that. He keeps changing the colors he uses." Frank stopped trying to separate the wires and called in to Joe, "Bring that knife in here, please, and use this key for attacking that hinge."

Joe traded his knife for Frank's key. But when he returned to the door, he changed tactics and probed the oversize keyhole to see if he could knock loose whatever was jamming it.

Frank delicately traced along each wire with one of the knife's smaller blades. The yellow wire went from the loop to circle around the box containing the explosive, tying it up like a Christmas present. There was no way into the box without cutting the wire. Frank looked at the timer. His vision was blurred with sweat running off his forehead. A finger cleared it. Less than a minute left. He'd have to chance it.

Heart thudding against his chest cavity and blood roaring in his ears, Frank scraped away the insulation on the yellow wire in two places. He wrapped in the piece of loose blue wire. That gave him a bypass circuit—maybe. He slipped the knife under the yellow wire, took what could be his last breath, and slowly raised the knife and snapped the wire.

He didn't even look at the timer as he slipped the box free and frantically dug his way through the plastique.

One deft probe with his fingers and an electrical lead came out of the gook. More careful digging, and a walnut-size metal ball was uncovered. "Booby trap," Frank said. "It's a mercury switch. Any attempt to move the box around would have set it—and the bomb—off."

Just then the noon gun went off far over their heads. Frank loved the quiet inside the bunker. No bomb exploded. It *was* disarmed. Frank smiled, slapped his brother on the back, and remembered to breathe.

"How does it feel to deface Parks Canada property?" Joe asked as they finally removed the hinges and the door.

Frank cocked an eyebrow at him.

Frank and Joe headed down the ramp, then across the drill field toward the exit. "I think an anonymous call to the cops should take care of what's left in there," he said. "And if our friends try to remove the evidence, all the better. Maybe they'll be caught in the act."

They took a different path away from the

Citadel, going down a flight of stairs cut into the hillside.

"How come we're leaving the bad guys' headquarters?" Joe wanted to know as he trailed Frank.

"That's not their headquarters," Frank said. "I started to say that when we saw our friend with the turban. There's too much staff and too many tourists around for any funny business. That bomb there just confirms it."

"I don't get it," Joe said.

"Would you set off a bomb in your base of operations? An explosion would be sure to focus too much attention."

Joe frowned. "Then how come that guy—*and* that bomb—were there?"

"We had to be followed. They brought something up to take care of us and led us right to it." Frank struck off on a downhill street, heading back to Halifax Harbor.

"You think this guy is still tailing us?" Joe asked, glancing over his shoulder.

"I hope so—and don't try to warn him off," Frank said. "Our next stop will give us a chance to isolate him."

They came down on the far side of the ferry terminal, out onto some docks where excursion boats were moored. Frank stepped up to a wooden shack to buy two tickets as a guy with sandy blond hair came screeching up on a bike.

"You guys are lucky that I held up our departure to go to the bank."

They pocketed their tickets, then followed the man to one of the excursion boats already filled with tourists. He led them across the deck, up a staircase, onto the top sundeck, then into the deckhouse. "Ready to cast off!" he called to his two crewmen.

Joe stared. "You're the captain?"

The guy grinned back. "Of the McNab's Island Ferry.

Joe turned to Frank. "So *that's* where we're going."

Frank smiled at Joe. "There're a couple of forts out there." Then he turned to the captain. "Can you hold off for a few more minutes?"

"Why?" the captain wanted to know.

Frank smiled. "I think you'll be getting one more customer."

Sure enough, the turbaned guy with the mustache came tearing down to the pier. The bad news was, there were about six other guys with him. Frank and Joe recognized most of them from their marathon to the ferry the day before.

"Well, you wanted to isolate him," Joe whispered to Frank.

"Looks like I've isolated us instead." Frank

asked the captain, "Mind if we stay up here? We'd like to see you work the harbor."

The captain grinned. "I'd like that. Most people are a little shy about coming up here."

Even the army of seven felt shy. They stayed down on the lower deck, glaring up at the Hardys.

Meanwhile the captain steered a course though Halifax Harbor to the island.

"You know, McNab's Island has a lot of history behind it," the captain said as they slipped into a wide cove with a single large pier. To the south, a neck of land jutted out, a lighthouse on its tip.

"That's Hangman's Beach," the captain said, nodding to the outthrust land. "They used to hang mutineers out there." He shook his head. "There're a lot of bodies—about ten thousand buried under that sand. The French sent an expedition here, and they based themselves on McNab's until storms and sickness nearly wiped them out."

"Where's the fort?" Joe asked.

"Which one?" the captain asked. "Fort Ives is at the north end, and Fort McNab is in the south." He grinned. "Fort McNab is the bigger draw."

Frank asked, "How far to McNab?"

"About a mile and a half from the pier," the captain said.

They were pulling up beside the pier now. A gravel road ran beside the beach, and Frank saw a pickup truck heading toward the pier.

Joe saw it, too. He turned to the captain. "Mind if we help tie up?"

The captain shrugged and reversed engines. Frank and Joe leapt from the sundeck to the pier, tossed the mooring ropes onto their pilings, and ran for the road.

They'd reached the beach before their pursuers had even gotten through the crowd gathered at the gangplank to the pier. Frank was already flagging the pickup down.

"Are you heading anywhere near Fort McNab?" he asked.

The driver leaned out the window. "I can take you partway," he said. "You in a hurry?"

Joe glanced at the thugs elbowing their way through people toward them—blood in their eyes.

"You *could* say that," he admitted.

Chapter
7

THE PICKUP PULLED away as Frank and Joe's
pursuers came tearing down the pier.

When he saw the newcomers, the driver
slowed. "They want to come, too?"

Frank talked fast. "Keep going—please! It's
a scavenger hunt—the first team to reach the
fort wins the point."

"Okay." The driver zipped off, leaving the
mob behind. So far, none of the pursuers had
pulled guns, although the Hardys had noticed
suspicious bulges under several of the guys'
jackets.

"Looks like they've been told to take us
quietly," Joe said. "No witnesses."

"Maybe," Frank said. "But where we're

going, there don't seem to be many tourists."
He stared over the top of the cab as they
bounced along the deeply rutted gravel road.
Ragged trees leaned over them, and the farther
they traveled, the more deserted the island
became.

About half a mile from the pier, another road
branched to the left. Their driver pulled up. "I
turn off here for the lighthouse. Just keep on
the main path," the driver said. "Take the first
branch to the right, it'll take you straight to the
fort."

"Let's get going," Frank said. "Those guys
aren't that far behind us."

"They're sure to see the pickup is empty
now—and this is the only way to go." Joe
pushed their pace to a jog.

The road skirted the lake and sank, turning
downright swampy. Some sections were more
mud than gravel. As they slogged along, they
could hear the sounds of the tide. "Great,"
Joe said. "We've got a lake on one side, and
what sounds like a cove on the other. All those
guys have to do is hang out here and we'll
never be able to get back past them."

"From the looks on their faces, I think we
can bet on their coming after us. Besides"—
Frank slapped at his neck—"if they stand still,
the mosquitoes might carry them off."

Joe slowed down for a second. "What if they

don't want to catch us?'' He turned to Frank. ''We came here to see if this is the fort Dundee meant. If it is, those guys could just be herding us to our slaughter.''

''I was wondering about that back on the truck,'' Frank admitted. ''But I don't think that mob was pretending to be in a sweat to catch us.'' He sighed. ''In fact, I think we may be heading for another dead end, but we've got to check it out.''

Joe gave his brother a quick look. ''Maybe you could find a better way to say that.''

The path began to lead uphill, then they reached the turnoff for the fort. The Hardys picked up the pace. Before their pursuers arrived, they had to investigate the fort and find a hiding place before circling back to the boat.

The path passed through a clump of trees, then opened out. A big sign read Parks Canada—Fort McNab—Danger.

''They got that right,'' Joe muttered as he looked around. He'd been expecting a smaller version of the Halifax Citadel—walls, defensive ditches, buildings, lots of hiding places.

Instead, the builders of Fort McNab had put up no walls at all. When Frank and Joe came out of the woods they were facing a hill, which was only broken here and there by huge, cement-walled rooms carved into its side.

''Bombproof storage,'' Frank said, peering

through a yawning hole where doors and windows had been. "This is where they probably kept the ammunition."

"Ammunition for what?" Joe stared around. "There's nothing here." Except for the dugouts, they were in the middle of nowhere—with nowhere to hide. Except the woods or around the back of the hill. But the thugs would be in the woods by now.

The road curved to their left, around the hill. So the boys hurried on, looking for a hiding place.

Reaching the far side of the hill, they came to a large open space, with three crescent-shaped concrete walls rising about six feet high.

"Gun emplacements," Frank said, chinning his way to the top of the wall. "I can see water down there—this must have been part of the harbor defenses. They could blow away any enemy ship from up here." He looked at the distant shore. "Right now, I wish we were over there."

Behind the first two gun positions was a concrete blockhouse built into the hillside. Frank shook his head as they jogged by. "Too open—nowhere to hide."

At the end of the path there were no more buildings—just a small collection of scattered gravestones. Joe looked at his brother. "A *real* dead end," he said.

Frank pretended not to hear that. "There's still one place we have to check out." He pointed to a pillbox rising on the crest of the slope.

They climbed to the top of the hill and saw a huge stretch of harbor. "This must have been where they aimed the guns," Joe said.

"Great view, but a lousy place to hide," Frank complained.

"Looks like this isn't the fort Dundee meant. And we've run out of places to hide," Joe said.

Frank was about to agree when he saw movement on the other side of the hill, back where the path came out of the woods. Their pursuers had finally caught up. "Down," he snapped at Joe.

Crouched in the tall grass, they counted seven guys, all toting guns. The turbaned leader and one of the others carried mini-Uzis.

"The gang's all here," Joe whispered. "What do we do now?"

Frank watched as the tracking party broke up. "Come on," he whispered. They slithered along until the old pillbox blocked them from sight, then Frank ran down the back of the hillside toward the abandoned blockhouse.

"We want to be lying down and ready when

the first guy comes around this curve," Frank said, pointing at the path. "They're all splitting up to search." He looked his brother in the eye. "We didn't do too well finding a hiding place—but how about grabbing a hostage?"

Moments later Joe lay motionless in the brush, the rank stink of weeds in his nose. He pinched his nostrils. This wasn't the time to sneeze.

They'd chosen their spot carefully—it left them hidden, with a clear view of the path. Now it was down to waiting.

They heard the crunch of footsteps on gravel. Please let him be alone, each boy prayed to himself.

The searcher rounded the curve—he *was* alone. He wore a striped shirt, had a deep tan, and carried a 9 mm Beretta in his right hand. The gun pointed at the ground. He was ambling as if he were on a picnic.

Frank and Joe both rose. This was their chance.

Joe's feet caught the guy in the back. The gunman flopped to the ground, but twisted around and raised his gun. Frank stomped his wrist, then kicked the gun away. Joe came down with a roundhouse right. The guy was out before he had time to yell.

Frank grabbed the gun while Joe dragged their prisoner out of sight behind the blockhouse. Now it all depended on timing. They had to cut down and across the hill before the rest of the seven made it around to their position at the back of the hill.

Just as the Hardys were starting off they heard a shout from quite near. The words didn't make sense—they were in some foreign language—but the message was clear. Someone had discovered that one of their men had disappeared.

The Hardys pulled their prisoner upright and dragged him around to the front of the hill. Now, if there wasn't a guard at the fort entrance . . .

Frank and Joe could hear shouting from the back of the hill now—loud, worried voices calling what was probably their captive's name. They were almost in the clear—the forest was only a few feet away and it would give them all the cover they'd need. But, no. One of the searchers must have backtracked, spotted them, and was now letting out a wild yell.

Frank pivoted and snapped off a shot that pinged against a concrete wall on one of the dugouts. The guy hit the dirt, still yelling.

"Let's hustle," Frank muttered. But their prisoner, who was awake now, did his best to hold them back. He dug in his heels as the boys yanked on his arms. "Look, stupid—"

Frank jammed the gun into the prisoner's side.

"No!" The bellow came from behind them. Frank glanced back to see that the pursuers had formed a line, all with weapons up and leveled straight at them. But they weren't shooting—their turbaned leader had shouted to hold their fire. Probably didn't want them hitting their guy.

The Hardys took off down the trail. This time their fear gave them superhuman strength, and their prisoner bounced easily between them.

But speed was impossible on the stones—either the small pebbles turned under their feet, or the mud slowed them. They could hear the crunch of shoes on the pebbles behind them.

"Don't know if we can beat them this way," Joe gasped. "Maybe we'd better take off for the woods."

"If we were alone." Frank glanced at the prisoner. "Couldn't manage him there."

For Joe, the escape was like a nightmare in which he had to run but his feet were stuck in glue. He plowed along, his head down, gripping the captive's right arm. Mosquitoes swarmed in his face. Just ahead, he heard a bird calling.

Then off to his right, in the woods, he heard the crackle of brush.

"They're circling around us," he said as

they stumbled down in the marshy part of the trail. "If they catch us where the island narrows . . ."

He didn't need to say any more.

The trio staggered a little faster, but Frank and Joe knew it was hopeless. The ambush was just ahead, any time, any place.

They had almost reached the shore of the lake when Frank saw the duck family he'd noticed earlier suddenly lift off from the water. What had scared them? Then, at the edge of the water behind a tree, he saw the telltale edge of a loud sports shirt.

"Joe," he whispered, nodding with his head.

Following Frank's eyes, Joe caught sight of the ambusher. He grinned. "Hold him here a second," he said, bending down to collect a few good-size stones.

He slipped off the path, skirting along the mucky edge of the lake. When he was behind the ambusher, he began hurling rocks at top speed.

The guy stepped back, lost his balance, and toppled into the lake with a splash.

Heads appeared from behind other trees, and Frank sent a couple of bullets whistling over their heads before dropping and taking cover.

The ambush disintegrated into wild shooting and shouting.

"Who's fooling with those blasted fire-works?" an angry voice demanded. From the turnoff leading to the lake stalked two angry tourists from the boat. "It nearly scared us to death."

Guns and ambushers disappeared at the first sign of witnesses. So did Frank, Joe, and the captive—straight for the dock.

Just before they emerged from the forest, Frank suddenly handed Joe the gun and pointed behind them. The prisoner turned to look—and when he did, Frank grabbed his neck, digging into two pressure points. The guy was out.

When the captain saw the Hardys carrying their new friend onto the boat, he asked what had happened to him.

"I don't know," Joe said.

The captain stood at the helm and steered the boat away from the dock. Frank sat beside the "patient" in the cockpit. The captive lolled in his seat, head down, hands dangling between his knees. Joe stood by the door, his eyes on the one stairway that led up to the deck they were on, his hand on the gun in his pocket.

"Captain," Frank said, "you may want to radio the Halifax police. This guy—"

Before he could finish the sentence, the prisoner bolted upright, slammed Frank to one side, and reached for his ankle. Then he was on his feet, four inches of gleaming knife blade in his hand.

"No radio," he said, threatening the captain with his knife. The guy spoke English all along. Then he turned to Joe. "You give me the gun."

Joe had the pistol in his hand, but there was no chance for a clear shot without endangering the captain or his brother. He stepped back out onto the sundeck. The prisoner grabbed the captain, using him for cover as he followed.

"The gun—before I lose patience."

His knife gleamed at the captain's throat now.

Joe had retreated all the way to the ship's rail. The escaped prisoner pursued, pushing the captain ahead of him.

"The gun," the man snarled.

Joe knew that once this guy had the pistol in his hand, it was all over. He had only one choice. . . .

Holding the gun out, he tossed it in a high arc over the rail and into the water below.

The thug's eyes followed the Beretta. And in that moment Joe's fist flashed out. He caught the guy in the side of the head, sending him staggering toward the rail. The captain batted his knife hand away, dodging in the opposite direction.

Before the guy could bring his knife up

again, Joe unleashed a sledgehammer right—
an uppercut that lifted his opponent high into
the air.

Then the guy tumbled back—over the rail
and into the waters of Halifax Harbor.

Chapter

8

"MAN OVERBOARD!" the captain shouted.

From the lower deck, Frank and Joe could hear running footfalls as crewmen and tourists dashed for life preservers.

They easily spotted the guy in the water by the brightly colored shirt he wore. He was floating facedown, the shirt billowing up and over his back. Frank and Joe watched as someone threw out a rope with a life preserver attached.

But the guy in the water didn't even make an attempt for it.

"Something's very wrong here," the captain said, slipping off his shoes and shirt. He dove into the water from the sundeck and swam over to the escaped prisoner. After hooking one arm around him and the other around the life preserver, he let the crew haul them back to the boat.

Frank and Joe ran down to the lower deck in time to help drag the limp form of the prisoner over the side. Laying him facedown, the crew brought his arms up over his head, trying to force any water from his lungs. Only a little came up.

"Let me," Frank said. "I know mouth-to-mouth."

The captain shouted to the pressing crowd, "Give us some room. We have the situation in hand." The tourists moved off.

Frank bent the guy's head back to open the breathing passage. Then he opened the man's mouth, took a deep breath, and pinching the guy's nose, leaned over to pump air into his lungs.

But before he reached the guy's mouth, he flinched and moved back, his eyes watering.

"What's the matter?" Joe demanded.

"He's dead," Frank said simply.

The captain knelt by the man, first feeling for a heartbeat, then for a pulse. "You're right," he said, abruptly standing. "Look at his lips."

Even as they watched, the man's lips were taking on a bluish tinge.

"Cyanosis—a typical indication of lack of oxygen," the captain said. He gave a half smile at Frank's surprised look. "During the school year I go to medical school."

He frowned down at the still form on the deck. "Get a blanket from inside the cabin to cover him up." Then he headed up the stairs, back to his cockpit. "I'd better get on the horn to the police."

His frowning gaze shifted from the body to Frank and Joe. "Shame about the poor guy," he said. "Drowning on such a small amount of water."

A crewman brought a blanket to cover the dead body. "What made you jump back like that?" Joe asked after he left.

"Something I smelled," Frank replied. "He was right about the cyanosis. But that guy didn't turn blue from lack of oxygen. I smelled cyanide on him."

Joe blinked. "Cyanide? You mean someone poisoned him?"

"Nope. I think he poisoned himself," Frank answered. "The smell seemed to come from around his mouth. He may have crushed a pill between his teeth."

"Come on," Joe said in disbelief. "The next thing you're going to tell me is that he's an Assassin." He shook his head and smiled at his brother.

The Hardys had crossed swords with the Assassins before, fighting desperate battles with these terrorists for hire. They'd thwarted an assassination attempt against a presidential candidate and an attempt to cut the Alaskan pipeline.

But those victories had come at a high cost. Iola Morton, Joe's first love, had disappeared in a fireball from an Assassin bomb, a bomb that had been meant for Frank and Joe.

Silence grew as Frank didn't answer his brother.

"I mean, let's get real," Joe said. "Assassins in Halifax?"

Frank shrugged. "You said the same thing about Assassins in Alaska," he said. "Think a minute. This guy follows their method of operation—he died rather than be captured and questioned."

They stood beside the covered form, silent for the twenty-minute ride back to Halifax.

It was dinnertime when the ferry docked, and since the boys were near, they headed for the Hungry Guardsman. Strange, they thought. There were no diners in the outdoor café area, and when Joe pushed against the door, it was locked.

Just as he was turning away, the door popped open, and the pert face of Shauna MacLaren appeared. "Sorry, we're closed—getting ready for a private party."

Then she recognized the Hardys. "Aren't you the guys who gave me a ten and left most of your dinners on the table last night?" she asked. "Are you hoping for a refund?" She grinned at Joe with a flirtatious look in her eye.

"Actually, we were hoping just to come in and finish a meal," Joe said. "But if you're closed—"

"Oh, come on in. I can make you a sandwich at least. I mean, we have a reputation to protect," she said, tossing the words over her shoulder on the way to the kitchen.

With sodas and two thick sandwiches of something called "smoked meat" in hand, Frank and Joe were soon sitting with Shauna in the empty restaurant. Most of the staff were still working in the kitchen, but she'd finished her chores.

They chatted for a few moments before Shauna asked, "So how do you like Halifax?"

The Hardys glanced at each other for a second, then Joe said, "It's not the easiest city we've ever visited." He went on to explain why they'd come there and what misadventures they'd had.

Shauna shook her head. "I heard about that

car exploding on the news. And you've been checking out forts ever since? I wonder if you met my friend Charlie Bell—he's a corporal in the Seventy-eighth this year. We go to school together.''

Her face grew more and more serious as she heard about the incident on the excursion boat. ''So you think he poisoned himself?'' She shuddered.

''What I don't understand is how they found us so quickly,'' Joe said. ''We changed hotels and didn't even get our luggage. When we started out today, we took a long walk, just to see if we did have a tail. And I'll swear we didn't.''

Frank nodded. ''I've been thinking about that, too. They couldn't just have picked up on us at the Citadel. There wouldn't have been time to rig that bomb. They had to have tailed us, or they just happened to see us at Fort Needham Park. And then they overheard our plan to go to the Citadel. It had to be that they just stumbled on us.''

Frank turned to Shauna, an idea forming. ''What's that area like?''

''By the park?'' Shauna asked. He nodded. She shrugged. ''I guess you'd say it was the poor side of town.''

''Well, that's where I think we should start looking.''

67

"For what?" Shauna wanted to know.

"Our attackers. Maybe their headquarters is *near* Fort Needham Park."

Frank looked down at his empty plate. "Whatever that sandwich was, it was great. Are you sure we shouldn't pay for it?"

"Just come back," Shauna said with a grin at Joe. "And, of course, tell all your friends."

Joe grinned back. "I don't know—the last time we brought people in here, they turned out to be pretty rough."

That got a laugh from Shauna.

Right then they were interrupted by a knock on the glass door. Shauna jumped up to answer it. A businessman in a blue suit and briefcase stood there.

"Sorry," Shauna said, shaking her head, "we're closed."

The man shouldered the door open, pointing to Frank and Joe. But Shauna just shook her head more determinedly. *"Closed,"* she said.

That seemed to get through. The man shrugged and set off down the street.

"Sometimes I have to be pretty firm." Shauna looked a little embarrassed, especially since Joe kept looking after the guy.

"There's something not right here," Joe said abruptly. "That guy left his briefcase right by the door."

Leaping up from his seat, he hustled them away from the door and windows—just in time.

The briefcase went up in a roar, filling the space where they'd been sitting with a hail-storm of jagged glass.

Chapter

9

THE BLAST NEARLY caught Frank, Joe, and Shauna in a part of the room that had been cleared for dancing. Joe managed to haul his brother and Shauna behind a table. Shards of broken glass rattled against it, points sticking into the wood.

Frank Hardy shook his head, his ears still ringing from the concussion. Then he began to hear the crackle of the flames. The wooden floor and tables by the door had caught on fire.

"We'd better get out of here," he said, getting to his feet.

"Out the back way!" Shauna grabbed Frank and Joe's arms, leading them away from the rapidly spreading fire.

70

The doors from the kitchen burst open, and a heavyset guy with a big bushy beard came charging up, holding a fire extinguisher. A quick look told Frank that wouldn't be enough to beat this blaze. He followed Joe and Shauna through the swinging doors and found himself confronting the whole kitchen staff.

"What's going on?" asked a young guy with carrot-colored hair. He wore an apron over jeans and a T-shirt and held a knife in his hand. Frank figured he must be an assistant cook.

"You wouldn't believe us if we told you," Shauna said.

"Have you called the fire department?" Frank asked.

The guy stared. "Why? Bob's out there with the fire extinguisher."

A moment later Bob came swinging back in through the doors, coughing his head off. "Too much," he gasped. "Call the fire—"

A blare of sirens cut him off. Someone else must have noticed the smoke.

"Out, out." Bob made shooing gestures, and the kitchen staff meekly headed out the rear door. Wisps of smoke were now coming through the thin gap between the swinging doors.

Frank and Joe followed Shauna out the door as the first wave of fire fighters arrived.

"Well," said Joe, "I don't think there'll be a party tonight."

Shauna nodded, a little forlorn. "Tonight—and quite a few other nights," she agreed. Then her face became furious looking. "Imagine the nerve of that guy! He could have killed us."

"I think that was the idea," Frank said a little dryly. Then to his brother he said, "Those other six guys must have sneaked back on the boat when we weren't looking."

Then his face grew even more serious. "Too bad we didn't get a look inside that case," he said. "I'd have liked to see if that bomb had a Fellawi loop."

"A who-what?" Shauna asked.

"My brother's a bomb buff," Joe told her. "He knows everybody's trademarks." More to Frank, he pointed out, "If you'd gone to take a look, the bomb would have blown up in your face."

Shauna poked them both. "So—what do we do now?"

Frank grinned. "That's usually Joe's line—and what do you mean, 'we'?"

"Well, these terrorists or whatever they are have just put me out of a job," she said. "It seems only fair that I should get a shot at revenge. Besides," she pointed out, "you really need someone who knows the town. Otherwise, you'll just waste more time looking at empty forts."

Frank looked at Joe. "Looks like we've got ourselves a native guide."

"A very *pretty* native guide." He turned to Shauna. "Okay, lead us to Fort Needham—a nice, confusing route, to give anybody following us a headache."

"Right." Shauna led them around the block, where an ancient stone facade hid an ultramodern hotel. She led them through the elegant lobby, past a row of shops, then up an escalator. They found themselves on another shopping arcade, with a walkway at the end leading to another building.

As they walked above the early evening traffic, Frank and Joe looked back to see if they could spot a tail. Nobody was there.

"I've seen a lot of these walkways downtown," Joe said. "Why do you use them instead of walking in the fresh air?"

"If you were here in the winter, you wouldn't ask," Shauna replied. "Besides, it beats climbing up and down hills, which isn't fun in ice and snow."

In the next building she led them through several shops and made a couple of unexpected turns, again to shake or isolate any tails. None showed up.

Shauna then took them out a back entrance,

around the mall, down several streets, three-quarters of the way around a churchyard, and then finally to Gottingen Street.

Joe shook his head in defeat. "If that didn't turn up anyone following us, I'd say we were in the clear."

"Right," said Frank. "Let's head for the park—and keep our eyes open."

They reached Fort Needham without seeing anything out of the ordinary. "I don't get it," Frank said, leaning against the strange bell tower on the bluff. His eyes bored out toward the harbor in the distance. "If they caught us once, why couldn't they catch us again?"

"Dumb luck?" Joe suggested, sitting on the grass to rest his feet. Shauna sat beside him.

"I don't like to credit things to luck," Frank said. "It's not logical, rational, or—I don't believe this!"

He stepped back against the cement of the bell tower, keeping out of someone's sight. "Joe," he said calmly, trying to keep the excitement out of his voice, "look who's here."

Easily—with no fast movements to catch anyone's attention—Joe rose to his feet. He turned as if he were talking to Shauna, then glanced over to where Frank was looking.

He couldn't believe his eyes. There, walking down a path in the park with the sun very low in the sky behind him, was their old pal, the guy in the turban. Now he was leaving the path and heading down a grassy slope to a side street.

From their position on top of the bluff, the Hardys and Shauna could see his course clearly.

"What do you think?" Joe said. "He didn't act like he saw us. He didn't act like he was looking for us. Maybe he's doing just what it looks like—maybe he's just cutting across the park."

"Or maybe," Frank said, "he's setting us up again. I'd hate to get locked up in a room with another bomb."

"I say we follow him." Joe started along the path, hands in his pockets, as if he were taking a stroll.

Mr. Mustache never looked back as the side street became a flight of stairs, leading down to the waterfront area.

"I wonder what he wants down by the dock?" Shauna said.

That end of the harbor didn't have the bustling energy they'd seen on piers on the rest of the waterfront. Railroad tracks, a warehouse or two, and what looked like a sheet-metal shop made up most of the landscape.

The building their quarry headed for was definitely a rundown warehouse. It took the three a little while to get close. The area was flat pavement, like a gigantic parking lot. They couldn't risk being seen by the turbaned man—even if he wasn't looking back.

Using what cover they could, they finally made it to the building. The door stood wide open.

"Shauna," Frank whispered, "you stay here as lookout. Give us a whistle if anyone comes along."

She nodded, taking a position by the corner of the building.

Frank and Joe stole inside. Dead ahead of them, across the vast room, were wide-open loading bays. No one was around. To their right were storage bays, with a hodgepodge of small-ish boxes, bales, and crates.

"So, can you tell me if the ship has finally been unloaded?" The voice came from a glassed-in office in the left corner of the floor. The Hardys didn't have to worry about being spotted—nobody had washed the glass in years.

Frank frowned. The voice had a trace of an accent. But he couldn't quite place it.

Joe and he darted for shelter behind some boxes when they heard the office door rattle.

"I knew it was important to you, Mr. Singh." A man in a stained jacket came out of the room, followed by the turbaned guy. "That's why I kept an eye out for it. Came in just this afternoon, so I kept it out special. You were lucky I decided to work late tonight."

The man stopped in the middle of the room to pat a long, bulky packing case. "See? She's right here. Pity you didn't bring your truck."

"Can I use your phone? I'll call for the truck."

"Fine, and then we'll go over the shipping papers."

Frank and Joe stayed low in the shadows as the two men headed back to the office.

As soon as the door was closed, they sneaked over to the crate. A shipping manifest was taped to the rough wood, along with a bill of lading.

Frank quickly scanned over entries like factor, port of embarkation, transshipment point, until— "Here it is—consignee. That's the person who's supposed to receive it."

He read the name typed beside the form entry. "Forte Brothers, Inc."

He raised an eyebrow at Joe. "I think we've found our fort."

Chapter

10

"BUT I'D LIKE to know what kind of presents these Forte Brothers are getting," Joe said. He looked around for a crowbar or anything to wedge the crate open.

Just then Shauna's whistle sounded from outside.

Joe dashed for the doorway, then back. "There're the lights of a car in the distance, and it seems to be heading this way."

Frank took off running for a corner of the warehouse, where he'd spotted a forklift truck. "Joe, start looking through those storage bays. We need a crate about the size and shape of this one."

While Joe darted down the alleyways of the

bays, Frank turned on the engine of the fork-lift. All this frantic action took place in nearly absolute silence. Joe's footfalls were smoth-ered by the rubber soles of his running shoes. And the forklift had an electric motor, which only gave off a low hum as Frank maneuvered it to the crate.

Frank lined up the blades of the forklift with the openings in the wooden skid under the box. It took him only a moment of fumbling to figure out how to lift the fork up so he could move the crate away. He quickly got the knack, and soon was trundling the crate to the back of a storage bay where Joe stood. Joe was beckon-ing frantically and pointing down the bay. Half-way down the alley was a crate nearly identical to the one Frank had just moved.

Frank dropped off his cargo and maneuvered in to pick up the new box. He whispered to Joe, "Go and take the papers off the crate—*carefully*. We don't want a torn packing slip making them suspicious when we put those papers on the new crate."

With the new crate secured on the forklift, Frank spun and drove out to the spot where the original crate had been. The car must be at the warehouse by now, and he hoped Shauna had sense enough to hide.

He carefully lowered the crate, disengaged the fork, and backed up. Joe ran over to the crate and smoothed on the papers he'd taken from the original crate.

Frank drove quickly to put the truck back where he'd found it. Just as he was jumping from the driver's seat, he heard the sound of a vehicle pulling up outside and the honk of a horn.

The office door opened, and Frank dove for cover behind the forklift.

Joe was out in the open, standing next to the crate. A good twenty feet of open space separated him from the nearest storage bay. Realizing he'd be seen if he made a run for it, he ducked down behind the crate.

The warehouse manager and Mr. Singh, as he was called, stepped out of the office. "These must be my people now," Singh said.

Joe held his breath. Would they notice anything odd? The forklift wasn't exactly where it had been. Neither was the crate. But the two men hardly gave the area a second glance.

Joe let out an inaudible sigh of relief as he heard their footsteps move away from him. He peeked around the side of the crate to see the backs of the two men heading for the warehouse door.

A van stood just outside, its doors open. This was the only chance he'd get. Rising to his feet, Joe darted noiselessly for the nearest bay—and safety. In seconds he had worked his way down an alley and found a nice pile of boxes to hide behind.

Frank had slipped from behind the forklift to find a hiding spot, too. He watched as Singh, the warehouse manager, and three other guys approached the crate in the center of the floor. The manager pawed around in his soiled jacket, finally coming up with a pen. "Sign here and here, and the shipment's yours."

He sighed. "Must be tough for the relatives to wait for it to come by boat. Pretty sad."

"Sadness is our business," Singh replied. "And it was a monetary decision for them. Air freight is so very expensive."

The manager was still shaking his head as he walked over to the forklift. He turned it on, then expertly whipped it around, bringing it over to the crate. "Better move your van to the loading dock," he said. "It'll be easier."

The manager then drove the forklift and its burden over to the open side of the warehouse. He was silhouetted against the darkening sky, easing the machine down to the end of the loading bay.

The van backed up to the dock, then Singh and one of the other guys stepped out of the back doors, carrying something between them. Neither Frank nor Joe could see it clearly. But it seemed to be a collapsible metal frame on wheels.

They set it up on the floor of the bay. Several grunts later, they had the box on their collapsible stretcher and wheeled it into their van.

Singh waved goodbye to the manager, then he took off.

After driving the forklift back to the far wall, the warehouse manager strolled back to his office.

Joe could hardly wait for him to close the door. He'd found a crowbar, and he was itching to get the top off the mystery crate. He popped out of his hiding place.

Frank appeared, too, and headed past Joe to the door. "I'm going to tell Shauna what's going on," he whispered. "She's probably getting worried out there."

"Uh, right," Joe agreed. He tapped the crowbar in his open palm. "Well, I'll get started on the crate."

"Just do it quietly," Frank said. "Any sound of splintering wood will bring our friend out."

As if on cue, a muffled noise came from inside the office—the sounds of a war. Joe grinned as he heard a cavalry bugle, gunshots, and war cries. "He must have a TV in there," he said. "As long as the shooting keeps up, we can afford a little noise."

Nothing appeared to be stirring outside— then Frank caught a flicker of movement. It was Shauna, peeking round the corner of the building.

"Frank!" she gasped. "I didn't know what had happened to you."

"We pulled a switcheroo," he explained to her. "The box they left with wasn't the box they came for."

"Where's Joe?" Shauna wanted to know.

"Inside, opening the real crate. We want to know what these guys were supposed to get."

Curious, Shauna started toward the door. Frank gently took her arm to stop her. "We need you out here still. Our box isn't going to fool those guys very long—just till they open it up. Keep an eye out for them. As soon as you see them coming, warn us. Okay?"

Shauna pouted for only a second but then had to admit that Frank was right. "But I want a blow-by-blow description," she warned.

Frank grinned. "Joe has an instant camera. He'll take pictures."

He went back inside to bring his brother up to date. Joe had loosened all the nails on three sides of the box, and was working on the last one. He chuckled when Frank told him of his promise. "Well, I've got the camera right here," he said, touching a pocket in his summer-weight jacket. "I suppose we'll need the evidence, anyway."

Joe pried up the last of the nails, then silently

pulled the lid of the crate free. He propped the lid against a pile of boxes, then turned back to watch Frank burrow through packing material.

"So, what is it?" Joe asked.

Frank had finally scooped enough of the packing stuff out of the way and stared down.

"Would you believe a coffin?" he asked.

Chapter

11

FRANK AND JOE both leaned in and began sweeping the packing material out with their arms. Together, they cleaned off the whole top, creating a snowstorm of polystyrene peanuts.

The box inside the crate was dull silver in color, about seven feet long and three feet wide. The top was in two sections, with a hairline crack between them.

As he stared down at the grim-looking shape, Joe Hardy had to admit that his brother's first guess was right. They were looking at a coffin.

"Well, this explains what Singh was talking about," Frank said. "Remember when he was talking with the manager? He said something like, 'Sadness is our business.'"

Joe nodded. "Yeah. I guess if we looked up Forte Brothers in the phone book we'd find out that they're funeral directors."

"Probably," Frank agreed. He stared at the coffin for a moment, poked against the top, and then looked over at his brother. "You have your Swiss army knife? I need a screwdriver."

"What do you need a screwdriver for?" Joe asked. Then, when he figured it out, he looked at Frank's determined face, appalled. "Oh, no," he said. "Wait a minute. You're not going to open this thing, are you?"

"Just the top half," Frank admitted.

Joe stared. "You've finally lost it completely. We *know* what's in there. Who are you expecting to find, Count Dracula?"

"We don't *know* what's in there," Frank replied. "But I think we ought to find out." He held out his hand for the knife.

Joe Hardy finally dug it out and handed it over. "This coffin has spent *weeks* on some freighter," he said. "Remember what the manager said about the relatives waiting. Are you sure you want to open it? I mean, after all, what would you expect someone to ship to a funeral parlor?"

"You're forgetting that these guys aren't normal funeral directors." Frank bent over and reached under the sides of the coffin, feeling for the screws that held the top closed. "They shoot guns and leave bombs around. That's not normal—unless Halifax has a shortage of dead people and they're drumming up business.''

"It all sounds weird to me.'' Joe shook his head in disbelief.

"No, it all makes a horrible kind of sense,'' Frank insisted as he worked on the screws. "A phony funeral home would be a perfect cover. I mean, who would bother a mortician? And if he has the odd body to get rid of, it couldn't be easier—''

He grunted as a tight screw resisted him for a second. "And if you were smuggling things into a country, what better way than in a coffin? Who'd check it out?'' A little more work, then Frank straightened up suddenly. "That's it. The top should lift off.''

Joe stepped away from the coffin. "What if you're wrong? This could be pretty gross.'' He shuddered. "Horrible, I mean.''

"Don't be silly.'' Still, Frank took a deep breath before he swung the top open.

He looked in and quickly shut the lid. The coffin wasn't empty—it did contain a body.

"See, I told you,''Joe said.

But Frank slowly eased the lid up again for another look. This time he reached in and dug his fingernail into the face of the body.

"Have you gone crazy?'' Joe said louder than he'd intended.

"Nope. And this isn't skin under my nail. It's wax. At first glance the dummy looks real, but it's made of wax."

When he pulled down the blanket covering the body, Frank found a little door in the left-hand side of its chest. Joe stared. The door was right where the heart would be on a living person.

"This poor guy isn't getting a very comfortable final rest." Joe tried a joke to cover up for his earlier nervousness. "I thought most coffins had padded silk linings. Look at this." He ran a finger along the dull, grayish black metal that lined the box. His fingernail scratched a line in it. "What is this stuff, anyway?"

Frank scratched at it, too, managing to break a thin piece off. "Lead foil, I think." He frowned, then quickly tossed the piece back into the coffin.

Meanwhile, Joe had pulled his camera out of his pocket. "I guess we ought to take some pictures," he said. "What do you think? Full face or profile? Should we shoot him lying down or sitting up?" he asked, his sense of humor returning.

Frank bent down, reaching across the coffin to the dummy's left side. "At least we should take out whatever's inside."

He hesitated a second. Something very unpleasant could be hidden inside the dummy.

Then he braced himself, grabbed the little handle on the door, and pulled.

"Huh!" Joe said, disappointed. "I thought we'd find jewels or something. But that—I don't even know what that is."

Tucked deep inside the cavity in the dummy's chest was a small metal cylinder, maybe two inches high and one inch wide. The outside was highly polished.

"Looks like stainless steel," Joe said. "I don't see any openings. Maybe it twists apart." He set his camera down on the dummy's chest and started to reach into the opening for the mysterious metal container.

Frank's hand moved like a striking snake, clamping on to Joe's wrist. "Don't touch it," he said.

Joe twisted in surprise and dropped his little instant camera into the opening. "Okay," he said. "Could I at least take a picture?"

He snatched up the instant camera and stepped back to snap the coffin, its strange inhabitant, and the bizarre opening with its mysterious cargo.

"Now don't move," he said playfully, his finger going for the shutter release. But he never took the picture.

"Hey, guys."

Joe turned at the sound of running feet.

Shauna was peering down the shadowy loading bay, trying to find them.

"Over here," Frank said.

She froze when she got close enough to see what they were bending over. Shauna stared for a second, then pulled herself together. "We've got to get out of here," she said.

Frank glanced toward the door. "They're back?"

Shauna nodded. "With reinforcements, it looks like. There's another set of lights behind the van's. And they're both driving like maniacs."

Frank slapped down the little door in the dummy's chest, then closed the top of the coffin.

He turned to pick up the wooden lid for the crate, then shook his head. "We don't have time to hide our tracks. Let's just get out."

The three of them turned and were dashing for the loading docks just as squealing brakes and angry horns announced the arrival of Singh and his men.

Chapter

12

FRANK, JOE, AND Shauna jumped from the loading dock down to the bay, where they'd be less likely to be seen.

Crouched down, they made their way toward the edge of the building. The sooner they put a brick wall between themselves and the uproar going on behind them, the better.

Leaning against the wall, Frank could hear Singh yelling and screaming at the warehouse manager. The poor manager, of course, couldn't understand the mix-up. At least six other voices joined in the shouting.

Then the voices split up, accompanied by lots of banging and crashing. "Sounds like they've decided to search the place," Frank said. "Let's get out of here while they're still busy."

With the warehouse behind them, they tried to figure an escape route. To their right was the harbor itself, to their left the bluffs that cut the dock off from the rest of the city. At the top of the bluffs was a heavily traveled street. But getting there wouldn't be easy. The wide-open spaces around the warehouse would make them easy targets even in the dark.

In the near distance rose a redbrick warehouse, with the name "Collins" in white letters over the well-lit door. In between them and the brick warehouse were a couple of old freight cars on a railroad siding. That was it for cover. They'd be as exposed as a bug on a clean tablecloth if they made a run for it. But it was their only choice.

The yelling inside the warehouse went up another notch. "They must have found the coffin," Joe said.

Frank started out for one of the freight cars. "Come on! They'll be looking for us in a minute. We have to be out of direct sight by then."

By the time they'd darted behind the first freight car, they could hear a car engine turn over. "I don't know how you expect us to outrun a car," Shauna said.

Frank didn't answer. He was calculating

their chances of making it to the next piece of cover.

About thirty feet on was an old piece of machinery that had been blocked by the freight car. The question was, could they reach it before the searchers got that far in their car?

He looked at Joe, who shrugged. "Let's go for it."

They took off, Joe in the lead, Shauna following, Frank bringing up the rear. About halfway to their goal, they heard the whine of an engine and the screech of tires.

A compact car was zooming up directly at them.

"You guys keep going," Frank said. "I'll try to get them off your backs."

Joe knew what Frank was up to. He took Shauna's hand, leading her in a wild dash to the far side of the rusted machinery.

Frank ran for the near side, staying out in the open. He'd seen what he wanted in the headlight beams—a metal bar sticking out of the side of the decaying mass. Once it had been a controlling lever, but now it was just a foot-long piece of garbage, held on by rust.

As Frank ran past, he grabbed the bar and heaved. It came off almost too easily, making him stumble.

The car veered after him. As it approached, Frank was caught in the glare from its headlights. He swung around, whipping the metal bar at the car.

His weapon flew true, working even better than he'd expected. It shuddered along the car's hood, leaving a long, jagged scratch, and then it smacked into the windshield, cracking it into a hundred tiny lines.

The little car veered wildly as the driver screamed something. Frank grinned. The guy jammed on the brakes, actually stopping the car so he could lean out the window to take a shot at Frank.

While the driver's friend hauled him back in, Frank tried to increase the distance between them.

In the meantime, Joe and Shauna were running for the warehouse. It was up to Frank to keep the bad guys' attention on himself so they could make it.

The driver was back in the car now, and he had only one thing in mind—to run Frank Hardy down. The scary thing was, his aim was good.

The little car's engine was gunned, and suddenly it seemed to roar at twice its size.

Fortunately, Frank had a better turning radius than it had. He jumped to the side, and started running back to the rusted-out machinery.

The driver jammed on the brakes, sent the

car spinning wildly in a tight turn, and came after him again. Apparently, he wanted to turn Frank into a large oil spot on the pavement.

Frank dodged again, away from the machinery this time, but the car plowed on in a straight line. The driver had misjudged the angles a little. His right fender caught and scraped on the rusted mass, letting out a hideous screech.

Frank paid no attention, running for a trailer someone had parked beside the redbrick warehouse. It would give Frank lots of room to maneuver and hide behind—if he lived to make it there.

Behind him, Frank heard the car scream to life again, and the driver continued his game of cat and mouse. He was sure to blow out his engine if he kept driving that way. Maybe, though, the driver felt that would be okay, if he could just run Frank down.

Legs pumping, Frank risked a look over his shoulder. The car was aimed straight at him. He looked ahead. That trailer was too far—Frank knew he couldn't outrun the little monster. He'd have to dodge. Last time, he'd dodged left. This time he'd go right.

From the sound, Frank knew the car had blown its muffler. It now sounded like a racing machine as it thundered on. Frank glanced back again. How could he have thought of that car as small? It was huge—and only twenty feet behind him!

He faked left, then dove right. The driver hooked his car left, missed Frank, and went into a hair-raising skid as he jammed on the brakes and his wheels locked.

Frank leapt to his feet and ran like a maniac. The car was now in a position to cut him off. All that mistreatment must be affecting the car's handling, Frank hoped.

He refused to look at the car, concentrating only on the trailer ahead. But his side vision caught the movement of the car. It was zooming straight for him.

He stepped into a pothole he couldn't see because it was so dark and he fell.

It was a lucky fall. If he'd gone two steps farther, he'd have been right in the path of the speeding car.

It fishtailed through another crazy U-turn to come back. Frank had barely enough time to get up and throw himself to safety under the trailer before the car flew past him again.

This time, instead of screaming into another turn, the car screeched to a jerky stop, and two guys got out. Frank wondered if they really wanted to catch him or if they were just afraid of their friend's driving.

Well, he couldn't stay there and let the ground troops drive him out of cover. While the guys were still getting out of the car, Frank sprinted for the warehouse.

This building was long and thin—a rectangle—with loading bays on both sides. As he ran for the nearest bay, Frank could see straight through the building to the other side. The perfect short-cut—provided the two goons didn't station themselves on the far side.

He heard the car spin its wheels, but he knew he had it beat to the warehouse. Catching a ragged breath, Frank threw himself at the nearest loading dock—and nearly went into shock as a pair of strong arms gripped him.

Joe grinned down at him. "I thought you'd done enough," he said, walking into the warehouse with Frank. "While you kept those clowns occupied, I managed to get Shauna all the way over to the bluffs. There's a sort of path up there, and this bozo won't be able to drive after us. I guess we're lucky they didn't know at the warehouse what we did. They had to split up to search for us. Speaking of which"—he pointed to the bays on the far side of the building—"those goons plan to catch you as soon as you go out over there."

His grin got wider. "But they won't be expecting two of us, and I'm rested, so I can take the heat from the driver for a while." He led the way across the warehouse floor. "I have a plan."

Joe was right—the two guys weren't expecting two people to come out of the warehouse. Guns in hand, they'd positioned themselves at either end of the building, so that if Frank came for one, the other could cover him. When an attacker leapt on both of them, however, they weren't ready.

Frank jumped on his guy from the loading dock. The gunman dropped like a sack of potatoes. Joe had his man pinned to the ground, grappling with him. He gestured with his head for Frank to get going.

As Frank ran, he heard the sound of the compact car's engine laboring around the warehouse building. This was bad. There was no place to hide at all—just a few stunted weed-trees, and beyond them, railroad tracks. The tracks could throw the car out of control if it hit them, but that wouldn't stop the driver from going for *him*.

Then, as the car swerved around to aim for Frank, two shots rang out. He turned back and saw Joe smashing his adversary's gun hand against the ground.

Frank couldn't believe it. One bullet had taken out the car's left headlight, the other, the left front tire.

The driver had a new target now. His car barreled at Joe, who jumped safely aside. The driver came close to hitting his own man, who now lay out of it on the ground.

Joe got up and trotted, tauntingly slow, toward the far end of the building. It took the driver a little longer to take his battered car through the turnaround. But when he saw Joe almost reach the corner of the building, he floored the gas pedal to get him.

The car shimmied wildly but moved as fast as a rocket. Joe pretended to be unaware that it was coming, as he strolled toward the corner.

But when Joe did turn and saw the car, a look of horror crossed his face. He'd made his move too late. Even if he got around the corner, the driver could cut him down.

Joe raced around the corner and flattened himself against the building as the little car pursued him on two wheels.

The car slammed into a telephone pole. It shuddered and fell down right on the hood of the car.

That ended the chase.

The steep climb up the overgrown path wasn't easy, but Frank, Joe, and Shauna handled it quickly. They didn't want to be hanging around when their pursuers regained consciousness.

Shauna found a pay phone to call the police to report the accident. If those guys needed any help, they'd get it. In the meantime, they hoped, the police would keep them off the streets for a while.

"Where to?" Joe asked.

"Back to Fort Needham for a moment," Frank said.

"But it's dark," Joe said.

"It's lit up at night and looks very beautiful," Shauna said.

"I just want someplace pleasant where I can think," Frank replied. While he'd been busy escaping and running for his life, he hadn't had a chance to put together all the things he'd seen. Now . . .

Frank sat on the grass, smiling as Joe shot a flash picture of Shauna with his camera. Joe frowned at the result.

"Look at this," he complained. "The picture's all foggy—as if it had already been exposed. What do you think, Frank? Is it bad film? Or did I break the cam—"

Joe broke off when he saw Frank looking at the film as if it were a nightmare come true. "Come on, it's just a bad picture."

"Take another one," Frank ordered him. "Just shoot—anything."

Shrugging at Frank's weird reaction, Joe took another picture of Shauna. It was just as foggy as the first.

"This isn't a new load of film, is it?" Frank sounded as if he were interrogating Joe. "You took a perfectly clear shot of me in the airport.''

"It's the same film," Joe said. "What's the big deal?"

"I know how the film got ruined," Frank said. "Remember how the camera fell on that little metal canister inside the dummy? That's what did it.''

"Did what?" Shauna asked.

"It irradiated the film." Frank looked at them with growing horror in his eyes. "That metal slug had a little pellet of something very radioactive inside. That's why those guys were so upset when we opened up the coffin and found it.''

His voice dropped lower as he stared at the ruined prints. "We just saw a piece of an atomic bomb.''

Chapter

13

"AN ATOMIC BOMB?" Shauna said, stumbling over the words in disbelief. "Here in Halifax? You must be joking."

Frank shook his head, ice growing in his stomach. "Actually, it makes a terrible sort of sense. Halifax is a big port city, with lots of ships—and people—passing through from all over the world. It's a Canadian city, a perfect place for the Assassins to launch a plot against the U.S. And there are three thousand miles of friendly border to smuggle it across—unless they bring it down by boat."

He looked slowly from the pictures to Shauna. "In fact, I couldn't think of a better place on the East Coast to assemble and build a nuclear bomb.''

She stared at him in complete shock. ''Well—we've got to do something about it! Tell the government! Tell the police!''

Joe sighed deeply. ''We can try,'' he said.

''Try?'' Shauna burst out.

''I think what Joe is trying to say is that we don't have much hard proof,'' Frank explained. ''A lot of things have happened— bombs going off, people getting hurt, even killed. But the police would have to take our word to pull it all together.''

''And cops aren't exactly eager to take a kid's word about something like this,'' Joe finished up for him. ''They think we get weird ideas from watching too many spy movies and just tune us out.''

Joe shook his head. ''The one contact we had on the force was Gerry Dundee. He found out something fishy was going on at Forte Brothers, and they shut his mouth for him.''

''We played it very straight, telling the police everything that happened since we arrived in town,'' Frank said. ''And the detective in charge just shrugged it off.''

''Think how he'd react if we came in and told him that his case ties in with some kind of nuclear terrorism plot.'' Joe's lips were a hard, thin line.

"But this is important!" Shauna wailed.

"Think about it for a minute," Joe said gently. "If you hadn't been along with us and we told you this story, would *you* believe it?"

"I . . . well, I would—" Finally, Shauna nodded. "I would think you were out of your minds. Back at the Hungry Guardsman, when you first started telling me all this stuff, I thought you were pulling my leg. Then that guy tried to blow the place up!"

Frank smiled. "Explosions are usually a good way to persuade people. But I'm afraid we can't depend on somebody planting a bomb at police headquarters when we go to talk to them." His smile faded. "We need some proof—something a lot stronger than foggy pictures and a story about a coffin. They won't go for a search warrant unless we have some solid proof."

"Luckily, we don't need search warrants— and we know where to find some proof." Joe began pacing back and forth. "So, where do the Forte Brothers do business?"

"I couldn't tell you that," Shauna said, heading out of the park. "But I'll lead you to the nearest phone book."

They found a telephone directory at a corner café a few blocks down from Fort Needham Park.

"Here it is," Shauna said, paging through

the directory. "It's about nine blocks from here, back the way we came, in the Hydrostone."

"The whozie-stone?" Joe asked.

"You know those houses behind Fort Needham Park?" Shauna said.

Frank and Joe nodded.

"It's a housing project," Shauna explained, "built in an area that was completely devastated. Hydrostone is a kind of concrete block—that's what they used to build the houses."

"Well, what do you say we head back there?" Joe said.

The others nodded. "But first I have to pick up a couple of things back at the hotel," Frank said.

Walking down the street that was listed as the address of Forte Brothers, they passed a line of closed and dark shops. The funeral home was in the middle of the block. No lights showed in the windows or on its porch.

Frank led the way to the end of the block and made a right. "There's too much street traffic to go in the front," he said. "Let's see how the back looks."

Joe had been expecting that. "It's the fourth house from the end. We'll just count our way up."

The stores backed up on a spacious alleyway, which they shared with the rear of a line of houses.

"Not as crowded," Frank muttered. "But we'll have to be quiet, unless we want the neighbors looking over our shoulders."

From the windows of one house, they could hear the theme music of a popular TV show.

"I think they've got other things to watch than us," Joe said.

"Let's hope so," Frank muttered, "because we're going in."

It turned out that they didn't need to count houses. Parked behind Forte Brothers was a dead giveaway—the company hearse. They hid behind it as they made their way up to the back door.

Frank slid the screen door open, bracing it with his knee. Then he knelt by the doorknob, slipping a little box with wires out of his pocket.

Shauna watched wide-eyed. "What's that?" she asked.

"It started out as a circuit tester. I made a few modifications." Frank touched the wires to the doorknob, then ran them up and down the space between the door and the frame. A light flashed on the box.

"Trouble," Frank whispered. "They've got an alarm on the door. Open it up, and a siren sounds."

"Does this mean we can't get in?" Shauna asked.

"It means we use the door as a last resort," Joe explained. He backed up to check the windows.

"Frank, look at the last window on the right—the one behind the bush."

Frank slid over, reached up, and felt around. "Bathroom window," he whispered. "We're in luck. Somebody left it open." Even so, he checked carefully for pressure pads or contacts in the window frame before he shoved the window up.

Then he switched on a miniflashlight, and shielding it with his hand, checked the tiled windowsill.

"People have a bad habit of leaving things on bathroom windowsills," Joe explained to Shauna. "If we knocked anything over coming in, it would land on the tile floor with a nice, loud crash."

"You think there still could be people inside?" She stared up at the dark windows.

"We don't know. So we'll play it safe."

Frank was leaning in the window now, playing his light around the room. He wasn't shielding it anymore. "The door's closed. I'm going in."

The creeping bush that grew up past the

107

window made the opening quite small, but Frank swung himself in.

Joe laced his fingers together to make a cup of his hands. "Put your foot in here," he told Shauna. "You're next."

With a boost from Joe, she made it in silently. Then Joe had to squeeze in.

He pulled out his own flashlight and glanced around the room. "Doesn't look like they're hiding the bomb in here," he whispered. "Where do we go next?"

Frank glanced back. "Kill the light." He stood with his ear to the door, listening. When he was sure no one was outside, he turned the doorknob and eased the door open. It made the slightest squeak, but no one came to investigate.

The hallway outside was carpeted—they could tell that much by feel. It was also totally dark. Frank and Joe flashed their lights in opposite directions. They saw a small sitting room by the front door, and two funeral chapels, one large, one smaller.

Joe also found a stairway with a small arrow pointing down and a sign that said Office.

"Let's check it out," Frank whispered.

At the foot of the stairs was a small, walled-in area with a door marked Private. Beyond that was a large, shadowy open area.

They tried the office first. It was a mess.

Piles of paper rose in one corner of the room. Frank went to check them, and they turned out to be nothing more than the business records of the firm. On top of the pile was a contract stating that the Forte Brothers had sold their business to somebody named Jihan Singh. He wondered if that was the Indian equivalent of John Smith.

Joe, in the meantime, was concentrating on a desk, which was littered with wires and tools. He touched a soldering iron, some resistors, and a digital timer, which he held up. "Look familiar?" he asked.

"I seem to remember disassembling something rather like that," Frank admitted. He flashed his light around. "This might be the workbench, but I don't see the finished product in here."

They stepped out of the office and into the larger space. As they flashed their lights around, they saw it was a salesroom. Racks lined the walls, with various styles of coffins on display.

Joe gave a low whistle. "I don't believe this," he said.

In the center of the room was what must have been the Cadillac of coffins. It was a metallic box about half the size of a luxury car and colored a carefully polished deep bronze.

The handles looked like solid gold, and probably cost as much as any three other caskets.

But unlike any of the other caskets, this one was closed. All the rest of the models were open.

Frank had a weird feeling the moment he saw this behemoth. He was stepping toward it, reaching out with his hand, when the lights suddenly snapped on.

Jihan Singh's voice rang out in the small room.

"It wouldn't be wise to touch that, Frank Hardy. There are conventional dangers as well as a nuclear one."

Chapter

14

SINGH WAS NOT alone. At least four other guys backed him up, all of them pointing Uzis or MAC-10 submachine guns at Shauna and the Hardys.

"How did you know we were here?" Joe asked, not caring about the firepower trained on him.

Singh smiled at him. "I'm surprised that you didn't notice the motion detectors. Each room has one. But, my dear Joe—you don't mind that I call you Joe?—we were *expecting* you." His smile got wider and brighter under his huge black mustache. "Why do you think we left that window open?"

Frank and Joe looked at each other, feeling like perfect chumps.

"So, now we have the famous Frank and Joe Hardy, and a lovely friend." Singh turned to Shauna. "Tell me, are you with the Halifax police? We know most of the local undercover forces. Or perhaps you represent the national forces? RCMP, perhaps."

"RCMP?" said Joe.

"Royal Canadian Mounted Police," Frank explained. "They handle a lot of security jobs—like the FBI back home."

Joe stared at the head terrorist. "You think she's a cop?" he asked in disbelief. "She's Shauna MacLaren, an architecture student and part-time waitress. One of your boys nearly blew her up when you planted that bomb at the Hungry Guardsman."

"Is this true?"

Shauna nodded, still staring silently at the four gun muzzles.

Singh nodded. "We worried that you might have gone to the authorities—especially when that unmarked police car came for you at Dartmouth. I had to use a local operative there who did not recognize Sergeant Dundee. But he did not know that his superiors no longer listened to the old man."

"Oh, yeah?" Joe said. "That 'old man' was the one who put us on to you."

"I knew he had started to ask some embarrassing questions." Singh shook his head. "He should have died of a heart attack, a stroke—something appropriate for a man his age. I'm afraid that bomb drew far too much attention."

"Why *have* you been trying to blow us up?" Frank demanded. "Ever since we arrived in this city—"

"Ever since I saw you arrive," Singh corrected. He stared at the Hardys. "You really don't know? Then, Frank and Joe, let me tell you about your rare honor—"

"You make it sound like 'This Is Your Life,'" Joe cut in.

Singh ignored him. "It's something the Assassins haven't used in nearly a hundred years. We've been ordered to kill you on sight."

The Hardys stared for a moment. Then Joe said, "Pretty heavy-duty. So you sicced your goons on us."

"Yes," Singh said. "You've been rather a drain on my local manpower. We have one dead, and three in local hospitals at this time. One is in the same Intensive Care Unit as is your friend Dundee. Luckily, none of these patients know the exact timing of our project."

"What's your rush?" Joe asked.

"It's *your* fault," Singh told him. "This is what you Americans call a crash project. I had just assembled my team when one of our most important agents was captured."

"Captured? I thought all you people would die to avoid that," Joe taunted.

"It was very bad luck," Singh admitted.

Frank, however, was staring at the head Assassin with slitted eyes. "Who was this agent?"

"His code name is Adyab. You knew him as Sandy White."

Sandy White led the Assassin task force working undercover to destroy the Alaska pipeline. During the *Trouble in the Pipeline* case, the Assassins almost succeeded in cutting the oil flow—except for Frank and Joe. In fact, Joe was the reason White had been captured. He'd literally punched the poison tooth out of White's mouth.

"We have word that Adyab is still resisting interrogation," Singh told them. "But for how much longer? He knows too many damaging facts about our organization. We can't allow him to be cracked."

"So you're going to take an entire city hostage," Frank said.

Singh nodded. "You live up to your reputation for having a quick mind," he said. "My project was pushed ahead as having the best chance of getting Adyab released."

"Well, it certainly raises the stakes," Frank

admitted. "You must have had a pretty tough job."

"With an international organization, much can be accomplished," Singh said. "We had already begun collecting fissionable material. I had a physicist for the theoretical design. All I needed was an explosives expert."

"And you got Omar Fellawi."

"You recognized his work." Singh smiled at Frank. "He was most impressed that you survived. I'll introduce you in a moment—after we make sure you can't cause trouble."

He gestured to a row of heavy metal caskets. "Please back up against them." Then he pulled sets of handcuffs out of his pocket.

Joe glanced at Frank. This might be the only chance they'd get to make a move.

But Singh was too experienced to fall into any traps. As his prisoners moved, so did the guards, keeping them covered at all times. And he was careful to stay out of the line of fire as he cuffed Frank, Joe, and Shauna. Not only were their hands behind their backs, but the chains between their cuffs ran through a handle on each of the three different coffins.

"It's just a small precaution to keep you from moving around," he said. "And don't bother screaming for help. This room is soundproofed. One of the first improvements I made after buying the place. It makes an excellent safe house, doesn't it?''

"Very clever," Frank said, complimenting him.

"My plan was well along, except for the problem of getting the nuclear materials into the city. Then I had the idea—"

Singh looked at Frank. "You may be aware of the sudden outbreak of terror in the Middle East?''

"I've been reading about it, yes."

"But have you noticed the number of Canadians who've recently lost their lives? There was one in that bus who blew up, another on that boat.''

Frank looked hard at the terrorist. "Now that you mention it, there have been quite a few.''

"Six, to be exact—six paper people that I created. Passports, tickets, visas, I arranged for them all. Then I gave them to agents who traveled under the identities. Since we knew where and when these—disasters were to occur, it was easy enough to plant the identification papers. Then other friends and agents took care of sending back the 'remains.' Of course, you saw what was really shipped.''

Frank nodded. "Dummies in lead-lined coffins, each carrying a slug of—what? Uranium? Plutonium?''

116

"Uranium-238," a new voice cut in. A short, thickset man thumped down the steps on stumpy legs. His coarse blond hair was shaved down to a brush cut, and his icy blue eyes crackled with intelligence. "Six slugs—sixty grams. Less than an ounce of fissionable material, but enough to make two nuclear bombs."

"Thank you, Herr Professor," Singh said. "Let me introduce Ranulf Lupec, our scientific advisor."

"So these are the people who kept you so busy these last few days?" There was the faintest trace of an accent in Lupec's words as he looked at the prisoners. He could just as easily have been examining a shipment of laboratory rats.

Another figure came down the stairs—a tall, gawky guy with a beak of a nose, wild black hair, and a receding hairline. He looked like the kind of person who wound up running the soda machine in a fast-food joint. Yet Frank found himself looking at the man's hands. The fingertips were stained with nicotine and acid. But the long, thin fingers were amazingly graceful, even grasping a heavy lead box.

"Omar Fellawi?" Frank asked.

The lanky man stopped and gave him a big grin. "You are the one who took apart my bomb," he said. "Very smart—I must stop using that loop."

He turned away to the coffin in the center of the room. "I would like to talk, but there is work to finish."

Frank watched as Fellawi ran his fingers over several places on the casket—on one of the locking bolts, behind a handle, and at the base. Then he carefully swung the coffin lid open.

Even the hardened killers shrank back; only Lupec, Singh, and Fellawi leaned over the revealed machinery.

"This is a gun-type atomic weapon." Lupec spoke to the prisoners almost as if he were lecturing a class. "An explosive charge drives a small piece of uranium into a larger piece at two thousand feet per second. When the two pieces are smashed together, they reach critical mass and explode with the force of thousands of tons of dynamite."

He smiled. "It's the simplest form of bomb. The Americans were so sure of this design, they didn't even test it before dropping it on Hiroshima."

"Yes, the design is simple," Fellawi said. "Making it work—*that* is hard. Especially when these young people try to steal our parts."

"The slug you tried to intercept was our final shipment," Singh explained.

"We didn't try to intercept anything," Joe told him. "We didn't even know what it was until after we left."

Frank had been thinking over something else Lupec had said. "You said you'd smuggled in enough for two bombs," he began.

"That's right," Singh told him. "We have the assembly for one bomb all ready to be brought across the border. Omar here is finishing our second one right now."

Fellawi had opened up the lead box and removed a short, fat cylinder, maybe four inches tall. He bent over the innards of the coffin-bomb and began working with his magic fingers. "I move it here, I shift here, slip it in—good. Now, I make the connections." He looked around. "Where is my soldering iron?"

A guard dashed into the office and came back with the tool. Fellawi leaned over again, using the soldering gun with all the brilliance of a brain surgeon. "We connect here, and here. Move this— No!" He almost slapped Lupec's hand away.

The scientist glared daggers at the gawky, almost clownish figure towering over him. But Fellawi shook his head fiercely. "You know about the fission and the critical mass," he said. "But me—I know about bombs."

A few more minutes' work, and Fellawi

stepped back. "Ready," he said. "We set the timer now."

Joe couldn't believe his ears. "Set the timer? How are you going to carry that thing when it's armed?"

"Oh, we're not going to carry it," Singh told him. "We're leaving it here."

He smiled at the horrified expressions on the young people's faces. "The other bomb, with the final assembly not completed, will head for the United States tonight. After we've landed in your country, this bomb will go off. When Halifax disappears in a mushroom cloud, your government will have to believe that we can— and *will*—destroy one of your cities. They'll have to set Adyab free."

Singh and Lupec watched as Fellawi set the timer, then started it. "Eight hours," the bomb maker said. "More than enough time."

He put the timer inside, then closed the top of the coffin. His hands were covered now with black graphite lubricant, and one of his knuckles was skinned and bleeding. "We go now?" he asked.

"I am afraid we'll have to leave you," Singh said to the prisoners. "This is why, of course, we were so willing to tell you so much. In an operation like this, we don't need to tie up loose ends." He smiled. "We've already tethered you."

Frank, Joe, and Shauna stood frozen. In less than eight hours the bomb would go off—and they would be vaporized.

"I'll mention your names to Adyab," Singh promised Joe and Frank. "He'll be so happy to hear that you helped gain his freedom."

Chapter

15

FELLAWI SMILED AT Frank. "Goodbye, smart boy." He wasn't making fun of Frank—he meant his compliment sincerely. "I wish I could show you this bomb. *Three* loops inside." He held up three fingers. "But now we go to the place with the funny name. Stony Strand?" He shook his head and went upstairs.

Singh smiled at the retreating genius's back. "For all his brilliance, he never connects the victim with his bombs."

"I think you are the first victims he actually talked to," Lupec added. He gave the prisoners a short, ironic bow. "Gentlemen, lady, our transportation to the States is waiting for us. Goodbye."

Singh just nodded his farewell and barked an order to the guards. Joe thought he had never seen people so happy to be getting out of a room.

At the top of the stairs, Singh paused. "I'll leave the light on, so you can see each other," he said. "We don't want to be cruel, after all."

"Of course not," Joe said sarcastically. "He just wants to light up our lives with this thing." He lunged like a crazy man, trying to kick out at the coffin-bomb. His cuffs and the weight of the coffin he was attached to kept him well short of his target.

"I don't want you to think I'm ungrateful, guys," Shauna MacLaren said. "But I'm starting to wish I'd stayed with the gang from the Hungry Guardsman. At least then I wouldn't know what was going to happen."

She shut her eyes and turned her face away from the coffin.

Joe stopped looking at the bomb, too. He was half-turned away from it, trying to get his left pocket in range of his bound hands. Singh hadn't searched his prisoners—and maybe, just maybe, he'd wind up paying for that oversight.

Twisting himself very uncomfortably, Joe finally managed to jam a couple of fingers into his pocket. He fumbled around until he found the short three-sided file.

He'd popped in a couple of tools when

they'd gone back to the hotel. There was no way—or time—to file through the chains on the handcuffs. But the handle on the file was thin enough to be used as a lockpick. Now, if only he could get it out . . .

His fingers groped for the end of the file. They touched it, lost it, grabbed it again, only to have it slip away. He rubbed his fingertips against his pants. They were getting slick with sweat. He tried again. Got it! Delicately, he pulled the file from his pocket, trying to position his other hand so he could get a better grip on it.

Up above, the cellar door suddenly slammed open. Joe jumped and lost his precarious hold on the file. It tinkled as it hit the floor, but the noise was lost as Fellawi skipped down the stairs.

"I forgot to turn off the soldering iron," he said, shaking his head. "Very bad habit. Dangerous."

He unplugged the tool, brought it back into the private office, then started up the stairs again.

"I don't believe this guy," Frank said. "He sets things up to fry us with an atom bomb, then worries about the dangers of electrical fires. Unbelievable!"

"It probably makes sense from his point of

view," Shauna said. "A fire might set the bomb off prematurely."

"Before he's reached Stony Strand, you mean," Joe said. "What kind of name is that, anyway?"

"It's a small town near the southwest tip of Nova Scotia," Shauna told him. "A fishing village, really. Some of my friends at school come from there. It's very pretty."

"Well, I think it's drawing the wrong kind of tourists," Joe groused.

Frank glanced over at him, his hands busy behind his back. "Did Singh give you any slack on your cuffs? Can you get a hand free?" He struggled a moment more, then shook his head. "Mine are on too tight."

"Mine, too," Joe said.

"How about you, Shauna?" Maybe Singh had taken it easy on the girl.

But she shook her head. "If they were any tighter, they'd be cutting my hands off."

"We've got to figure some way out of this," Frank insisted.

"I almost had one," Joe said, "but it slipped through my fingers." He explained what had happened.

Joe threw himself again at his bonds. "If I get my hands on that Fellawi . . ."

"That's a pretty big if right now," Shauna said. But seeing that the Hardys hadn't given

125

up trying to escape shook her out of her own misery.

"Are there any other tools in your pocket you could use as a pick?" she asked.

Joe shook his head. "That was the only thing thin enough to reach inside."

"Where did it fall?"

"It came down behind me somewhere." Joe scraped around with his running shoe. Then he heard a tiny grating sound beneath his heel. "Here it is."

Carefully scuffing his foot forward, he brought the file into sight.

"It sure looks skinny," Shauna said.

"Let's not mention how useless it is sitting down there." Joe tried a couple of contortions, seeing how close he could get a hand to the floor. But he couldn't even get within two feet of the floor.

"There's no way to reach the stupid thing." Joe brought his foot back, ready to kick the file across the floor. But Shauna stopped him, stretching out her foot to tap his ankle.

Joe looked down at her foot, beginning to get an idea. He waited until he heard the front door slam and a car pull away—final proof that the Assassins were really gone.

"Look," he said to Shauna. "I've got an idea that's pretty far-out, but it might just work to get us out of here."

An hour and a half later they were still working on it. Joe and Shauna had kicked off their shoes and scraped off their socks. Now, with their bare feet, they were trying to pick up the file and get it into Joe's hands.

It was like a stupid summer game they'd play to pass the time at the beach. Shauna would wrap her long toes around the file, and try to lift up her leg. The file would slip away and fall to the floor. They'd both scrabble desperately to make sure it didn't bounce out of reach. They they'd start all over again.

Finally, miraculously, Shauna had caught the file between her toes. She stuck her leg out almost straight from her hip, stretching as far toward Joe as she could.

"That's pretty incredible," Joe said. "How can you do that?"

"Twelve years of ballet classes." Shauna's voice showed a little tremor of strain. "How about doing your part now?"

Joe bent over, straining against his cuffs, aiming with his mouth for the file that wavered so temptingly in front of him.

He had it! The rough part of the file grated against his teeth, but he had a definite hold on it. He straightened up, the file sticking out of his mouth like a long, thin cigar.

"So far, so good," Shauna said. "But how do you get it down to your hands?"

127

Joe turned back, leaning his head as far over his shoulder as he could. Back, back . . . he pressed against the side of the coffin. Then he opened his lips and let the file fall inside.

Shauna gasped. "All that, and you let it get away from you! We've had it!"

"It didn't get away from me." Joe continued to twist around, looking over his shoulder. "I pulled the little pillow over here to catch the file. And now—" He grunted, straining against the cuffs. "If I can just— Got it!"

Picking the cuff wasn't easy. But it was a lot easier than getting the improvised lockpick into position.

At last, all three of them were out of the cuffs, massaging their wrists.

"Well, let's call the police," Shauna said. "We've got more than enough proof for them now." She stared at the closed coffin-bomb as if she could hear it ticking away.

"That may be too dangerous," Frank said. "This is an Omar Fellawi bomb. His crazy ways of putting them together have blown up a lot of bomb-disposal types. It may take better experts than can be found in Halifax. And I don't think there's enough time left to fly anyone in."

"So what are you saying?" Shauna cried.

"He's saying that he's probably the only person in town who's beaten an Omar Fellawi bomb." Joe stared hard at his brother. "Do you think you can do it?"

Frank took a deep breath. "I don't think we've got much choice."

He approached the coffin, remembering how Fellawi had touched it first. Running his fingers along to find the tightening bolt, he found a small button and pushed it. Then, behind the handle, another button. And there was another one, down at the foot of the casket.

Frank picked up the cover. Nothing happened. He gasped when he saw the timer. More time had passed than he thought. "Okay," he said, "we know where the final assembly went in. If we get that out, and cut the detonator for the charge that's supposed to blow it into the other chunk of uranium, we should be home free."

He pulled out the circuit tracer from his pocket. "Joe, see if you can find me some wire clippers. And bring back that soldering gun."

Frank spent an hour of agony crouched over the big bomb, tracking circuits, disconnecting wires, slowly undoing what Fellawi had built. He'd found the cylinder of the final assembly. Fellawi had surrounded it with a maze of circuitry, including two of those infamous loops.

He found trap after trap and cut those circuits out. Sweat ran down his face, burning his eyes. He had to be absolutely perfect. It wasn't just his life on the line, or Joe's, or Shauna's. Frank was carrying an entire city on his shoulders.

At last he was ready to slide out the final assembly. He eased the cylinder out of its sleeve, the graphite lubricant making his fingers black and slippery.

Then he stopped. What was that over there, against the blackness? Frank traced along the outside of the cylinder with his finger. He could hardly see it, but he could feel it. Fellawi had set a booby trap like the wires looped around the plastique in his bomb in the Citadel. But this time he'd used a black wire against the black graphite.

Holding the assembly exactly where it was, he turned to Joe and said, "Get me some wire from the desk, please. And get your knife out for me."

With a nice big piece of wire and Joe's pocketknife, Frank was able to construct a loop of his own—a bypass loop. Now he had lots of room to slip the deadly cylinder out.

"Okay. One down, one to go." He let out a deep sigh. Whatever happened now, the city was safe.

It took another forty minutes to disarm the detonator. By the time he was done, Frank's hands were black, bruised, and scratched from fumbling around the insides of the bomb. But

Omar Fellawi's deadly creation was now just a lot of junk machinery in a fancy coffin.

"Now it's time to call the cops," Frank said.

Maybe he was too tired from tackling the bomb. He should have foreseen the police reaction.

They'd gotten Detective Otley out of bed. He wore a suit and tie, but Joe had the suspicion that his shirt was actually a pajama top. Sitting in the office of the funeral parlor, he listened as the kids explained the connection to the attack on Dundee.

"So this is the fort he was talking about, huh?" He sleepily nodded his head.

His eyes opened a lot wider when they mentioned what was in the coffin in the storeroom. "An atomic bomb? And you disarmed it?" His tone was frankly disbelieving. "Well, if it won't go off, we may as well leave it for later this morning. I'm leaving a guard at this site, going home to sleep, and expect to see you this morning—at a more decent hour."

"But the Assassins will get away with the other bomb!" Joe burst out.

"Kid, I'm having a very hard time believing any of this," Otley told him. "And you're not helping things by yelling. I'll see you in the morning. *Period.*"

"You might at least call the RCMP," Frank suggested.

"And wake them up at this ungodly hour with a story like this? Later for you, pal—much later."

Joe, Frank, and Shauna stepped out of the house into the predawn darkness.

"They'll be long gone by the time you get to see Otley," Shauna predicted gloomily.

"That means it's up to us to stop that bomb from leaving for the States." Joe turned to Shauna. "Do you know the way to Stony Strand?"

Chapter
16

"SHOW YOU HOW to get to Stony Strand?" Shauna said. "I'll do better than that. We have to find a phone."

They got a lift back to their hotel from the police. While Frank and Joe got some soda from the machine in the hallway, Shauna went to work on the phone.

"All set," she said, smiling mysteriously when they returned to the room. "We have to be downstairs in half an hour to catch our ride."

"So, tell us more about this Stony Strand place," Joe said.

"It's about thirty miles from here, on the south coast," Shauna said. "About twenty thousand years ago, the last Ice Age scraped away all the topsoil from the area. Settlers called the place Stony Strand because the beaches are ledges of solid rock."

"Solid rock?" Frank said.

"*Solid*," Shauna repeated. "The first time I went down there, someone pointed out a graveyard. It was the last place in about twenty miles where the soil was deep enough for burying people."

Joe gave her a look. "That's a nice, pleasant thought to start off this little jaunt."

Half an hour later they stood outside the hotel in the predawn chill. They'd dressed as warmly as they could, and Shauna looked a little like a refugee in Joe's jacket.

The ride Shauna had promised turned out to be two rides—a car and a van. The guy who leaned out from the driver's seat of the car looked vaguely familiar.

"Frank and Joe Hardy, meet my friend Charlie Bell," Shauna said, taking care of the introductions. "He's a corporal up at the Citadel."

"*That's* where we saw you before," Joe said.

"I'm harder to recognize out of uniform," Charlie said with a grin. "But there are some good things about being a corporal."

He led the way to the van and opened the back door. Five guys sat in the back, besides the driver. "This is my squad," Charlie said. "Will's behind the wheel, and these are Robert, Ken, Doug, Jack, and Harry. Guys, meet Frank and Joe Hardy."

His corporal's guard was out of uniform. But Frank noted that each of the guys in the back of the van clutched the antique rifle he'd been using up at the Citadel.

"When Charlie called and told us what you'd done for us," one of the guys—Ken—said, "we thought you could use some reinforcements."

He grinned as he patted his big rifle. "It's a hundred and forty years old, but this is all the firepower we could get our hands on."

"Let's hope we don't need to use it," Frank said.

"Well, let's get this show on the road," Charlie said. "You guys will be riding with me. I'll be guiding Will."

"Remember how I said I had friends from Stony Strand?" Shauna said. "Well, Charlie's one of them."

Frank nodded. "I'm glad we have someone who knows the area."

They set off west from the downtown area, skirting an arm of the harbor, then heading inland for a while. The road looped its way to the south, then curved west again as it approached the south shore.

Charlie drove steadily through the murky dawn. Joe could hardly make out the landmarks Shauna pointed to. Frank was asleep in the back seat beside him.

Rolling to a stop at the crest of a hill, Charlie said, "We're here."

Frank roused himself to look down on a scene that should have been on a postcard. Stony Strand was little more than a village, a handful of gaily painted and weather-beaten houses scattered along the shore of a small cove. Piers lined an inlet from the cove, where fishing boats bobbed at anchor.

The sun still wasn't all the way up, but fingers of telltale gray were appearing in the east. Stony Strand's fishermen had been up and about for at least an hour. Charlie was invaluable. As a local boy, he was able to ask if any strangers were staying in the area.

One grizzled old salt nodded. "Someone's renting the old Garth place—you know, the cottage on the headland."

Charlie knew it all too well. "When we were kids, that was the town's haunted house. Somebody fixed it up to rent to summer tourists." He frowned. "They couldn't have chosen a better spot for themselves."

"Why?" Joe asked.

136

"You'll see."

They drove as close as they dared, hiding the vehicles behind a house that belonged to friends of Charlie's family. Then they marched on through the murky early morning light to the foot of the headland.

Wet fog blew in from the bay as they made their way across rocky terrain that looked as if it would be more at home on the moon. They had to place their feet carefully—the fog had made the naked rock slick underfoot.

Finally they reached the headland. A light breeze tore a hole in the curtain of fog, and Joe understood what Charlie had been talking about.

The cottage perched on a slight rise at the tip of the headland. To get to it, they'd have to move across a hundred feet of naked, broken granite. The neck of land was only fifteen or twenty feet wide in places. One man with a pistol could hold off a small army.

"This fog is a lucky break," Charlie said, kneeling behind a clump of boulders and peering out at the house. "They won't be able to leave until it begins to clear."

"You live around here. Can we use it to get closer to the house?" Frank asked. "Or will it lift too soon?"

"We'll have to try," Charlie said with a shrug. He started setting up his tiny force.

"Robert, Jack, and Doug, you're our best marksmen. Stay here behind these rocks and lay down cover fire if we need it. The rest of you will move up with me and the Hardys."

He glanced at Shauna, but she just smiled and shook her head. "I've had enough playing with guns tonight."

"Okay," Charlie said. "Load your firelocks."

His men grounded their guns, pulled out little paper cartridges, poured the powder down the muzzles, then pushed a bullet down with a ramrod. Placing a percussion cap under the hammer of the gun, they were ready.

"Takes a while to load those guys, doesn't it?" Joe said.

"It's worse than you think," Charlie said as he shoved a bullet home in his own gun. "To use this ramrod right, you almost *have* to stand up."

Joe looked at the uneven, rocky surface they'd have to move across. Anyone standing to reload would be a sitting duck. "You guys better hold your fire until we know it will do some good."

Rifles at the ready, Charlie and his troops set off down the headland in a ragged skirmish line. To the rear, the covering force hunkered down behind the boulders. Frank and Joe, crouching low, crept ahead of Charlie's force.

They made it almost three-quarters of the way to the house before they bumped into a guard.

The guy was sitting against a rock, half-asleep, when Frank came upon him. Caught by surprise, the man half rose, trying to bring up his Uzi.

Frank snapped out a kick that knocked the guy back against the rock, out cold. His gun clattered to the ground.

That was enough noise to wake up another guard closer to the house. He asked something in a foreign language while Frank groped for the lost weapon.

The man spoke again, a nervous edge to his voice.

Then the worst happened. The fog began to lift.

Charlie and his troops appeared through the thinning grayness like ghosts. The guard yelled and leveled his Uzi. But Joe popped up from behind a rock, his arm already swinging in a roundhouse right. Now they had two down, but that left two guards from the funeral home unaccounted for.

They soon put in an appearance, firing wildly with their machine guns. Charlie and company ducked to the ground, finding whatever cover they could among the rugged rocks. The three guys left in the boulders opened fire, driving the guards back indoors.

It was a weird sort of battle—the latest in automatic firepower against weapons that were antiques a century ago. The Assassins could spit three bullets a second at their enemies. Charlie's guys were lucky to manage two shots in a minute.

One of the Assassins took advantage of the long reload time to lean out the window and spray bullets around the rock where Charlie lay. Frank answered with half a clip from his Uzi, driving the guy back inside.

A moment later the other guard tried a charge, throwing open the door. The heavy bullet from one of Charlie's guys hit the door, sending the man staggering back.

The firing died down as a sort of stalemate developed. The Assassins couldn't come out of the house, but the Hardys and their friends couldn't get in.

"Is Frank Hardy there?" Singh's voice rang out in the sudden silence.

"Yes," Frank shouted back.

"So, you disabled our bomb. And all this shooting will surely bring the authorities. A pity." The rock Frank hid behind was spattered with machine-gun fire.

In fact, bullets were flying all along the headland from the windows of the house. It was as though the people inside weren't worried about saving ammunition.

Then Frank saw why, as the last of the fog cleared away. The guards were wasting bullets as a delaying action. They had to keep the attackers' heads down so the brains of the operation could escape.

And escape they would if the Hardys didn't do something about it. Beyond the house stretched a small pier.

And at the end of the pier was a seaplane, and the plane's props were already beginning to spin.

Chapter

17

FRANK HARDY POPPED up, fired a quick burst from his Uzi, then ducked behind the rock again as the Assassins sent a hail of bullets his way.

He had slid behind a different rock, working his way back to Charlie and the guys from the Citadel. The problem was, the next stretch of rock behind him was bare and flat. There was no cover at all. How could he get across?

Joe must have seen the problem, because now he popped up to fire a couple of shots. That drew the enemy's fire his way as Frank dashed across the open space.

Covering each other, the Hardys finally managed to reach Charlie's position.

"Take this," Joe said, handing over his Uzi. "It will help even up the sides a little." He pointed at the pier, where even now three figures had appeared. "Use it to pin them down, to keep them from reaching the plane."

"What are you going to do?" Charlie asked.

"I'm going for a swim," Joe replied. "With luck, I may be able to convince that pilot to delay his departure."

"I'm doing the same," Frank said, passing his gun to another of the student soldiers. "Do the best you can till we get out there."

"You're going swimming—here?" Charlie said. "The undertow can kill you."

"The undertow isn't the only thing," Joe said with a grin. "You worry about keeping those guys from crossing the pier. We'll worry about getting to the plane."

"Of course, if they start shooting at us, we wouldn't mind a little covering fire," Frank added.

Charlie nodded, rising for a second to deliver a quick burst from his Uzi. The three figures on the pier scattered and hit the deck.

"You'd better get going," Charlie said. "The bullets in this clip won't last forever."

The Hardys made their way to a rocky ledge

by the water, concealed by a big upthrust boulder. They took off their shoes and socks, then Joe stuck a foot into the water. "Cold," he announced. "And that undertow is— Whoa!" The force of the current sucked him right off the slippery rocks.

Frank slid in after him, bracing himself for the sudden cold. The undertow pulled hungrily at him, trying to take him out to sea. But that's where Frank wanted to go. He didn't have to fight to get back to land. As long as he headed for the seaplane, he'd be all right.

Of course, if the seaplane took off before he reached it, it would be a long swim to Maine.

Frank tried not to think about that. He just concentrated on the seaplane. Both he and Joe spent most of their time swimming underwater, rising only to catch a breath of air and to make sure they were heading the right way.

Once when he broke the surface, Frank heard gunfire. He glanced over at the pier. The three figures were making it closer to the plane. Could he beat them?

He struck out a little stronger as he swam.

Now he began to feel all the exhaustion he'd held back while he worked over the bomb. Fighting the undertow was a little trickier than he'd expected, too. It pulled at him like a hungry beast that wanted to be fed.

Frank sucked air and kept struggling. Then

. . . what was this in front of him? The pontoon for the seaplane!

He reached up to grab on—and his hand slipped off. The undertow tore at him now, as if it were afraid he might escape. He was going down. . . .

A strong hand grabbed onto his collar, hauling him back up to the air. Joe Hardy grinned down at him, one hand on a strut of the plane, one still twisted in his shirt.

"Hey, big brother," he whispered. "You don't want to miss the party now."

They crept along the pontoon, concealed from the Assassins by the fuselage of the plane. It was very slippery going—one wrong move would leave them at the mercy of the undertow. Finally Joe reached the passenger door.

He pulled it open and swung in on the astonished pilot. By the time Frank got in, the pilot lay in the back of the plane, deep in dreamland.

Frank settled himself in the pilot's seat. "Okay," he said. "Let's see if those ground-training classes were worth the money Dad paid."

He checked the instruments, trying to find the engine controls. Outside on the pier, the shooting suddenly reached the proportions of a small war. The nasty rattle of submachine guns had a desperate sound.

The group on the pier had almost reached the plane now. Frank recognized them at once. Lupec, pale and staring, scuttled along. Tall, gangling Fellawi moved carefully, his hands cradling a lead box like the one he'd carried the night before.

Frank realized that must be the final assembly for the second bomb. He glanced in the back of the plane and saw a big crate. So, the rest was already on board.

Singh was the last of the three. He kept facing the headland, a MAC-10 in his hands, spraying bullets to keep the Citadel kids down. The whiteness of his gritted teeth showed against the dark of his mustache.

There was no more time to study the situation. Frank reached out, flicking switches, adjusting controls. The engines, which had only been idling, roared into life. The propellers began to turn in earnest now. Leaping against its moorings, the seaplane was ready to fly.

Frank let out the throttle on one engine, while pulling back on the other. He jockeyed the stick. Slowly, the seaplane began to swing around.

Singh caught the movement and turned around, his eyes becoming round when he recognized Frank and Joe in the cockpit.

He didn't have a chance to do anything else. The seaplane's wing swept over the pier, scraping Singh, Fellawi, and Lupec straight into the water.

"You're lucky those three didn't drown," Detective Otley told the Hardys a little later. The headland was now crawling with police, Halifax cops, provincial police, even some RCMP—although Joe was disappointed to see they weren't wearing their snappy red uniforms.

"None of these guys would have been any great loss to humanity," Joe said. "Besides, we caught them all before they went out to sea."

They'd dragged the three chief terrorists out of the water like drowned rats. Singh had lost his gun, but Fellawi was the most upset. The final assembly for his bomb had slipped from his fingers. Who knew where the undertow would take it?

"We'll have divers looking for that piece of the bomb," Otley said, almost reading Joe's mind. "But what about these guys? The head Mountie told me that Assassins take poison rather than be captured."

"Well, Lupec and Fellawi weren't really Assassins," Joe explained. "They were only working on contract. As for Singh—I guess he was in too much shock to do the job. We had his poison pellet out of his hollow tooth before we gave him mouth-to-mouth."

"I had some professors from Dalhousie University looking that bomb over early this morning," Otley said. "They nearly had fits when they realized what it was." He glanced over at Frank. "They also told me that we have a lot to thank you for."

Frank waved that off. "Just make sure my name doesn't get into the papers—that is, if the papers ever get to write anything about this."

"You don't think they will?" Joe said.

"Governments get a little nervous about announcing things like this," Frank said. "This whole story could just become another nuclear secret."

"That's fine with me," Shauna MacLaren said. "I'd prefer to forget about the whole thing. Halifax doesn't need to know it just escaped an atomic explosion." She managed a smile. "Besides, my thing is building stuff, not blowing it up."

She winked at Joe, who smiled back. "You'll have to come back and have another free dinner," she said to him. "We can't have you going around saying that the Hungry Guardsman blows up at the least little thing."

Joe laughed. "I'd like that," he said.

She got a little more serious as she looked

up at him. "I would, too. Well, maybe you'll have more depositions to collect—"

"Oh, no!" Frank said. "We haven't even gotten the ones we were sent here for!"

"Don't worry," said Otley. "They're on Gerry Dundee's desk. You can have them by this afternoon."

"How is Sergeant Dundee?" Frank asked. "We checked in on him yesterday, but since then . . ."

"I know," Otley said. "Things got a little hectic. Well, the good news is that he's going to pull through."

"That's great," said Joe.

Otley went on. "The bad news is that he's through as a cop. He suppressed your report, went off on his own, and nearly got himself killed. Like it or not, he's going to retire."

"Sounds tough on him," Shauna said.

Otley nodded. "You said it. This guy is all cop."

"Still, he'll go out in a blaze of glory. He smashed a terrorist ring," Joe said.

"Maybe more than we know." Frank thought of Sandy White in a prison somewhere. He wasn't going to get out. The questioning would continue. Maybe the questioners would get the information they needed to smash the terrorists once and for all.

"And, of course, he helped save Halifax," Joe went on. "That's nothing to sneeze at."

Frank nodded. "There are worse ways to go," he said. "Much worse ways."